D0306954

FLAME

IN THE

MIST

Also by Renée Ahdieh

The Wrath and the Dawn
The Rose and the Dagger

Renée Ahdieh

FLAME
IN THE
MIST

HODDER &
STOUGHTON

First published in Great Britain in 2017 by Hodder & Stoughton
An Hachette UK company

1

A CIP catalogue record for this title is available from the British Library

Hardback ISBN 978 1 473 66442 5
Trade Paperback ISBN 978 1 473 65797 7
eBook ISBN 978 1 473 65799 1

Printed and bound by CPI Group (UK) Ltd, Croydon, CR0 4YY

Hodder & Stoughton policy is to use papers that are natural, renewable and recyclable
products and made from wood grown in sustainable forests. The logging and manufacturing
processes are expected to conform to the environmental regulations of the country of origin.

Hodder & Stoughton Ltd
Carmelite House
50 Victoria Embankment
London EC4Y 0DZ

www.hodder.co.uk

To 엄마 and Mama Joon—
For teaching me that true weakness
is weakness of the spirit.

THE SEVEN TENETS OF BUSHIDŌ:
THE WAY OF THE WARRIOR

Gi—Integrity

Yūki—Courage

Jin—Benevolence

Rei—Respect

Makoto—Honesty

Meiyo—Honor

忠
義

Chūgi—Loyalty

"In this age of decadence that we live in, people's minds are twisted and only words are loved but not practical deeds."

—from Vol. I of the *Bansenshukai*, the ancient manual on the *shinobi no mono*, or the art of the ninja

FLAME
IN THE
MIST

The Beginning

———✴———

In the beginning, there were two suns and two moons.

The boy's sight blurred before him, seeing past the truth. Past the shame. He focused on the story his *uba* had told him the night before. A story of good and evil, light and dark. A story where the triumphant sun rose high above its enemies.

On instinct, his fingers reached for the calloused warmth of his *uba*'s hand. The nursemaid from Kisun had been with him since before he could remember, but now—like everything else—she was gone.

Now there was no one left.

Against his will, the boy's vision cleared, locking on the clear blue of the noon sky above. His fingers curled around the stiff linen of his shirtsleeves.

Don't look away. If they see you looking away, they will say you are weak.

Once more, his *uba*'s words echoed in his ears.

He lowered his gaze.

The courtyard before him was draped in fluttering white, surrounded on three sides by rice-paper screens. Pennants flying the golden crest of the emperor danced in a passing breeze. To the left and right stood grim-faced onlookers—samurai dressed in the dark silks of their formal *hakama*.

In the center of the courtyard was the boy's father, kneeling on a small tatami mat covered in bleached canvas. He, too, was draped in white, his features etched in stone. Before him sat a low table with a short blade. At his side stood the man who had once been his best friend.

The boy sought his father's eyes. For a moment, he thought his father looked his way, but it could have been a trick of the wind. A trick of the perfumed smoke curling above the squat brass braziers.

His father would not want to look into his son's eyes. The boy knew this. The shame was too great. And his father would die before passing the shame of tears along to his son.

The drums began to pound out a slow beat. A dirge.

In the distance beyond the gates, the boy caught the muffled sound of small children laughing and playing. They were soon silenced by a terse shout.

Without hesitation, his father loosened the knot from around his waist and pushed open his white robe, exposing the skin of his stomach and chest. Then he tucked his sleeves beneath his knees to prevent himself from falling backward.

For even a disgraced samurai should die well.

The boy watched his father reach for the short *tantō* blade on the small table before him. He wanted to cry for him to stop. Cry for a moment more. A single look more.

Just one.

But the boy remained silent, his fingers turning bloodless in his fists. He swallowed.

Don't look away.

His father took hold of the blade, wrapping his hands around the skein of white silk near its base. He plunged the sword into his stomach, cutting slowly to the left, then up to the right. His features remained passive. No hint of suffering could be detected, though the boy searched for it—felt it— despite his father's best efforts.

Never look away.

Finally, when his father stretched his neck forward, the boy saw it. A small flicker, a grimace. In the same instant, the boy's heart shuddered in his chest. A hot burst of pain glimmered beneath it.

The man who had been his father's best friend took two long strides, then swung a gleaming *katana* in a perfect arc toward his father's exposed neck. The thud of his father's head hitting the tatami mat silenced the drumbeats in a hollow start.

Still the boy did not look away. He watched the crimson spurt from his father's folded body, past the edge of the mat and onto the grey stones beyond. The tang of the fresh blood caught in his nose—warm metal and sea salt. He waited until his father's body was carried in one direction, his head in another, to be displayed as a warning.

3

No hint of treason would be tolerated. Not even a whisper.

All the while, no one came to the boy's side. No one dared to look him in the eye.

The burden of shame took shape in the boy's chest, heavier than any weight he could ever bear.

When the boy finally turned to leave the empty courtyard, his eyes fell upon the creaking door nearby. A nursemaid met his unflinching stare, one hand sliding off the latch, the other clenched around two toy swords. Her skin flushed pink for an instant.

Never look away.

The nursemaid dropped her eyes in discomfort. The boy watched as she quickly ushered a boy and a girl through the wooden gate. They were a few years younger than he and obviously from a wealthy family. Perhaps the children of one of the samurai in attendance today. The younger boy straightened the fine silk of his kimono collar and darted past his nursemaid, never once pausing to acknowledge the presence of a traitor's son.

The girl, however, stopped. She looked straight at him, her pert features in constant motion. Rubbing her nose with the heel of one hand, she blinked, letting her eyes run the length of him before pausing on his face.

He held her gaze.

"Mariko-*sama*!" the nursemaid scolded. She whispered in the girl's ear, then tugged her away by the elbow.

Still the girl's eyes did not waver. Even when she passed

the pool of blood darkening the stones. Even when her eyes narrowed in understanding.

The boy was grateful he saw no sympathy in her expression. Instead the girl continued studying him until her nursemaid urged her around the corner.

His gaze returned to the sky, his chin in high disregard of his tears.

In the beginning, there were two suns and two moons.

One day, the victorious son would rise—

And set fire to all his father's enemies.

Illusions and Expectations

※

Ten Years Later

On the surface everything seemed right.

An elegant litter. A dutiful daughter. An honor bestowed.

Then, as if to taunt her, Mariko's litter lurched, jouncing her shoulder into the *norimono*'s side. Its raised mother-of-pearl inlays would undoubtedly leave a bruise. Mariko took a deep breath, stifling the urge to grumble in the shadows like an angry crone. The smell of the *norimono*'s varnish filled her head, bringing to mind the Dragon's Beard candy she favored as a child.

Her dark, sickly sweet coffin, bearing her to her final resting place.

Mariko sank farther into the cushions. Nothing about the journey to the imperial city of Inako had gone well. Her convoy had left later than intended and stopped all too often. At least now—by the way the *norimono* listed forward—Mariko could tell they were traveling down an incline. Which meant they'd moved past the hills around the valley, more than halfway to Inako. She leaned back, hoping her weight would help balance the burden.

Just as she settled in, the litter halted suddenly.

Mariko raised the silk screen covering the small window to her right. Dusk was starting to descend. The forest before them was shrouded in mist, its trees a jagged silhouette across a silver sky.

As Mariko turned to address the nearby soldier, a young maidservant came stumbling into view. "My lady!" the girl gasped, righting herself against the *norimono*'s side. "You must be famished. I've been remiss. Please forgive me for neglecting to— "

"There's nothing to forgive, Chiyo-*chan*." Mariko smiled kindly, but the girl's eyes remained wide with worry. "It was not I who halted the convoy."

Chiyo bowed low, the flowers of her makeshift hairpiece falling askew. When she stood once more, the maidservant passed along a neatly wrapped bundle of food to Mariko. Then Chiyo moved back to her post beside the litter, pausing only to return Mariko's warm smile.

"Why have we stopped?" Mariko asked the nearby member of the *ashigaru*.

The foot soldier wiped the perspiration from his brow, then switched the long pole of his *naginata* to his other hand. Traces of sunlight glinted off its sharp blade. "The forest."

Mariko waited, certain that could not be the extent of his explanation.

Beads of sweat gathered above the soldier's lips. He opened his mouth to speak, but the clatter of approaching hooves stole his attention.

"Lady Hattori . . ." Nobutada, one of her father's confidants and his most trusted samurai, reined in his charger beside Mariko's *norimono*. "I apologize for the delay, but several of the soldiers have voiced concerns about traveling through Jukai forest."

Mariko blinked twice, her features thoughtful. "Is there a particular reason?"

"Now that the sun has set, they fear the *yōkai*, and they worry—"

"Silly stories of monsters in the dark." She waved a dismissive hand. "Nothing more."

Nobutada paused, doubtlessly taking note of her interruption. "They also claim the Black Clan has been seen near here recently."

"They claim?" A dark eyebrow curved into Mariko's forehead. "Or they've sighted them in truth?"

"They are merely claims." Nobutada lowered the chin guard beneath his horned helmet. "Though it would be unusual for the Black Clan to rob us, as they do not generally attack convoys containing women and children. Especially those guarded by samurai."

Mariko lingered in consideration. "I defer to your opinion, Nobutada-*sama*." Recalling the foot soldier from a moment ago, she attempted a smile. "And please see that the *ashigaru* have time to rest and take in water soon, as they appear overtired."

Nobutada scowled at her last request. "If we are forced to go around Jukai forest, it will add a full day to our journey."

"Then it will add a full day to our journey." She was already beginning to lower her screen, the awkward smile still pasted across her face.

"I'd rather not risk angering the emperor."

"Then it is an easy choice. We must lead so that others may follow, Nobutada-*sama*. You taught me that, even as a young girl." Mariko did not look away as she spoke. Nor did she attempt to apologize for the sharpness of her retort.

His scowl deepened. Mariko smothered a sigh. She knew she was being difficult. Knew Nobutada wished for her to make a decision. At the very least, wished for her to offer an opinion.

To make a useless play at control. A play Nobutada could then smugly subvert, as her elder.

As a man.

Try as she might, Mariko could not help the resentment simmering beneath the surface.

Control is an illusion. Expectations will not rule my days.

Not anymore.

"Perhaps not easy," Mariko amended, her fingers toying with the edge of the screen. "But it *is* simple." She softened her tone—a pitiful attempt to mollify him. One that was sure to chafe, as her contrary nature so often did. Her brother,

Kenshin, frequently gave her grief about it. Frequently told her to be less . . . peculiar.

To conform, at least in these small ways.

Mariko dipped her head in a bow. "In any case, I defer to your wise judgment, Nobutada-*sama*."

A shadow fell across his features. "Very well, Lady Hattori. We shall proceed through Jukai forest." With that, he urged his charger back toward the head of the convoy.

As expected, Mariko had irritated him. She'd offered no real opinion on anything since they'd left her family's home that morning. And Nobutada wanted her to play at directing him. To give him tasks befitting such a vaunted role.

Tasks befitting the samurai in charge of delivering a royal bride.

Mariko supposed she should care she might be arriving at Heian Castle late.

Late to meet the emperor. Late to meet his second son—

Her future husband.

But Mariko did not care. Ever since the afternoon her father had informed her that Emperor Minamoto Masaru had made an offer of marriage on behalf of his son Raiden, she'd truly not cared about much.

Mariko was to be the wife of Prince Raiden, the son of the emperor's favorite consort. A political marriage that would elevate her father's standing amongst the ruling daimyō class.

She should care that she was being exchanged like property in order to curry favor. But Mariko did not.

Not anymore.

As the *norimono* lurched forward again, Mariko reached above to adjust the slender tortoiseshell bar speared through her thick coils of hair. Tiny strips of silver and jade dangled from its ends, snarling with one another in a ceaseless war. After Mariko finished sorting them into place, her hand fell to the smaller jade bar below.

Her mother's face took shape in her mind—the look of determined resignation she had worn as she slid the jade ornament into her only daughter's hair.

A parting gift. But not a true source of comfort.

Just like her father's final words:

Be a tribute to your family, Mariko-chan. *As you were raised to be. Forswear your childish wishes. Be more than . . . this.*

Mariko's lips pressed tight.

It doesn't matter. I've already taken my revenge.

There was no reason for Mariko to dwell on these things anymore. Her life was on a clear path now. Never mind that it was not what she wanted. Never mind that there was so much left to see and learn and do. She'd been raised for a purpose. A foolish one at that—to be the wife of an important man when she could easily have been something else. Something more. But it did not matter. She was not a boy. And—despite being barely seventeen—Hattori Mariko knew her place in life. She would marry Minamoto Raiden. Her parents would have the prestige of a daughter in Heian Castle.

And Mariko would be the only one to know the stain on that honor.

As dusk fell and the convoy made its way deeper into the

forest, the scent of warm, wet air took on a life of its own. It mixed with the iron of the earth and the green of newly trod leaves. A strange, heady perfume. Sharp and fresh, yet soft and sinister all at once.

Mariko shuddered, a chill taking root in her bones. The horses around the *norimono* whickered as if in response to an unseen threat. Seeking a distraction, Mariko reached for the small parcel of food Chiyo had given her, staving off the chill by burrowing into her cushions.

Perhaps we should have gone around Jukai forest.

She quickly dismissed these doubts, then turned her attention to the parcel in her hands. Within it were two rice balls covered in black sesame seeds, along with pickled sour plums wrapped in lotus leaves. After unfolding her meal, Mariko shifted her fingers to light the tiny folded-paper lantern swaying above.

It had been one of her earliest inventions. Small enough to hide in a kimono sleeve. A special slow-burning wick, suspended by the thinnest of wires. The wick was fashioned from cotton braided with river reeds dipped in wax. It kept its shape despite its size, all while burning a steady light. Mariko had made it as a child. In the heavy dark of night, this tiny invention had been her savior. She'd placed it beside her blankets, where it cast a warm, cheery glow by which she'd penned her newest ideas.

Smiling in remembrance, Mariko began to eat. A few black sesame seeds fell onto the painted silk of her kimono;

she brushed them aside. The fabric felt like water at her fingertips. The color of sweetened cream, its hem bled through with darkest indigo. Pale pink cherry blossoms crowded the long sleeves, unfurling into branches near Mariko's feet.

A priceless kimono. Made of rare *tatsumura* silk. One of the many gifts sent to her by the emperor's son. It was beautiful. More beautiful than anything Mariko had ever owned in her life.

Perhaps a girl who prized such things would be pleased.

When more sesame seeds fell onto the silk, Mariko didn't bother brushing them away. She finished eating in silence, watching the tiny lantern sway to and fro.

The gathering of shadows shifted outside, growing closer and tighter. Mariko's convoy was now deep beneath a canopy of trees. Deep beneath their cloak of sighing branches and whispering leaves. Strange that she heard no signs of life outside—not the caw of a raven nor the cry of an owl nor the chirr of an insect.

Then the *norimono* halted again. All too abruptly.

The horses began to pant. Began to stamp their hooves in the leafy earth.

Mariko heard a shout. Her litter teetered. Overcorrected. Only to strike the ground with a vicious thud. Her head smacked against varnished wood, throwing stars across her vision.

And Mariko was swallowed into a void.

The Nightbeast

---※---

Mariko woke to the smell of smoke. To a dull roar in her ears.

To shooting pain in her arm.

She was still in her litter, but it had toppled to one side, its contents smashed into a corner.

The body of a familiar maidservant lay across her. Chiyo, who had loved to eat iced persimmons and arrange moon-flowers in her hair. Chiyo, whose eyes had always been so open and wide and honest.

The same eyes that were now frozen in Death's final mask.

Mariko's throat burned. Her sight blurred with tears.

The sounds of movement outside brought her back into focus. Her right hand pressed into a tender lump on the side of her head. She gasped into full awareness, the sound a strangled sob. Her arm pulsed sharply, even with the smallest of movements.

Mariko shook her head clear. And looked around.

From the way Chiyo was positioned across her—and from the way Mariko's lacquered *zori* sandals had fallen from the maidservant's hands—it was clear the girl had tried to free Mariko from the wrecked litter. Tried to free her and died in the attempt. Blood was everywhere. Splashed across the shining inlays. Spilling from the nasty gash in Mariko's head. Pooling from the fatal wound in Chiyo's heart. An arrow had pierced clean through the small girl's breastbone; its tip dug into the skin of Mariko's forearm, a trickle of crimson in its wake.

Several arrowheads were embedded in the wood of the *norimono*. Several more were fixed at odd angles across Chiyo's body. Arrows that could not have been meant to kill a kind maidservant. And had it not been for this kind maidservant, these arrows would undoubtedly have struck Mariko.

Mariko's eyes brimmed with more tears as she clutched Chiyo tight.

Thank you, Chiyo-chan. Sumimasen.

Blinking away her tears, Mariko tried to shift her head. Tried to seek her bearings. The ache near her temple throbbed, keeping time with the rapid beat of her heart.

Just as Mariko began to move, a rumble of male voices drew near. She peeked through a break in the mangled screen above. All she could discern were two men dressed in black from head to toe. Their weapons shone bright in the light of nearby torches, their blades oiled a sinister red.

It can't be . . .

But the evidence was irrefutable. The Black Clan had over-run her convoy.

Mariko held her breath, wincing into the corner as they moved closer to the litter.

"She's dead, then?" the tallest one said in gruff fashion.

The masked man to the right considered the overturned litter, his head cocked to one side. "Either that or she passed out from the—"

A howl in the distance swallowed the last of their conversation.

The men eyed each other. Knowingly.

"Check once more," the first man said. "I'd rather not be forced to report we failed in our mission."

The second man gave a curt nod and moved toward the litter, his torch held high.

Panic took hold of Mariko. She clenched her rattling teeth still.

Two things had become clear as these masked men spoke:

The Black Clan obviously wanted Mariko dead. And someone had tasked them with killing her.

Mariko changed position, ever so slightly, as though it might conceal her from their prying gazes. As though it might shrink her into nothingness. Chiyo's head slumped forward, thwacking against the battered wood of the *norimono*. Mariko bit back an oath, cursing her thoughtlessness. She inhaled through her nose, willing her heart to cease its incessant pounding.

Why did it suddenly smell so strongly of smoke?

Mariko's eyes darted around in alarm. The edges of Chiyo's bloodstained robe were blackening. Brushing against the crumbled wick of Mariko's tiny lantern.

Catching flame.

It took all her restraint to remain quiet and still.

Terror pressed in on her from all sides. Pressed her to make a final decision.

If Mariko lingered, she would be burned alive. If she moved from her hiding place, the masked men outside would undoubtedly finish their dark task.

Flames licked the hem of the maidservant's robe, grasping for Mariko's kimono like the tentacles of an octopus.

Her panic rising, Mariko shifted once more, stifling a cough in her shoulder.

It was time to make a decision.

How am I to die today? By fire or by the sword?

The advancing man halted a hairsbreadth away. "The litter is on fire."

"Then let it burn." The taller man did not flinch. Nor did he look their way.

"We should leave." The man just outside glanced over his shoulder. "Before the scent of blood and singed flesh draws the nightbeasts." He was near enough to touch. Near enough to strike, had Mariko the courage.

The taller man nodded. "We shall leave soon enough. But not before you check to make sure the girl is dead."

The mournful baying grew louder. Closer. Hemming them in.

When the man nearby reached for the mangled screens, one of the *norimono*'s damaged poles split in two. The broken wood struck his arm, sending a flurry of sparks every which way.

Leaping back, he cursed under his breath. "The girl is as good as dead." The man spoke more forcefully, his torch whipping about in the wind. Heat from the mounting fire sent sweat down Mariko's neck in steady trickles. The growing blaze near her feet crackled as it seared Chiyo's skin.

Mariko's stomach lurched at the smell. Sweat poured onto her stiff white collar.

Make a decision, Hattori Mariko! How do you wish to die?

Her teeth chattered. With a forceful swallow, Mariko dug her fingernails into her palms, her eyes flitting about the small, shattered space. Bravery did not come to her naturally. She spent too much time weighing her options to be brave. Too much time calculating the many paths before her.

But Mariko knew it was time to do more. Time to be more.

She would not die a coward. Mariko was the daughter of a samurai. The sister of the Dragon of Kai.

But more than that, she still held power over her decisions.

For at least this one last day.

She would face her enemy. And die with honor.

Her sight blurring from the thickening smoke, Mariko pushed Chiyo aside, her hands trembling despite her best efforts.

A shout rang out in the darkness. The man near the *norimono* twisted around at its cracking toll.

The cries were followed by the snarl of an animal. The growl of several more.

Another shriek. The echo of a death knell. With it came the cries of feasting animals.

"The nightbeasts!" The man with the torch pivoted again, his flame leaping with his motions. "They're attacking our flank!"

"Check the girl," the first man insisted. "The girl is more important than—"

"The prince's bride is as good as dead!" With that, he threw his torch on top of Mariko's *norimono*, whirling away as he sealed her fate. "Collect our fallen. Leave nothing behind," he yelled to men she could not see.

Mariko bit back a scream as clanking metal and rustling bodies converged in the nearby shadows. Chaos grew with each passing moment. The flames in the *norimono* leapt higher. Faster. Their heat turned her skin pink. She clasped her fingers tight, smothering her coughs as she shrank farther into the corner. Tears streamed down her face, leaching her of all resolve.

Coward.

The torch above crackled to fire against the varnished wood of the *norimono*.

It wouldn't be long before Mariko would burn along with it. The lacquered tinder around her popped and fizzed, the melted resin burning into blue flame.

A shuddering breath flew past her lips.

I am not *a coward. I am . . . greater than this.*

Her tears stained the front of her kimono silk. She refused to die like an animal locked in a cage. Like a girl with nothing save her name.

Better to die by the sword. Better to die at the mercy of the nightbeasts.

To die in the night air. *Free.*

Her pulse trilling in her fingertips, Mariko shoved Chiyo's body away in final decision. She kicked open the *norimono's* door. One glossy sandal fell as she struggled to heave herself through, gulping air to quench the burn in her throat. Mariko reeled from the ruins, her eyes wild as she glanced about, frantic.

The forest was full dark.

And her kimono was on fire.

Her mind worked quickly. Instinctively. Mariko wrapped the silken material around itself, robbing the fire of the air it needed to burn. Her wrist seared beneath the kimono's folds, smoke curling from the watered silk in grey wisps. With a rasping cry, Mariko tore at her obi, cursing the way it had been wound about her waist. So intricate. So unnecessary. Stumbling through the underbrush, she ripped the beautiful kimono from her shoulders, lurching away from the burning *norimono* like a drunken fool.

Her eyes sought the darkness for any beacon of light. All she could see was her litter, engulfed in flames. Her kimono smoldered against the forest floor.

If the men return, they will see the kimono. They will know I escaped.

Without hesitating, Mariko took hold of the hem and hurled the silk back at the pile of hissing flames.

It flared as it touched the melting varnish. Burning silk and scorching lacquer. Melting Dragon's Beard candy.

Mingled with the scent of searing flesh.

Chiyo.

She blinked hard, struggling to remain steady.

All around her were the bodies of her father's convoy. Maidservants. Samurai. Foot soldiers.

Slaughtered as one.

Mariko stood swathed in shadow, her chest heaving as her eyes flew across the damp earth.

Anything of value had been taken. Swiftly. Efficiently. Trunks had been emptied. Imperial chargers had been yoked as chattel, leaving nothing but their tasseled reins behind. Ribbons of red and white and gold littered the ground.

But Mariko knew robbery had not been the primary objective.

The Black Clan tried to murder me. Even though they knew I was to marry Prince Raiden, they still carried out their task.

Someone with sway over the Black Clan wishes me dead.

Cold shock descended upon her in a sudden rush. Her shoulders began to wilt. Again—as if on instinct—Mariko set them straight, her chin braced against the threat of further tears. She refused to succumb to shock. Just as she refused to grant refuge to her fears.

Think, Hattori Mariko. Keep moving.

She staggered forward, intent on fleeing without a glance

back. Two halting steps were all she managed before she thought better of it. Thought better about the odds of proceeding through a darkened wood, unarmed and dressed in nothing but her underclothes.

Shielding herself from the worst of the carnage, Mariko moved toward a fallen samurai. His *katana* was missing, but his shorter *wakizashi* was still in its scabbard, bound to his waist. She took the small, wieldier weapon in hand. Pausing only to kick soil across her tracks, she moved through the forest, without direction, without purpose. Without anything, save the need to survive.

The darkness around her was oppressive. She stumbled on roots, unable to see. After a time, the lack of one sense heightened all the others. The snap of a twig or the scuttle of an insect rang through the air with the resonance of a gong. When the bushes nearby rustled—steel grinding against stone—Mariko pressed into the bark of a tree, terror finally taking the last of the warmth from her blood.

A low growl crawled from the earth, cutting through her like the thunder of an approaching army. It was followed by heavy paws padding over dead leaves.

A savage sort of stealth.

A nightbeast, stalking the last of its prey.

Mariko's stomach clenched, and her fingers shook as she prepared to meet her end.

No. I will not cower in a corner.

Never again.

She scrambled away from the tree, her ankle catching on

a scree of rocks. Each movement jolted through her as she landed on the forest floor, only to claw back to her feet. Her body felt alive, energy rolling beneath her skin in waves, all while her blood coursed through her body. There was nowhere to hide. The white silk of her underrobe did nothing to shield her from the forest's most sinister monsters.

The growling behind her had become a steady grumble. Undeterred. Moving ever closer. When Mariko spun around to face her attacker, two saurian yellow eyes materialized in the darkness. Like those of a giant snake.

The creature that formed around these eyes was immense, its features resembling a jaguar, its body as massive as a bear. Without further provocation, the beast rose on its hind legs, saliva dripping from its bared fangs. It threw back its head and howled, the sound ricocheting into the night.

Her knees turned to water as Mariko fought to brace herself.

But the creature did not attack.

It looked to one side, then back at her. Its yellow eyes glowed bright. It canted its head, as though glancing past her shoulder.

Run! a voice within Mariko cried out. *Run, you silly little fool!*

She inhaled, taking a slow step back.

Still the beast did not attack. It glanced again to the same side, then back at her, its growl rising in pitch and ferocity.

As though it was warning her.

Then—without another sound—the beast glided toward

her. Like a ghost. Like a demon of the forest, flying on a whorl of black smoke.

Mariko's scream tore through the night sky.

The creature disappeared in a whoosh of air. In a swirl of inky darkness.

"Well." A gruff voice resonated from behind her. "Fortune has indeed smiled upon me tonight."

Not a Girl

---✷---

A dirty man materialized from the shadows. He stalked toward her, twigs snapping at his bare feet.

"What are you doing here, girl?" His lips glittered with saliva. "Don't you know this part of the forest is dangerous?" Beady black eyes raked over her trembling form.

No man had ever dared to look at her like this before.

With such unchecked evil alighting his gaze.

"I'm . . ." Mariko paused to think before answering. To devise the safest tack. She could not admonish him as her mother would have done. This was not one of her father's vassals or servants. Indeed—after what she'd just witnessed—there was no way for her to know if the man was of flesh and bone at all.

Enough of this nonsense.

Fear would not drive her to discern shape from smoke and shadows.

Mariko stood tall, angling the *wakizashi* against her under-robe. Out of sight. Instead of adopting her mother's imperious tone, she spoke calmly. Softly. "In truth, I'd rather not be here. Which is why I'm trying to find my way out." She met his eyes with a silent challenge.

"Dressed like that?" He leered at her, his smile a jumble of grime and missing teeth.

She said nothing, though every bone in her body stretched thin.

The man oozed closer. "I take it you're lost, then?" His tongue leapt out of his mouth, a lizard questing for purchase.

Mariko swallowed the urge to reply. The urge to take him to task. Kenshin would have led him away in chains, with nothing more than a nod to the men at his back. The men bearing the crest of the Hattori clan. But Kenshin had the might of a soldier. The will of a samurai.

And it was unwise for Mariko to provoke an unknown.

So then, what should she say?

If threats were not a weapon in her arsenal, then perhaps cunning would serve her instead. Mariko stayed silent. Though her free hand shook, the palm wrapped around the *wakizashi* remained steadfast.

"You're lost." The man paced nearer. Near enough for Mariko to smell the scent of unwashed skin and sour rice wine. The copper of recently spilled blood. "How did you manage to get lost, lovely creature?"

Her breath caught. The grip around the short sword

tightened. "I imagine if one knew the answer to that question, one would no longer be considered lost," she said in an even tone.

The man chortled, suffusing the air with his acrid breath. "Smart girl. So very careful. But not careful enough. If you were truly careful, you wouldn't be lost in the woods . . . all alone." He rested his *bō* in the earth between them. Fresh blood stained one end of the wooden staff. "Are you sure you're not part of the convoy less than a league from here? The one with all the dead bodies"—he leaned even closer, dropping his voice to a whisper—"and no money?"

He'd tracked her. Even with the care Mariko had taken to cover her trail, this man had managed to find her. This shiftless crow who fed on the scraps of his betters. Again she chose to keep silent, secreting the *wakizashi* completely behind her.

Words would not serve her well with a man such as this.

"Because if you are lost," he continued at his leisure, "I'd consider it quite a fortunate omen for you. The Black Clan doesn't take prisoners. Nor does it leave survivors. It's bad for business, you see. Both theirs and mine."

Understanding settled on Mariko, its grasp all too tight. As she'd suspected, he was not a member of the Black Clan. Even from the little she'd gathered earlier, the band of masked murderers was far more organized.

Far more precise.

This man—with his filthy feet and soiled garments—was anything but.

When Mariko failed to reply yet again, he furrowed his brow, agitation beginning to take root.

"What if I delivered you to them?" He sidled closer—an arm's length away—dragging his *bō* haphazardly through the dark loam at his feet. It should have been threatening, but the man lacked the necessary focus. The necessary discipline of a true warrior. "I'm certain the Black Clan would appreciate me bringing you to them. I can't imagine they would want word of this failure to reach their employers. Or their competitors."

As she watched him lose footing on a root, Mariko couldn't suppress a soft gibe: "Well then, I'd be much obliged if you would lead me to them. It appears they've taken a few things of mine. And I would like them back."

He rasped another laugh, and—even with its lazy resonance—the sound chased down her spine. "You'd almost be amusing if you smiled more." His lips curled upward. "In case your mother never told you, pretty girls like you should smile. Especially if you're trying to get a man to do your bidding."

Mariko stiffened. She hated his words. Hated the suggestion she needed a man to do anything for her.

Hated its truth.

"Don't worry." The man swung his *bō* slowly, directing her to walk before him. "We'll find the Black Clan. It might take some time. But I happen to know their favorite watering holes ring the western edge of the forest. They're bound to turn up there sooner or later. And I'm a patient man." With a sly grin, he removed the coil of fraying rope dangling from his waistband.

Mariko prepared to fight, easing her feet apart. Bending slightly at the knees. Anchoring herself to the earth.

"Besides—" His deepening smile caused her to shudder internally. "You look like excellent company."

As he uncoiled the rope, Mariko readied her blade. Kenshin had taught her where to strike. Soft places unhampered by bone, like the stomach and the throat. If she could slash above the inside of his knee, his blood would spill fast enough to kill him in mere moments.

Mariko calculated. Considered.

She was so busy in thought that she failed to anticipate his sudden movement.

In an instant, the man had grabbed Mariko by the forearm, jerking her toward him.

She shrieked, pushing back at him. The *bō* was knocked from his grasp, clattering against the base of a tree trunk. In the ensuing tumult, Mariko sought an angle to slash at his grip. She swung the *wakizashi* wide, not even caring to aim, hoping to strike anything at all.

Callous laughter rolled from his lips as the man grappled for the *wakizashi*. His elbow caught the side of her face, bringing Mariko to the ground with no more effort than it took to subdue a mewling calf.

One of her wrists in his filthy grip, the man attempted to bind her hands together.

There was no time for fear or fury or emotion of any kind

to steal upon her. Mariko screamed loudly, kicking at him and wrestling for control of the blade. Its tip sliced into her upper sleeve, cutting the fabric away from her body. Revealing more skin.

The man shoved Mariko's cheek into the dirt.

"It will do you no good to fight, girl," he said. "There is no reason for you to make this unpleasant for both of us."

"I am *not* a girl." The rage collected in her chest. "I am Hattori Mariko. And you will die for this. By *my* hand."

I swear it.

He chuffed in amusement, his lower lip jutting smugly, saliva pooling in its center. "The one marked for death is you. If the Black Clan wants you dead, you'll never make it through this forest alive." Wiping his mouth on a shoulder, he paused as if in deliberation. "But I might be willing to consider other options." His eyes stopped on the swath of naked skin above her elbow.

The look she found on his face made Mariko want to tear out his throat with nothing but her teeth. "I do not make deals with thieves."

"We're all thieves, girl. Your kind most of all." He placed the blade of the *wakizashi* beneath her chin. "Make your decision. Barter with me, and I'll return you to your family in one piece. For the right price, of course." His foul stench washed over her. "Or wait to barter with the Black Clan. But if I had a preference, I would choose me. I'm much nicer. And I won't hurt you."

In the lie she heard the truth. Saw it, buried deep in his gaze.

I will not be bandied about by men any longer. I am not a prize to be bought or sold.

Mariko let the desire to fight ease out of her, as though she was contemplating. Capitulating. The *wakizashi* dropped from beneath her chin just as her palms fell to her sides. Without a second thought, she threw a handful of dirt in the man's eyes. He flailed, his fingers swiping at clumps of earth, his soft underbelly exposed. Mariko promptly punched him at the base of his throat, then rolled away as he coughed and gagged, struggling to catch breath. Mariko tried to stand—tried to run—but her thin white robe was tangled around his legs. She fell atop him, and he made a blind grab for her.

Without thought, Mariko snatched the tortoiseshell bar from her hair—

And stabbed it through his left eye.

The ornament pierced through its center, a needle through a grape.

His scream was slow. Tortured.

With its sound came a sudden rush of clarity. It blossomed in Mariko's chest, spreading like a swallow of perfectly brewed tea.

Simple. Instinctual.

She took hold of the *wakizashi* and slashed the man's throat from ear to ear.

His scream was swallowed by gurgles. Crimson bubbles

sloshed past his lips as he tried to form his final words. After a few moments, he fell silent. Motionless, save for the blood dripping from his eye and throat.

Mariko crawled away, heaving the contents of her stomach into the underbrush.

Hattori Mariko crouched against the rough trunk of an ancient pine tree. Her body rocked slowly in place. She watched her white *tabi* socks dampen in the misted moss. The brambles around her had become a refuge, the lichen at her sides a cloak. Soughing pines swayed above her head. Their echoing moans brought to mind the disquiet of lost souls. The many lost souls that had met their doom in the shadow of Jukai forest.

Less than a stone's throw from her lay one of these lost souls.

Thank the stars I am not among them.

Not yet, anyway.

Mariko wrapped her arms about her legs. As though she could hold herself together.

The forest may not yet have claimed her for its own, but it was clear she was horribly lost. Beyond all comprehension. In a wooden maze filled with creatures—both human and inhuman—that could kill her with only the wish to do so. The darkness that had recently become her refuge would also likely bring about her ruin. Its pressing menace reminded her of the time ten years past when Kenshin had challenged her to dive with him beneath the surface of the lake at the edge of their family's land. It had been the afternoon following a summer storm. The water was a muddy color, the silt at its floor a constant swirl.

Though she typically eschewed such mindless challenges, Mariko had always been an excellent swimmer. And Kenshin had been particularly self-important that day. Had been especially in need of a lesson. So she'd dived for the bottom, her hands spreading through the murky water with assertive strokes. As she'd clawed toward her goal, a branch of twisted leaves had brushed her cheek, disorienting her. In that instant, she'd lost her bearings. Mariko could no longer tell which way to swim. Could no longer make out a path in either direction. She'd taken in mouthful after mouthful of water as the terror had frayed away her confidence. Had rubbed its edges raw until it all but fell apart.

Were it not for the pull of Kenshin's steady hands, Mariko could have perished that day.

It felt like that here. In this darkness thick with threat. In this forest, harboring in its folds the nightmares of millennia.

A hooting owl broke through the quiet as it swooped lower. As it prowled for its evening meal. Glancing to her left, Mariko caught sight of a spiderweb in a bend of branches nearby. Dewdrops clung to its silken strands. She focused on the way they welled. Collected. Slid down and across the twinkling silk to pool at its center.

Before she could blink an eye, the water splashed from the web in a cascade of diamonds. Its maker had returned, eight long legs stretching across its surface.

Lying in wait for its prey.

Mariko wanted to run from her skin. Be anything, be *anywhere* but where she was.

A brush of wind raked through the thorny brambles around her. Its breeze coiled beneath her hair, lifting the unbound strands. They caught in the stickiness on her cheeks. The salty wetness left there by trails of tears.

She needed to find her way home. Back to her family. Back to where she supposedly belonged.

But Mariko could not silence the thrum of her thoughts.

Could not squelch her curiosity.

She wanted—no, *needed*—to find out why the Black Clan had been sent to kill her.

Who wished her dead? And why?

She inhaled carefully. Gripping her knees as they pressed into her chest, Mariko forced herself to stop swaying.

And start thinking.

What would Kenshin do?

The answer to that was simple. Her older brother would stop at nothing to learn who had tried to kill him. Who had robbed his family and nearly brought an end to his life. Kenshin wouldn't rest until he brought the heads of his enemies home in sacks stained red with their blood.

But her brother was allowed such discretion. Such freedom

to choose. After all, he had not earned the name the Dragon of Kai by remaining safe within the walls of their family's home.

He'd earned it on the field of battle. With every swing of his sword.

If Mariko returned home, her family would promptly dry her tears and send her back on her way. Back down this same path. Any word of the events that had transpired in Jukai forest would be guarded to the death. If the emperor or the prince or any member of the nobility learned that Mariko had been attacked on her journey to Inako, the royal family might cancel their marriage arrangement. Might claim this misfortune was a bad omen. One that could not be risked on royal blood.

Never mind the cold question that would undoubtedly follow. The whispers that would trail at her back.

The question of Mariko's virtue. Lost in the forest, alone with murderers and thieves. A question that would linger, despite her family's heartfelt protests.

Mariko pressed her lips to one side.

The same question she'd already answered in revenge. In an afternoon of calculated fury. But if . . .

If.

If she learned the truth—if she learned who was responsible for sending the Black Clan to murder her—Mariko might be able to spare her parents the embarrassment of having their daughter turned away. Might spare them the risk of having their family name soiled under a cloud of suspicion.

Her thoughts began to wind through her mind with the slow squeeze of a snake.

What if someone in Inako had sent the Black Clan? What if a rival family in the nobility had arranged her death to ruin the Hattori family's rising fortune?

If such a feat could occur, then anyone in the imperial city could be called to question.

If Mariko learned the truth behind tonight's events, then perhaps she could bring to light her family's detractors, proving herself useful to the Hattori name, beyond securing an advantageous marriage. Moreover, she would have a few days—perhaps even weeks—to spend roaming at her leisure.

Then she would return and be the dutiful daughter evermore.

Mariko swallowed. She could almost taste the air of freedom. Its sweet promise, tantalizing the tip of her tongue.

Again a cool breeze cut through the air, twisting her hair in another frenzy. The light scent of camellia oil filled her nostrils. The oil used to tame her thick strands. To coil them into obedience.

Reminding her.

Hattori Mariko could not roam the Empire of Wa at her leisure.

A girl from a noble family could never attempt such a thing. Not to mention the fact that Hattori Kenshin was among the best trackers in the empire. As soon as her brother discovered Mariko had gone missing, he would begin his search, without question. That was how it had always been. Though Kenshin was only a few moments older than Mariko, he had cared for her—watched out for her—since they were children.

Her brother would find her. Of that there was no question.

Exasperated, she swiped a white sleeve across her forehead. A streak of black powder rubbed onto the silk. The burned paulownia wood that had been used to enhance her eyebrows. Mariko scrubbed at the stained sleeve, then gave up with a silent oath, her moment of happiness swallowed by the inevitable crush of truth.

Her eyes fell on the bloodied *wakizashi* lying nearby. No longer caring about the loss of her fine underrobe, she wiped the blood on its hem. Smeared it further. Blood and blackened paulownia.

It was true Hattori Mariko could not roam the empire at her leisure. But if . . .

If.

Mariko removed the jade bar from the last ring of hair at her crown. The black tangles tumbled around her shoulders, unfurling to her waist in a fall of scented ebony. She gathered her hair in one hand, near the nape of her neck.

Later she would marvel at how she did not hesitate. Not even for an instant.

Mariko sliced through the gathered strands in one blow.

Then she stood. With only a passing glance of remorse, Mariko scattered her hair across the thorny brambles, careful to conceal the strands deep in the shadows.

She felt lighter; her shoulders eased back.

Mariko glanced around with a new sight, as though her

eyes could penetrate the heavy darkness. See through the thick veil of night. Her gaze locked on the motionless figure to her left—the twisted scavenger she had recently killed.

Strange how she did not feel any pity. Did not feel even a shred of remorse.

Kenshin would have been proud.

She'd fought off her assailant. And in doing so, she'd displayed one of the seven virtues of *bushidō*:

Courage.

The way of the warrior.

Mariko knelt beside the pool of congealed blood. As with everything else, the man's garments were filthy. The collar of his hemp *kosode* was stained with rice wine and dried millet, and the linen of his trousers was threadbare.

But they would serve one last purpose.

Her thoughts unnervingly clear, Mariko untied the sash of her underrobe. Let it drop from her shoulders to the ground. Then she reached to untie the knot of his *kosode*.

Hattori Mariko was not just any girl.

She was more.

The Dragon of Kai

———✳———

The massive warhorse stalked through the predawn mist. A curtain of vines parted in its wake. Mounted samurai moved from the darkness, resuming their formation at the beast's flank. Its heavily armored rider led them inexorably forward. The horse huffed through its nostrils, its eyes wild as its breath mingled with the mist—two steady streams of barely checked rage.

The samurai atop the sorrel horse was a stark contrast to his mount. He appeared calm. Collected. His helmet sported twisted horns. A gaping dragon's maw adorned the front, fashioned of bloodred lacquer and polished steel. The breastplate of his *dō* was molded from rectangular plates of hardened leather and iron. It bore a hexagonal crest, with two arrow feathers affixed like dashes in its center. Opposite each other. Ever watching the other's back. Ever promising a balance between light and dark.

Silently the men and their beasts crept through the rapidly fading darkness. An early-morning fog encircled the horses' hooves, unraveling with each step as they cut through Jukai forest. Ever forward. Ever onward.

The samurai leading the contingent rode through the ghostly wood, his eyes scrutinizing the ground before him.

Missing nothing.

After a time, they came upon a clearing. The same clearing they had sought for the past two days. Recently arrived vultures circled above in slow downward spirals, drawing the men closer.

Drawing them toward a scene of death and devastation.

Before the band of samurai lay the remnants of a wealthy convoy, recently plundered.

The men reined in their horses. Their leader dismounted without a word. He was so light of foot, his steps could barely be heard. The white fog swirled around him as he moved forward soundlessly.

Though he could have paused to take note of the men lost—the bodies of the fifteen samurai left to rot in an ignominious predawn—the leader instead moved with unfailing purpose toward a heap of wood that looked to be the remains of a recent bonfire. As he neared the charred traces, the shadow of an elegant, lacquered *norimono* formed before his gaze. The samurai adjusted the swords at his belt and removed his helmet.

A rosy light began to crest through the trees at his back. Unbidden, he turned to face its blushing warmth. He took in a careful breath. A breath mindful of the life he was still privileged to live. A breath mindful of the good death he was destined to have—

On the field of battle.

He was young. His face was lean. Hawkish. With a pointed jaw and eyes blacker than pitch. His topknot was perfect, every strand aligned in elegant submission. As he inspected the ruins, another armored samurai moved to his side, carrying a fistful of burned *boro* and silk—two singed banners, one bearing the same hexagonal crest and another bearing the crest of the emperor.

The second samurai passed along his confirmation. "I am sorry, Kenshin-*wakasama*." Though his words were apologetic, he did not speak with remorse. He spoke with an understood promise.

One of bloody retribution.

Instead of meeting the samurai's promise with one of his own, the young man with the dragon helmet did not even glance his way. Expressionless in the face of the horrors perpetrated on his own men—on his own family—he gripped a blackened piece of wood and yanked it aside with vicious precision. It splintered, its ends crumbling to dust in his grasp.

The young samurai peered inside.

The scorched body of a girl lay within. What remained of her skin was crackled black by the fire. When he studied the carnage further, Hattori Kenshin noticed the glint of several arrowheads buried beneath the girl's remains, a suspicious stain darkening the *norimono*'s floor. Tarry. Thick.

Blood.

She had not died by fire.

He paused.

Then continued in his search, his eyes unceasingly roving.

Wedged into one of the only remaining corners of the richly appointed *norimono* was a small triangle of burned fabric. The same sort of *boro* fabric his family used to fashion their pennants. The same *boro* the peasants and maidservants wore.

He looked harder, scouring the embers for further glimpses of truth.

Mariko's kimono. Not even a hint of the distinct *tatsumura* silk could be seen anywhere.

Kenshin's eyes moved to the bare earth at his feet. Drifted to the left, then slowly to the right.

A *zori* sandal—all but hidden from his eyes—lay on its side a few steps away from the *norimono*. It shone, even in the dim reaches of the early-morning sun. A lacquered finish unmarred by flames. Kenshin stepped toward his sister's shoe, kneeling to retrieve it.

"My lord," the samurai at his back began in a hesitant tone, "I know—"

Kenshin silenced him with a glance, then returned to his work, his eyes still searching. Ever hunting.

Soon he found what he was looking for.

Tracks.

Two sets. One made in pursuit of the other, the second set of far less interest to Kenshin than the first.

The first set were the tracks of a woman's split-toed *tabi* socks. Tracks like those of a wounded deer, staggering away from its inevitable demise. It was clear an attempt had been made to cover them. But few who traversed these woods possessed the dogged determination and unfailing skill of Hattori Kenshin. He knew these tracks. The shapes pressed into the earth were too small to be those of a man. Too delicate.

Though his twin sister was anything but delicate, Kenshin knew they belonged to her with the same sort of certainty he felt in his heart. In his every breath. She'd been alive three days ago.

And these tracks led to the left.

Away from the massacre.

Without a word, Hattori Kenshin returned to his wild-eyed warhorse. Born to the motions of a warrior—to the movements of a hunt—he replaced his dragon helmet and chin guard, then swung onto his oiled saddle.

"My lord," the samurai protested again, "though it may be difficult to accept, I am afraid it is clear Lady Hattori—"

Kenshin raised his left hand. Curled his fingers into a fist. Then he signaled his men onward.

Following the tracks into the forest.

From his perch at the head of the convoy, the Dragon of Kai grinned slowly. Darkly.

His sister was not dead.

No.

She was much too smart for that.

The Golden Castle

His Imperial Majesty Minamoto Masaru—direct descendant of the sun goddess, heavenly sovereign of the Empire of Wa—was lost.

In his own gardens, no less.

But there was no need for him to worry. It was not the kind of lost to cause alarm. Today he'd intentionally wandered too far. Wandered away from those who hovered around him like flies to a carcass.

He often became intentionally lost on afternoons such as this.

The season was beginning its slow shift from spring to summer. Everything around him was in bloom, the air stirred by a soft breeze. An ocher sunset gilded the waters of the pond to his left. Its gently lapping shore rippled like molten amber. Fallen cherry blossoms littered its surface, pale pink petals strewn across slate-grey waters.

The flowers were beginning to die. To fall under the weight of the sun.

It was his favorite time of year. Warm enough to wander the royal gardens of Heian Castle without feeling the threat of a chill, yet cool enough to forgo the nuisance of an oiled-paper umbrella.

Perhaps he would venture to the moon-viewing pavilion tonight. The sky had been unusually clear today. The stars, too, should be unusually bright.

He took his time across the squared stepping-stones encircling a miniature pagoda. Its tiered eaves were sprinkled with birdseed. A heron strutted near the shore, blasting a warning to the black swan gliding by: *Keep clear of my domain.*

The emperor smiled to himself.

Was he the heron, or was he the swan?

His smile fell as quickly as it rose.

A familiar warble cut through the silence at his right shoulder. A swallow soared toward him, landing on a corner of the miniature pagoda, its wings an unearthly shade of iridescent blue. The diminutive bird puffed out its stomach and shook out its feathers, tilting its head to one side.

Waiting for the emperor.

The emperor took two steps toward the swallow. Leaned in close, his left ear angled near the swallow's bright orange beak. The small bird tilted closer, unafraid. Unnatural. Its familiar warble faded to a hushed whisper. A melodic sigh.

The emperor nodded. The swallow preened. Once more the bird took flight on a wisp of wind.

Vanishing into the clouds above.

Without even a moment's pause, Minamoto Masaru turned from the shore, back in the direction of his castle. After wending down a few misguided paths, he finally saw the topmost gable of the imperial palace rising above the trees.

In honeyed moments like these, the emperor understood why Heian Castle was often called the Golden Castle. A sea of gilded roof tiles spilled from tier to tier, catching the light in slowly descending waves. Along each hipped eave were carved figurines of cranes, fish, and tigers. Cherry trees lined the eastern foot trails; orange trees bordered the west. The covered walkways leading from building to building were constructed of citrus-scented cypress wood, their paths formed of neatly raked white gravel.

He stopped to watch his castle become awash in the colors of a setting sun.

If he didn't take time to enjoy such sights, they would soon be lost to him.

Like tears in rain.

The emperor proceeded to walk by a granite monument resting on a hillock to his right. His eye caught on the flapping pennants adorning its four corners.

A trio of gentian flowers above a spray of bamboo leaves.

The Minamoto clan's royal crest.

His frown deepened as he continued onward.

In a few months it would be time for the festival of Obon. The time each year when all the empire's citizens returned to their ancestral homes to honor their deceased. Soon the emperor would be making the journey to Yedo for this very reason. To clear his ancestors' graves of weeds and pay homage to them with food and drink.

But would his forefathers feel pride at his return?

Or would they feel disdain?

The emperor could not answer these questions. Not yet. For he had not yet accomplished all he meant to accomplish. All his greatest aspirations had yet to be realized. Yes, it was true he'd maintained power over the Empire of Wa for the entirety of his reign. But it was a muddled sort of power—much like a loosely tied ribbon, its ends trailing the ground. He had not achieved half of what his father had achieved before passing on the crown; he had not made the Empire of Wa bigger or stronger.

He had not managed to build a greater legacy for his sons.

Indeed, it could even be suggested that he'd left his empire in worse condition. One far weaker than before. One that would rely on the strengths of *both* his sons.

Roku's intellect.

And Raiden's fist.

Strange that all this had come to pass. Come to pass despite the emperor having sacrificed so much to give his sons more. He'd gone as far as to execute many of his childhood friends to keep them from challenging his reign.

The emperor halted again in his stroll, as though the wind had been cracked from his chest. He took a slow breath. A pinching one, heated tongs clenched tight around his heart. He still felt it, even after all this time; the weight of his friends' deaths would always be a heavy burden. A constant reminder. But he could not afford to feel remorse for his past decisions.

They had not been made lightly.

The Emperor of Wa could not be openly challenged by any man, not if he ever meant to achieve his greatest desires. And his friends would undoubtedly have challenged him. Naganori would never have remained quiet in the face of the emperor's most recent edicts. His most recent attempts to consolidate his holdings. To raise taxes on his lands. To collect his due. All before striking out on his grandest of conquests:

Waging war for dominion over the sea and all its spoils.

Yes. Naganori would always have been a problem. An Asano man, through and through. Married to the law and its pervasive sense of justice.

But perhaps Asano Naganori could have been controlled in time.

Were it not for others . . . less willing to bend.

Takeda Shingen.

A cloud of yellow butterflies wafted across the white gravel before him. They took flight on a twist of air, curling and unfurling into themselves like a beating heart.

No. The emperor's childhood friends would have been far too problematic.

Better he keep his council small.

Better he keep it amongst his family. And no one else.

He pushed through the cloud of butterflies, leaving them to scatter in disarray.

Alas, the deaths of his friends had not succeeded in putting an end to the whispers at his feet. The murmurs of those who would prefer to see a man with military skill at the helm of the empire. Especially of late, the emperor had witnessed the pomp and grandeur of the royal court being cast in a weak light. The weak light of undue opulence. Of unnecessary excess.

Awareness flared in his throat. Pulsed in his ears. The grandeur of the court was the grandeur he knew well. It was the grandeur of his son, the crown prince of Wa, Minamoto Roku. Second born, but first in line to rule.

It was not the grandeur of his other son, Raiden. Firstborn.

Yet destined to rule nothing.

Indeed, Destiny was a fickle beast.

"There you are, my sovereign."

Warmth riffled through the emperor at the sound of this voice. A stirring that began in his bones and thrummed to his fingertips. The comfort of a loved one. Of an embrace he need never question.

But he did not turn at its sound.

The husky female voice continued. "I thought I would find you here."

He did not face her. The emperor did not need to look to see her face. Its image lingered ever in the forefront of his mind. It was the face of the woman he had loved all his life. The mother of his elder son, Raiden.

Not his empress. Not his wife. But the woman of his heart.

She was here. With him. Though he'd failed to make her

his empress, she'd stayed by his side as his royal consort. Stayed by his side and never questioned anything.

"You know me well, Kanako," he said without looking her way.

"Yes." Her laughter was the music of a softly strummed shamisen. "I do."

Finally he turned toward her. Time had not weathered her features as they had his. Her figure was willowy, her skin like smooth ivory. She was still beautiful. He would always find her beautiful. From the moment he'd watched her conjure animals from the stuff of shadows, he'd found her to be the most beautiful woman he'd ever beheld.

They'd been young then. Not much older than children. He'd loved her still. And she'd loved him still, even when his father had forced him to marry a different young woman. One from a wealthy family with a million-*koku* domain.

The emperor did not reach for Kanako, though he wanted to. It was impossible to know who watched them, even now. Which servants reported to which master.

Or mistress.

And it would not do for anyone to witness the emperor in a moment of weakness, no matter how insignificant.

Blossoms from a nearby cherry tree slanted their way. Kanako wove her slender fingers through the shower of petals, catching several in a grasp of magic. A swirl of sorcery. Almost absentmindedly, she conjured the petals into slowly churning eddies. Shapes. First a dragon. Then a lion. Then a snake.

Transfixed, the emperor watched the snake consume the lion. Kanako smiled, her lips curving into a gentle crescent.

"Did my little swallow deliver its tidings?" she asked softly, letting the snake roll between her fingers.

The emperor nodded. Waited to hear more of what he craved.

"The daughter of Hattori Kano is nowhere to be found," she continued. "She was due here two nights past. Many are saying her convoy was ambushed near Jukai forest." A pause. "By the Black Clan."

He waited further.

Kanako let the petals drift away. "It is not clear if the girl lives."

Though a tic rose in his jaw, the emperor nodded carefully. Then he resumed his stroll toward his castle.

"You have told our son?" he asked under his breath.

"Not yet." Kanako glanced sideways at him, her dove-grey kimono silks parting like waves at her feet. "Not until we decide what must be said. What must be done."

They rounded a bend in the white gravel walkway. The empress's pavilion bloomed into sight. The emperor could hear the tittering of female voices, the undoubted condescension passing through the ranks of his wife's countless attendants.

The emperor is walking through the gardens with his witch whore.

Again.

He refrained from sneering. From showing any reaction at

all. Those foolish women knew nothing but this. They were the reason his reign had been tarnished by the stain of weakness. Of excess. These insipid young nobles and their families, forever grasping for favor.

The emperor had to transcend this stain. He had to have a tribute worthy of his lineage. He knew now—more than ever—how much he needed the might of both his sons to achieve this. No matter how improbable that may seem. No matter how unlikely his wife would be to acquiesce.

Her beautiful, obedient Roku would never be allowed to work alongside the son of the witch whore.

When a burst of nearby female laughter caught his attention, the emperor's eyes flitted to a covered walkway across the courtyard. The empress's billowing pink kimono pooled against the white stone as she bowed low, then spun away before he could catch her gaze.

Before he could see the hurt in her eyes.

Unmoved, the emperor watched his wife float away, her back rigid and her tittering minions trailing in her shadow.

"What of my wife?" he asked Kanako in a low voice.

A hesitation. "She knows." The edge in her voice could cut through steel.

The emperor straightened his spine. Hardened his will.

"And so it begins."

A calculated risk

———✳———

Foolhardy. It was not a word people often attributed to Hattori Mariko.

Curious had been the word most often ascribed to her when she was younger. She'd been the watchful sort of child. The one conscious of every mistake. When Mariko had erred, it had usually been intentional. An attempt to push barriers. Or a desire to learn.

Usually it was that. A wish to know more.

As she grew from a curious child into an even more curious young woman, the word she most often overheard at her back was *odd*. Much too odd. Far too prone to asking questions. Far too apt to linger in places she wasn't meant to be.

The sort of odd that would bring her—and her family—nothing but trouble.

She sighed to herself. If her detractors could be present

now, they would be pleased to admit how right they'd been. Pleased to see her in obvious distress.

True, what Mariko planned to do tonight was foolish. But it could not be helped; she'd already lost nearly five days. Five days of precious time, especially as there could be little doubt that Kenshin was now on her trail. Mariko had doubled back on her path several times. Even resorted to deliberate misdirection.

But her brother would find her soon.

And after five days of creeping through villages and outposts on the westernmost edge of Jukai forest—five days of making quiet inquiries—and having bartered the exquisite jade hairpin her mother had gifted her, Mariko had finally found it late last night.

The favored watering hole of the Black Clan.

Or so that old crone two villages over claims.

After achieving this hard-won victory, Mariko had spent all evening hiding behind a nearby tree a stone's throw from where she now sat. Hiding behind that tree and determining how she could best use this newfound information. How she could best manipulate it to learn why a band of cutthroat thieves had been sent to murder her on her journey to Inako.

When not a single black-clad man had bothered to show his face last night, Mariko had come to terms with a second, harsher truth: the old crone could very well have fleeced her for the priceless hairpin.

But Mariko would never know if she didn't try.

This was an experiment, and experiments of all sorts

intrigued her. They offered a way to glean knowledge. To use it—shape it, mold it—into whatever she needed it to be.

And this was a different kind of experiment. A different way to collect information. Though it was an admittedly foolish one, and could also have disastrous results.

The watering hole in question was not as grand as Mariko had imagined it would be.

Which makes sense. After all, it's not exactly one of the fabled geiko *houses of Hanami.*

She smiled to herself, amending her initial impression. Favoring it for facts.

Sequestered near a farm, the watering hole was awash in the scent of refuse and dank river water. Mud seeped from between a series of misshapen flagstones leading to a weathered lean-to. The structure was fashioned from rotted cedar and bamboo greyed to stone by the sun. Several rickety benches and square tables littered a circle of cleared land enclosing the lean-to. A small fire rose from a lopsided brick oven that served as part of the structure's only standing wall. Bamboo torches ringed the clearing, bathing everything in a warm, amber light.

In truth—despite its smell, which Mariko would never find acceptable, not even if she lived for an age—it had a certain charm all its own. Hattori Mariko had lived a life disdaining much of the silk and luxury her status had afforded her, and there was a delicious comfort in no longer having to put on airs that had always seemed so foreign to her.

She slouched lower on her bench. Scratched unabashedly

at her shoulder. Sat with her feet spread. Ordered whatever she wanted, without hesitation. And met every man's gaze full on when addressed.

Mariko had been waiting for the past four hours. Upon her arrival, she'd ordered one small earthenware bottle of sake and had nursed sips of the lukewarm rice wine from a chipped cup, watching as the sun took refuge beyond the horizon.

Now it was dark; now the day had given way for the creatures of the night to come slithering from their holes.

Alas, the particular creatures Mariko sought were not of the punctual sort.

Her knee began to jounce beneath the low slab of crooked wood. It was a crude table, perched atop four unevenly sliced tree trunks. If she leaned too hard on one end, the entire structure wobbled like her old nursemaid walking in the wind. To her left, horses drank from a large canvas tarp suspended between bamboo poles staked in the ground.

A watering hole built for both beasts and their drunken burdens.

Speaking of which, where are they?

The more time passed, the more Mariko's nerves reached a feverish pitch.

The copper pieces she'd won off a drunken peasant in a game of *sugoroku* two nights past would not last her into tomorrow if the Black Clan did not arrive. She might have to trick more money from someone else tonight. But—though she was beginning to understand the necessity and value of this skill—Mariko did not possess a true taste for thievery, even if she did display a certain knack for it.

Sleight of hand. But faint of honor.

The same kind of thief she'd mocked in the forest.

Before murdering him.

The remembrance pulled at her insides. Washed her cheeks an unbecoming pallor. Not from remorse—as she still did not feel any—but more from the harshness of such actions. The coldness with which she'd taken a life. It unseated her in these quiet moments of reflection. Made her uncomfortable in her own skin.

She took another sip of the sake and stifled a grimace. Despite its warming effects, Mariko had never quite developed a taste for the brewed rice wine. She preferred chilled *umeshu*, with its sweetly sour plum flavor. But a traveling soldier or a wandering peasant would be unlikely to ask for such a thing. Especially not in a watering hole downwind of a smelly farm.

Mariko let her eyes wander skyward. And breathed deep.

Though she was surrounded by the unknown, that same sense of freedom washed through her, lush and heady. Irrespective of the refuse around her, it could not be denied that this part of Jukai forest was lovely. Lacy red maples fringed the border of the wood, coming together to frame the watering hole on all sides, like a mother embracing a child. The scent of the maples was rich. Earthier than the sharp bite of the pine. Beside the lean-to was a willow, its drooping branches dusting the battered roof in a ceaseless caress.

Mariko had always found willows profoundly sad.

Yet deeply beautiful.

Just as she noticed the willow branches begin a new dance—a slow-swaying undulation—a sudden burst of motion erupted from behind her.

She turned in time to watch the elderly man who had been stoking the lopsided fireplace hobble from its shadow, his hands rubbing at a linen cloth dangling from his waist, removing whatever traces of grime lingered.

"Ranmaru-*sama*!" he called, his grin wide and his eyes bright. "I'd wondered where you'd disappeared to these last few days."

A tall figure dressed solely in black bounded toward the elderly man, pulling him into a warm embrace. When the newcomer's head turned, Mariko caught a brief flash of his features.

He was a boy not much older than she!

But his clothes were unmistakable—black from his chin to his toes. Even his straw sandals and thin socks had been dyed to match.

A tingling awareness flared through her. Mariko was all but certain now; she'd found a member of the Black Clan.

A member of the band of men who'd tried to murder her.

Fury surged beneath her skin in a heated rush. She gritted her teeth, forcing herself to remain steady. Anger was a reckless emotion. And she needed all her wits about her if she intended to outmatch this boy.

More men clad in black moved to join him. They were all unmasked and well-kempt, ambling at the leisurely pace of those without worry. The pace of panthers sated from a recent hunt. Another boy and a girl with no more than twenty years to each of their names rushed behind the elderly man, bearing earthenware jars of sake and many small cups, some of them rather worse for the wear.

Curiosity chased after the hot fury still coursing through Mariko's veins.

She tried her best to avert her gaze. To convey a sense of general disinterest. It would do her no good for any member of the Black Clan to suspect she'd been waiting for them.

To suspect she'd lain in watchful preparation these past two nights.

One immediate realization granted her reprieve. If they thought it was possible someone was on their trail, the Black Clan surely would not have come tonight. But Mariko had taken special pains not to draw anyone's notice. To their eyes, the circular clearing surrounding their favorite watering hole was being patronized this night by two older men playing Go, one slovenly young drunk snoring at his own table, and what appeared to be a dirty peasant boy of no more than fourteen or fifteen, distastefully swallowing sips of lukewarm sake.

Indeed, there was not a single threat to be seen here.

Mariko watched surreptitiously from behind another swig of sake as the men in black took their places at the tables nearest to the lean-to. Her eyes roamed with thoughtful slowness. Deliberate languor.

I am a reed in a river, bending and moving with the current. For now.

Something brushed past her, startling her from her attempt to remain inconspicuous.

It was a final straggler. She did not see his features as he glided past, but did observe several things of note. Unlike many of the other members of the Black Clan, his shoulder-length hair was unbound. Unkempt. Forgoing the traditional topknot of a warrior. He also did not carry a sword. At first glance, it appeared he had no weapon anywhere on his person.

This straggler did not offer any warm greeting to anyone present. No one came running from the lean-to to offer him an embrace and a bottle of sake. Instead he promptly stretched out on a bench and turned his hood backward to cover his face. With his hands stacked atop his chest, he remained at a distance, taking in some rest.

A man of obvious repute.

At the sound of more laughter, Mariko's eyes drifted back toward the first boy. The one the elderly man had called Ranmaru. A part of her wished to move closer. To be within striking distance. But caution commanded that she keep her distance.

The boy sat as he stood—straight as an arrow. His jaw was strong and squared, his lips broad. Though he was clean-shaven and smiling—oddly affable for a supposed mercenary—he still gave off the distinct feeling of power. A checked sort of power, like that of a strong undercurrent. One that could drag you beneath its depths in an instant.

Ranmaru stood once more, speaking in hushed tones to the elderly man, who nodded and replied just as furtively.

Then Ranmaru resumed his place of deference at a rickety low table near the center of the clearing. Even while he continued speaking with the men in black gathered around him, Mariko watched him rearrange his bench, positioning it with care. A care that put to question the unconscious laughter emanating from his lips.

He's moving the bench into a position where he can see anyone or anything attempting to approach him unawares.

He was smart, despite his age. Exceedingly watchful. A trait Mariko prized in herself. She leaned in, attempting to connect the voices present to those in her memory.

Attempting to prove her suspicions true.

The other black-clad men took their seats, encircling Ranmaru as their earthenware bottles and cups were filled and refilled at steady intervals. From beneath lowered lashes, Mariko also noted that—though he continued drinking and joking alongside everyone else—Ranmaru's eyes were in constant motion.

Eyes that soon fell on her.

Mariko was struck by how neat and clean he appeared. How . . . proper. Not at all like a member of a notorious band of thieves and murderers. Though his attention lingered on her for no more than a breath, the faintest of flushes crept up her neck. Soon this flush touched the edges of her temples, and Mariko realized not a moment too soon that her fingers were dangerously clenched around her small cup of sake.

Another wash of anger. Mixed with that same, strange curiosity. Again she fought back the desire to situate herself in the center of things. For it was far safer to remain alert and apart.

If Ranmaru was indeed the leader of the Black Clan, this boy was the one responsible for the attack on Mariko's convoy. For the deaths of Chiyo and Nobutada and countless other lives lost in a darkened wood only five days before.

She lifted the sake to her lips and squeezed her eyes shut. Though she knew for certain she did not appear to be a threat, Mariko could not afford for any member of the Black Clan to linger on her for too long. To study her and find an enemy. Or worse, find a prize.

Focus on the task at hand. But never forget.

Now came the difficult part.

Now came the time to put her musings to action.

Mariko had spent the better part of the last few nights writhing beneath a woolen blanket. Plotting through a haze of anger. For these past few days, she'd lived the life of a poor vagabond. And though it had been strangely peaceful to be beholden to no one save herself, she'd still been acutely aware of her purpose. Each night, she'd taken in careful breaths from beneath her blanket—a blanket that had smelled of iron and dirt and had felt even worse against her skin. One of many items she'd pilfered from the stable of a comfortable farm in a nearby province.

A horse blanket. In a horse stable.

She'd climbed into the loft and fallen asleep amongst stale bales of hay. The only time Mariko had paused in her efforts to find the watering hole of the Black Clan was when she'd washed her stolen clothes in a nearby creek, rubbing away the dried blood and musty smell of sweat until her knuckles chafed raw.

All her efforts culminated in this. Everything was risked for this.

Risked on her ability to endear herself to the Black Clan. To ply one of its lowliest members with food and drink until she could befriend the poor bastard and move on to a bigger catch. One that could provide Mariko the direction she desperately needed to keep her family's honor intact and prove her worth beyond the marriage market.

Prove her worth beyond that of a mere girl.

Of course this all hinged on the Black Clan never discovering she was in fact their intended target. It was all unfathomably frightening. Darkly fascinating.

Her parents would be horrified.

Kenshin would undoubtedly disapprove.

Mariko continued her careful scrutiny of the Black Clan. A group of twenty or so men of all ages surrounded Ranmaru— the boy she suspected to be their leader, despite his surprisingly young age. Everything about him indicated so, from his natural deportment to their natural deference.

She squared her shoulders and coolly assessed those present, her attention fixed on the most pliable: its youngest and oldest members.

The ones most likely in need of a listening ear.

To Ranmaru's right stood a one-legged man of middle age, balancing his weight on a crude false limb. Alas, this man did

not present a good target; he, too, seemed entirely too obser-
vant, his fingers drumming against any hard surface within
grazing distance. At one hip were multiple small knives of
varying size and shape. A pouch with dried leaves peeking
from its folds rested at the opposing hip. A cook, if Mariko
had to hazard a guess. Or the Black Clan's resident poisoner.
Regardless, she would need a far more pliable target than
he. All the cooks Mariko had met in her short life labored to
notice even the most insignificant detail. Labored to understand the basic ingredient of all things.

Another, smaller boy around her age was also not a good
option. He moved erratically, hovering on the fringes, the
tips of his otherwise immaculate topknot standing on end. His
eyes had a dull stare to them. An almost haunted look. Glazed
over from a past Mariko was not ready or willing to hear.

The straggler sleeping on the bench could be a decent
choice. If she could successfully rouse him to drink, which
at this rate did not seem likely. His chest rose and fell in a
rhythm of total relaxation. Perhaps an anvil dropping from
the sky might awaken him. Perhaps.

Along the periphery, another young member of the Black
Clan studied the leaves in the nearby trees with such serenity
Mariko was certain he'd stepped from a story she'd once
heard her mother tell—one about a boy who floated through
the sky, carried on the wind by an umbrella of oiled paper. His
face was smooth and shiny, almost like a pebble shimmering
beneath the surface of a stream.

So intent was Mariko in her mission to learn everything

she could possibly manage about everyone present that she did not see the elderly man looming over her until he was nearly stooped at eye level, the scent of burning charcoal emanating from his wrinkled skin.

"Another?" the elderly man asked bluntly. It appeared his congeniality was reserved only for Ranmaru and his troupe of murdering miscreants.

"I—" Mariko paused to clear her throat. To deepen the note of her voice. "Yes."

The man pursed his lips, forming radiating lines all around his mouth, much like a judgmental dumpling. "Are you quite certain, young man?"

Immediately Mariko assumed what she hoped was a distinctly masculine posture. She lengthened her spine. Craned her neck to the right as though she were peering down her nose. For this one blessed moment, she was glad to be taller than most girls her age. Glad to be not so delicate. "I'm quite certain. Are you not in the business of selling wine?"

"To those who like to drink it, yes." A mischievous glint took hold of the old man's gaze.

Mariko blinked. "I like it just fine." In her periphery, she noticed the boy with the haunted, almost murderous eyes draw closer, his expression tight.

The old man rasped a laugh. "You might have a lot of water in you, boy, but it doesn't make you a good teller of tales. The words don't form well on your lips. They don't take shape as they should. You should practice more."

Water? She'd always lacked the fluidity to be water. The

natural grace. Her mother claimed she had too much earth in her. That she was far too grounded. Far too stubborn. Almost like a rock, half buried beneath the soil. If Mariko was anything outside of earth, she was wind—disruptive at times, and invisible always.

Never a day in her life had she been water.

"You are mistaken," Mariko said gruffly. "Both about the water and about the drink."

"Akira-*san* is rarely mistaken about anything."

Mariko froze. Refused to turn around. Then thought better of it.

Now was not the time for indecision of any kind. *Death follows indecision, like a twisted shadow.* It was something her brother said. A word of caution too often levied her way.

Though she could not immediately connect the voice to any in her memory of that night, Mariko knew it belonged to the leader of the Black Clan. To Ranmaru.

Far from its most pliable member.

But if I can save myself the work of deceiving my way into his graces . . .

The same instant Mariko turned to face him, Ranmaru walked into her line of sight. Again she sensed a leashed sort of power, like a coil about to spring.

"If Akira-*san* says you are water, you are water," he continued.

Mariko's right shoulder lifted, emulating one of Kenshin's many nonresponses to her frequent questions. She held fast to her composure, though her pulse ratcheted in her throat. "If it gets me another bottle of sake, I can be water."

His smile was pointed. "Allow me." He put his hand out to one side without even glancing to his left or right. The boy with the spiked topknot and the haunted gaze surrendered his bottle of spirits before Mariko had a chance to blink.

Why do they obey him so unflinchingly?

Ranmaru leaned close, and Mariko caught the faint scent of pine and steel. He poured a thin stream of rice wine into her cup with steady hands. Hands that were remarkably clean. Hands that made Mariko want to conceal her own filthy fingers in the folds of her nonexistent kimono.

Just as this realization settled upon her, Mariko fought against it. Fought against the urge to be the proper young woman she'd been raised to be. Hands trembling, she lifted the cup in a salute, then downed its contents in a single gulp.

Of course this would be the moment she coughed from the burn. A hacking, wretched sort of cough. The men at Ranmaru's back let loose a chorus of raucous laughter. Save for the boy with the murderous eyes. Mariko shuddered to think what he might find amusing.

A box of paralytic scorpions? A jar of venomous snakes?

"This little runt can't hold his drink," a burly man with arms of knotted pine and a *kosode* of burnished black leather announced through his laughter. Though tinged by amusement, the look he gave her bordered on dismissive. Indifferent.

Unease sparked once more within her. If the Black Clan

thought her unworthy of their attention; Mariko would lose this precious opportunity to endear herself to their leader.

The leader of the men charged with murdering her.

But she could not readily pretend to be something she wasn't. And she wasn't a skilled drinker. Nor was she a skilled fighter. On the surface, she wasn't a fearsome enemy at all. Mariko was . . . odd. Curious. Clever. Perhaps too clever, as her father always said. It had never been meant as a compliment, though she had always taken it as one.

But perhaps it was better this way. These men would not want to see Mariko as odd or curious or clever. Those were characteristics that would warrant concern in any unknown. Maybe it would serve her well to don a different disguise. One of a bumbling fool desperately in need of direction. Desperately in need of the Black Clan's most esteemed guidance.

Anything to keep them in her thrall.

Mariko set down her cup, then cleared her throat with a series of raps against her chest, willing her nerves silent. She grinned up at Ranmaru sheepishly. "I've recently left home to seek my fortune along the road. And I have not yet spent enough time in such places. Even still, I'm most grateful for the drink. Would you allow me to return the favor?" Her grin widened. "Then perhaps I can learn from you how better to enjoy such things."

Ranmaru watched Mariko as he refilled her cup, his gaze thoughtful, his broad lips pursed to one side. "While I would normally—"

Just then a series of booming footsteps crashed through the underbrush at the edge of the forest, disrupting the peaceful grove of maple trees across the way.

"Takeda Ranmaru!" An enormous man, standing nearly three heads taller than anyone present, shouted into the night sky. "I will not bear this insult a single day more!"

Ranmaru straightened. The men at his back stood silent. Unmoving.

A moment passed in stillness. A moment laced with tension. The sort meant to be bowed by a sword.

"Then, by all means, state your grievances." Ranmaru's smile was wide. Unaffected. "And we shall *both* face the consequences."

Fall Forward to Keep Moving

——✳——

Takeda.

Mariko knew that name.

It sifted through her mind, dredging up a faded memory.

One of a boy standing in a bloodied square, silently crying to the heavens.

"Consequences?" Sporting a look of amused incredulity, the giant of a man stepped toward Ranmaru. The thunder in his voice dashed away Mariko's memories before they could fully take shape.

In his meaty right hand, the giant held an immense *kanabō*. He swung the huge club into the light of a nearby torch. "Did you not think I would know it was you?" The metal barbs studding one end of the *kanabō* flashed dully. "Did you not think we would come to seek retribution?" He nodded to the men at his back. To their generous array of weaponry. These men were exactly what Mariko had pictured a passel of cut-throats to be. Bearded. Unwashed. Uncouth.

The complete opposite of the Black Clan.

In fact, Mariko would have staked the rest of her copper pieces—even an entire gold *ryō*—on the fact that the wretched soul she'd killed in the forest five days ago might have known these intruders.

Might even have been well acquainted with them.

Her discomfort rose in a sharp spike. She looked back to the Black Clan. Two sides of her continued their silent war: the part that wished to remain in the thick of things and the part that wished to observe from a distance.

Ranmaru stayed relaxed. His hands were at his sides, his posture easy. As though a giant bearing a studded club had not stepped into his world, intent on beating him to a bloody pulp.

"Did you hear me, *rōnin*?" The giant spat the last word, hurling it into the air with the venom of a curse.

Rōnin.

More scattered pieces aligned in Mariko's mind.

A reason for Ranmaru's proper, almost noble comportment.

Takeda Ranmaru was a masterless samurai. Or the son of a samurai fallen from grace within the nobility. He was—or had been—part of Mariko's world once. Judging by his age, it could not have been so long ago.

Again that image of a boy not many years older than she, standing beside stones rusted brown with blood, came into brief focus. Then blurred away, like a reflection rippling across a pond.

Mariko narrowed her eyes at the *rōnin*. The idea intrigued her with its ludicrousness.

A noble thief. A mercenary of samurai lineage.

Though Ranmaru continued to appear unaffected, she saw his right hand twitch, as if it was aching to take hold of a sword.

"I heard you." Ranmaru leaned back on his heels, once more the picture of calm, his words a mocking pronouncement. "Both times, you bumbling colossus."

The giant grunted. He swung his *kanabō* again. It cut through the air with a shrill whisper.

An unmistakable threat.

Mariko sank lower in her bench.

This would not end well.

She should leave. The last thing she wanted to be was collateral damage in a tavern brawl. But that cursed boy with the murder eyes continued to stare at her intently. It made it difficult for her to think straight.

The group of men previously standing behind the giant began to unfurl into a line, standing shoulder to shoulder on either side of their leader. Each of their weapons was coated in layers of dried blood.

They . . . did not appear to be in a negotiating mood. Mariko caught the distinct sound of air being sucked through teeth, as though in anticipation of a thrill. When her gaze fell upon one of the cutthroats closest to her, she understood something she'd only heard of in passing.

Bloodlust.

A hunger nothing but slaughter could slake.

Her heartbeat quickened.

Ranmaru sighed. Mariko noted that—though his men did not step forward in response to the giant's threat— many had placed hands on their own weapons. Ready and willing to strike. Ready and willing to defend their leader. The masterless samurai.

The *rōnin*.

Odd that a rōnin *inspires such loyalty.*

A boy who would kill an innocent girl for money.

She took in a measured breath, slowing the speed of her pulse. Her resolve hardened once more. Hardened like folded steel shaped and reshaped under a red-hot flame for countless days and nights.

Until nothing could best it.

I will be a reed in the current. A reed of folded steel.

Even if Ranmaru's men found him worthy of admiration, Mariko *never* would.

Chiyo.

Nobutada.

This boy deserved to be hung upside down and drowned in Yedo Bay. Disgraced, for all the world to see.

Just as the vision formed in her mind, the one-legged man previously standing to Ranmaru's right stepped between the boy and the bumbling colossus, placing his restless fingertips on the hilt of a dagger. Several more men moved to shield their leader from view. To take whatever blows may come his way, with the honor a samurai would espouse for his lord. Try though she might, Mariko could not understand such reverence.

Not amongst murderers and thieves.

As the members of the Black Clan readied themselves for a fight, Mariko recalled something her tutor had said. He'd been a scholar from Kisun, well versed in alchemy and metallurgy. A lover of ancient philosophy.

One winter afternoon in their tenth year, Mariko had overheard their tutor say something to Kenshin that had taken root in her heart. That had left her in a state of quandary for most of the night.

Sometimes we must fall forward to keep moving.

Mariko had not understood it at the time. Only recently had she begun to grasp its meaning.

Remain motionless—remain unyielding—and you are as good as dead.

Death follows indecision, like a twisted shadow.

Fall forward. Keep moving. Even if you must pick yourself up first.

That was what this young *rōnin* must have done. Fallen forward to keep moving.

Into a life of savagery.

A heated exchange of words tore Mariko from her thoughts. The men on both sides had drawn closer. Bridged the gap even farther. The giant's men were being stirred into a slow-moving frenzy.

A charge gathered in the clearing. Like that feeling right before a summer storm. A flash of light, crackling across the night sky. A flare of magic, snapping through the air.

When the giant took a threatening step toward Ranmaru, all the members of the Black Clan moved in tandem. All—Mariko noted—save the one still sleeping on the bench. Apparently the anvil had yet to fall.

"This is becoming tiresome." Ranmaru moved toward the men positioned protectively before him. They parted to let him pass. Several of them unsheathed their swords, their blades gleaming blue and orange in the light of the nearby torches. "If I remember correctly, I already sent word through one of your"—his nose twitched—"*men*. As we were unaware that particular outpost had fallen under your domain, I offered to repay you the exact amount lost. You demanded more. Try though you might, that will never happen. Even you must know . . . the arm bends only inward." He spoke in an idle tone, though Mariko caught his dark eyes flashing.

"An insult!" hissed a scrawny man with a face like a vulture. "You sully our name while stealing our livelihood, and you think a few copper pieces tossed in the dirt will be enough?"

"I did not sully your name."

"You did!"

Ranmaru frowned. "I most certainly did not."

Interesting. Mariko could not help but think this fight too

closely resembled a childish squabble. The like of which she'd had many a time with Kenshin. Over such things as the last of the sweetened rice cakes.

"Since you won't give us what we are due, you've forced us to resort to such measures," the hissing vulture continued. "Forced us to take you to the nearest daimyō and collect the reward money for your capture."

Again Ranmaru sighed. It was almost exaggerated in length and breadth. "If you think the daimyō will gladly hand over fifty *ryō* and smile as you ride away in triumph, you are sorely mistaken."

"Enough of this ridiculous chatter!" the giant bellowed. "Either come with us now, or force us to kill each of your men and take you prisoner anyway."

A mirthless smile cut across Ranmaru's face. "If you intend to take anything, then take my advice," he said. "This one time only, I'll offer it without cost: the best way to win a fight is to avoid it."

"The words of a thieving coward."

Ranmaru grinned. "Despite what you may think, I believe in honor amongst thieves. And I thought we were all in agreement; the enemy is them, not us."

The giant spluttered, confusion still marring his brow. "Lies."

When the giant heaved his *kanabō* over his shoulder—readying to strike—Ranmaru lifted a hand. Momentarily staying the killing blow. "I'll go with you on one condition," he said. "We shall let it come down to a fight. If you win, I'll go without a word. If I win, you leave and never come back to this part of the forest. Under pain of death." The last was spoken with a harshness Mariko had not heard thus far in Ranmaru's voice.

A harshness that sent a shiver down her spine.

The giant grinned. "You want to fight me?" His chest puffed like a sweet bean cake.

"Best on best." Ranmaru nodded.

The sound of the giant's laughter brought to mind a dog choking on a bone. It made Mariko swallow hard. Once his laughter died down, the giant rested his *kanabō* across his shoulders. His fingers dangled on either edge. They flexed once. Twice.

"I'm going to enjoy this, *rōnin*. Maybe even more than I'll enjoy the gold I collect from your bounty." While he spoke, the giant began to step sideways, taking stock of his prey.

Ranmaru did not unsheathe either of the blades positioned at his left side. Instead his feet moved automatically, mirroring his opponent, as though in a deathly dance.

After both he and the giant had taken three steps in a matched circle, Ranmaru halted. Cocked his head. And began to laugh.

The giant's pockmarked brow furrowed.

"I just realized"—Ranmaru paused, as if he was still considering his thoughts—"you think you're fighting me."

His eyes narrowing, the giant heaved a great breath. "What?" It was a stutter of air and sound.

"I said best on best." Ranmaru grinned. "What made you think I was talking about me?" He backed away, his body

77

never once turning from his opponent. These movements seemed second nature to him.

Proving that no one ever stood at Takeda Ranmaru's back.

Mariko refrained from bristling. It troubled her greatly that she could not readily recall the voices of the men beyond her *norimono* the night her convoy was attacked. Their sounds had been too muffled, her nerves far too fraught.

But she was certain one of them *had* to belong to the leader of the Black Clan. As certain as she was of the sun rising in the east. Takeda Ranmaru and his men had been sent to kill her. And Mariko intended to do whatever needed to be done to learn why.

She narrowed her eyes at the unflinching boy across the way.

It's a shame you don't realize another enemy is merely waiting for you in the shadows, rōnin. *Perhaps not a fearsome one, but nevertheless an enemy far craftier than the bumbling colossus before you.*

Mariko took stock once more of the other members of the Black Clan.

Several of them had stood taller at Ranmaru's declaration. Then a ripple of amusement passed across their collective gazes, save for that of the boy with the haunted eyes and the spiked topknot. His eyes had not once left Mariko's face until now. Though even he was distracted—unable to hide his anticipation—wetting his lips with a swipe of his tongue.

Mariko could believe this boy to be the Black Clan's best.

His eyes screamed murder with every look. Two hooked swords were laced across his back. The type Mariko knew could be linked and swung, severing head from body in a single blow.

Just as she became certain this boy was to be the giant's opponent, he, too, stepped aside.

Only Ranmaru continued watching the giant, his expression a strange mix of hard and soft. Punishing and pitying.

The Black Clan turned their gazes behind them in force—

To their lazy comrade, still fast asleep on the bench.

An Unmerited Blessing

———✳———

K enshin smelled the body before he saw it.

A sickly sweet scent, mingled with the odor of decaying meat. It caught in the uppermost portion of his throat, scratching at his senses.

Sending his heart thundering through his chest.

His sister was not dead. Mariko could not be dead.

He would not allow it.

Undeterred, Kenshin continued his low prowl through the darkened underbrush of Jukai forest. Continued searching for his sister's tracks.

Then—in the thorny brambles at the base of a pine grove—Kenshin came across the source of the smell. The body of a dirty man, rotting in the underbrush. Unclothed, save for a filthy loincloth.

At this realization, his heart slowed. Kenshin crouched

beside the dead body, on the hunt for any detail, no matter how seemingly insignificant.

For the third time that night, he was glad to have left his men behind at their makeshift camp. After tracking for nearly two hours, he was now deep in Jukai forest. Had he not taken care to mark the trees as he made his way, the journey back to camp would have been treacherous.

Despite their assurances otherwise, Kenshin knew none of his men rested well in Jukai's shade. Three of their horses had already bolted. Only his own sorrel steed, Kane, remained unshaken. The whispers of the *yōkai* ever chased at their heels. Kenshin himself had yet to see a single demon of the forest, but—as such things often did—one man's story had mushroomed into many. A single tale of a headless deer clomping at their flank. A single sighting of a silver snake with the head of a woman.

One story was all it took. Superstitions were quick to become truths in a night of ghostly sighs and shifting shadows.

Kenshin knew he could order his men to follow him. To obey his every command. But it was far easier for him to march on alone. Much like his father, he did not care to hold council with anyone, no matter how much respect the man might be due. Nor did he care to address anyone's fears. Kenshin knew better than to even try.

Curbing his distaste for such absurdity, the Dragon of Kai squinted at the body lying supine on the forest floor. The man's skin was stretched. Bloated from the first flush of decay.

Maggots wriggled through a slit across his throat, their tiny bodies the color of rice paste. One of the man's eyes had been punctured by a small weapon. Some sort of needled blade.

No.

Kenshin leaned closer.

Not a weapon.

He reached to take hold of the slivers of jade dangling from its end.

A tortoiseshell hairpin. One he quickly recognized.

For the second time that night—two occasions too many—Kenshin felt a wave of distress unfurl beneath his skin.

If this man had been pierced through the eye by this particular hairpin, there could be no doubt as to who had placed it there. Which meant his sister had been pushed beyond the realm of reason. Kenshin did not know Mariko to lose her temper on a whim. Nor did he know her to be inclined to violence. His sister had always been a scholar of reason, devoid of emotion.

If Mariko had murdered this man, he had undoubtedly deserved it. What he had done to deserve it Kenshin could only begin to guess.

Could only begin to imagine.

The wave of distress crested into full-blown rage.

Such a clean death. Such an unmerited blessing.

Had Kenshin been present, this man would have suffered far worse.

His chest pressed against his breastplate as he took in a calming breath. The time for anger had long passed. Far more urgent now was the need for action. Kenshin sank lower in his crouch, resuming his search through the underbrush. As his palm grazed across the thicket—brushing the edges of a swallow's nest —his fingers caught on what at first glance appeared to be a tangle of fine, dark thread.

When Kenshin lifted his hand into the moonlight, he found strands of black hair twisted around his knuckles.

His sister's hair had been scattered across the underbrush. It was clear someone had tried to conceal it beneath the brambles, but the attempt had not escaped the clutches of the forest's most resourceful creatures.

He stood without a sound. The strands of hair drifted from his fingertips, fading into the darkness. Puzzlement flared through him.

Then his gaze fell again on the body at his feet.

The body of a dead, unclothed man.

Kenshin's head lifted. His eyes softened. It took him no more than an instant. No more than a moment of understanding. He reached down and yanked the tortoiseshell hairpin from the man's rotting eye.

Then he spun back toward his horse.

Back on the trail.

Of a girl dressed as a boy.

———————

He did not notice the pair of yellow eyes trailing behind him.

The choice

———❋———

Mariko's brows gathered in confusion.

That lazy boy cannot possibly be the Black Clan's best fighter.

As if in answer to her thoughts, the lazy boy in question inhaled with exaggerated slowness. As though he were beyond annoyed. As though the mere action of taking in air involved too much effort. He knocked away the hood covering his face, then unfolded to his feet in a languorous stretch, much like that of a jungle cat.

With a swipe of his left hand, he pushed back the long strands of hair from his brow. Then he cleared his throat.

His sight now unencumbered, the boy turned toward his quarry. Turned into Mariko's vantage point. Her confusion deepened as she took in his features.

The boy was tall and lean. A body of angles and sinew. A diagonal scar cut through the center of his lips. He blinked sluggishly, as though he'd been startled from a stupor, his hooded, heavy-lidded eyes lifting open then shut. Open then shut. In such a charged moment as this—when his very life could be at stake—Mariko could not fathom his expression, for it was as lax as his demeanor. One that did not match a face of hard edges and graceful slopes.

A face of contradiction.

After another stretch in the opposite direction, the boy's gaze drifted toward the assemblage of men and weapons to his right. Then he began a measured stalk toward the giant.

His steps were instinctual—the gait of a young man with a natural awareness of his surroundings. If a gale were to suddenly descend upon them—or a tree branch to fall from the sky—it would be unlikely this boy would be caught off guard.

The way he moved reminded Mariko very much of Kenshin. Which meant that—despite this boy's lazy comportment—he could well prove to be a formidable opponent. Mariko's brother had been a student of battle for much of his life. She knew such innate prowess was not gifted at random.

Yes. It was possible this boy could best the giant. That is, if he could be bothered to procure a weapon. He still did not appear to have a single blade on his person.

As the boy came to a halt near the gathering, Mariko realized something else of import. Though this boy's movements were similar to those of Kenshin, there was also a distinct difference. One that made Mariko amend her earlier comparison. Her brother moved precisely, each foot placed with deliberate intent. This boy did not take steps.

He glided like a shark through the water.

And like the sea, the members of the Black Clan parted around him as the boy took position before the giant.

The charge that had begun to collect earlier rose again in earnest.

Even though the giant appeared perplexed at this turn of events, he swung his *kanabō* from side to side. Attempting to frighten his new opponent with another show of bravado.

When the boy did not react—did not even attempt to dodge—the giant scowled.

"Don't you need a weapon?" he grunted.

The boy shook his head. Yawned once more. "No." He rolled his shoulders. Cricked his neck.

A chuff passed the giant's lips. "Arrogant fool."

"Not arrogant." The boy scratched along his jaw nonchalantly. "Just accurate."

The giant laughed again, goading his men to join in his amusement. A smattering of uneasy laughter spread through their ranks. It did little to leaven the mood. If anything, it only darkened it.

Mariko's pulse quickened. Should this fight develop into something more than a mere exchange of posturing, it was possible she would never obtain her answers. Never spare her family undue embarrassment. Or prove her worth beyond the marriage market.

It was also possible she might die.

Yes. That, too, was a fact of which she was keenly aware.

Her knowledge of how to win a fight was purely theoretical.

The scuffle with the drunken fool in the forest had confirmed one thing: Mariko's best asset in any altercation was her mind. And even with that advantage, she'd barely managed to best a man heavily encumbered by spirits. She had a strong suspicion of how she would fare against a seasoned warrior in an actual fight. And with men of any sort, Mariko had always found brute strength to be given the greatest weight.

But in a battle of wits?

It could be any man's—or woman's—game.

Mariko weighed her options. Whether she should run or stand her ground.

I should simply take shelter and watch these fools kill each other.

There could be a certain satisfaction in that.

But if that were to happen, she would never know who had plotted her death.

And why.

The sharp whistle of the *kanabō* being swung through the air tore her from her thoughts. She blinked toward the fight—

Just in time to see the lazy warrior dodge the giant's first swing. With not a moment to spare. The breeze from the blow tossed the boy's hair back into his face.

The giant laughed. "Too slow."

An easy smile touched the boy's scarred lips. As though he possibly shared the giant's amusement. Shared his unfavorable opinion. Just as Mariko began to consider this possibility, she noticed a change in the boy's body.

It had begun to tremble.

Is he . . . afraid?

Anticipation curled through her center. She fought to tamp down the rising curiosity. The rising interest. No. Mariko could not be the least bit entertained by any of this. Being entertained meant she could be easily distracted. And she refused to die in a watering hole this night.

Careful to remain beyond anyone's notice, Mariko rose to her feet, still clenching her small cup of sake tight. Being certain not to make any sudden movements that might draw attention her way.

The giant swung his *kanabō* in a vicious backhand. As it rose, its tip grazed the boy's shoulder. Mariko winced reflexively when the boy barely managed to escape the full impact of the blow. He rolled through the dirt—away from the giant— then spun to standing. Once he righted himself, he noticed a tear in the arm of his black *kosode*. He proceeded to launch into a series of curses Mariko had only heard the lowliest of stable hands utter in moments of great vexation. Vile, vulgar sorts of words that would have made her mother gasp into her palms and her father nod in warning to his subordinates.

The boy gripped his bare shoulder tight, wincing through the pain as blood began to well onto his fingers. As his shaking grew worse.

This was the best the Black Clan had to offer?

How had this lazy fool ever managed to best Nobutada?

It was as though everything Mariko had experienced in the last week had been in jest.

Her lips pulled into a frown.

If this battle wasn't in jest, Takeda Ranmaru was going to lose his wager.

And Mariko was not ready or willing to see him lose to anyone but her.

She waited for a member of the Black Clan to come to the boy's aid or put an end to this farce of a fight. It took her only a single glance to realize that none of their ranks appeared to be the least bit alarmed by the sight of their comrade on the verge of risking their leader's life.

The men in black continued standing to either side of the fight. Unworried. Ranmaru reached for his drink. Almost as though he was disinterested. The one-legged cook leaned on his *bō*, studying its polished wood surface as though he were seeking something with which to occupy himself.

As though there could be something more pressing for him to consider.

A blaze of triumph flashed across the giant's face. Raising his *kanabō* once more, he clomped toward the injured boy, set on proclaiming his victory.

Mariko edged away from her table, sidestepping in surreptitious fashion. Certain this fight was at an all-too-swift end.

The boy did not prepare himself to strike back. Did not so much as flinch from the coming blow. Instead he remained in one place. His hand dropped from his wounded shoulder.

His head fell forward, his dark hair veiling his features.

The trembling took hold of his body. Quickened into a

blur. The air around him began to hum. Distort. Like the space surrounding a lantern flame.

Just as the giant unleashed his killing strike, the one-legged cook launched his *bō* in a graceful pitch toward the boy. He caught it in one hand without even turning to see it.

Then the boy leapt into the air, far out of the giant's reach. He hovered—suspended on a spume of sound—before he came crashing back to earth, the soil at his feet exploding in concentric circles.

Mariko halted in her tracks. Anchored to one spot.

She had never before seen anyone move as he did.

Almost like that creature in the forest. The one that had tried to warn her.

Like a dark ghost. Or a demon of the night.

Disoriented by the sight, the giant stumbled, nearly collapsing to the dirt. The boy rippled through the air once more, far out of his reach, the hum around him growing in fever and pitch. Only a breath passed before he spun in place, crossing his arms above his head. The *bō* whirled, collecting momentum, cracking through the air like reverberating thunder. It arced toward the giant's wrist in a punishing downward blow. Bones crunched as the giant dropped his studded club to the ground. He yowled so loudly the trees around them shook their limbs in disapproval.

Or amusement. Mariko could not be certain which.

To her dismay, she was uncertain as to her own reaction.

This was not entertaining. It was not entertaining to witness a man of greater brawn fall to a smaller, cleverer foe.

Especially one clever enough to conceal his advantage so adeptly.

Mariko was not entertained by this sight. Not at all. Despite what the race of her pulse had to say otherwise.

The dark ghost of a boy blurred to a halt. The vibrations around his body lessened to a slow tremor. His chest rose and fell as he took in great drafts of air. As though he had been submerged in water for longer than any human could possibly bear.

He stood rooted to the ground, seeking a center.

Ignoring the giant still howling on the ground.

A sudden hush descended on the clearing. And Mariko could once again feel the threat of a storm on the air. About to ignite, like the strike of flint against stone.

She shifted into the shadows along the periphery, her fingers still wrapped around her earthenware cup. Her last resort of a weapon. *Something* with which to defend herself. Mariko knew if she even attempted to remove the *wakizashi* at her side—if anyone saw her moving through the darkness with a blade poised at the ready—it might further provoke the bloodlust around her.

As she continued folding into the fringe of branches along the forest's edge, Mariko's eyes stayed trained on the circle of men poised around the wailing giant and the dark ghost. The champion of the Black Clan continued to shudder in place. Continued to heave great breaths. His comrades appeared grim. Contrary to what she thought would happen, they did not cheer at this victory.

For it was clear the victory had come at a cost.

The giant's men took hesitant steps toward him, as though converging on a wounded bear—one just as likely to bite off a helping hand as it would be to lick it.

Mariko moved with great care, scuttling away from the watering hole like a crab into its shell. Her gaze stayed locked on the men across the way. Continued scanning for any notice of her retreat. Or her position.

Then she saw. Saw what no one else sought. What no one else thought to see, preoccupied as they were.

The hissing vulture. The one who had helped the giant provoke the fight.

He stood in a pool of torchlight a body's length to her left. She watched him slowly ease his hand behind his back. When he shouldered past the brute of a man at his side, Mariko caught a flash of metal.

The vulture's gaze was fixed on Takeda Ranmaru.

The fear that had been pressing Mariko to flee blossomed into outrage.

He's cheating.

If they could not win by the rules they themselves had created, they did not deserve to win at all! And Mariko would never allow herself to lose her prey to such inept, unworthy imbeciles.

Without pausing to think, Mariko tossed back her earthenware cup and took in a mouthful of lukewarm sake.

Then she sputtered it in the direction of the torch.

A burst of flame jetted in the hissing vulture's direction,

startling all the men around him. Catching on the sleeve of one nearby.

Cries of outrage emanated from their ranks.

The jet of fire had heightened their awareness. Had forced them from their trances.

All eyes searched for the source of the outburst.

That was . . . an unwise decision, Hattori Mariko.

Either make good on these actions, or flee from this place. Immediately.

Something in the back of her mind told her she would not get far.

The blood draining from her face, Mariko pitched the empty, earthenware cup toward the hissing vulture. It smashed against the back of his skull, knocking him beyond the safety of the shadows. Into the fray.

"He has a dagger," she accused in a coarse voice. "He's trying to cheat!"

It took all the work of a moment for the men in the Black Clan to process her words. The hissing vulture lifted his dagger into the light, intent on finishing his task, whatever the cost. Hands and elbows shoved at his back. At his chest. His weapon was ripped from his grasp. None of the men in his company fought to save him. Nor did they attempt to raise their weapons in revolt.

As soon as Mariko glanced toward Ranmaru, she understood why.

While the chaos had unraveled around them, the dark ghost of a boy had taken position before his leader. Though blood still dripped from the wound in his right shoulder, he managed to aim a cutting smile their way. One tinged by cruelty. His *bō* spun through the air.

Daring anyone to challenge him.

There is no such thing as honor amongst thieves.

"You cheating bastards." The one-legged cook spat in the dirt. "Leave. Now. Unless you'd care for a real fight." He unhooked two of the small daggers along his waist, twirling them between his fingertips with all the grace of a master.

The giant began to howl anew, still clutching the shattered bones in his hand. He yelled for his men to help him to his feet, hurling obscenities every which way.

His fury stirred the embers around him. Soon his men began pointing fingers at one another, riling themselves into another frenzy.

Mariko shrank beneath the branches. Away from view.

I should leave.

But she could not. Not yet.

Not until she knew . . . something of value. Something of surety.

"Enough!" Ranmaru yelled above the fracas, his voice aimed at the giant's men. "Leave here at once, as you agreed. If any of you show yourselves again—if I even smell one of your ilk on a passing breeze—expect that to be the last day you draw breath on this earth."

The fervor died to a whisper. A moment of decision.

With a grunt, the giant directed his men to depart. Unintelligible grumbling trailed in their wake.

Once they'd left, Ranmaru shifted into view. He glanced at the ghost boy now at his side, a brow raised in question. The Black Clan's champion lifted his uninjured shoulder. As though his wound were merely a scratch.

Ranmaru nodded.

The one-legged cook threw a dagger into the dirt with a grunt. A moment later, a gold *ryō* landed in the earth beside it.

"You're the devil, Ōkami," he muttered harshly.

The ghost boy eyed him askance. "You would know." A grin curled up one side of his face, rendering the scar through his lips white. "Since we both came from hell."

Concealed in her post beside the tree, Mariko watched the exchange, unsure of where she should go. Of what she should do. Perhaps it would be wisest to heed her own advice and leave at once. When she attempted to back away into the cover of the forest, a rough hand clapped on her forearm.

"Don't run just yet," the boy with the murder eyes and the spiked topknot said, his tone flat. "Boss will want to talk to you."

The consequence

————✳————

A rush of fear took hold of her heart. Of her every breath. Mariko's first inclination was to push off the boy's grasp. Panic set in when his grip on her arm tightened. The whites of his eyes were yellowed. Glazed. Like those of the dead.

"Don't even think about running. We'll hunt you down like a looting fox." He pulled her close, his whisper a brush of ice against her ear. "I especially like it when we catch them alive. It's much more . . . interesting."

Mariko forced down her terror, though her pulse quaked in her ears. The voice of her tutor admonished her once more:

Our greatest enemy can often be found within.

She would not be her own worst enemy. The only control Mariko had now was control over herself. If she could not flee, then she had to make the best of her situation.

The boy was taking her to his boss. To Ranmaru. This could be her only chance to learn the truth.

She would not waste it on fear.

Gritting her teeth, Mariko fought for a point of clarity through a haze of terror. She thought quickly. Kenshin would not allow himself to be handled in such a manner, even if it brought on punishment.

Mariko tried to tear away from him. The boy responded by twisting her wrist behind her left shoulder. She nearly gasped at the burst of pain that radiated down her arm and into her side. Hot, searing pain. The sort that brought immediate tears.

But she did not cry out. Refused to reveal even a hint of weakness.

A warrior is never weak.

Seemingly satisfied by her show of resistance—as though he relished the thought—the boy with the murder eyes released his grip. "Next time you try to run, I'll break your fingers, knuckle by knuckle." He leaned in. "One by one."

She choked out a retort. "Do you think I intend to run?"

"Only a fool would stay."

"Are you hoping to gain my cooperation by threatening me?" she blustered awkwardly.

He did not respond. He merely shoved her forward, hard. She almost tripped, catching herself at the last instant. When the boy yanked her into the light of the nearest torch, she thought she saw him smile.

Alternately yanking and shoving her along, the boy led her toward Ranmaru, who had once again taken his seat at the table seemingly reserved for him and him alone.

The leader of the Black Clan studied her in silence for several breaths. "Well, it seems I am in your debt . . ." Ranmaru paused, waiting for her to offer a name.

Thankfully Mariko had one at the ready.

"Takeo." She deepened the note of her voice. Roughened its edges. "Sanada Takeo."

Ranmaru smiled slowly. "It appears your parents had rather lofty designs when they named you."

"Because they named me after a warrior?"

"No. Because they gave their tactician son a warrior's name."

Mariko sniffed. Furrowed her brow to offset her mounting distress. "I'm a warrior. Just like you."

He laughed. The lines around his eyes crinkled in consideration. "Perhaps you are just like me."

She frowned at his mocking tone.

"I won't call you Takeo, though," Ranmaru continued. "I can't in good conscience call a scrawny boy a valiant warrior."

His judgment echoed in her ears. Forcing her to choose a path. Courage. Or fear. Standing taller, Mariko chose the path of courage—a tenet of *bushidō*. "I have not yet made comment on *your* name. But I can, if you like. And since Takeo is my given name, I insist you call me—"

"Lord Lackbeard," a voice behind Ranmaru declared. Mariko stiffened once more, her courage wilting. It was the Black Clan's champion. Ōkami. The boy named after a wolf. "It suits this little upstart far more than *Takeo*."

Ranmaru grinned. "I agree. If you wish to be called by your given name, you must first earn it, Lord Lackbeard."

At that, the men around him laughed.

"You can call me whatever you like," Mariko said over their laughter, knowing all too well how much she sounded like a petulant child. "But it doesn't mean I will respond."

"Is that so?" Ranmaru's grin widened.

Mariko stayed silent, eliciting another bout of laughter from the men nearby. As they amused themselves at her expense, knots began twisting in her stomach. Color began creeping up her neck, into her face. She hated this feeling. The feeling of being vulnerable. Mocked. It was the first time in a long while she'd had to stand still and experience abject ridicule. It was true many people found her odd, but her family's position and influence had spared her from being met head-on by the judgment of others. When she did hear it, it was at her back, whispered behind lacquered fans or in the shadow of elegantly papered screens.

She tipped her chin upward and bit her tongue.

A warrior is never weak.

Mariko repeated the refrain in her mind, letting it feed her, like kindling to a flame.

Frowning, Ōkami glided toward her, passing along an earthenware bottle of sake to Ranmaru as he walked by. The men grew silent while he circled her slowly, no doubt searching for blood in the water. Mariko fought to conceal the rush of indignation that bloomed in her cheeks at his silent appraisal. At the obvious latitude the Wolf was granted as the Black Clan's champion.

He stopped in front of her. Stared down at her. She could almost feel that same low hum hovering in the air about him.

It unnerved her.

"Now"—Ranmaru raised the bottle of sake in her direction—"I do believe I owe Lord Lackbeard a drink." He waited for her to respond, the picture of patience.

My best chance to learn the truth.

Making no effort to conceal her wariness, Mariko took a seat on the bench across from him. She did not fail to notice how Ranmaru's men watched her like hawks would a dove.

The leader of the Black Clan poured rice wine into a small cup, then handed it to her.

She stared at him over the lip of the cup. Sniffed its contents.

Smiling at her distrust, Ranmaru poured himself a drink from the same bottle. He knocked it back pointedly.

In response, Mariko took a small sip from her own cup.

"So," the knife-wielding cook said in a conversational tone, all while twirling the hilt of a dagger between his fingertips, "what sort of fortune is a young boy like you hoping to find along the western edge of Jukai forest?"

Mariko attempted a lazy, satisfied kind of smile. The kind she'd seen many of her father's younger vassals adopt in moments like these. "The sort that makes me rich." She knew she sounded foolish, but that, too, seemed appropriate.

"There are many kinds of wealth," the cook mused.

She nodded as she took another sip of sake. "But there is only one kind that matters."

The cook tilted his head to one side. "And what kind is that?"

"The kind that buys freedom."

His lips pursed together. Not in judgment. No. She did not think he disagreed with her. Though Mariko was not yet sure he agreed. Perhaps she should not have been so forthcoming with her answers. Or quite so clever when she decided to spare Ranmaru from the hissing vulture. Her gaze drifted toward Ōkami. The Wolf looked through her. Past her. He leaned against the table, one hand resting on a knee. Dried blood tracked the veins of his right forearm, like the tributaries of a sinister river. Once again, he seemed wholly uninterested. Utterly bored. But of all those present, the Wolf was the most difficult to read. Mariko had been wrong in her initial assessment of him, and that made her . . . uncomfortable in his presence.

In an attempt to conceal her sudden unease, she took another sip of sake. It warmed through her, heating her blood. Tingling her skin.

Tingling her skin?

"Is freedom important to you, Lord Lackbeard?" Ranmaru asked as he rolled the bottle of sake along the rough-hewn table's edge. His expression was light. Easy.

Knowing.

The tingling along Mariko's skin intensified. A burst of warmth flooded her face, clouding her vision.

No.

The sake.

Mariko stood suddenly. "You—" she spluttered. "You cheated. You're . . . you're . . ."

Ōkami floated before her, the dark ghost once more.

The last thing she remembered was a clear pair of onyx eyes.

———————

Mariko was jostled awake by the sway of an animal beneath her.

When she raised her eyelids, a smudge of brown muscle came into focus before her face. The muscles of a warhorse. Hattori Mariko had been thrown across the back of a steed, like a sack of grain. Realization surged through her. Remembrance clawed at her senses.

She'd been drugged by the leader of the Black Clan!

Mariko struggled to right herself, only to discover her hands bound. Swinging below her head. Her distress mounting, she tried to shift her body upward. To take stock of her surroundings.

They were still in the forest. Walking along a muddy embankment. She breathed deep. The air here was thinner. Crisper. They were now at a higher elevation.

Near a body of freshwater.

It was likely near dawn. And the—

A hand smacked the back of her head, chastising in its suddenness.

She could not help it. She cried out in frustration.

"Keep whimpering," Ranmaru said. "It amuses my horse."

Mariko lifted her arm to peek beneath it.

This was not possible.

She'd been thrown on the back of Takeda Ranmaru's horse.

"Where—where are you taking me? And why would anyone want to amuse your horse?" Mariko croaked.

Ranmaru began to whistle a tune faintly familiar to her. "Because if you don't, I'll gut you and feed you to the brute. His favorite meal is the flesh of tiresome young men. Especially ones who whimper."

"You routinely feed him whimpering young men?" Mariko attempted to twist into a better position. To see where they were.

"Not routinely. If he ate such a delicacy all the time, it would eventually lose its appeal."

"How would you know?" she grumbled, swallowing the lump of distress gathering in her throat.

"I myself no longer have a taste for it." With that, Ranmaru resumed whistling.

Her concern taking root, Mariko struggled to sit upright. Again a hand thwacked across the back of her skull.

Mariko shouted, the panic setting in. *A warrior is never weak.* "I must ask you to refrain from—"

"Listen to the little Lord Lackbeard, issuing orders like the damned emperor himself." Ranmaru laughed.

Mariko clenched her teeth. It was easier for her to admit

defeat. But she knew now was the time she most needed to appear strong—when she was at her weakest.

"Why have you drugged me?" she asked. "Where are you taking me?"

"More questions. In their depths, you'll find the answer."

She waded through Ranmaru's words. Let her thoughts settle into straight lines.

More questions?

Understanding dawned on her, as chillingly bright as a winter sun.

The old man at the watering hole. He must have told Ranmaru I'd been asking after the Black Clan.

"Akira-*san* whispered something to you when you first arrived last night," Mariko said, careful to conceal the defeat in her tone. Despite all her best efforts to evade notice, she'd been undone by the wily observations of a grumpy old man. "What did he say?"

"I knew you were smart." Ranmaru spoke loudly, ignoring her question. "Even if you were as untried as a newborn colt."

I lost my best chance.

I'm as good as dead.

Her body fell against the horse, loose in the face of failure. "So what do you intend to do with me?" she asked. "Besides feed me to your horse."

"Stop asking questions. Truly you don't learn."

If I'm going to die, what is there left to learn?

No. She needed to be brave.

And there was always something left to learn.

Mariko wrapped her fingers around the rope knotted about her wrists. "One must ask questions if one intends to learn anything." While she spoke, she searched for any slack in her bindings.

"I grow weary of your curiosity, Lord Lackbeard." Ranmaru glanced to his right. To a person Mariko could not see. "Take this thing from me."

A hand grabbed at the scruff of dirty fabric around her neck.

Mariko refrained from crying out again as she was hauled from one beast to another. This time she was not thrown on the back of the horse. No. This time she was tossed on her stomach before the rider, the breath momentarily knocked from her body.

As she was thrown about, she caught a flash of unbound dark hair.

Ōkami. *The Wolf.*

Before she had a chance to settle, Mariko thrashed about like a flailing fish. She knew it was foolish, but she refused to be handed off from one murderer to the next, as though she were a spoil of war.

"Stop fighting me." Though Ōkami's voice was softer, it was no less harsh. "I'm not Ranmaru. I won't hit you."

Again the feeling of being near him unnerved her. That same all-but-undetectable hum. "I'm not surprised." Venom tinged her retort, while blood rampaged through her body. "Based on my observations, you don't hit much."

The instant she mocked him, a jolt of fear passed through Mariko.

Laughter rippled around them. The front ridge of Ōkami's saddle dug into her stomach and chest. If Mariko hadn't thought to bind her breasts tight in a long length of muslin, she knew she would have been suffering far more discomfort.

"The little lord is right," the gruff voice of the cook called out from behind them. "What took you so long to best the giant, Ōkami? Are you losing your touch?"

"The little lord didn't let me finish." Ōkami bent forward. "I said I wouldn't hit him . . ." He was so close, his words pulsed across her skin.

"But that's not the only way to punish someone."

Fear knifed through Mariko's center, its aim hot and true. She knew she could not afford to let a boy like Ōkami see even a hint of distress. She had to get free of these men. Had to gain the upper hand somehow. Seeking a way to distract herself—any weakness in the strength surrounding her—she studied Ōkami's fingers. They were long. Strong. His forearms were corded with muscle. His hold on the reins was loose. Easy. Which meant he was likely an accomplished rider. Any attempt to unseat him would be ill-advised.

But perhaps Mariko could unseat him in other ways.

"What kind of a name is Ōkami?" she began, her tone low and brusque.

"You really don't learn, do you?"

"You mocked my name, even though your parents named you after a wolf?"

"They didn't."

Despite all, her curiosity took hold once more. "Then it's a nickname?"

"Stop talking," Ōkami said. "Before I pass you to someone who really will beat the impudence out of you."

She paused. "Wolves are pack creatures, you know."

Another rumble of coarse laughter rang out from behind them. "I must admit that boy is tenacious, even in the face of doom."

Mariko felt Ōkami shift in the saddle to address the cook. At that, she took the opportunity she'd been waiting to catch him unawares.

She bit into the skin just above Ōkami's knee. Hard.

He cursed loudly, causing his horse to rear. Mariko almost slid headfirst from her perch, but Ōkami took hold of her in a firm grip, catching her at the last possible moment.

He yanked her toward him, chest to chest, grasping her tight by the collar of her threadbare *kosode*. Mariko expected to find fury in his eyes. Instead she was met with an impenetrable expression. Not the cold sort. But rather carefully veiled, though his eyes were remarkably clear. Like glass in a cavern at midnight.

Mariko returned his stare, her heart thrashing wildly. "If you were me, you would have done the same thing." She could not prevent her voice from quavering on the last word.

"No, I wouldn't." Ōkami's dark brows lowered. Shadowed his gaze. Something tugged at his lips. "I would have succeeded."

"And how would you have gone about doing that?"

His mouth dipped again, the scar through its center white. "I gather you routinely think you possess the most intelligence of any man around you."

She shook her head slowly.

"A word of warning . . ." He bent closer. The scent of warm stone and wood smoke emanated from his skin.

Mariko blinked.

"Don't bare your neck to a wolf." With that, Ōkami heaved her off his horse into the shallows of the nearby pond.

Mariko gasped as the cold water enveloped her, the mud clinging to one side of her body. She sat upright, using her bound wrists to brush vines and muck from her brow.

Ōkami waited along the bank. Then he twisted his horse away, without a glance back.

"Welcome home, Lord Lackbeard." Ranmaru smiled.

"Home?" she choked. "What are you—"

"Clean yourself up. You were badly in need of a bath anyway. Then fetch me some firewood." He clicked his horse from the embankment. "And don't think of escaping," Ranmaru said over his shoulder. "There are traps everywhere. You won't make it a league from our camp."

I'm at the Black Clan's encampment.

"Why have you brought me here? What do you intend—"

"Today you work. Tomorrow . . ." Ranmaru shrugged. "I feed you to my horse."

jewel steel and night rain

✳

He'd lost track of her.

Lost all sight of where his sister might be.

Kenshin had followed her trail along the westernmost edge of Jukai forest. Followed it even as her steps doubled back and across the many small villages there.

He'd pursued it nevertheless. Doggedly. Ignored the twinges of frustration that cut through his chest. But Mariko's trail had disappeared this morning in the shadow of a run-down watering hole.

Inexplicably.

The elderly man Kenshin had prodded awake had ignored him at first. Ignored his queries while pushing him from the threshold of his ramshackle lean-to.

"Do you know how many travelers wander through here each day, young man?" the old man had finally rasped while cringing away from the sun. "Now I'm meant to recall each of them in vivid detail?" His laughter had greatly resembled a hacking cough. "You'd do better to ask me the position of the clouds at any given time." Then his expression had puckered as though he'd been sucking on the meat of a yuzu fruit.

Kenshin had almost accused him of lying. Something about the way the old man had brushed him aside so easily. Brushed aside such a respectful request from a celebrated young samurai.

In his concern for his sister, Kenshin had almost threatened an elderly man. But he'd forced his muscles to relax. His mind to settle. He'd caught himself before his thoughts could become irrevocable action.

Kenshin would never commit such a dishonorable deed.

For though he definitely thought the old man to be lying, he had no proof.

His sister's trail now hopelessly lost, Kenshin had been forced to return to his camp. What he'd found when he arrived was even more disheartening. His men had grown restless in his absence. Their supplies were dwindling.

Their direction was now lost as well.

Kenshin had realized it was time to return home. To re-supply and devise a different tack.

His men had been thrilled with the news. Far more thrilled than Kenshin wished them to be. After all, they'd failed in their task to rescue their lord's only daughter.

They—and he—had failed Hattori Kano.

It was true Mariko had never been greatly beloved amongst

his father's men. She'd been a curious sprite of a girl, armed with unceasing questions. Mariko had never shied away from an opportunity to learn. She'd pestered metalsmiths. Peered over the shoulders of alchemists. Stood unnervingly still as she'd watched Nobutada—the most gifted swordsman of his father's samurai—practice his kata.

Kenshin had always known how irritated the men riding under his father's crest had been. These were not the places for a young girl. Not the proper interests for the daughter of their esteemed daimyō.

Nevertheless his father's men needed to fall in line. Now of all times. Mere words would not be effective enough today.

An example would need to be made. One his father would undoubtedly approve.

As their convoy crested the hill leading into the valley of his father's domain, one of the *ashigaru* began singing a tune in time to their march. A melody offering tribute to the beauty of home, sung by a humble foot soldier. The men at Kenshin's back became jovial at its sound. Like the rolling swell of the sea, the melody carried through their ranks.

Jubilant. Boisterous. Even in the face of failure.

Kenshin's long-simmering irritation reached a boiling point. He yanked his reins to one side, curving his horse around the vanguard of the convoy. Kane reared once before driving his hooves into the fragrant earth. The convoy came to an abrupt halt.

The singing died down.

As the melody faded, Kenshin took a moment to seek out

his quarry. Then he prodded his warhorse alongside the neat formation of *ashigaru*.

"You," he said to the young foot soldier who'd been singing. "Step forward."

The *ashigaru* on either side stepped back as one, still maintaining their neat formation.

The singer was a boy. Possibly younger than Kenshin's seventeen years.

Beads of perspiration collected beneath the young singer's *hachimaki*. Kenshin watched the thin band of hemp around the boy's forehead start to slide, the Hattori crest in its center darkening.

Before stepping forward, the boy straightened his *hachimaki*. Stood tall.

Kenshin briefly admired his bravery. Briefly regretted what he was about to do. The image of his father's stern visage glimmered through his mind.

And his regret vanished.

"Why were you singing, soldier?" Kenshin's voice sliced through the silence. A sheaf of ice cleaving from a mountain.

The boy bowed low. "I apologize, my lord."

"Answer my question."

"I—I sang in error, my lord."

"A resounding truth. But still not an answer." Kenshin urged his steed closer. "Do not make me ask again."

The boy's *hachimaki* was soaked through now. "I sang because I was happy."

Kenshin's horse stepped impossibly closer. Close enough

for the horse's nostrils to flare at the boy's scent. As though Kane had smelled his next meal.

The boy recoiled from the wicked gleam in the warhorse's gaze.

"Happy?" Kenshin's voice dropped. "You were happy to have failed in your mission?"

"No, my lord." The slightest of hesitations.

Frustration warmed across Kenshin's skin. "Your purpose on this earth is what, soldier?"

"To serve the honorable Hattori clan." He said the words loudly, in rote fashion.

Kenshin leaned forward in his saddle, an unsettling twinge slicing through his stomach. "And serve them you shall." Without warning, he kicked the boy in the face. The crunch of broken bones echoed in time to the boy's startled yelp. He hit the mud beside Kane's hooves with a splat. Bright blood dripped from his nose and mouth.

As Kenshin watched the boy try to swallow his pain—to accept his punishment—another whisper of regret rose in his throat.

An unfamiliar uncertainty.

He swallowed it quickly. Then lifted his gaze to the rest of his convoy.

"There is no cause to be happy here." Kenshin let his voice carry across the ranks of *ashigaru* and mounted samurai. "No cause to celebrate. We have failed in our mission. But know this: that failure will not stand. You will each have a night's rest. On the morrow, we shall depart once more." Kane stamped his hooves in place, the battered boy cowering further into himself with every thud. "And there will be no singing—no laughter, no celebration—until we are successful."

Kenshin spurred Kane back toward the head of the convoy. But he did not pause there. Instead he kicked his steed into a full gallop. Shifted him toward a different path.

One that would grant them a moment's reprieve.

Hattori Kenshin did not want to be greeted at the main gate as though he was a victor returning from war.

He did not deserve it.

The path he chose led to the back entrance of his family's compound. An entrance unfrequented by those in the nobility.

Before him rose a wicket gate, its wooden slats tightly pressed into an arch. Stacked stones enclosed the perimeter; stones arranged with such precision as to render mortar unnecessary.

The rear courtyard housed many of the Hattori clan's most important servants and vassals. It also served as residence for a few of the scholars and artisans Kenshin's father hosted, many for years at a time. All with the desire to further his reputation as a lauded daimyō with growing influence.

In truth Kenshin often preferred to return home to this entrance. It offered him an opportunity to be present without being seen. If he were to arrive at the main gate, his mother would be waiting for him, with countless servants in tow. His father would follow only a few steps behind.

The wicket gate swung open, and Kenshin directed Kane

toward the back stables. The moment he dismounted, a stable hand rushed to assist him.

"I'll curry my horse," Kenshin said to the servant. "And please wait to inform my mother of my arrival until after I'm done."

Stepping back, the young servant bowed low.

Kenshin led Kane into the first empty stall, taking his time to remove the boiled leather armor from the horse's sweat-slicked back. In response to no longer being restrained, Kane whickered, pawing at the ground. He had always been a restless beast. With a smile, Kenshin took hold of a wide brush and began tending to his horse.

Another task he enjoyed. Another task he too rarely was given the chance to do while at home.

Behind him, light footsteps rustled across the woven mats strewn across the stable floor.

He did not turn. "Mother, I—"

"You are the last kind of beast I expected to find in the stable."

A smile ghosted across his lips again. "The last kind of beast I expected to find in the stable, *my lord*." Kenshin turned as he spoke, not even trying to conceal his pleasure at the arrival of this unexpected visitor.

A young girl in a simple kimono of deep blue silk leaned against the gate door. She wrinkled her pretty nose in playful distaste at his words.

Their titles had long been a source of amusement for them both.

For this girl was not in fact one of Kenshin's servants.

Despite what his father frequently said in private.

"It's not often that you surprise me, Hattori Kenshin." As the girl spoke, her tone became flatter. Almost morose.

Her amusement had already begun to wane. So quickly.

Too quickly.

Kenshin cleared his throat, letting his smile drop, despite his wish to remain lighthearted. There were smudges across her cheek and nose. He'd have wagered ten gold *ryō* they were from the dust of polishing sand. Just like when they were children. Just like when she'd helped her father—celebrated artisan Muramasa Sengo—polish weapons in the nearby smithy.

Memories stirred through Kenshin, pleasant and warm. He should not—would not—smile at this particular girl so familiarly again. No matter how much he wished to do so.

Such a gesture would not serve them well.

A grip of doubt took hold of Kenshin's throat. A terrible sensation that only ever came about in this girl's presence. "Would you like me to leave?"

"Well, I have no intention of currying your horse for you, even if you are the fearsome Dragon of Kai." Though her words were crisp—plinks of water against clay—her voice was calm.

It suited her. Amaya.

A night rain.

Crisp. Yet calm.

Kenshin gritted his teeth. "You should not—"

"You haven't brought your sword to be polished in quite some time." Amaya stepped toward him. "My father mentioned

it only yesterday." She held out her left hand. "Give it to me."
She spoke as though nothing were between them.

As though Kenshin meant nothing to her.

That same grip of doubt tightened its hold. Kenshin threw
it off with a roll of his shoulders, like an unwanted burden.

Better Amaya think he was nothing to her. Better for them
both.

The longer he thought it, the sooner it would become true.

Without a word, Kenshin removed his *katana* from its
bindings and passed it to her.

Amaya unsheathed the blade from its ornate *saya*. Her
eyes flitted across the intricate *tsuba*—across the copper-gilt
filigree of the Hattori crest worked into the hand guard. Over
the gaping dragon's maw inlaid with turquoise enamel. She
stopped to *tsk* at the sight of the sword itself. "Do you not
know by now?" Amaya scolded lightly. "Art such as this is
meant to be cared for."

Kenshin watched her study the grooves in the painstakingly crafted jewel steel. The notches of wear and neglect.
Her eyes were soft puddles of grey. Concern etched a groove
between them. One he desperately wished to smooth with a
quick pass of his thumb.

It was this groove—this concern for something Amaya
should no longer trouble herself with—that tempered the
anger in Kenshin's veins.

Despite her efforts to conceal it, Muramasa Amaya always
cared about things far more than she should.

"You're right," Kenshin replied. "Anything made by

Muramasa-*sama* is meant to be cared for." His words were laced with tender meaning.

Those same soft eyes lifted to his. Unhesitatingly. "Father would agree." She paused, then glanced away. "I'll see to it that the blade is sharpened and returned to you tonight."

"There's no need."

"No." Amaya returned the *katana* to its *saya* with a smooth flick of her wrist. "Father would not want a blade he fashioned to remain in such disrepair." She spoke as if her father— perhaps the most famed metalsmith in all the empire—would personally hone and polish the sword, but Kenshin knew Amaya would be the one to do it.

Knew it with the certainty of the rising sun each dawn.

A sharp pang carved a path around his heart.

But he said nothing. Did nothing.

It was better this way.

As Amaya turned to take leave, she looked over her shoulder. If he hadn't known her better, Kenshin would have sworn he saw Amaya hesitate.

"Mariko . . . isn't dead, Kenshin. She can't possibly be dead."

"I know."

"Good." Amaya nodded once. "Don't give up in your search for her."

"I won't."

A small smile curled up her face.

His resolve broke at the sight.

"Amaya . . ." Kenshin closed the gap between them. He wanted so badly to wipe the smudges from her cheek. To press the groove between her eyes until it vanished beneath his touch. His hand rose to her face.

She pulled back. "Good evening, *my lord.*" Amaya bowed low.

In the gesture, Kenshin saw none of her teasing. None of their usual humor.

He missed it more than he could ever say.

But Kenshin knew better. He stepped to one side. Dipped his head in a bow.

When she turned to go, Kenshin found himself moving forward, his feet obeying his heart's unspoken commands.

He could not watch her walk away.

Not again.

Instead Kenshin brushed past her coldly, back into the afternoon sun of the courtyard. He almost stopped short when he saw his mother standing there. Waiting. She was not looking at him. Her knowing eyes were trained on Amaya. Their piercing centers followed the daughter of Muramasa Sengo until the girl's slender shadow vanished around the nearest corner.

Kenshin did not falter as he approached his mother. He bowed before her.

"Mother."

"Son." She searched his face. For what, he could only hazard a guess. "Your sister?"

Kenshin shook his head.

His mother's regal shoulders sagged the smallest fraction. Only someone standing close by could ever have detected it.

Here, at least, Kenshin could offer comfort. He placed a hand against her cheek.

"She is alive, Mother," he said. "I promise you. Mariko lives."

The fire of truth blazed in her eyes. "Bring her back to us safely, Kenshin."

"I will."

"Then you have a plan?"

Kenshin nodded. "Tomorrow I leave for the imperial city."

"You hope to find your sister in Inako?"

"No." His lips thinned into a hard line. "I hope to find answers."

Many Kinds of strength

—✳—

Mariko had never known she could hate anyone with such deep-scated ferocity. She'd long considered the sentiment an exercise in futility. Hatred served no purpose, except to plague its bearer.

But these last few hours had proven her wrong.

She hated all these men. Every last one of them. With more fervency than she'd ever imagined possible. Even the recent edicts of her parents had not elicited this kind of furor. Of course her arranged marriage had provoked a reaction. Certainly bitterness. Even rage. A rash of emotions Mariko had struggled to contend with for several weeks.

But hatred?

Never.

Today her thoughts were consumed by murderous retribution. Mariko had dreamed of setting fire to the Black Clan's camp no less than ten times in the past hour.

She'd plotted. Allowed a plan to weave through her mind like a tapestry across a loom. Mariko had fantasized about laying kindling through the brush with great care, under cover of night. She'd imagined rigging her own set of traps. Naturally ones far more ingenious than any the Black Clan could ever concoct. In her mind, she'd carefully trailed a thin string soaked in pitch to a previously devised shelter. Then she'd calmly set the string to flame. Pausing only to watch the Black Clan burn, like the hell-fiends they were.

The vision materialized, a welcome respite from her reality.

Just as a small rock descended from the sky, pelting her on the head.

The pain blossomed across her skull like a dribble of steaming water. Her dream of revenge took shape once again, growing ever more vivid in detail. Now the very demons of the forest rose at her command, ready to wreak their ghostly havoc.

Another rock glanced across her shoulder.

A bigger one this time.

Mariko refused to cry out. To fall to the ground in abject misery.

"Move faster, boy," a harsh voice intoned nearby.

Her lips were parched. Her knees were trembling. Nevertheless Mariko picked up four more logs and braced them against her chest. She tried to channel bravery as a source of strength, but it did not answer. Strangely, it was fear that drove her forward. Fear that she would fail in her task to learn the truth.

Fear that the Black Clan would discover she was not a boy.

She hadn't eaten since yesterday afternoon. Unless she counted the muddy pond water she'd spat from her lips this morning, the last thing Mariko had had to drink was the sake from the night before. That same terrible night she'd fallen into captivity.

Her tormentor ambled alongside her, kicking dark soil into her path with undisguised relish.

"Only four?" he said. "At this rate, we'll be here all day." The boy sneered, his yellowed eyes cutting in half. "I've never seen a weaker excuse for a man." Mariko's chest hollowed at his words, her heart missing a beat. The boy's gaze did not leave hers, even while he tossed another small rock into the air. Only to catch it. And toss it again.

Toying with her.

Mariko braced herself for the pebble's inevitable strike. Sure enough—even as she quickened her pace—the stone hit the back of her leg, biting into her calf with all the menace of a tiny woodland creature.

Indignation bubbled in her throat. The same throat that desperately needed a drink of water.

Her tormentor stepped before Mariko, savoring her obvious distress.

Ren. The boy with the murder eyes and the spiked top-knot.

It turned out her earliest suspicions had been correct: Ren's haunted gaze did indeed mask something far darker within—a boy who smiled in the face of suffering, as though

123

he derived great joy from it. Ren had been designated Mariko's watcher, and he'd taken to the task as only a boy such as he undoubtedly would.

Like a fox to a swallow's nest.

"Did you hear me, Lord Weakling?" Ren angled closer, his expression increasingly sinister. A small log dangled from his fingertips.

Mariko closed her eyes, her posture rigid.

So far she'd managed to maintain her composure. She hadn't cried once. Hadn't so much as asked for a drop of water. When Death inevitably came for her, Hattori Mariko would not be sniveling and wretched. She would be in control of her emotions, no matter the cost.

With his free hand, Ren rapped his knuckles on the side of her head. Mariko's eyes flew open. He'd touched her. Struck her. A wash of anger reddened her vision. She quickly blinked it away.

Hattori Mariko was a warrior now.

And a warrior is never weak.

Ren smiled down at Mariko, as if he could see past her eyes, into the ugly truth of her soul. Though the boy stood scarcely taller than she, he reveled in the fact. Mariko suspected he did not always come across men of shorter stature.

Unfortunately this near parity of height did not grant her any advantage. Ren was stockier, his musculature hard-earned. She could see the scars and calluses along his hands and forearms. This boy was used to punishing work.

When Ren caught her studying him, he snorted derisively. "I said, did you hear me, you pathetic excuse for a—"

"I heard you."

Ren's smile faded. He plopped the log in his hand atop the four already pressed against Mariko's chest.

She faltered for the first time. Nearly lost hold of her burden.

"Move faster." Ren unsheathed one of the hooked swords from his back. A deadly pair of weapons, modeled after garden sickles. "Boss said if I don't like your work, I can cut you into pieces and feed you to Akuma." He pressed the flat end of the sickle to his own neck. Mocking her even further.

Mariko breathed deeply. She continued on her way, ignoring the pain building in her arms. Ignoring the dry burn in her throat and the sudden threat of tears. Sweat marred her sight. Slicked her palms.

How she wished she could run away. Vanish into the woods, like a ghost. Never once look back. The thought gripped her. Took hold of her for an instant.

Chiyo. Nobutada.

The chance to prove my worth.

Four steps.

Four steps were all Mariko could take before she crumbled to the forest floor, the logs tumbling from her grasp.

Ren laughed darkly. "This will be a long day for you. Too bad it will also be your last."

Mariko pushed her face into the earth, her pulse thrumming in her ears. The soil smelled fragrant and alive. She wanted to burrow into it. Disappear. Dig her way through to the other side.

"Get up."

A new tormentor. One whose voice Mariko readily recognized.

Readily hated. Without question.

"Get up." He was closer now. His voice even more gruff.

She pressed her hands into the earth and lifted to her knees.

Ōkami peered down at her, his arms crossed, his expression odd. A mixture of boredom and predatory amusement.

"Stand."

A brief moment passed in silent revolt. Mariko met his gaze, surprised to feel a sudden flare of courage ignite within her. The same courage she'd sought to channel all day. Ōkami did not look away, though one of his brows rose in question.

"Useless." He inhaled through his nose. "Utterly useless."

With that, the Wolf turned. Dismissing Mariko in almost the same breath.

The anger that had been lying dormant for so long erupted in her chest. Mariko staggered to her feet, gripping a log in one hand. She wielded it like a club, aiming for his imperious head.

Ōkami leaned out of the log's path without missing a step. His expression did not even register her attempt to strike. Still bored.

But perhaps a tad less amused.

He thinks I'm pitiful.

Worthless.

Fury tingling in her fingertips, Mariko hurled the log again. The force nearly took her from her feet.

Ōkami rolled across the forest floor, quicker than lightning over a lake. When he stood, he brandished a long branch in his left hand. With it, he struck Mariko once on her elbow. A burst of prickling pain shot down her arm. The log fell to the ground.

When Mariko curled her fingers into a fist—readying to lunge—Ōkami hit her on the shoulder with the same branch. Her hand opened of its own volition. Resisted her attempt to re-form it into a fist. For the first time since she'd been tasked with moving logs from one forsaken corner of the forest to another, Mariko yelled in guttural protest.

Not out of pain. But out of hatred.

Pressure points. The hellspawn was abusing her pressure points.

"You've had enough, then?" Ōkami said as he calmly brushed forest debris off his black *kosode*.

Mariko exhaled in a miserable huff. "You're cheating."

"You're useless."

"I am *not* useless." She began scrubbing away the dirt from her face, wiping it on her sleeve, as she'd often seen soldiers do.

Ōkami raised the branch before him, level with his shoulder. "Prove it."

"What?" She blinked. Beside her, Ren laughed ominously, stepping aside to lean against a gnarled tree trunk.

"Take the branch from me," Ōkami said.

Mariko's eyes went wide. Her mind opened to a myriad of possibilities, each of which she dismissed in rapid succession. She scanned the length of him. His impressive height. A body trained for warfare, wrapped in sinuous muscle. The long arm extended her way, fingers expertly coiled around the branch.

Fully prepared to teach her a lasting lesson.

Trying her best to convey disdain, Mariko spat the last of the soil from her mouth. "What will you give me if I take the branch from you?"

"You are not in a position to negotiate." He angled his head, the scar through his lips appearing silver in a shaft of sunlight.

"At least tell me why I was brought here. What you intend to do with me."

"I have no intentions to do anything with anyone." His black eyes glittered. "Besides sleep and eat and drink away my days."

Mariko refrained from frowning in judgment. Why such a lazy boy would choose to work in service to the Black Clan was beyond her. "If you won't answer any of my questions, there's little incentive for me to fight you." She let the words fall from her lips like rocks down a mountainside. In a rough and coarse tumble. "Especially since I know I will lose."

"You will lose because you are slow and untrained."

"I suppose that is what makes me useless in your eyes," she said. "That and my obvious lack of strength."

Another bout of dark laughter arose from Ren. A laughter that only served to irritate Mariko further.

"There are many kinds of strength, Lord Lackbeard." The branch dropped to Ōkami's side; his tone was thoughtful. "Strength of the heart. Strength of the mind."

Though she was surprised to hear these sentiments uttered by this boy, Mariko was careful to conceal it. "Show me a warrior who believes that to be true, and I will endeavor to take the branch from you."

A wry grin began to curl up Ōkami's mouth. "Be as swift as the wind. As silent as the forest. As fierce as the fire. As unshakable as the mountain. And you can do anything . . . even take this branch from me."

Mariko snorted, catching herself before crossing her arms as her mother would. "Needlessly cryptic. Especially since mere words make all things possible."

"I'm glad we agree." He raised the branch again. "Take the branch from me, Lord Lackbeard."

Her eyes narrowed to slits. "Words do *not* make all things possible. Ideas are the seeds of possibility."

"Without words, ideas are nothing but voiceless thoughts." Ōkami held the branch steady. Unflinching.

"Without ideas, words would never have come into being."

"Fine, then. Without words, give me an idea." Another slow, taunting smile. "Now take the branch."

Her ire spiking, Mariko returned his unwavering stare. Though Ōkami's expression remained one of detached amusement, a flame sparked behind his eyes like a sun at midnight. The sight prompted her to make a final decision. One of dishonor. One she was sure to regret.

"I prefer to fight battles I know I can win." With that, Mariko bent to pick up the log closest to Ōkami. Just as he lowered the branch a second time, she shot to standing, ramming her full weight into his injured right shoulder. The one she knew still bore a fresh wound from the giant's *kanabō* swing the night before.

The Wolf grunted loudly as they both fell to the ground in a tangled heap. Mariko landed on top of him—lunging for the branch—but Ōkami flipped her onto her stomach, forcing every last bit of air from her body by leaning on her with unnecessary intensity. Damp soil trickled into her mouth, causing her to sputter and retch and flail.

Mariko tried to shove her elbow into his face, but was met with nothing more than wry laughter.

"I owe you an injury, Sanada Takeo," Ōkami whispered in her ear. "And I pay my debts." He hauled her to her feet as though she were nothing more than a sack of air. "Now get back to work."

Humiliation took root in Mariko's chest, tugging at her center like a fishhook. She swiped the soil from her mouth and straightened her dirty *kosode*, hoping to pierce his resolve as he had hers. "This is a waste of time. If your glorious leader had granted me use of a wagon, I would have been done moving these logs hours ago."

It was a sound argument. One he—of all people—should readily agree with, as the Wolf did not relish expending unnecessary effort.

Ōkami paused to rub his shoulder. For an instant, Mariko

thought he would agree. Especially when she caught a trace of humor on his face. Then he swept his black hair from his forehead, as though he was banishing the thought. "If this is the last task of your life, it's never a waste of time to do it thoroughly."

A cold current of fear overshadowed Mariko's anger. "You—you don't truly mean that. If you intended to kill me, you would have done it already. Why have you brought me here? To what end?" She focused the last of her fear into something pointed. Sharp. "And if this is indeed the last task of my life, I'd rather be doing anything else—thinking anything else—than this."

"You'd waste your last day in thought?" Ōkami stared down at her, unblinking.

"I would spend it thinking something meaningful. Doing something honorable."

Like exposing the location of your camp.

Or bringing about an end to your band of bloodthirsty thieves.

"Thinking?" Ren interjected as he spat in the dirt by her feet. "Knowledge feeds no one. Nor does it win any wars."

"I find your position on this matter unsurprising." Mariko did not even bother glancing toward the boy with the spiked topknot.

"Honorable?" Ōkami shifted closer, his hand still pressed to his shoulder. The coppery scent of fresh blood suffused the air. "Do you consider attacking a wounded man without warning an act of honor?"

Color flooded Mariko's cheeks. She'd known she would

regret that decision the moment she'd made it. Honor was a fundamental tenet of *bushidō*. And her choice to deceive Ōkami and take advantage of his weakness was—without a doubt—a dishonorable one.

"I"—she swallowed—"was pushed to that action."

"As many men often are."

"I—"

"Don't trouble yourself by explaining. Honor bears no weight with me." The Wolf continued studying her. "And I find knowledge a poison to a weak mind."

A litany of retorts collected in Mariko's throat, but none seemed good enough. Wise enough. Instead she chose to defeat words with silence.

With an idea.

"Never doubt. Never fear. Never overthink." Ōkami watched her as he spoke. As though he was searching for something beyond her. "That is the only way to stay alive."

A glimmer of reason shone in his words. It unsettled her even further. Mariko's lips pressed together. The skin in their centers cracked as the salt of her blood touched her tongue.

Anger tingled across her skin. Anger at him. Anger at herself.

How she wished she had a perfect retort at the ready. One she could fire back, like a polished stone.

Wordlessly, she bent to retrieve the fallen logs.

When Mariko stood once more, she thought she saw Ōkami wince as though a lantern had been shined in his eyes.

He stretched, then yawned. "On second thought, take

Lord Lackbeard to Yoshi," Ōkami said to Ren. "Make sure he eats something. A well-watered tree yields sweeter fruit."

As the Wolf turned to leave, courage pushed Mariko into his path a final time. "Answer at least one question. After drugging me and dragging me here against my will, I'm owed that much."

He waited, his features coolly indifferent.

Mariko breathed deep. "Am I prisoner, or am I a servant?"

Ōkami paused before responding. "We choose what we are in any situation, be it a word or an idea." With a small smile, he walked away.

I dislike this boy. Immensely.

Before she had a chance to organize her thoughts, Ren yanked her to his side. Mariko watched from the corner of her eye while Ōkami strapped his *bō* across his back. The Wolf mounted a grey horse and rode from camp, nodding in salute to the guards patrolling the perimeter.

How Mariko wished she could best him at *something*.

Wished she could trounce him in all things.

The Wolf wasn't as clever as he believed himself to be. Mariko found herself contemplating ways to destroy him. To watch him struggle.

And beg for mercy.

But she could not waste her focus on such petty emotions. Not when there were so many more pressing concerns at her heels. Mariko needed to learn why the Black Clan had brought her to their encampment. Was it possible they'd somehow discovered who she was? Had she been taken hostage?

Ice curled down her backbone at the thought.

As quickly as the fear rippled over her, it melted away. If the Black Clan had known who she was, they would have killed her already. And Mariko would not have been allowed even the limited freedom she'd been granted thus far.

Mariko sighed. Each step she took brought with it another question. She needed to know why the Black Clan had taken her to their camp. Who they were exactly. But most of all, she needed to discover why they'd been sent to kill her.

And by whom.

She glanced at Ren sidelong as they made their way toward the center of the encampment. Through the haze of the afternoon sun, his yellowed eyes reminded her of a snake lying in wait in the summer grass. How it would slither in the shadows while it pursued its prey, lulling everything around it into a false sense of safety.

Perhaps the best way for Mariko to gain answers was for her to do the same. To stop being difficult. To start paying attention.

Follow orders. Engender trust.

First she needed to find a way to be useful to the Black Clan. Then—when the men were lulled into a false sense of safety—she would strike. Discomfort twisted through her chest as she pondered this course of action. For it was not one of honor; it was one of deceit. Unsettlingly more so than her choice to don the garments of a boy and seek out the Black Clan.

A true warrior would face her enemies without flinching. Not slither about in the shade.

But there was so much Mariko wished to know. So much she wished to learn.

And she was beginning to realize that honor did not serve her well in a den of thieves.

Briefly Mariko toyed with the idea of asking Ren how Ōkami's powers worked. The fool thought knowledge did not win wars? Knowledge was everything in a war. Especially in a war of wits. She could trick the evil twit into revealing damaging information. Learn how Okami was able to move as he did. Why the use of his powers seemed to take such a harsh toll on him.

As she glanced one last time over her shoulder, Mariko discovered she also wanted to know where the Wolf was going.

And to whom.

But for now she would lie in the shadows and wait.

weakness of the spirit

———— ✳ ————

The man with the wooden leg hovered over a steaming pot, peering into its contents with the focus of a mother hen. He paused to stoke the fire beneath the iron cauldron. A sooty box bellows groaned as he fed the flames with a blast of air.

As Mariko had first suspected, this Yoshi was the cook.

When another gust of steam rose from the pot, Yoshi stepped away, something akin to a smile spreading across his face. He was slightly portly in the middle. His reddened forehead shone with sweat, and one of his ears appeared larger than the other.

Yoshi leaned forward when Mariko and Ren approached. His eyes were still fixed on the contents of the pot.

"Yoshi-*san*." Ren prodded Mariko closer by digging his shoulder into her back. She refrained from scowling when she stumbled forward.

"Are you still here?" Yoshi muttered without even turning around.

His dismissive tone reminded Mariko of her father, though Yoshi appeared several years younger than Hattori Kano. She pursed her lips. "I'm not certain I have a choice." She pitched her voice low. Gave it a grating quality, as though she'd swallowed a mouthful of sand. It was true Mariko had decided to cooperate, but she knew only a fool would appear pleased to be the Black Clan's captive. At least not so soon after being taken prisoner.

"Of course you have a choice," Yoshi said.

"I fail to see what it is."

He turned to face her fully, a long wooden spoon hanging from one fist. "You could run." His tone was circumspect, the lines around his mouth deep-set.

Mariko paused in consideration. Wondered what could prompt Yoshi to make such a point. "I'd be caught."

"It's true." He nodded, drumming the spoon against his thigh in almost rhythmic fashion. "You would likely be caught."

"Then why bother with the risk?"

"Without risk, life is far too predictable."

Mariko stared at him, forcing her expression blank. She had not expected to find a philosopher buried beneath the cook's worn exterior. "We are born. We live. We die. All that matters in life is predictable. A rock settles into the soil. A blossom gives off a fragrance. A—"

"A blossom can split through a rock, given enough time."

"And enough sunlight. Enough water. Enough—"

Yoshi laughed sharply. The sound warmed through her in a way that troubled her. Mariko did not want to like any member of the Black Clan. Much less this portly fellow brandishing a wooden spoon. Yoshi continued laughing, his surliness causing the sound to spike into the patches of light above. He turned back toward his precious pot of steaming liquid, lowering the spoon into its depths with that same sharpened awareness.

Her curiosity growing with each passing moment, Mariko leaned closer to peer into the boiling vat, determined to see what Yoshi labored so painstakingly to prepare.

The bubbling liquid shifted as he stirred. A familiar object swirled into view.

Eggs?

"You seem disappointed." Yoshi eyed her askance.

Mariko frowned. "They're just eggs."

His lips protruded in a scowl as Yoshi removed one egg from the pot and gingerly dropped it into another bowl of water nearby. "These are not just any eggs." Using the tip of his spoon, Yoshi began rolling the egg in the water.

The silence that descended on them stretched uncomfortably thin. Mariko could no longer keep quiet. "Why are you washing the egg after boiling it?"

"This is cold water," Yoshi said as he took the egg from its chilled bath and raised it into the light. "Two extremes make for one perfectly cooked egg." He tapped the rounded end of the egg against the side of the pot. Then he did the same to the pointed end. He lifted the egg to his lips and blew hard, as though he meant to cool it entirely in a single breath.

The egg flew from its shell into Yoshi's waiting hand.

"Eat it." He offered it to her.

The last time Mariko had consumed an offering by a member of the Black Clan, she'd awoken to find herself thrown across the back of a horse. Nevertheless hunger overcame her the instant she took hold of the egg. A stronger warrior would have refused to eat any food offered by the enemy. But in this case she was not a strong warrior. She was a starving sparrow.

Mariko took a small bite. The white of the egg was cool and creamy. Light as a feather. Its center was the warm yellow of a dandelion. Steam rose from it in a perfect curl. In short, it was quite possibly the most delicious thing Mariko had eaten in her entire life. She opened her mouth to swallow the remaining bite whole.

"Wait!" Yoshi said, startling her still. From a small, earthenware jar, he removed a piece of pickled ginger half the size of his palm. Moving faster than Mariko's eyes could follow, Yoshi yanked a hooked dagger from the collection at his belt and sliced two paper-thin slivers of ginger on top of the egg. Then he prodded her to eat by raising his brows.

Mariko had been wrong before.

This was the best thing she'd ever eaten in her entire life.

Though her mouth was full, Mariko began offering muffled words of gratitude. It galled her to be giving thanks to a member of the Black Clan, but she'd already made her choice. For however long they kept her here, she would follow their orders. Find a way to be useful to them.

And wait in the grass to strike.

As Mariko started to speak, a rock pinged against the side of the iron cauldron, surprising her. The precious egg spilled from her mouth onto the earth. Before Mariko could think to react, Yoshi yanked another dagger from his belt and hurled it into the bushes at her back.

Ren shouted as the dagger struck the tree trunk a hairsbreadth from his shoulder. The branches around him shuddered from the impact.

"Mealtime is sacred," Yoshi scolded. "You know this better than anyone."

"Boss said I could do as I pleased with the new recruit," Ren fumed. "Even told me I could kill him if he broke any of our rules."

New recruit? Rules?

Mariko struggled to stay emotionless as a flurry of thoughts whirled through her mind. Yoshi's already flushed face reddened further. In that moment, Mariko knew she was right to keep silent.

Ren had just revealed something he was clearly not meant to divulge.

Yoshi took a deliberate step in Ren's direction. A step laced with warning. "He did not say you could do as you pleased with me. And as long as Sanada Takeo is with me, I insist you leave him be."

"Fine," Ren said, anger flashing in his yellowed eyes. "Enjoy your meal, Lord Weakling, for it might be your last!" As he yelled his threat, he fought to untangle himself from the brambles at his feet. Then he spun away, his expression promising a fierce reprisal in the near future.

Predictable, at all turns.

Mariko stared at the ruined egg lying on the ground. She contemplated picking it up and finishing it, dirt and all.

Such a shame to waste something so delicious.

"If that was to be my last meal," Mariko murmured, "how fitting is it that it fell from my lips before I could eat it?"

The previously rough timbre of Yoshi's laughter was gentler now. "Despite what I thought at first glance, you do have a flair for the dramatic. As to this being your last meal, that will depend on what Ranmaru decides." He transferred another egg from the boiling vat into the cool bath. "Though I must say, for someone on the brink of death, you do appear remarkably calm."

Mariko gnawed at her lower lip, once more considering what kind of information Yoshi intended to wheedle from her with his surly brand of kindness.

What kind of information she could, in turn, wheedle from him.

"I am not calm," she said finally. "It's a constant effort to quell my fear."

"Then why bother?"

"Because I do not wish to appear weak."

Another smile tugged at his mouth as Yoshi unshelled a new egg for Mariko.

His kindness could be a tactic. A way to wear down her defenses. Extreme cruelty tempered by extreme consideration. Much like the egg.

It could all be a trick.

But the egg—that simple egg—was so wonderful. So perfect.

How could anyone who would take such care to prepare a simple egg truly be bad?

Mariko sighed to herself.

If Yoshi's kindness was a lie or a trick, she would let herself fall prey. All in service to a greater goal.

Follow orders. Engender trust.

Strike when they least expect it.

She would learn who these men were. Whom they served.

And why they'd tried to kill her.

When the bushes behind Mariko rustled once more, Yoshi yanked another small dagger from his belt and took aim. A yelp and the scurry of fleeing feet followed.

While she chewed, Mariko marveled at the fluidity of his movements. His wooden limb did not hamper him. Nor did it grant him any advantage, in that heedless way of stories. It was not a gift, nor was it a blessing.

It simply was. Just as he simply was.

And Yoshi threw daggers as though he was born to it, like an eagle taking flight.

This realization prompted her to consider a new idea:

Perhaps true weakness is weakness of the spirit.

"How long did it take you to learn to throw a *kunai* like that?" Mariko asked with unconcealed admiration.

"Most of my life."

Her eyes dropped to the intricate leather belt at his hip. To the array of polished blades, each of varying shape and size. "What is the purpose behind having so many different kinds of daggers?"

"Some *kunai* are better to throw short distances. Others are better for longer ones. The remaining ones? Well, that's among the many secrets I possess." He snorted.

Mariko thought of Ren and his pebbles. "I wish I possessed this skill." Her lips quirked to one side. "Today of all days, a skill like this would have served me well."

"You could learn. Given enough training, anyone could."

"I'm not so sure." Lines of doubt settled across her face. "Are you also going to inform me I need to be as swift as a fire so I may move mountains in the wind?"

Yoshi laughed loudly.

Mariko caught herself before she could smile. "And you shouldn't dismiss your abilities. It insults both you and me at the same time."

Another raise of his brows. She suspected people did not often speak to Yoshi in such a direct manner. "Is that so?"

"Yes. You insult yourself by dismissing skills that took you a lifetime to develop. At the same time you insult me by stating that I need only try—as though the only hindrance is my own lack of effort." Mariko's speech grew more rapid with each passing word. She took a deep breath before continuing. "To even attempt something, one must first believe in the possibility. And *then* be granted an opportunity." As Mariko finished, she glanced meaningfully at the portly fellow.

Yoshi's grin turned knowing. "Alas, Sanada Takeo, you will not be granted the opportunity to throw a dagger here. But your attempt to try is duly noted. And appreciated."

"Not an attempt. Rather an unceasing challenge of life," she mused. "To learn, even when knowledge itself may fail you."

"Rather the unceasing challenge of youth," Yoshi said drily as he lowered more eggs into the simmering pot. "Not to worry; I can promise that all great opportunities in life follow some form of struggle."

"May I ask what it is you struggle with most?" Mariko prodded.

Yoshi rubbed a sleeve on the sweat gathering above his brow. Then he wandered to the bushes to retrieve the blade he'd thrown at Ren, prying it from where the *kunai* was embedded in the tree trunk. He lifted the dagger into the light, then lovingly restored it to its place at his hip.

"Learning a new blade," he replied.

A groove formed at the bridge of Mariko's nose.

Yoshi said, "Every blade has its own path. Every handle is different. Every tang is unique. The balance of every dagger is its own."

Again Mariko lingered in thought. "Would consistency

not make it better? Consistency in the forging of the steel. In the forming of the blade."

"Consistency is not enough. It doesn't account for chance, and there is always a chance the handle will strike the mark instead of the blade. No amount of skill can thwart it every time."

Mariko studied the hooked dagger Yoshi had used to shave slices of pickled ginger. "Two blades affixed in their centers like a cross would work better." She considered further. "Or perhaps even three. Like a star."

"Why not four?" Yoshi said with amusement. "Alas, you will never see me wielding a cumbersome thing like that. Any effective *kunai* would need to be light." In one flowing motion, he whipped a blade from its sheath and hurled it toward the same branch. "Quick."

Mariko considered the quivering handle. Yoshi had thrown it to strike the exact same place as before. It fit into the previous divot at a near-identical angle. The way the handle shook—trembled into solid motion—brought to mind Ōkami and his mysterious abilities. Mariko frowned.

She did not wish to be reminded of anything she did not yet understand.

Especially something pertaining to the Wolf.

Mariko lowered into a crouch. Picked up a twig. Began to draw.

Indeed.

Why *not* four?

Jubokko

———✳———

That night, Mariko woke from her slumber to the sound of screaming.

It startled her into awareness, like a splash of icy water. Her forehead grazed the rock she'd been using as a pillow. Her fingernails dug into the damp soil.

The screams echoing through the forest were the screams of a tortured animal. Not a man.

It couldn't be a man.

No human could make sounds like these.

As the screams continued, each beat of her heart crashed through her, a drum pulled taut beneath her skin. She opened one eye, trying to focus on the forest's shadows. Trying to drown out the sounds of pure suffering.

Men with torches were massing in the distance. Several rings of fire blurred through the trees.

For a moment, Mariko considered running. The Black

Clan was distracted. Perhaps they would not notice her slipping into the night. Perhaps she could find her way out of the forest without tripping any of their supposed traps.

Perhaps.

A foot kicked the small of her back, frightening her all the more.

"Get up." It was Ren. "Now." The tenor of his voice was surprisingly sad.

Mariko scrambled to her feet, too unnerved by the screams to protest. She followed Ren as he wove through the trees, his torch held high.

Save for the screaming, the forest had grown eerily silent. The wind did not stir through the branches. Nor did Mariko hear the sound of any life in the air about her. Only the crackle of Ren's torch. The snapping of twigs beneath her bare feet.

And the screams.

Ren walked silently, Mariko at his back. As they made their way toward the cluster of torches, the screaming grew louder.

Mariko refrained from covering her ears.

They approached several members of the Black Clan, standing around the base of a tree, its branches twisting into the darkness like skeletal fingers stretching for the sky.

At first glance, the tree appeared completely normal.

What Mariko saw once her eyes adjusted to the shadows almost elicited a scream from her own lips.

At the base of the tree was a young man. His limbs were tangled in the roots. Roots that had risen from the soil, wrapping around him like a thorny vine. Thin rivulets of blood dripped down his face. Down the skin of his arms. Across the meat of his stomach.

The thorns had pierced through the young man's skin. All over his body, the vines squeezed tight, their thorns cutting deeper and deeper.

But the horror did not stop there.

When the thud of her pulse lessened, Mariko heard a slurping sound emit from the vines, followed by the rustle of dark leaves bursting to life in its skeletal branches.

The vines—the tree itself—was *feeding* on the boy.

The tree was draining him of blood.

He screamed again, the sound amplified by raw anguish.

Ranmaru and Ōkami stood before him, watching.

Mariko wanted to plead for mercy. Surely they could cut the boy away from the branches. Save him from such a slow, horrific death. She reached for a thorny branch, with a mind to rip it from the ground itself.

Quicker than a spark, Ōkami seized her by the elbow. "Don't touch it."

She blinked, the warmth of his hand searing through the thin hemp of her stolen *kosode*. He looked strangely severe. Much more so than ever before. His dark eyes roved across her face. Whatever he saw there briefly softened his expression.

"If you touch it, the *jubokko* will snare you, too," he said.

Horrified by this revelation, Mariko's jaw fell slack. Her eyes widened at the dying boy before her.

Ranmaru glanced her way. "Don't look on him with pity."

The boy screamed again. His cries were becoming weaker with each passing moment. "He was sent to find our camp. To find it and murder us in our sleep, like a treacherous snake."

"Even the most treacherous of snakes doesn't deserve to die this way," Mariko said hoarsely.

Ren started at her words. His glazed eyes flickered toward her, his expression unnerving even in the darkness.

"He is not a snake. He is something far worse." One of Ōkami's fists clenched around a piece of stained cloth. Mariko caught the edge of a white crest in its folds, but she could not make out the family. Nor could she make out anything of note.

The young man's screams had become soundless. His mouth hung open for a beat, only to shudder shut, his teeth chattering like insects scuttling across stone. The tree slurped again, and a sundry of black flowers burst into bloom.

Her horror abounded with each passing moment. Mariko wanted to tear her eyes away from the sight. Tear them away from the truth. She briefly considered asking Ren why he had brought her here.

Why they had forced her to witness this horror.

"You could end it." Mariko looked toward Ranmaru. As she struggled to keep her voice level, her eyes drifted to Ōkami's face. To the torchlight wavering around its carved hollows.

"You could end his suffering," she said to him, drawn to a sudden need for goodness in the ghastliness around her. "Don't leave him to die like this. He's just a boy." Mariko chewed her lower lip. "A boy . . . like me." As soon as she uttered the words, understanding dawned on her.

Understanding of why she had been brought to witness this horror.

Ōkami's gaze remained level and clear. His eyes—so focused, even amidst such suffering—locked on hers. Black and shining, like the onyx embedded in the hilt of her father's sword. "We are what we do." Though Ōkami's words sounded fierce, weariness tinged their edges. "This boy came to our home, intent on murdering us. He and his kind must pay." Again his fist tightened around the stained cloth and its obscured crest.

"We are so much more than what we do!" Mariko drew closer, as if nearness could invoke a sense of truth. "We are . . ." She searched her mind for the right things to say. "Our thoughts, our memories, our beliefs!" Her eyes dropped to the dying boy. To the evil tree, slowly draining him of life.

"This tree is not the forest," she said softly. "It is but one part."

"No. A murderer is a murderer. A thief is a thief." Ōkami bent his head toward hers, equally firm in his conviction. "In this life, believe in action and action alone."

Mariko's fingernails dug into her palms. She resisted the urge to grab Ōkami by the shoulders and shake him into reason.

He did not balk. Nor did he move to help.

It was Ranmaru who finally crouched before the dying boy. When the leader of the Black Clan spoke, his voice was gentle. Almost soothing. "Many years ago, there were three young men who grew up together near a forest not so dissimilar to this one." He mopped the sweat from the boy's brow with a clean piece of muslin.

The boy gasped. Mariko's chest pulled tight.

"When they were children, they played together. Studied together. Challenged each other as only friends can do. When they became older, one turned toward justice, another toward honor." Ranmaru's voice lowered. "The last toward ambition.

"In time, the three young men became warriors in their own right, each with sons of their own. As they settled into age and influence, the ambitious man realized his friend who valued honor above all else would never compromise on anything, even for the sake of those dearest to him."

With quiet solemnity, Ranmaru reached for the glittering hilt of the *katana* at his side. "So the ambitious man manipulated his remaining friend—the one who valued justice above all. With the skill of a tailor, the ambitious man threaded lies into truth. Planted seeds of doubt. He made the man who valued justice believe their honorable friend would undermine all they tried to achieve."

The boy's gaze was riveted on the leader of the Black Clan. As Ranmaru unsheathed his *katana*, he inhaled through his nose. Understanding softened the lines on the dying boy's face. He nodded feebly.

"When their honorable friend was accused of treason, the ambitious man turned to the last of their trio, hearkening to that same, pervasive sense of justice." Ranmaru stopped in his speech. Wordlessly asking for permission. The dying boy's eyes darted from the sword to Ranmaru. He nodded once more. Gratefully.

With a gentle nod of his own, Ranmaru pressed the tip of his *katana* above the boy's heart. "And so the friend who valued justice above all else executed his honorable friend . . . in front of his friend's only son. But when he realized what he had done—the mistake he had made—he tried to balance the scales. To right this terrible wrong and bring about renewed justice."

From where he stood before her, Mariko watched Ōkami's jaw harden. The sound of a blade slicing through skin rose into the night as Ranmaru pushed forward. Swift. And sure. A thankful smile upon his lips, the boy's eyelids opened sluggishly one last time as the life fled from his body.

"For his efforts to right this wrong, the man who valued justice was hung by his feet in Yedo Bay. Drowned before his family." Ranmaru slanted his head. As though he wished to speak directly to Ōkami. But could not. "In the dead of night, the son of this drowned man—a wolf in his own right—set fire to the tent of his father's accuser and fled into the mountains."

The air around them churned with unspoken thoughts. Countless unuttered sentiments, across years and generations.

Yet Mariko understood, all the same.

The tale Ranmaru told was of him and Ōkami. A tale of two boys who had lost their fathers to an ambitious man. A man who had once been their dearest friend.

Ōkami's father had betrayed Ranmaru's father. This was the reason Ōkami served Ranmaru. The reason he held such unswerving allegiance to the Black Clan. These two boys were inextricably linked by this betrayal. Linked by life and death.

A friendship forged in blood and fire.

As Ranmaru's story faded like a ghost into the night, the image from several days past—the memory of the boy standing in a courtyard, staring at stones stained red with his father's blood—formed in Mariko's mind.

As she'd first thought, this boy was Takeda Ranmaru.

Not a boy anymore. Now a young man, imbued with a shadowed purpose. One Mariko had only begun to grasp. Against her will, her curiosity abated, like a tide pulling from a desolate shore. In its place rose a tentative sadness—a halting kind of sympathy. She could not imagine what it would be to lose her family right before her eyes. To lose all she held dear, in an instant. Her mother. Her father. Kenshin . . .

But it could happen.

This forest had taught her that, even in a few short days.

As Mariko considered the possibility of such loss, a heaviness settled onto her skin. A burn began to rise in her throat.

The burn of injustice.

Ranmaru had killed her father's men. And Chiyo.

He'd tried to kill Mariko.

And she would never forget it.

Follow orders. Engender trust.

Strike when they least expect it.

"Watch closely, Sanada Takeo." Ranmaru slid his sword

from the dead boy's slumped body and stood tall. "This forest protects us. These trees—the *jubokko*—are everywhere. Our forest is guarded by *yōkai*, and they will not look kindly on you, should you attempt to run. Should you attempt to betray us in any way." He turned to face her. "But if you stay true, one day Jukai forest may serve you as well."

Mariko stared down at the lifeless young man. His skin had taken on a waxy hue.

To her left, Ōkami finally spoke, his words a whisper on a dying wind—

"Never forget, Sanada Takeo: in this forest, there is no place to hide."

the throwing star

---✶---

Over the course of the next four days, Mariko listened. Followed orders without complaint. She learned that many of the twenty or so members of the Black Clan left the camp at odd hours, often returning laden with small trunks of silk. With leather satchels of gold *ryō* and countless tins of copper pieces. Then they would leave again under a cloak of darkness, taking their stolen spoils deep beneath the trees. Disappearing from sight.

In this forest, there is no place to hide.

Ōkami's words echoed through Mariko's mind like a haunted refrain. They gave her leave to shudder when she thought no one was watching. To embrace her fears as she never had before.

Mariko discovered there was wisdom in facing her fears headlong. Acknowledging them made her cautious. Made her smarter. Perhaps these fears would help her obtain a shred of information. Something to warrant all this effort. Anything to justify the horrors she had witnessed four nights ago in Jukai forest.

She needed a way to earn the Black Clan's trust. If not their trust, then at least a semblance of their admiration. With it, she could then begin digging her way to the truth, like an army of termites set to decimate a structure from within.

If the incident with the *jubokko* had taught her anything, it was that one way to gain Ranmaru's confidence was through Ōkami. Their bond seemed unshakable. The kind of trust built over time. Alas, Mariko could not begin to understand how to earn the Wolf's favor. He was not exactly the demonstrative sort.

Now she was left to fight for Ranmaru's attention on her own.

So intent was she on devising the best way to impress the leader of the Black Clan that it had taken her five days to work up the courage. To take action.

And though she now possessed a plan, Mariko still remained uncertain. Whatever free time left to her had been spent mulling over the details. Considering the possibilities. All while putting aside the likelihood that—at any moment—her great secret might be revealed.

That a member of the Black Clan might learn she was not in fact a boy.

Fear again took hold of Mariko, leaving her immobile for a breath. Leaving her weakened. The only remedy was to return its cold embrace once more.

It fed her. This fear.

It gave her a sense of will.

Mariko straightened her shoulders. Reshaped her thoughts.

Ranmaru had paid her no attention today. As far as he was concerned, Mariko could be a single leaf among many. Ōkami was equally hopeless. An endless well, covered by years of neglect. Only two members of the Black Clan continued to pay Mariko mind—Ren and Yoshi. The former plagued her at every turn. The latter made it his duty to instruct her on the most inconsequential of lessons: how to light a fire, how to boil water, how to dig for edible roots. Ever since the night the *jubokko* had drained the young intruder of life, Mariko had been left to handle the most trivial tasks around the camp.

Washing pots. Plucking feathers.

And of course collecting firewood.

This lack of attention only hardened her resolve. Drove her toward a loftier goal. Now that she had successfully infiltrated the Black Clan's ranks, Mariko endeavored to gain access to its inner circle. Only by doing so would she ever obtain any information of import.

And discover the truth of why they'd been sent to kill her.

The most valuable knowledge she'd gleaned in the last few days was learning that Ōkami left camp alone every other morning, armed with nothing but a *bō*.

And did not return until well after nightfall.

Not that his absence mattered much to her. The Wolf spent his time in camp hidden in his tent. But Mariko was not fool enough to think he wasted any effort. These repeated absences were definitely a matter of note.

Where was he going?

Was it possible he was meeting with those holding sway over the Black Clan? With those who wished her dead?

As Mariko delved through the countless possibilities before her, she continued to fight with a bundle of dirty hemp cloth that had been left by her feet while she slept. Gritting her teeth, she wrangled the rough bolt of fabric straight, struggling to anchor a length of it onto a bamboo pole. Someone— likely Yoshi—had left her the means with which to build her own tent.

Mariko had felt strangely elated to discover this gift.

The tent proved that at least one member of the Black Clan found her useful. Wished for her to stay. She was reminded of Ren's error in divulging Ranmaru's plans to make her their newest recruit. Perhaps this was a sign she had made progress to that end. Though Ren's nasty attitude indicated otherwise, it was obvious someone in the camp supported the notion. She'd even been given a place to call her own. Tonight would be the first night Mariko would not have to sleep on a pile of rocks and debris.

If she could ever put together the cursed thing.

Just before Mariko succumbed to the desire to fling the hemp fabric into the underbrush, a hand scored by numerous burns reached out, snatching the bundle from her grasp.

Yoshi loomed above her, his red face mottled by irritation.

"Are you *still* trying to put that tent together?" He sat on the ground, swinging his wooden limb into position before him. Mariko considered it for a spell. Many times in the last few days, she'd wanted to ask Yoshi how he'd lost his leg. But she was learning to expect two things from the surly cook: He did not reveal information without intention.

And he did not permit anyone to make excuses for anything.

"As you undoubtedly know by now, Yoshi-*san*, I have never been in possession of this skill. Likely because I have never been granted the opportunity," she joked awkwardly. "But even so, I do feel as though I am missing something."

Yoshi rummaged through the bamboo rods and the knotted ball of twine by their feet. "Who gave these to you?" His lower lip pouted in a frown.

"I thought you did." She blinked. "But if it was not you, then perhaps it was Ren. His concern for my welfare has been nothing but consistent," Mariko said bitterly.

The creases vanished from his blotchy brow as understanding settled on Yoshi. "You're missing two key pieces of framing."

Perhaps it was indeed Ren who had left her the tent. Only he would have enjoyed watching Mariko suffer through trying to accomplish such an impossible task. "That—that miserable little fiend."

"Don't be angry with him." Yoshi sent half a smile her way. "Ren has led quite a difficult life. He's less a fiend and more a wounded cat."

Mariko mumbled, "Wounded cats still possess claws."

"True." He laughed. "I'll retrieve the missing pieces." Yoshi peered at her through one narrowed eye. "Have you shared your idea with Haruki yet?"

She shifted uncomfortably. "No."

"Then tell him about it while I piece together your tent." He spoke as though there was not even a question of Mariko following his directive.

A strange mix of comfort and concern rippled through her. Of course she disliked being told what to do. But she also appreciated someone—anyone—caring enough to try.

Despite the murmurings of her mind, Mariko's heart would not permit her to dislike Yoshi. "Perhaps you shouldn't help me," she said. "*Someone* might steal your tent frame as punishment."

"Someone?" He barked a laugh.

"I won't disclose who." Mariko smiled in return. "But a certain someone might seek retribution for you showing me this kindness."

"No one would dare. Lest that certain someone find himself perishing of starvation. You idiot boys don't even know how to cook rice properly, much less anything of substance." With this final pronouncement, Yoshi pushed her in the direction of the hillock to her left. Then he rolled the bundle of hemp cloth and took to his feet once more, intent on finding Ren and the missing lengths of bamboo.

Distress flashed through Mariko. She briefly considered flouting Yoshi's orders. Or perhaps even lying about it later.

But the churlish cook would learn the truth, and he would not be pleased that she'd failed to meet with the metalsmith for yet another day. Not to mention the dishonor of unnecessary deceit. It wasn't that deception by its very nature troubled her. Mariko realized its necessity, especially when paired alongside survival. But bald-faced lies were not the same thing. So, with a sigh, she began walking toward the small hill nearby, drawn to the feather of smoke rising from the fabric wall at its crest. One side of the hill was shaded by a looming stone protuberance—one of the many small outcroppings that eventually burgeoned into the snowcapped mountain in the distance. On her second day there, Mariko had realized how strategically positioned the camp of the Black Clan was. This collection of outcroppings offered them natural fortification, preventing anyone from attacking their flank.

She dug her heels into the soft earth and pressed onward, her calves burning from the steep incline. As Mariko walked, her mind continued its unceasing mutterings.

It was Yoshi who'd first pushed her to take her rendering of the throwing star to the Black Clan's metalsmith. He'd told her the idea had merit. And he'd not once called her foolish or found her efforts unwanted or out of place. It was a strange feeling. To have one of her enemies be the first among her acquaintances to appreciate her ideas.

Mariko paused before the wall of smoke-stained fabric, taking in a breath. Seeking courage of a lasting kind.

"Hello?" she said in a brusque voice.

When the metalsmith emerged from behind the fabric wall of his *jinmaku*, Mariko released a pent-up breath, allowing the relief to flood through her.

Haruki the metalsmith was none other than the boy she'd noticed that first night at the watering hole. The one with the shining skin, who looked as though he'd been taken from a childhood story about a boy who floated through the sky, buoyed into the clouds by an oiled-paper umbrella. Mariko recalled him watching the leaves sway through the maple trees with an almost otherworldly kind of serenity.

At least *this* boy would not take it upon himself to torment her as Ren had.

At least she hoped.

Haruki was tall and lean, with a narrow face and wide-set eyes. The front part of his hair was too short to fit into its topknot. The strands hung straight and loose. Only his hands and his *hachimaki* appeared marred by soot. He stood in silence as he studied her. Not a judgmental kind of silence. Not even a silence laced by curiosity.

He merely gave her leave to speak first.

"Yoshi said—"

"I was wondering when you would come here." Haruki smiled with his eyes, his voice pleasing and precise. "Yoshi told me about you last week."

Startled, Mariko stood still. "I didn't realize he'd said anything."

"One thing we all learn early on is to say very little to Yoshi. He likes his gossip almost more than he likes his food."

He wiped both his hands on a cloth hanging from his dark leather belt. Then he mopped the sweat from his neck. When the collar of his *kosode* shifted, lines of scarred skin became visible, wrapping around his shoulder like a set of monstrous fingers.

He was badly whipped in his past.

Mariko caught her voice before it could speak out of turn. And ask questions to which she did not need answers.

I should not care. I do not care.

"My name is Haruki." He dipped his head in a small bow.

Steeling herself, Mariko returned the gesture. "Sanada Takeo."

"I know."

She pursed her lips. Was it always necessary for boys to prove they knew more than anyone else around them? "I suppose Yoshi also told you why I wanted to come here."

"He said you had something you wished to show me."

It was a hedging kind of answer. One that made Mariko immediately wary.

"And you weren't . . . curious?" she said.

"You *do* ask a lot of questions." Haruki smiled calmly. "And no, I wasn't curious. I expected you to come my way when you were ready." Again he waited for her to speak.

It was time for Mariko to stop being worried that everyone she met harbored hidden agendas. That Haruki the metalsmith would laugh at her. Or dismiss her. Yoshi had said her idea was a good one. And this was the only way to see if both he and she were right.

Mariko lifted her gaze to meet Haruki's. "I wanted to ask if you could make a kind of . . . *kunai* for me."

"A throwing dagger?" He studied her once more, but she could not read his expression. "For you?"

Yes. Ultimately.

"No. Not for me." She inhaled deep. "I meant to say a *kunai* based on my design. One with many edges." As she spoke, Mariko knelt before him and began sketching in the dirt with a small stick. "Almost in a circle." She drew what at first glance appeared to be a sun with six rays curling away from it. "If you curve the blades in the same direction, it can be thrown in a rotating fashion, thereby allowing it to fly farther and faster."

Haruki crouched beside her. Considered her design.

"This would be difficult to make," he pronounced after a time. "And the amount of steel necessary would be quite costly, especially for a weapon a warrior might discard."

"What if you used iron instead? It's softer and less expensive than steel."

Haruki's eyes grazed over her drawing a second time. Still considering. "Even if it were made of iron, a weapon like this would take far too much time to fashion. I'm sorry. Each of these spikes would need to be individually sharpened."

Mariko nodded, trying to tamp down her disappointment. Having a weapon of this sort would have been an advantage to her for many reasons, most of which she meant to conceal in the darkest recesses of her mind. For now. Before she could succumb to disappointment, she shored up her resolve. Recalled this thought:

True weakness is weakness of the spirit.

She refused to give up so easily. "What if we could make a mold instead? Perhaps even reduce the number of blades?" Mariko used her stick to smooth the ground over her previous rendering and fashion another. "The mold could first be cast in beeswax, similar to an arrowhead. That way it could be sharpened with relative ease."

Haruki stood. Walked around the newest drawing, his head canted in consideration.

Quite suddenly, the metalsmith stopped pacing. "Come with me," he said, his tone crisp. Haruki proceeded to march down the hill, his long legs carrying him fast. Mariko ran to keep up as he strode toward another tent across the way. A larger tent, with a guard posted at its entrance. The tent to which Mariko had been trying to gain access ever since she was first brought to the Black Clan's encampment against her will.

The tent of Takeda Ranmaru.

Outside the entrance, several younger members of the Black Clan watched two weathered veterans play a game of Go. All appeared to be betting on the outcome, copper and silver links dotting a worn tatami mat. Several smaller coins had been thrown to the wayside, almost slipping out of notice. Mariko slid one beneath her sandaled foot, to surreptitiously pocket it later.

There could be a time I might need money.

Before Mariko had a chance to collect the coin, Haruki paused near the entrance, waiting for her. With what Mariko hoped was an innocent smile, she moved forward, quickly dragging the copper coin beneath her straw sandal.

Haruki began speaking to Ranmaru even before Mariko came to a stop beside him. Despite what she'd initially thought, the metalsmith was not one to linger without purpose. "His idea isn't a bad one. The weapon itself would be small. Light. Much easier to aim than a traditional *kunai*. But the time and cost it would take to make it almost negates its value."

Of course the leader of the Black Clan did not look surprised to see them. Nor did he appear surprised to learn of Haruki's conclusion.

As Mariko had suspected, Yoshi had told Ranmaru about her invention.

Mariko opened her mouth to speak. And was unceremoniously pushed forward by the tent's newest arrival. An arrival whose scent made his presence known even before he came into view.

Warm stone and wood smoke.

By the grace of the old gods, Mariko managed to remain mostly in place when Ōkami rammed an elbow into her side, clearing the path before him.

"I sincerely apologize," she said to Ōkami, trying her best to keep her store of sarcasm in reserve. "I guess it must be quite difficult to see that which is directly in front of you."

Well. She did try.

"No." Ōkami's face wore a silent challenge, his eyes glinting as he glanced back at her. "I saw you." For an instant, Mariko thought she also caught a trace of amusement as he brushed by. "And even if I hadn't seen you, I definitely smelled you. When was the last time you bathed?"

That same awful feeling of being mocked took hold of Mariko. Vicious, unrelenting hold. Making her feel so much smaller than those around her. So much *less* of everything when all she wished to feel was taller and stronger and braver. So much more. It made her afraid to be herself. Afraid these men would see how every step she took each day was a lie.

Enough. This is not the time to be weak.

Instead of letting the fear allow her to shrink into herself, Mariko let it feed her.

It collected in her stomach. Twisting in her throat.

Reshaping into anger.

No. She did not have time to be angry with Ōkami. Being angry with him meant she cared. And she absolutely did not care. It was far easier not to care.

Mariko pursed her lips, glowering at the leanly muscled back before her.

When Ōkami realized she'd kept silent at his provocation, he peered at her over one shoulder. The confusion that passed across his face almost made Mariko's efforts worth the trouble.

Absentmindedly ruffling his hair, the Wolf glided toward a corner of the tent, settling on a pile of silk cushions. Then he closed his eyes as though he meant to rest.

"How was Hanami?" Ranmaru asked Ōkami, disregarding his friend's obvious desire to sleep.

At her right, Mariko heard Haruki sigh to himself.

Ōkami ignored the metalsmith's quiet judgment. "As one would expect." With a yawn, he burrowed into the cushions.

Hanami?

Of course this lazy boy with little regard for honor frequented the most infamous pleasure district in Inako. That, at least, offered Mariko an answer as to where he'd been disappearing every other day.

Hot on the heels of this newest realization came a different series of questions.

Inako was several hours' ride from the forest.

"You went to Inako?" Mariko asked automatically. "Why would you journey so far simply to go to Hanami? Are there not pleasure houses nearby?"

"Pleasure houses?" he scoffed. "It's clear Lord Lackbeard does not have the first clue about the joys Hanami has to offer." Though his eyes remained closed, one side of Ōkami's lips curled upward. Ranmaru frowned in response.

Mariko bristled. "Though I've never seen Hanami myself, I have every idea what happens in a—"

"Liar."

She crossed her arms. Irritation snaked through her chest. Yet Mariko made the decision to say nothing, as she'd found it to be the best response in situations like these.

When she knew words would not serve her well.

Ōkami's dark eyes flashed open. Mariko had to admit it was an admirable feat. How he was able to shift from casual

apathy to absolute awareness in a single breath. "Interesting."
He unfurled to standing. Glided toward her, once more the
shark seeking blood in the water. "I called you a liar, yet
you've said nothing to refute that. Unusual, considering your
regard for all things honorable."

The closer Ōkami moved toward her, the more Mariko's
worry collected. The more she wished to retreat. Sometimes
he saw her too clearly for comfort.

Again the irritation gathered in her stomach. Knotting
into anger.

I will not yield to my emotions.

Ōkami stared down at her, just as he had that night they'd
first met. Mariko stood her ground, disregarding her desire
to flee.

"It's obvious you haven't the faintest clue what Hanami
is," he said softly. "You lie as freely as you breathe, yet claim
to value honor above all else." His laughter was a brush of air
and sound. "What other secrets are you hiding beneath that
cool head of yours, Sanada Takeo? And what would it take to
steal them from you?" he whispered, his eyes shimmering like
black ice.

Blood rushed up Mariko's neck, into her face. As before,
she stoked her fear into fury. Into a strange kind of heat that
began to swirl in the space between them.

"You don't know the beginning of me." She trembled as
she spoke. "And . . . you will never see the end." It was as close
to a threat as she dared.

His smile was cool. Appreciative. "I've made you angry."

"Anger can be a good thing," Ranmaru interjected, his features unreadable. "It can harden you. Make you stronger."

"Perhaps my kind of strength isn't the same as yours. Perhaps my kind of strength is as light as a feather." *As deadly as an idea.* Her hands continued to shake beneath their gazes, yet she returned Ōkami's measured stare.

The Wolf nodded, but Mariko did not see mockery in the gesture. Merely the same strange intensity. As though he truly approved. "Master your anger, Sanada Takeo. Anger is an emotion that poisons all else."

"I am not angry. It's possible you do not know me as well as you think you do." Mariko willed him silent, determined not to argue with him any further.

Arguing with Ōkami was like trying to catch smoke.

His only reply was another half smile punctuated by a white scar. But his smile was not the playful sort. No. Despite his barbed attempt at banter, the Wolf was not playful. Not at all. He was a boy who liked to set fire to things and watch them burn. Mariko's anger quickly slid to animosity. It irked her that Ōkami could provoke such strong emotions from her with so little effort.

Ranmaru stepped between them. Separating them. Dissipating the heat that had risen in the air. "I'll make you a deal, Lord Lackbeard," he said. "If you succeed in helping Haruki find a way to make this—what do you call it?"

The metalsmith moved to reply, his lips already forming the words.

"A throwing star," Mariko said before Haruki could speak, her words clipped. Her attention lingered on Ōkami as he returned to his cushioned corner, his hands now laced beneath his head. At this moment, it did not behoove Mariko to look away from him.

As he'd once warned, she should never bare her neck to a wolf.

Ranmaru continued, his manner contemplative. "Successfully fashion a throwing star, and the next time Ōkami travels to Hanami, we will accompany him."

At this, the Wolf stood again, unfailingly graceful, despite a glimmer of annoyance. A snakelike smile spread across Ren's face just as Ranmaru broke into a pleased grin. It was clear this newly formed proposal appealed to the leader of the Black Clan. Perhaps simply because he was antagonizing his best friend. A feat Mariko guessed to be rather difficult.

In answer, Ōkami stepped closer, his jaw tight.

A tacit threat. For her benefit or for that of Ranmaru, Mariko could not be certain. Nor did she care. For it pleased her, too, to rankle the Wolf.

Ranmaru's grin widened. "While in Hanami, we can—how did you say it that night, Lord Lackbeard?—teach you how to *enjoy* such things."

At the flagrance of his words, the blood began to drain down Mariko's neck. "I—don't think that's necessary." Her eyes flitted around the tent; her skin now cast a sickly pallor. "As I said before, I am fully aware of what happens in Hanami, and—"

"When you're about to lie, don't look to the skies first," Ōkami said. "The old gods won't help you."

"In the future, I'll be sure to heed your advice," she retorted quickly. Curtly. Her gaze locked on the scar slicing through his lips. "But I was busy making a promise to remedy their past mistake."

His brows raised in question.

"This time, I promised to cut out your tongue instead of simply leaving a warning." Mariko almost gasped as the words fell from her mouth.

These were the words of a different person.

Wild. Dangerous. Without fear.

Perhaps Sanada Takeo had far more nerve than Hattori Mariko. Perhaps Takeo didn't mind risking punishment if it meant earning respect. Though the beat of Mariko's heart raced through her veins, she kept her expression fixed. Unmoved.

The Wolf's eyes narrowed. The muscles along his jaw twitched. Whether it was from anger or amusement, Mariko dared not guess.

A spell of tense silence passed. Then Ranmaru laughed. Loudly. A thoughtless, heedless kind of laughter. Different from any she'd heard pass his lips before. Even Haruki and Ren seemed startled by its sound. When Mariko's tormentor made to shove her as punishment for her insult, she shifted beyond his reach. Ren pressed forward, intent on teaching her a lesson. His persistence forced Mariko to step in the space occupied by either Ranmaru or Ōkami.

Without thought, she shifted to the left.

Beside her sandaled foot, a copper coin winked into view.

A harrowing beat passed before Ōkami bent to retrieve it. He did not move away as he aimed a bladed smile at her. Mariko bumped against him, suppressing a cringe. He returned the coin to her, all while standing close enough that she smelled the wood smoke on his clothes. Felt the warmth radiating from his skin.

A low hum began to form around him. Immediately Mariko swallowed the urge to cower, grateful for the shadows that concealed the color in her cheeks.

Was it from anger, then? Did anger unleash Ōkami's abilities?

Was he angry with her? Or amused? Why was it so hard for her to read this accursed boy?

"So now you've become a thief as well," he said softly, his dark gaze filled with an uncanny light. "Fashion your throwing star. Take your winnings to Inako. But don't feel fortunate when you do. The streets of the imperial city are only slightly less forgiving than I."

The leader of the Black Clan waited until Ren, Haruki, and Sanada Takeo were far beyond earshot. He glanced at his best friend. His closest confidant since the darkest of times.

"What do you think of our newest recruit?" Ranmaru asked.

Ōkami scowled in the direction of the tent entrance before replying. "He's . . . quite smart. And equally odd."

"Oddly smart, then."

"Two qualities that engender concern. I don't trust him."

"What's to trust?" Ranmaru tossed a silk cushion onto the packed earth, then took position over the ledgers strewn across the scarred low table. "Anyway it's unlike you to care about such a thing."

Ōkami remained standing. "We should leave him in Inako. He won't last a day in its bowels."

"Or perhaps we should simply let the forest have him." Ranmaru shrugged.

"Perhaps." The Wolf did not sound convinced.

Ranmaru stopped skimming through the ledger. "Do you suspect he knows anything?"

"No. But he makes me feel . . . uncomfortable. I'm not certain why you wanted to bring him here. Why you thought he would make a good addition to our ranks."

Ranmaru paused. They were both aware that very little made the Wolf uncomfortable. Ōkami had spent his formative years impressing a sense of discomfort onto others. Impressing it and taking advantage of the aftermath.

It was far easier to bend the will of those amid strife.

"Sanada Takeo is different from anyone else in the Black Clan," Ranmaru said. "He's lost in a way that intrigues me. Intelligent in a way that could make him quite useful to our cause." He paused again. "What about him makes you feel uncomfortable? It's odd for anyone this insignificant to bother you so." The beginnings of a smile began to cross his lips. "Or for anyone to remain unchecked after repeatedly challenging you."

Ōkami said nothing for a time. "Does the boy not make you uncomfortable?" he finally asked, his voice inexplicably hesitant. "Does he not—make you ask yourself strange questions?"

"No," Ranmaru replied. "Not any more than usual. I'll agree he's strange. But have you seen Ren?"

"Ren is a boy lost between two worlds. That tends to happen when you witness your parents being butchered before your eyes," Ōkami said. "Of course Ren would be strange."

"Well, it's possible Sanada Takeo has seen such things as well."

"Possible. But unlikely. He's far too green to have witnessed anything truly horrific. Did you see how long it took him to put together a simple tent?"

"I thought you left that tent to test him."

"That's immaterial. For someone as smart as he, Sanada Takeo should have realized he was missing pieces long before Yoshi brought it to his attention. It's obvious the boy has never had to fend for himself in his life. He's coddled in a worrisome way. Likely the son of a wealthy man—book learned and world foolish."

Ranmaru sighed. "I leave it to you, then. Whatever decision you make as to whether the boy stays or goes, I support you." His left brow arched high into his forehead. "But he's your responsibility in Inako. You earned that privilege by antagonizing him as you did today. And if I were you, I would be far more vigilant about how much you allow Sanada Takeo under your skin." Ōkami turned at this, clearly intent on disavowing the notion. But Ranmaru raised a hand, cutting him off before he could speak.

"Take Takeo to the teahouse as promised, then do what you will with him afterward." Ranmaru flattened a blank sheet of *washi* paper and began rubbing a dampened ink stick into the inkwell beside him. "Though I'm inclined to let Takeo stay, as he might prove to be quite an asset. Oddly smart ideas notwithstanding."

Ōkami did not respond immediately.

"We shall see."

Rivets of Gold and Petal Pink Waters

Inako.

A city of a hundred arched bridges and a thousand cherry trees. A city of mud and sweat and sewage. A city of golden cranes and amber sunsets.

A city of secrets.

The imperial city had changed in the four years since Kenshin had last been within its walls.

It was clearly bigger. The outskirts of Inako now pressed beyond the fields and forests that had ringed its borders in the past. Snaking through the city's center was a gently flowing river littered with dying blossoms. Its petal pink waters were a painted stroke separating the tiled roofs on either shoreline—a swell of blue-grey clay, rising like the sea, bandied about by a storm.

Kenshin's mother had once said the entire story of the

imperial city could be told by its roof tiles alone. The curved clay marked where the grandest sections of Inako gave way to its poorer thoroughfares. Its downtrodden lanes. Where the rounded tiles and the gleaming angles dipped into dusty disrepair. Where they vanished into the parts of the city Kenshin had never frequented.

The number of cracked and misshapen rooflines had become even more staggered and crowded in the last four years. Strange how—regardless of wealth or circumstance—they all appeared to use the same kind of tile. The same color. The same shape.

A strange marriage of chaos and conformity.

In that same way, Inako looked smaller to him now. Despite its obvious growth.

Kenshin mulled over this as he rode with his men past the main gates of the city. Vendors lingered on either side of a long dirt lane, selling neatly stacked fruit and freshly washed produce. Several children hawked small hemp sacks of crisp rice crackers, their faces and hands clean despite the ragged appearance of their clothes. A stall displaying perfect rounds of sweet *daifuku* caught Kenshin's eye as he passed by. He smiled as he remembered how much Mariko had loved to eat the fluffy rice cakes filled with sweetened bean paste. How they'd always fought over the last of the *daifuku* whenever their father had brought home a box from Inako.

As children, Kenshin and Mariko had squabbled quite often, their fights becoming the stuff of legend. As epic as the wars depicted in their history lessons, replete with subterfuge and elegant misdirection. Kenshin had always tried to best her physically, while Mariko had always fought to unseat him mentally.

His sister had won more times than Kenshin had cared to admit.

He smiled to himself as a shower of memories descended on him.

Mariko was not dead. She was simply fighting a different kind of war. Though Kenshin had yet to understand her purpose, he believed in his younger sister. Supported her.

Just as he knew she believed in and supported him.

They would always be there for each other. Whatever may come.

Kenshin's small convoy paused as imperial guards inspected the endless line of wagons and weary travelers entering Inako.

As soon as the Hattori crest was seen, he and his men were waved past the line. Kenshin had elected to take only fifteen of his best soldiers with him to the imperial city. Five samurai and ten *ashigaru*. Before he'd left his family's domain at dawn, Kenshin had realized a larger contingent of men would draw more whispers. Elicit further speculation.

He did not want anyone to suspect the truth behind why he'd journeyed to Inako. Though it was unlikely, there was still a small chance not everyone at court knew about the events that had befallen his sister in Jukai forest. When he'd returned home, several of his father's advisors had informed him it was possible the Black Clan was to blame for plundering Mariko's convoy and setting fire to her *norimono*. The notorious band of thieves was known to haunt that section of the woods. Initially Kenshin had thought to seek them out. To feather his soldiers throughout the hills and hunt them down.

But doing so without hesitation almost felt . . . too easy. The Black Clan did not usually attack convoys containing women and children. Assigning them immediate blame felt pre-arranged. As though someone intended all along for Kenshin to split his forces and lose his footing in a relatively short time. The suggestion reeked of the same elegant misdirection he had grown accustomed to while warring with his sister.

Except that now, the battle was not over a sweet treat. But over lives.

If Kenshin could be certain of anything, he could be certain of this: such machinations had been and always would be the purview of those in power.

First he wanted to hear what the nobles in the imperial city had to say. He hoped the story of the Black Clan had not spread too far. Hoped it remained within the inner circles of Inako and stayed that way for however long it could. At least until Kenshin was able to recover Mariko safe and sound. And before word of their family's misfortune spread throughout the empire and ruined the Hattori name beyond repair.

Apprehension gripped Kenshin as he rode through the winding streets of the imperial city, his back straight and his features impenetrable. Behind him, mounted samurai and foot soldiers bearing banners emblazoned with the Hattori crest trailed in neat formation.

The scent of fresh water and swirling dust suffused the air as their convoy neared the deep moat enclosing Heian Castle. Kenshin left his ten *ashigaru* and three of his samurai in a clean set of barracks just beyond the curved stone wall at the edge of the moat. Then he and his two remaining samurai crossed the wooden drawbridge, pausing before the first set of towering black gates at the castle's entrance. Gold-plated hinges and round-ringed handles glistened in the late-afternoon sun as Kenshin and his men waited to speak with the imperial troops manning the guard tower. When two of the soldiers stepped forward to address Kenshin formally, he noticed the silk banners flying on either side of the glossy black gates. Even the rivets were plated in gold.

No expense had been spared to make Heian Castle a worthy seat for the empire's heavenly sovereign.

The imperial guards stood rigid, inspecting all the weaponry Kenshin and his men wished to bear with them. As samurai, Kenshin and his men were allowed to enter the castle bearing two customary swords each—a *katana* and a shorter *wakizashi*. Hidden weapons were considered dishonorable. As was the act of unsheathing a blade in the emperor's presence.

Just before the second pair of gates, Kenshin and his samurai were instructed to leave their horses with one of the stable attendants waiting nearby. Then they began to ascend the immense stone staircase leading to the imperial grounds. The weight of his armor and the heat of the early summer sun slowed Kenshin's pace. But it also offered him a chance to take in the splendor of the imperial castle rising before him, each of its seven gabled stories and gilded rooftops flashing, catching, throwing endless rays of light.

When the first of eight concentric baileys rose into view, Kenshin paused. This series of *maru* was famous even beyond the reaches of the empire. Its inner workings were said to be enchanted. Crafted by an ageless kind of sorcery. The first and largest *maru* was complete with a pond and mazelike pathways graveled by white stone. The pattern of its spiraling walkways served two purposes—one of beauty and one of befuddlement. It was designed to confound, for the entrances and exits did not flow in logical order. At all hours of day and night, the concentric circles moved in different directions, at different speeds, like wheels turning within each other. Absent a knowledgeable escort, a guest could get lost at Heian Castle without even trying.

And an intruder?

Would never make it out alive.

Kenshin halted before taking the final step onto the trimmed grass of the first *maru*.

This marked the only occasion he had ever been to Inako without his father. Without his family. Today would be the first day he and he alone would represent his clan before their emperor.

Kenshin had not expected to feel so uneasy at this realization.

But he did not show it. Would never show it.

Instead he took the last step, careful to remain steady. To enjoy these brief moments to himself.

While he still could.

———————

Contrary to what Kenshin had expected, he was not instructed to go before the emperor upon his arrival.

A fact that gave him pause.

Instead Kenshin and his men were told to wait for a time on the enchanted *maru*. They crossed the perfectly manicured lawn, stopping only to watch the hundred-year-old carp and its gaggle of orange-and-white koi flit beneath the waters of an azure pond. One of the emperor's attendants then bowed low before Kenshin, calmly leading him toward another *maru*, past another series of inner gates. As they moved through the arched entrance, Kenshin felt the ground beneath him shift. Felt it turn slowly to conceal their trail and keep him and his men from view. They quickly exited the second bailey and flew down a staircase leading to a grassy field ringed by a gathering of richly garbed onlookers.

Soon Kenshin understood why he and his men had been brought here instead of being formally received by the emperor.

They'd arrived at Heian Castle at a moment of spectacle.

Beneath an eight-sided silk canopy—resting atop a tiered dais—sat Emperor Minamoto Masaru upon his black lacquered throne. The balustrades on either side of him were painted vermillion. Eight silver phoenixes were mounted at every post. Hanging between these posts were flashing mirrors and curtains of spun silk, stamped in their centers with the imperial crest of the Minamoto clan.

Strange that the emperor had chosen to display the phoenix alongside his own crest. The Minamoto crest was one of gentian flowers and bamboo leaves—a crest that signified prosperity and granted its bearer protection against evil. The phoenix crest had always been associated with the Takeda clan—a long line of shōgun that had fallen from grace under a cloud of shame. When the last of the Takeda line had disappeared ten years ago, the thousand-year joint reign between emperor and shōgun—an emperor to rule the people, a shōgun to lead the army—had disintegrated.

Had faded into remembrance.

A part of Kenshin understood why the son of Takeda Shingen was unwilling to come forward, even following a decade of exile. His clan had collapsed in disgrace. His father had been compelled to end his life after conspiring to commit treason against the emperor. The emperor had been generous indeed to offer a traitor the honor of a warrior's death. A chance to die so that his son might live.

No one knew for certain where this disgraced boy—this _rōnin_—might be. If he was still alive, he would be around Kenshin's age. Perhaps a year or so older. In time, rumors had spilled from the lips of drunken soldiers. Had rippled through lantern-lit gardens and spread like wildfire behind fluttering fans. The son of Takeda Shingen had become a beggar. A thief. A pirate. A whoremonger. He and his lost family had become the stuff of legend. A warning to all those who dared consider speaking out against the emperor.

No matter how high a man rose in life, death was the greatest of equalizers.

As a result of Takeda Shingen's treachery, both the might of the army and the will of the people now rested with the emperor. Perhaps that was why Minamoto Masaru had thought to marry the two symbols under his own banner. A phoenix flying alongside a crest of gentian flowers. A bird risen from the ashes of a bloody history.

The thunder of stampeding hooves tore Kenshin from his thoughts. Cheers erupted from the throng of onlookers seated on plush cushions, their servants balancing colorful silk umbrellas above elaborate headdresses. The noblemen sat nearest to the emperor. The empress and her female attendants were gathered on a lower dais positioned to the right.

On the grassy field before them, the *yabusame*—the imperial army's elite force of mounted archers—conducted an exhibition. Most of the imperial court had come to partake in the scene. Kenshin had heard from others who frequented Inako that the emperor often invited those in the nobility and their guests to witness the might of the empire's army.

The skill of its best soldiers and finest samurai.

Though Kenshin was mildly interested in watching the display, he kept beyond the gathering of noblemen in their silken finery and the ladies of the court fluttering their folded fans. Kept apart and removed, as he often felt in such company.

Kenshin had never been at ease around those in the imperial court. It was not that he harbored any judgment against
them. He knew these shows of extravagance were necessary.
They offered outsiders a glimpse of the empire's glory, and
they gave its citizens a chance to revel in its greatness.

As he continued watching the exhibition, Kenshin's
expression began to sour.

These were skilled riders. Skilled archers. The best the
empire had to offer.

But it was still a show. And such immodesty did not sit
well with the ideals of *bushidō*. Was not in keeping with the
way of the warrior.

Weapons were not meant for show.

They were meant for war. Meant to be used in defense of
a samurai's lord. In defense of one's family.

And, above all, in defense of the emperor.

A member of the *yabusame* soon drew every onlooker's
notice. The young rider sat atop a dappled steed. One side
of his fine silk robe hung from his right shoulder—revealing
the armored silver *yoroihitatare* beneath—freeing his arm for
unencumbered movement. With a rattan-reinforced bow, he
fired whistling arrows at a notched post, three times in rapid
succession, all while riding faster—and more fearlessly—
than any of his peers. Not once did the young warrior reach
for the reins, but directed his horse entirely with his knees.
Even from a distance, Kenshin could see how he rode—heels
down, locked in placed, steady. Excellent horsemanship was a

requisite of being in the *yabusame*. As was the ability to fire arrows at high speeds with uncanny accuracy.

Not once did the warrior miss his target.

Whispers of admiration rippled through the crowd. They unfurled into a steady murmur when a slight boy clad in silks stained a rare shade of yellow—almost like burnished gold—took position at the opposite end of the field.

Kenshin did not immediately recognize him, but he felt certain the boy had to be the crown prince, Minamoto Roku. Though he'd never met him before, Kenshin had heard from both his father and from Nobutada that the crown prince did not possess a striking appearance, yet nevertheless managed to hold his own at court.

Kenshin could see why now. There was a noble bearing to the boy. A distinct haughtiness to the set of his thin shoulders and the tilt of his pointed chin. The only member of court with finer robes was the emperor himself.

The crown prince drove three *kaburaya* into the ground. Kenshin immediately noticed how the whistling arrowheads did not appear to be the blunted sort generally used for practice. Without pausing for thought, the crown prince fitted one of these arrows to the string of his bow. At that exact moment, the finest archer of the *yabusame*—the one who had caught everyone's attention earlier—broke ranks and began riding toward the crown prince.

With no sign of stopping.

Concern flared through Kenshin. Several members of the

nobility took to their feet, alarm spreading across their faces.

Without even a glimmer of concern, the crown prince fired an arrow at the warrior on the grey-and-white steed. The warrior dodged it, effortlessly sliding from his saddle as the horse continued its wild gallop. He clutched the reins as his feet sluiced through the soft earth. When the crown prince fired another shot, the warrior vaulted back onto his saddle, easily avoiding the arrow's mark. He continued riding toward the crown prince, undeterred.

The crown prince's shots were well timed. Well aimed.

Meant to strike.

But the rider drew closer and closer to the crown prince, refusing to veer. Refusing to yield.

At the last possible second, the crown prince fired another arrow, straight at the warrior's chest. The warrior yanked it from the air and—quicker than a flash of lightning—nocked it to his bow. He fired it back at the crown prince.

The arrow embedded in the dirt at a perfect angle, a hairsbreadth from the prince's feet.

The crown prince smiled.

As soon as the warrior reined in near him, he dismounted and removed his helmet. Then he bowed low. Grinning at one another, the two young men clapped each other on the back appreciatively.

The smattering of awkward applause became cheers.

Only members of the royal family would be permitted to touch the crown prince with such impunity.

Kenshin saw the resemblance. Despite the fact that the

member of the *yabusame* was nearly a head taller. Considerably broader.

The rider was Prince Raiden.

His sister's betrothed.

"I was very sorry to hear about your sister's untimely death, Kenshin-*sama*," Minamoto Roku said as he dropped to his cushioned seat before a low table in the corner of his chambers.

Though the crown prince's words sounded heartfelt, Kenshin did not feel any warmth in them. The statement was coolly pronounced. Said with the same inflection Roku might have offered when commenting on a spate of bad weather. The contrivance in the prince's tone bothered Kenshin, but he stifled his irritation. After all, he was in the presence of royalty. At audience with the emperor's two sons.

Mariko's betrothed.

And the future heavenly sovereign of Wa.

A future sovereign who was—at the moment—far too concerned with arranging sheets of ivory *washi* paper on the table before him. Smoothing their surfaces. Anchoring their edges with weights. Preparing to practice his calligraphy.

Roku looked at Kenshin—as though he expected Kenshin to elaborate further on the matter of Mariko's untimely death—before smiling to himself and slowly circling an ink stick in the well of a carved inkstone to his right.

In moments like these, Kenshin wished Mariko were at his side. She would be thinking far in advance of what anyone might do or say. Holding her emotions close and in check. His sister was leagues ahead of anyone in most conversations. Far past anyone's present. In contrast, Kenshin often found himself crashing through the underbrush of conversations Mariko skirted with ease. It was not that his sister was a particularly gifted conversationalist. It was more that she always seemed to know what people intended to say even before they did.

She read people much like she read books.

Such ability would be of great use to Kenshin right now.

But he was a warrior. Not an envoy or a strategist.

Kenshin cleared his throat. "I do not believe Mariko to be dead, Your Highness." He glanced toward his sister's betrothed to see if he could sense any reaction. Minamoto Raiden exchanged a wordless conversation with his brother, but Kenshin could not glean the sentiment behind his expression.

It could be worry. It could be anger. It could be suspicion.

Or perhaps it could be all of these things.

It never ceased to frustrate Kenshin how he was able to notice tangible things with the eye of a hawk. How the smallest detail was never missed. But when it came to analyzing the unseen—the unspoken subtleties of life—he was far from being a hawk. He was more of a mole, wandering through a world of darkness. Even with Amaya, he'd been painfully unaware of her feelings until it was far too late.

After a time, Minamoto Raiden took a steadying breath. He traded another glance with the crown prince, whose expression remained neutral. Then he leaned forward almost conspiratorially. "Kenshin-*sama*," his sister's betrothed began,

"I was told Mariko's convoy had been attacked in Jukai forest by a band of thieves. Several members of my father's personal guard believe it to be the work of the Black Clan—though I'm not as inclined to agree. It seems far too . . . simple. Far too predictable. Not to mention beyond the typical behavior of the Black Clan." He rested an elbow on a knee, inclining toward Kenshin even farther. "Is it possible your sister still lives, despite all the evidence to the contrary?"

As Raiden spoke, concern seeped into the small lines framing his mouth. He was only nineteen years old, but the effect of this concern made him appear battle-hardened. Weary. The sight strangely comforted Kenshin. As did the words his sister's betrothed spoke. They were in keeping with Kenshin's earlier thoughts. But it was also possible this was a ruse meant to earn his trust. Meant to plant seeds of unforeseen doubt.

Yet Minamoto Raiden did seem far less calculating than the crown prince. Far less conniving. And Kenshin appreciated how he appeared to value forthrightness more than his younger brother. Raiden's character was more in keeping with his own. Since this marked Kenshin's first interaction with his sister's betrothed, these feelings set his mind somewhat at ease. At this moment, any sign of subterfuge remained solely in the black eyes of the crown prince. The slight, pale boy clad in golden silk, calmly practicing his *shodo*.

Perhaps Minamoto Roku had been the one to orchestrate the attack on Mariko's convoy.

And yet . . .

A part of Kenshin did not quite believe the crown prince

would strike out at his own brother by murdering Raiden's future wife. After all, what would he have to gain by doing so? Roku was already first in line to the throne. And not once in all his years had Kenshin heard of Raiden having designs to usurp his younger brother. They could easily have been at war with each other. Brothers in similar situations had often killed each other for power in the past. But that did not appear to be the case here. By all accounts, these two brothers—despite the enmity between their birth mothers—were close friends. Trusted confidants.

Perhaps Kenshin had been wrong to suspect that members of the nobility had plotted to murder his sister. That someone in Inako had tried to thwart the nuptials between the emperor's firstborn son and the daughter of an ambitious daimyō.

Or perhaps Minamoto Raiden was merely good at reading people as well.

As though he could hear the tenor of Kenshin's thoughts, Raiden smiled reassuringly. He began to speak again, but was immediately silenced by his younger brother.

The crown prince shot a pointed look their way. As soon as Roku made certain he held their attention, his eyes drifted toward the beautifully carved folding screen to his left. "This is not the place to discuss such things," he said in a harsh whisper. "The walls of Heian Castle possess ears." The last was said in a barely audible tone.

A cultivated whisper, belying his earlier disinterest.

Following this admonition, the crown prince took hold of his right sleeve and dipped his brush in ink once more, positioning the bristles above the *washi* paper at a perfect angle. "Perhaps it would be nice to share some tea with us later, Kenshin-*sama*," he said, his voice as mild as before. Filled with that same feigned lack of interest.

But spoken in a tenor meant to be overheard. Meant to be interpreted by attending servants and chance observers alike.

In his zeal to learn the truth, Kenshin had almost forgotten.

Inako was—first and foremost—a city of secrets. Ones to be stolen and sold off to the highest bidder at first chance.

Nodding in understanding, Raiden stood swiftly. "Will you be our guest this evening, Kenshin-*sama*?"

Kenshin was not fool enough to question the conversation's rapid change in course. He may not be well versed in recognizing emotion, but he was the Dragon of Kai, and he knew the sharp tang of fresh blood. Of a path to be followed. Quietly. Carefully.

"I would be honored, my lord," Kenshin said. "Where is it you wish to go?"

Raiden grinned, and the sight greatly reminded Kenshin of a snarling bear. His voice dropped until it became more breath than sound.

"The finest teahouse in Hanami."

Hanami

———✳———

Mariko had been to Inako once, when she was younger. As a girl.

As a boy, the sights of the imperial city were entirely different. And it was not merely because a blindfold had been torn from her eyes only moments before.

Everything seemed crisper. Colors seemed more alive. Scents flooded her nostrils, and sights flashed across her vision—marinated squid sizzling over an open flame, vividly dyed paper lanterns strung above bolts of lustrous silk, displays of painted fans and freshly sliced persimmons, creamy bean curd floating in barrels of cold water. She smelled and tasted everything in the air with the abandon of a girl in a fevered dream.

Mariko felt free. Freer than she could remember feeling in quite some time.

Her current situation notwithstanding.

At least in Inako there's little chance of me being snared by a blood-draining tree. Or being pelted by sharp rocks.

Ranmaru studied her. Caught her grinning with open glee. "Is this your first visit to the imperial city?"

Mariko thought quickly. "Yes." Her answer more easily explained how enthralled she was. It also helped circumvent any further inquiries about her past. The Black Clan had been blessedly uninterested in who she was before she came to the forest, and Mariko wished to keep it that way for as long as she could.

"Try not to appear so green once we arrive at the teahouse," Ōkami said from his perch atop his warhorse to her right.

Mariko wrapped her fingers tightly around her reins, struggling to bite her tongue. To ignore the rope trailing from Ōkami's horse to hers, keeping her tethered to the Wolf's side.

At her left, Ranmaru laughed, his brown eyes sparkling. "Or when you first set eyes on Yumi, the most beautiful girl in the empire."

"I doubt Lord Lackbeard has ever seen a *geiko* before in his life," Ōkami said. "Much less been with a beautiful girl." Even as he provoked her, Ōkami maintained a cool affect. One of careful indifference.

A geiko?

So they were not traveling to a mere house of ill repute, as she'd initially surmised. A *geiko* would never set foot in such a den of iniquity.

Regardless Mariko kept silent. Stewing in unspoken reprisals.

Ranmaru's brows arched. "Tell us, Lord Lackbeard. Are you indeed untried?"

She shifted uncomfortably in her seat. Of all the questions for Ranmaru to ask, of course he would choose that one. Men left to their own devices were so sadly predictable. "I am not untried. I have been with . . . many women." Her words were half true, at least. She was no longer a maid. Though the one and only occasion had not involved another girl.

It had involved rebellion.

Mariko recalled the face of the young stable boy fated to accompany his master to her father's province one spring morning not so long ago. She remembered the boy's kind smile. His enthusiasm. His obliviousness.

It was his smile that had drawn Mariko to him. Drawn him into a sun-drenched hayloft to while away a moment in her embrace.

He'd been kind. Gentle.

Only hours later had a horrible realization shaken Mariko to her core. Her actions that afternoon could have resulted in this kind and gentle boy's death. Not once—not in the entire time they'd spent lazing about in the fragrant hay—had she paused to consider what might happen to the boy if they were caught. Her anger with her parents had been too sharp. Her wish for control far too blinding.

She considered Ōkami's words from a fortnight past:

Anger is an emotion that poisons all else.

Even in Mariko's thoughts, it did not sit well to admit the Wolf might be right about something.

The morning of her undoing, she'd dressed in the clothing of a peasant. In this disguise, Mariko had seduced the stable boy. Given him the gift her parents had recently traded for the emperor's favor. The gift her parents had calculatingly sold.

Despite the risks, not once had Mariko regretted her decision, though the act itself was awkward. Not unpleasant, but definitely not worth the fuss. And absolutely not worth ceding control.

But it had been Mariko's first time, and—for that one time only—she'd wanted her body to be her own. The decision to be hers and hers alone. Her body was not for sale. It did not belong to her parents to sell to the highest bidder. Nor did it belong to Minamoto Raiden or to any other man.

She remembered Chiyo telling her that finding one's match was like finding one's other half. Mariko had never understood the notion.

She was not a half. She was wholly her own.

A hand waved before her face. When Mariko's vision cleared, Ranmaru's features came into focus as he attempted to draw her back into the present.

"What were you thinking about just now?" the leader of the Black Clan asked. "You disappeared." Though his words were nonchalant, his look was as sharp as a razor.

"Family," she said smoothly. "And entitlement."

Ahead of them, Mariko thought she saw Ōkami slow his horse. But he did not look back. Nor did he lean toward their conversation. It was possible she had imagined him easing up on his pace.

Ranmaru continued studying her sidelong. "Interesting that you link the two together."

"I don't find it interesting at all. Family can entitle you to many things. It can also feel entitled to much from you in return."

"Is that why you ran away from yours?"

Mariko swallowed. She'd known all along she could not escape answering questions about her past. Men like Ranmaru—even ones as young as he, with such ready charm—did not rise to positions of power on blind faith alone.

A simple lie—threaded from truth—could be Mariko's best answer. "My father arranged for me to marry. I wished to do otherwise. When we could not come to an agreement on the matter, I left." She kept her explanation unembellished. Abrupt.

"You wished to marry someone else?"

"No."

"So then you are not one of those poor fools enamored by the idea of love?" he teased.

She scowled. "Certainly not." At least in this, a lie was unnecessary.

"You don't believe your great love is out there, simply waiting to be found?"

"Do you?" Mariko pitched her voice low. Graveled with disbelief.

Ranmaru's broad lips spread into an easy smile. "I believe the stars align so that souls can find one another. Whether they are meant to be souls in love or souls in life remains to be seen."

Mariko found herself momentarily at a loss. It was . . . a lovely sentiment. Were she dressed in the fine silks of a young girl, she would have felt her gaze soften. Her cheeks grow pink.

Beautiful words were beautiful words, even to the most practical of minds.

Instead Mariko focused on the worn fabric of her reins. Coughed with undisguised discomfort.

"There," Ranmaru pronounced, his tone one of supreme self-satisfaction. "I've managed to embarrass Lord Lackbeard simply by talking about love. And not once did I mention anything about women." He turned toward Ōkami, his palm outstretched. "You owe me five *ryō*."

Mariko froze in her saddle, her posture rigid. "That—is a lie."

"Which part?" Ranmaru blinked.

"You mentioned Yumi." She sniffed. Deepened her speech to a drone. "The most beautiful girl in the empire."

At that, the Wolf started to laugh. It began softly, like the rumble of a drum. Then it rose to a steadying rain. It wasn't a rich kind of laughter. Its sound didn't fill Mariko's ears with its honeyed resonance. But it was clear and deep, much like the color of his eyes.

And a part of her couldn't help but think—were he another boy, in another time, in another place—Mariko would have liked to hear Ōkami's laughter.

Would have enjoyed being the cause of it.

But he was a member of the Black Clan. The band of

mercenaries who had tried to kill her. Who had slaughtered Chiyo and Nobutada.

She hated this boy and all he stood for.

It was dangerous for her to consider anything else, even for a moment.

Mariko grasped her reins tighter. As though she were taking firm hold of herself. "Do I receive any share of the gold?" She looked to Ōkami, her features expectant.

"No." He didn't hesitate before responding.

"I saved you money. Shouldn't I receive at least half of it as a reward?"

"Taking half my money isn't saving me anything."

She spurred her horse closer to his. "You thought Ranmaru could embarrass me by talking about *love*?" A sneer touched the edges of her lips.

"I think it's remarkably easy to provoke certain reactions from you."

Mariko flinched. Opened her mouth. Closed it.

Ōkami smiled. "It's better when you say nothing. That way I don't have to point out how freely you lie." He rode on, the rope behind him losing its slack.

Mariko gritted her teeth, willing herself silent. Her nose scrunched as a cart filled with manure passed by. Flies buzzed before her face, and she fended them off with a wave of one hand.

She did not care if Ōkami found her dishonest. She found him dishonorable.

Which was far worse.

In an attempt to drown out her irritation, Mariko pitched her voice louder. "All matters of love make little sense to me anyway. As do most things that cannot be proved as fact."

"Why is that?" Ranmaru asked.

"Love is—" She shifted in her saddle, fighting to sit taller, to convey a larger sense of self. "It isn't something that can be understood or explained. It's intangible. Like magic. Those who do not possess its power can never fully grasp it."

Ranmaru inclined his head. "That sounds rather sad."

"And smells like horseshit," Ōkami said over his shoulder. "Like the words of a boy with a great deal left to learn."

Once more, Mariko bristled at his judgment. "Only a boy with a great deal left to learn himself would ever think that of someone else."

"Or one with a great deal of regret," Ranmaru said softly. Soberly.

Ōkami did not look their way as he spoke. "There is indeed a great deal of regret in my life." Even from a distance, Mariko saw a shadow descend on his face. For once she thought she might catch a glimpse of vulnerability in the Wolf. She leaned in closer. Waiting. Her breath bated.

If something—anything—made the Black Clan's champion weak, Mariko desperately wished to know what it was.

Follow orders. Engender trust.

Strike when they least expect it.

"My life has been filled with death and lies and loose

women." Okami pushed back a fall of black hair, meeting her gaze. Holding her there. Rapt. "I regret everything else." He smiled, his hooded, heavy-lidded eyes brimming with mockery.

Truly he was hopeless.

Mariko almost snarled in frustration. She bit down on her cheek to keep silent. To control her need to rebuke. This time Ōkami definitely slowed the pace of his horse to match that of Mariko. He drew alongside her, though he did not glance her way for some time.

"So you don't believe in silly sentiments like love." He fixed that same appreciative look on her from before. The one tinged in approval.

It only compelled Mariko's need to disagree. "I didn't say that."

"You said you preferred things that can be proved as fact."

"I meant that it's difficult to prove a feeling as fact. But I've seen it happen before."

Mariko had watched Muramasa Amaya—the daughter of her father's famed metalsmith—fall in love with Kenshin. Foolishly, desperately in love with him. When they were younger, her brother had failed to notice the signs. But Mariko had seen them. In moments when Amaya thought no one was looking, her attention would flit to Kenshin. Linger for a spell. The look Mariko saw there often left her feeling hollow.

Often left her wishing someone would look at her that way. Just once.

"Did it look like magic?" Ōkami asked, his tone circumspect. Mariko expected him to mock her again, but when she turned toward him—bracing herself for his biting scorn—she did not see any evidence of it.

His eyes were clear pools of deep water, hiding nothing. Two black mirrors, drawing her in. Making her question.

A brush of heat danced across her skin.

"It did." Mariko fought to keep her voice even. "She looked at me as though I were magic."

Ōkami's eyes remained constant. A sky without stars.

It was Mariko who turned away first. Only to catch Ranmaru laughing once more.

With a click of his tongue, Ōkami prodded his horse forward, well beyond earshot, the rope between them going taut. Again Mariko fidgeted in her seat, wishing for all the world that she'd changed the subject. That she could turn back time and begin this conversation anew.

"Have *you* ever loved anyone?" she asked Ranmaru bluntly, pleased to see him startle, if only for a heartbeat.

Serves him right for starting this mess.

Ranmaru hesitated before replying. "Yes."

"Did it feel like magic?" Irritation bled into each syllable.

"Sometimes it does." But his smile was not from the heart. "Other times it feels like an endless siege."

She shot him a quizzical glance.

Ranmaru smiled brighter. As though he were coaxing himself beyond the truth. "I suspect you will understand what I mean soon." He sat forward again. Cutting off their conversation before it could start. No longer willing to permit Mariko any glimpse into his life.

Despite her growing curiosity, Mariko knew not to press further.

They continued toward the center of Inako. Toward a winding river, covered in layers of drying petals. When they rounded a bend in the road, an arched bridge of dark grey stone emerged before them, its gritty surface stained green with lichen, dripping with moss. Before crossing, the trio tethered their horses to a post and paid a hunched old man to watch their steeds.

Mariko's eyes passed over the row of horses already under his care.

At first, it all seemed so silly to her. Anyone with the smallest dagger could rob the old man at any time. But the types of horses left in his charge were fine beasts bridled with brightly colored reins. With tassels fringed in gold and silver. Emblazoned with the crests of Inako's finest families.

Only fools would steal from the most powerful people in the imperial city.

Fools like the Black Clan.

The river before Mariko flowed at a leisurely pace. The lanterns hanging from the balustrades on either side of the bridge swayed brightly. At its end—along the opposite riverfront—a line of dogwoods interspersed with cherry trees shaded everything from view. Kept it hidden. Secret. The scent of jasmine and musk curled its invisible fingers toward them, beckoning them closer. When Mariko followed Ōkami and Ranmaru across the bridge, a shower of pink and white petals caressed her skin before cascading into the water like thick flakes of snow.

She had never seen anything like this before.

Without being told, Mariko knew they were crossing into one of the most fabled districts of the imperial city.

Hanami.

At a distance, the single-storied structure appeared to be nothing more than a teahouse. Mariko, Ōkami, and Ranmaru waited outside a simple gate. Rang a simple, unremarkable bell.

Its liquid chime coiled into an almost summer sunset. A sky lingering in the blue hour, just beyond nightfall. The wicket gate creaked open, and Mariko trailed behind Ōkami and Ranmaru as they followed a clean-faced young woman clad in a silk kimono. Her steps were light. Quick. As though she were skimming across the clouds. She led them to a sliding door, pausing only to allow them passage.

When the sight before her centered, Mariko stopped short. Fought to keep from gasping.

This was anything but a simple teahouse. Not once in her life had Mariko ever dreamed of anything its equal.

The pavers winding across a lush, green garden were smooth and black. Perfectly rounded. Some ingenious system— completely obscured from view—had redirected a bubbling brook and sent it churning down a set of three waterfalls, each no higher than the length of Mariko's arm. At the base of these falls, swirling foam gathered around glossy lily pads and snow-white lotus blossoms. Tiny golden koi darted beneath the surface of a small blue lagoon.

Every outer wall of the main teahouse was constructed of sliding screen doors framed in latticed wood. When Mariko looked closer, she realized the screens were not made of rice paper, as was typical. Instead they were made of thin silk.

Decadent to a fault.

Interspersed between the low-hanging eaves of the roof were many cast-iron lanterns made to look like miniature pagodas. Tongues of blue flame licked between their honey-combed slats. Squat brass braziers perfumed the air with an intoxicating mixture of night-blooming jasmine and clean white musk. Though dusk had only just fallen, the teahouse was ablaze in warmth and light. The sounds beyond the screens were ones of lilting music and shared merriment.

Mariko had expected to find this teahouse in Hanami somewhat sordid. A place men went to lose themselves in fantasy.

Thus far she had seen nothing of the sort. She'd seen only tranquil beauty. Felt nothing but serenity. But Mariko knew better than to trust these feelings. They were obviously part of a ploy to disarm even the most critical of patrons.

Time would soon reveal the truth.

When Ranmaru removed his sandals and stepped onto the landing of the teahouse, Mariko followed suit. She straight-ened her robes, suddenly conscious of a discomfiting fact:

she was not dressed appropriately. Her clothes were far too big. After the garments had first been loaned to her, Mariko had suspected they belonged to Ren. He was the only member of the Black Clan with comparable height. At the time, it had not bothered Mariko to wear something ill-fitting and past the fashions of the imperial city. Nor had it bothered her to wear Ren's clothing. She'd seen no reason to care what anyone thought of her appearance.

Until now, Mariko had not even paid attention to what her compatriots wore, for it, too, had seemed immaterial. When amongst men, she'd found fine clothing to be of blessedly little concern.

But now—as Ranmaru and Ōkami turned to wait for her—Mariko suddenly felt acutely aware of her appearance. Almost self-conscious. A feeling she disdained.

So much like a girl, despite all her efforts to the contrary.

Ranmaru's knee-length robe was made of fine, dark green silk. He'd layered it over pleated *hakama* trousers, and had managed to keep himself immaculate and unrumpled all throughout the long ride from the forest into the imperial city. Ōkami wore a similarly styled robe of rich deep blue, except that his *haori* hung open, layered atop a *kosode* of white silk, belted by a black cord.

Though these young men were in truth nothing but a pair of *rōnin*—and notorious thieves, to boot—they looked as though they belonged here, in an elegant teahouse of wonder and mystery. While Mariko greatly resembled a scraggly alley cat, wrung out to dry after a long spring rain.

I suppose it can't be helped.

Donning a mask of fortitude, Mariko forced herself forward. Stopped short just beside Ōkami.

He turned away just as swiftly, pausing only to rinse his hands in a basin filled with water, scented by fresh rose petals. Mariko mimicked his actions, feeling all the while as though she did not belong. As though at any moment, someone would tear the mask from her face and reveal her to the world as the fraud she was.

A silk-screened door slid open before them, unveiling another layer of the hidden splendor of Hanami. Another layer of this place of beauty and excess.

Mariko had quietly sneered at the tales of this excess for many years.

Geiko were referred to as living, floating works of art. The very idea had ruffled her sensibilities. That a beautiful woman could be nothing more than a form of entertainment, left to the vices and pleasures of men.

But as Mariko watched—transfixed—while a *geiko* clad in layers of *tatsumura* silk drifted across the spotless tatami mats, she realized her first mistake. This young woman did not stand or move from a place of subservience. Nor did she convey any sense that her existence was based solely on the whims of men. Not once did the *geiko's* gaze register the newest arrivals. Her head was high, her gait proud. The poise with which she moved—the grace with which she took each of her steps— was a clear testament to years of training and tradition.

The young woman was not a plaything. Not at all.

As she walked, she tantalized. Performed each step as a dancer would on a stage. Painted as an artist would across a canvas. With nothing but the simplest of motions.

Once the *geiko* had crossed to the other side of the long rectangular tearoom, she turned with studied elegance and knelt in one corner, smoothing the folds of her kimono beneath her knees in one even swipe. An attendant handed her a gleaming wooden shamisen. When the girl closed her eyes and began to strum its strings with a carved ivory pick— her music soft and glowing with the same amber light emanating from the hanging lanterns—Mariko fell upon a second realization. She'd judged something before she'd ever given it an opportunity, the same opportunity Mariko had requested from Yoshi that first day at the Black Clan's encampment.

The music the *geiko* played was haunting. A song filled with veiled feeling. Its rhythm was torrid, yet its melody did not burn; rather it hypnotized. The low, constant buzz of the shamisen's deepest string rumbled throughout the space, lulling Mariko into a near stupor.

There was such pride in the way the *geiko* performed. Such passion. She played for herself, first and foremost. And Mariko appreciated it more than she could ever have put to words.

Once the song was finished, Mariko, Ranmaru, and Ōkami took their places at a set of individual tray tables on one side of the rectangular room. Two neat rows ringed the perimeter, parallel to each other. The floors were covered in freshly woven tatami mats, their edges trimmed in deep purple silk.

Mariko sat before one of these trays, again catching herself thoughtlessly imitating each of Okami's motions. Hating herself for it. As though she could ever wish to emulate anyone like him. Anyone so smug. So uninterested in anything of import.

Just as Mariko had finished arranging the hem of her robes around her, a bowl of glazed black porcelain—filled with fragrant rice—was placed before her. Lacquered chopsticks were rested atop a stand of polished jade. More female attendants in the same simple silk of the girl at the teahouse gates bore individual servings of food—fillets of amberjack covered in a sauce of fresh sorrel and white miso paste, a cut of creamy bream served alongside a small bowl of ponzu, cool abalone marinated in sweetened soy sauce and topped with finely diced chives.

When Mariko touched the tip of her chopsticks to the amberjack, the fish fell apart in flakes. Flakes that melted in her mouth, buttery and rich on her tongue. Hand-painted flagons of sake and matching cups were set before each of the teahouse's guests. Soon the room was filled to capacity. And the topic of conversation descended to winking suggestion. Became bawdier. Louder.

Men. Mariko shook her head and looked around, staving off the flush creeping into her cheeks.

Slants of light emanated from matching miniature pagoda lanterns hanging at intervals around the room. The flames within flickered through the intricate slats, creating shadows that danced through the screens, throwing light across the silk-covered walls.

After Mariko finished consuming her food, the sliding door at the opposite end of the main tearoom slipped open. At first, Mariko thought the girl standing before them was simply younger than all the other *geiko* present. Perhaps even younger than Mariko herself. When the girl began gliding by—each of her steps a gentle brush across the woven mats—Mariko saw the flash of padded red silk positioned in the center of her hair, just above her nape. It was the sign of a *maiko*—an apprentice *geiko* who had not yet established her place among the official ranks of floating art in Hanami. The train of the *maiko*'s long kimono rippled behind her, like a soft swirl of wind. On her best day, Mariko could not imagine the skill it took to walk with such grace when burdened by the weight of three undercrobes and a heavily embroidered kimono of brocaded turquoise and pale pink silk. Her obi alone looked as though it weighed nearly a stone, its knot at her back ornate and immense.

Just as she passed Mariko, the *maiko* leveled a smile at her. A smile that made Mariko think this girl knew the answer to any question ever asked. The *maiko*'s prowess in the art of flirtation did nothing to hide the calculating intelligence in her painted eyes. If Mariko had had to guess, she'd have said this girl possessed a formidable mind as well. The touch of hardness in her gaze made her appear all the more mysterious.

Every man in the room was entranced. Ōkami watched the *maiko* float to the other side of the room and nodded once when she looked his way. Ranmaru followed her with his eyes, ready and willing to catch her should she begin to fall, even from across the room. Though Mariko did not miss the glimmer of pain—the undercurrent of unhappiness—that lingered on the leader of the Black Clan's face as he watched the *maiko* pass him by without a single glance in his direction.

This must have been what Ranmaru meant earlier. This *maiko* had to be the source of his endless siege.

And a possible weakness.

Her interest heightened at this realization, but Mariko held her emotions in check. Just as cool and as even as the Wolf.

Once the *maiko* faced the wall on the opposite side of the tearoom, she stopped. Turned slowly, her movements perfectly timed with the strum of the shamisen. From the pocket of one long sleeve, the *maiko* removed two folded silk fans. With a quick snap, she opened them, striking a lingering pose, glancing over her shoulder at the rapt audience behind her. As she faced them, the girl twirled one fan around her first finger in a spinning circle, like a delicate windmill. The other she fluttered across the sea of mesmerized faces, wafting the scent of sweet plum and honeysuckle their way.

She continued floating across the mats, coiling and catching her fans in perfect unison with the rise and fall of the music. Though Mariko did not see anything sensual about the dance, she nevertheless felt titillated at its sight.

Something about it seemed forbidden. Illicit.

Mariko knew she'd been granted a remarkable opportunity. How many noblewomen before her had been inside a teahouse in Hanami? Had witnessed firsthand the famed art of the *geiko*—an art that had been carefully controlled and kept secret from her kind for so many centuries.

The experience opened Mariko's mind to several new considerations.

This girl could not be older than her own seventeen years. Briefly she wondered if the *maiko* had had a choice in her future. Or if—like Mariko—the choice had been made for her by another. A sister. A father. A mother. An aunt. But for a twist of fate, this girl could have been Mariko. And Mariko could have been her.

Something about the *maiko*'s performance struck Mariko in the way willow trees often did. So profoundly beautiful. Yet hauntingly sad.

A smattering of applause rang through the room when the *maiko* finished her fan dance. She bowed, then swished in their direction. Again the beautiful girl ignored Ranmaru, sweeping past him almost coldly. Ignoring the flash of hurt that rippled across his face. Then the *maiko* fired another winsome smile at Mariko before settling beside Ōkami.

Was this girl the one Ōkami visited every other day in Inako? Would Ōkami knowingly conduct an affair with the girl of Ranmaru's heart? Even for the Wolf, this seemed needlessly cruel. Not to mention a waste of time and money and energy.

When the lovely *maiko* leaned toward Ōkami's ear—brushing the snowy petals of her hairpiece across his angled jaw—a faintly unsettling sensation took hold of Mariko's stomach. She questioned it for an instant, and annoyance quickly rose in its place.

She was not angry at the *maiko*. The mere thought was ridiculous. Whether or not the girl took advantage of Ōkami and Ranmaru—spending the former's coin and breaking the latter's heart—was not Mariko's concern.

Unless of course she could use either to her advantage.

Mariko conceded that perhaps a part of her was merely annoyed by the way the girl manipulated one boy to cause another boy pain. Chiyo had often gossiped about servant girls who behaved in such a manner, and Mariko had never liked it.

But why should she care what these idiot boys did with their time and their money?

The sake was clearly taking root in her head.

"Ōkami-*sama*," the *maiko* said, her voice a perfect mixture of shy and coy. "Thank you for coming to see me tonight." Her exquisite eyes slid toward Ranmaru with absolute intention. Then her gaze hardened once more, if only for an instant.

Another ripple of exasperation shot down Mariko's spine. The *maiko* knowingly played with fire. Knowingly toyed with Ranmaru's feelings.

But to what end?

And was there a way Mariko could leverage the girl's end to achieve her own goals?

The *maiko* inclined her head—drawing even closer to Ōkami—and continued whispering in his ear. After a time, he nodded indulgently, and the girl smiled. She drew up one kimono sleeve to pour him a cup of hot tea, each of her movements like liquid smoke.

The more time transpired, the more it became apparent: irrespective of the *maiko's* ulterior motives with regard to Ranmaru, she and Ōkami shared an obvious connection. Their conversation was hushed. Intimate. Not once did an awkward moment pass between the two. Ōkami never needed to ask for anything. The *maiko* anticipated his every wish, all while gazing at him with perfect trust.

The sight faintly disgusted Mariko. Was this how every young woman appeared in the company of handsome young men? How ridiculous. No wonder young men craved spending time in places like Hanami. Mariko would have wagered everything she had that this *maiko* was the reason Ōkami traveled so often to Inako.

A lock clicked open in Mariko's mind.

Perhaps this girl was also the one connecting the Black Clan to its employers. Providing the mercenaries entry to the imperial city's many secrets. *Geiko* were famous for keeping and disseminating some of the most valuable information amongst the nobility. Their unfettered access to men of power often gave them advantage in matters of state.

Perhaps this girl had the answers Mariko so desperately sought.

The *maiko* unfolded to her feet in a whisper of silk. As she passed Ranmaru, he began to stand.

"Yumi," he said softly, "please . . ."

The girl shot a biting glare at the leader of the Black Clan before quitting the tearoom entirely.

As Ranmaru fidgeted beside him—his features marked by distress—Ōkami finished his tea in silence. The only comfort he offered his friend was to pour him another cup of sake. Then Ōkami stood, following the path the *maiko* Yumi had taken not long before.

Once Ōkami took his leave, Mariko debated how best to proceed, her mind a tangle of thoughts. It was clear Ranmaru and Ōkami were in love with the same girl. Strangely this conflict had yet to seed any obvious enmity in their friendship. The only reason Mariko could gather for this was that Yumi served a far more important purpose.

The unlocked door in Mariko's mind swung open.

Yumi *had* to be someone of great significance to the Black Clan.

In that moment, Mariko was gripped by the need to know what purpose the girl served. The need to know anything and everything about the *maiko*.

This undeniable weakness.

Awareness forcing her to take action, Mariko tossed back a final cup of sake, then decided to take advantage of Ranmaru's distressed state of mind. She stammered as she asked one of the attendants to direct her to a place where she could relieve herself. Once Mariko left the tearoom, she made her way down a connecting corridor toward an enclosed courtyard with an elegantly raked footpath and a tiny brook snaking through its center. She whipped around the next corner before crashing to a halt.

Across the courtyard, Ōkami and Yumi stood swathed in shadow beneath a low-hanging eave. They spoke in subdued tones, the *maiko* within embracing distance of the Wolf. Mariko's breath drew short when she saw the expression on Ōkami's face as he listened to the beautiful girl speak.

It was an expression of warmth. Understanding. Compassion.

Undeniably of love.

The Wolf wore the look well. Surprisingly well, considering his earlier disdain for the sentiment. Had she not seen it with her own eyes, Mariko would never have believed it. In contrast, Yumi appeared strangely conflicted. Her shoulders sagged, and Mariko saw the girl's fingers grip her silken sleeves.

When Yumi's head fell forward—some invisible weight taking its toll—Ōkami took her in his arms, pulling her close.

Offering her comfort.

Another pang of annoyance cut through Mariko, just beneath her heart.

She could not understand what Ōkami saw in this girl, beyond the embarrassingly obvious. Frankly Mariko expected better of him. It was unwise of him to flaunt his affections in such a manner. Earlier he'd claimed to appreciate Mariko's stance on love. Claimed to understand her position on emotions in general.

This entire display was foolish. A waste of his time,

especially on a girl who was a potential source of conflict with Ranmaru.

Mariko pursed her lips. It did not matter if Ōkami and Ranmaru were at odds with each other. Indeed it might be better if they were, for her purposes.

With a roll of her shoulders, she pressed into the shadows, trying to determine a way to move within earshot of Ōkami and Yumi. She recalled what she and Kenshin had done as children when they'd wished to spy on their elders. They'd licked a finger and pressed it to one of the rice-paper screens, forming a tiny hole through which to eavesdrop. But of course the screens in this teahouse were fashioned of silk. As if its builders realized the need for utmost discretion in all corners of Hanami.

With no obvious way to intrude at hand, Mariko looked upward. The low-hanging eave on this end of the courtyard was within reach. She could grab hold of it and shimmy along the roofline. If she could get close enough, Mariko might be able to hear all that passed between Ōkami and Yumi.

Mariko studied the intricately formed copper lanterns dangling at intervals along every wooden eave. They mirrored the lanterns along the exterior of the main teahouse, only these were smaller. Some were not yet lit, for it seemed the proprietors of the teahouse believed the silver light of the full moon was more than enough to illumine its inner courtyard, despite the fleece of clouds gathering above.

She braced a foot along a support beam and clambered onto the tiled roof, her movements masked by the steady din from below. Once Mariko settled in place, she considered standing, but realized the *tabi* socks on her feet would not provide the necessary traction to move about freely. So instead she crawled like a spider across the curved roof tiles, keeping her head low.

When she glanced over the ridge at the crest of the roofline, Mariko almost slid from her perch, her pulse on a sudden rampage.

It's not possible.

There—standing by the waterfalls near the entrance of the finest teahouse in Hanami—stood a face to mirror her own. A face Mariko had been raised alongside. A face she understood as no one else ever could.

Hattori Kenshin.

The Dragon of Kai had finally found her.

The swinging Lantern

—✳—

Mariko thought quickly, her mind ablaze.

What is Kenshin doing here?

It was possible her brother had tracked her to Inako. Though it did seem highly unlikely anyone could follow her bizarre trail through a mountainous forest, back to the imperial city. But if there was even a remote possibility, Mariko knew Kenshin would be the one to do it. Which meant it was also possible he knew the Black Clan was responsible for the attack on her convoy.

Now Mariko was met with the consequences.

Impossibly, here her brother stood.

Kenshin waited beside the blue lagoon as his two hooded companions spoke to the attendants at the gate. Even from a distance, Mariko could see the concern on his face.

The deep-seated worry.

She scrambled to make sense of it all. Scrambled to form a plan.

However Kenshin had managed to track her here, Mariko could not allow him to find her. She'd risked too much to get this far.

I am not ready to cede control. Not yet.

Nor am I ready to go back home.

Her brother had not arrived at the teahouse alone. Two other nobles had entered the gates with him. Ones from an extremely wealthy family, judging by their clothing. The way several other attendants materialized from the shadows to assist their every need only further proved the point.

When four members of the imperial guard stepped beneath the glow of the lanterns to their right, Mariko's heart crashed into her stomach: the two young men accompanying Kenshin were from the inner ranks of the imperial court. Possibly even members of the royal family itself. Mariko searched for signs of their crests. Tried to see past their resplendent cloaks.

Was it possible one of these hooded men was her betrothed, Minamoto Raiden?

Mariko swallowed, her nerves wound tight, her pulse trilling through her veins.

If her brother and his royal companions found Mariko here—in the company of the empire's most notorious thieves, scrambling on the rooftop of Hanami's most fashionable teahouse—the ensuing scene could prove disastrous.

It would undermine all her plans. Undermine her wish

to spare her family any embarrassment and prove her worth beyond the marriage market. Undermine her chance to discover who had plotted to murder her.

Not to mention the scandal that would unfold when it was revealed that Minamoto Raiden's bride-to-be had disappeared only to reemerge . . .

Dressed as a boy.

Lastly Mariko did not even want to consider what might happen if a fight were to occur between Kenshin and any member of the Black Clan.

Much less with Ōkami.

Mariko shuddered as she contemplated the possibility. Kenshin was the finest samurai she'd ever known. But not a single warrior she knew moved like the Wolf.

No. Mariko could never allow the two to cross paths.

As her panic continued to rise, the taller of Kenshin's companions lowered the hood of his cloak. Even from her perch along the roofline, Mariko saw the silver crest stamped into the hood's silken inlay.

A trio of gentian flowers and a sprig of bamboo leaves.

The crest of the Minamoto clan.

Her terror spiked in a white-hot flash. In an uncontrollable plume.

She'd never seen Minamoto Raiden before. But she knew from past accounts that he was tall. A gifted member of the *yabusame*. Chiyo had all but swooned when Mariko's betrothal had been made official.

Even without proof, Mariko could easily surmise that her

brother's taller, broader companion was likely her betrothed. Which meant that . . .

The slighter companion. The reedier boy still cloaked and shielded by imperial guards.

Mariko's body went numb, as though a wintry gale had blown across the rooftop.

The crown prince of Wa.

Takeda Ranmaru had been exiled by Minamoto Masaru. Though Ranmaru had not specifically said the emperor's name that night by the *jubokko*, Mariko was not a fool. Ōkami and Ranmaru believed their fathers had been betrayed and murdered by the emperor.

Nothing good could come of their sons meeting by chance in a teahouse deep within Hanami on a dark summer night.

Consumed with worry, Mariko watched from her perch as Kenshin rinsed his hands in the same basin she'd used a few hours ago. Watched as he waited to enter the same teahouse. It was now impossible to return to her place in the main room. If Kenshin saw her, he would recognize her before she could swallow her next breath.

Panic took hold when Mariko realized that Ōkami was doubling back toward the teahouse, with Yumi at his side. Which meant his path would soon cross that of her brother. If Ōkami returned and discovered Mariko missing, he would undoubtedly ask Ranmaru where she had gone. The two would begin making inquiries. They would learn she had not simply disappeared to relieve herself.

And her brother would hear everything.

Without knowing exactly what information Kenshin already possessed, it was leaving too much to chance.

Mariko had to get the Black Clan to leave the teahouse with her in tow. Before Kenshin caught wind of anything that might be afoot. Because if the Dragon of Kai was here to find her, he would find her. Her brother would not give up until he did.

And she could not allow that to happen.

Not yet.

The way she saw it, Mariko had two immediate options:

She could either attempt to distract her brother by creating a commotion in his vicinity—perhaps by flinging the single throwing star she'd pilfered from Haruki—or she could create a diversion around Ōkami, away from the main tearoom. The kind of diversion that would grant them a chance to summon Ranmaru to their side, so they could all escape without being seen.

When faced with the decision to possibly threaten her brother—and coincidentally the crown prince of Wa—or Ōkami, Mariko's choice was easy. She grabbed the chain of an unlit copper lantern behind her. Hauled it onto the roof. Took careful aim.

As soon as Ōkami came within range, Mariko swung the lantern into his path, intent on catching him off guard. She hoped that—with the sliver of time this small distraction bought her—she would have a moment to clamber off the rooftop unnoticed and quietly inform Ōkami of the teahouse's most recent arrivals.

She could, of course, simply say something. Simply shout down at him from her perch. But if Mariko could help it, she did not wish for Ōkami to know she'd been spying on him. And she could not risk Kenshin hearing her. Or worse, seeing her.

So she was left with nothing but a lantern.

Unfortunately Mariko miscalculated two things when she boldly swung the lantern at the Wolf:

The surprising weight of metal suspended from a chain.

And the quickness of the Wolf's reflexes.

As soon as he heard the grate of swinging metal from above, Ōkami shoved Yumi away and looked up in the same motion.

The *maiko* screamed as the rogue lantern struck the Wolf hard in the face, causing him to topple over the railing into the burbling brook. Orange-and-white koi darted in every direction as the splash resounded through the courtyard, drawing the attention of everyone within earshot.

Mariko blinked, her eyes and mouth forming perfect ovals. Ōkami swiped the hair from his face and immediately leveled a look of pure hatred up at her.

As though he'd known where she was all along.

That did not exactly go as planned.

Yumi stared down at Ōkami's drenched body, one hand covering her perfectly painted lips.

At the gate's entrance, Mariko's brother stepped from beneath the overhang outside the teahouse's sliding doors, drawn by Yumi's bell-like scream and the sound of splashing water. Minamoto Raiden wandered from the shadows, following in Kenshin's footsteps.

Mariko ducked lower, hiding herself from any eyes that might think to drift upward.

Hoping Ōkami would not draw attention to her.

Praying for a miracle.

When the Wolf stood suddenly—recrimination in his dark eyes, water sloshing from his fine clothes—Mariko cut him off with a sharp look, before he could begin yelling. Then she jerked a thumb over her shoulder, as though that offered a sufficient explanation. As though it offered her a valid reason to swing a metal box at his head. Ōkami peered over the connecting walkway leading toward the main tearoom, toward the row of richly clad figures now proceeding in their direction. Though his fury remained intact, he narrowed his eyes. In less than an instant, understanding settled across his features.

From where it had fallen beside him, Ōkami reached for the chain of the lantern Mariko had swung. Then he whistled once, the sound like that of a waterbird.

Again the terror gripped Mariko's throat, catching her voice in a vise.

Each second brought her brother a step closer. If Kenshin had trailed her this far—trailed Mariko all the way from Jukai forest to the imperial city—her brother likely suspected the Black Clan of kidnapping her. Did he know the identity of the exiled boy who led this band of mercenaries?

Would he recognize Ōkami or Takeda Ranmaru?

Mariko kept to the edge of the roof, her pulse roaring in her ears.

She felt powerless. Helpless. Her blood surged on, ignited by fear.

Kenshin and his companions rounded the corner beneath where Mariko crouched. Soon they would see Ōkami. Be within striking distance. The Wolf did not look perturbed at this. Nor did he attempt to flee. He merely motioned for Yumi to leave. Then he vaulted the balustrade, trailing an arc of crystalline water behind him.

Her fingers shook. Mariko could not be certain what the Wolf intended to do. But it was obvious he meant to stand his ground, even against imperial guards. Even against the celebrated might of the finest member of the *yabusame*.

The Wolf's eyes were locked on the advancing party.

Locked on the Dragon of Kai.

An icy chill brushed across Mariko's skin.

Ōkami must recognize the Hattori crest on Kenshin's garments.

Which meant he had to know the reasons Hattori Kenshin had trailed him here. Because the Black Clan was guilty of trying to murder his sister. Guilty of attacking her convoy.

Guilty of everything, as Mariko had always suspected.

And now Ōkami intended to face Hattori Kenshin. Intended to finish it, once and for all.

In that instant Mariko knew—beyond the shadow of a doubt—

No amount of information was worth her brother's life.

She removed the throwing star from her sleeve. Positioned it between her fingers. Mariko would kill Ōkami if he so much as reached for a sword. If his hand so much as twitched in suggestion. As she raised the throwing star into the light, a blur of motion erupted from the patch of darkness at the end of the walkway. A shadow crossed the beams, its steps soundless, its features masked.

A silver blade sliced through the air.

And Mariko's scream echoed through the night.

An Honest Exchange

Everything happened all at once. Before Ōkami had a chance to attack, the moonlit blade arced from the shadows again. It barely missed Kenshin's head as he dodged the blow with uncanny reflexes, whipping his *katana* from its scabbard in a sinuous motion.

Mariko stifled a gasp when the same figure darted into the light of a nearby lantern. Though it was only a moment—and though a black mask concealed the lower portion of his face— she recognized the warrior's clothes.

Ranmaru.

The leader of the Black Clan avoided Kenshin's parrying blow, then made to sidestep him entirely. As though he had no intention to engage her brother, but meant to disable him. With clear designs on the warrior at Kenshin's back.

Minamoto Raiden. Mariko's betrothed.

At that, Raiden unsheathed a gleaming *katana*, then

shoved his younger brother back before barking for the four imperial guards already swarming in their direction.

Ōkami engaged Raiden the instant Mariko's betrothed brandished his sword. A black mask now obscured the Wolf's face as well, though his weapon was still nothing more than a copper lantern swinging from its slender chain.

The imperial guards raced down the walkway, and the hiss of swords being torn from their scabbards reverberated on all sides. Ranmaru attacked the first of the imperial guards. The two guards in the back had already taken hold of the crown prince, leading him away from the fray.

When a low hum began to collect in the air, Mariko's eyes cut to Ōkami.

The lines of his body had begun to blur. To ripple into unchecked motion.

No.

Mariko flung the throwing star into the melee, watching it spin toward Ōkami's back. It dug into one of his shoulder blades, and he yelled once—more from fury than from pain— as the tremors across his body only intensified. Ranmaru parried another blow from Kenshin, fighting to make his way to his injured friend's side.

"Get out of here," Ōkami said to Ranmaru as he ripped the throwing star from his back. "Now!"

Ranmaru hesitated.

"Now!" Ōkami repeated, his voice hoarse, his bloodied fingers grasping the long lantern chain, intent on using it as a weapon.

With an unmistakable expression of guilt, the leader of the Black Clan disappeared, melting into the darkness like smoke into the night sky.

Mariko saw the exact moment Kenshin realized an opportunity. With deadly resolve, her brother shoved aside one of the remaining imperial guards and charged Ōkami.

The low hum in the air spiked to a feverish pitch. And Ōkami became a blur of movement, striking out at anything he could see, his lantern swinging in perfect circles.

Without hesitation, Mariko launched herself from the edge of the rooftop, directly onto her brother. Trying to shield him. He fought her off, twisting in midair as they lost balance and toppled to the wooden walkway.

Kenshin's head struck the edge of a pillar. His body slumped forward, motionless. Mariko's icy, trembling fingers flew to his mouth, checking for breath. A sigh escaped her lips when she realized her brother had only been knocked unconscious.

Before Mariko could do anything else, she was grabbed by the waist and hurled into darkness, the night breeze whipping across her face as she flew away from the scene, borne on a wicked wind.

Mariko was flung against a plaster wall.

As soon as she caught a lungful of air, she realized they were behind the teahouse. Ōkami had grabbed her and run, faster than a shock of lightning. He must have taken a hidden exit to get them to the other side of the compound so quickly.

The Wolf shoved his forearm beneath Mariko's throat, the sleeve of his elegant *haori* still damp from his recent swim.

"What are you doing, Sanada Takeo?" he demanded, his chest heaving. Anger flooded his voice. Corded the muscles in his neck. "Are you trying to kill me?" She could feel him shaking even now.

Her pulse jumped to a martial beat. Mariko thought quickly. "No! I was trying to save you, and I misjudged—"

"Don't lie to me." His fingers curled into the collar of her *kosode*, yanking her close, the hum still rolling off his skin. "No more lies, Sanada Takeo." Above his mask, his eyes flashed like obsidian. Two stones of fathomless black, cut from molten fire.

"I'm not lying," she whispered around the knot in her throat.

"This night only, speak the truth." A light spring rain began to mist around them. His hands moved to either side of her head, caging her between his arms, the veins there tensing in silent threat.

"Only if"—she swallowed—"only if you agree to do the same. The price of my truth is your own."

Ōkami's tone descended into lethal quiet. "You're still trying to negotiate."

Her heart flew into her throat, its beat crashing through her ears. "I have the answers you seek." Mariko steeled herself, the rain turning into a steady trickle. "Take off your mask, and I'll take off mine."

His lips twitched. Then—without warning—he gripped her throat once more, the pressure light, but unyielding. "That's the problem with wearing a mask." He flexed his fingers, pressing her into the plaster wall. "It can be torn off at any time."

Mariko wanted to fight back, but she kept her body still. Her hands clamped around his wrist. If the Wolf wished to see her struggle—as predators so often did—she refused to give him the satisfaction. When she looked into his hooded, starless gaze, she failed to see a trace of the sleepy-eyed degenerate she'd first met that night beside the watering hole.

Instead she found something infinitely more. Of everything.

Yet she no longer felt any fear. In its place she felt nothing but strength.

"I'm not afraid of you." Mariko removed her fingers from around his wrist.

And tore the black mask from his face.

"Good," he said softly. He began to smile, leveling a cool look at her. "An honest exchange."

Mariko blinked. "What?" Confusion stole the breath from her body.

He whispered through the driving rain. "I still owe you an injury, Sanada Takeo."

With that, Ōkami released her.

Only when her feet fell flush with the worn cobbles of the empty alleyway did she realize Ōkami had suspended her in midair. Mariko knew she should have felt afraid when faced with such ruthlessness. Such control. Yet strangely she still did not feel fearful.

She felt powerful.

Powerful to have met his black gaze with one of her own.

"Stay close. If you try to run, I will wring your scrawny neck," Ōkami warned as he whirled into the darkness. Mariko followed him as he crossed another winding alleyway. Then another. Two more before they emerged onto the main thoroughfare of Hanami. Then Ōkami whipped off his blue kimono jacket, turning it inside out to reveal a *haori* of rich brown silk. A color to mask the blood of the wound on his back, at least from a distance. He removed the black cord from around his waist and handed it to Mariko.

In the same stilted silence, she reversed her jacket and altered her own appearance.

For a time, they proceeded through the rain-slicked streets, pausing only to steal new pairs of sandals. Then they made their way toward a dilapidated bridge. Toward a section of town where the scents were raw, the people distinctly more ragged. A section starkly different from Hanami. Many of the windows were littered with holes. The stench of fetid water and flowing sewage twisted through the night air. It seeped down the open conduits before carving through the center of the streets.

Though Mariko desperately wanted to ask Ōkami where they were now going—where Ranmaru had gone—she knew better than to press him. He did not often show anger or emotion of any kind. And he was not prone to fits of rage. In the past she'd always found him to be uninterested in almost everything.

But it was clear he'd been furious with her beside the teahouse, if only for a moment. Furious enough to let his guard down. To show her he did care about *something* beyond himself.

He'd warned her not to run away.

That statement had surprised her the most.

If Mariko was such a nuisance to him—a source of so many injuries—why would Ōkami not want to be rid of her? Why had he not left Mariko behind to fend for herself?

After all, she *had* swung a lantern at him. And struck his back with a throwing star. Another man might have killed Sanada Takeo for less. At the very least struck him in return.

She glanced at the tall, capable figure striding before her. An odd feeling of warmth settled over her chest. Almost akin to trust.

In the same instant, Mariko banished the traitorous thought, letting horror slide into its place. Ōkami had nearly attacked her brother, intent on inflicting untold damage. He'd nearly killed *Kenshin*. After nearly killing Mariko and decimating her convoy.

He deserves everything I do to him. And more.

She glared at his back, seeing the capable figure in a different light. One tinged in sinister tones. The reds of violence, the blacks of death, the greens of vengeance. Blurring lights and slashing weapons. Trailing bands of smoke.

"How are you able to move as you do?" Mariko blurted.

Okami did not answer.

"Were you born with this ability?" she continued.

His reply was curt. Not once did he look her way. "No."

Which meant it was the sort of magic gifted to him.

Though Mariko knew it was foolish to press him further, she ached with the need to know who—or what—had gifted such power to Ōkami. Ached with the desire to know what this power was. But she also knew better than to ask at this moment.

Soon they paused before a gate surrounded by broken latticework. The timbers used to construct it were greyed, their edges warping. Mariko was certain a solid kick would render the lock at its front useless.

When Ōkami paused to knock softly at the entrance, Mariko permitted herself to glance at his face.

In its depths she could discern nothing.

Unsurprising, as always.

The gate unlatched with a rusty whine. A small lamp dangled from the overworked hand of a woman around the same age as Mariko's grandmother. Her face was kind, but fatigued.

"Tsuneoki-*sama*!" she said, briefly peering over Ōkami's shoulder at Mariko. "My lord Ranmaru is not with you?"

The use of Ōkami's given name startled Mariko.

Tsuneoki. If he is the son of Asano Naganori—as Ranmaru revealed that night beside the jubokko—then Ōkami's real name is Asano Tsuneoki.

"We were separated in a skirmish." Though Ōkami kept his voice level, Mariko could hear the undercurrent of irritation in his words.

One side of the woman's mouth dipped lower as she peered closely at the dark stain on his *haori*. Close enough to notice the telltale signs of blood.

"I see."

Ōkami ignored her frown of concern. "I wanted to apologize in person, Korin-*san*." He reached into the folds of his white *kosode* and drew out a drawstring pouch. With both hands, Ōkami passed it to the woman. "This is all I can give you now, as a result of this evening's . . . events. The rest of the funds have been waylaid for now."

The lines on her already weathered brow deepened. "What happened? Have we been . . . betrayed?" Her voice nearly broke on the last word.

Which answered the first of Mariko's many unuttered questions. This woman was not affiliated with the teahouse. Ōkami had not brought her money as restitution for tonight's damages.

"No." The smallest of sighs passed Ōkami's lips. "It's only that we've been faced with a few complications."

"By members of the nobility? Or by imperial soldiers?"

He almost smiled. "Both, actually. It appears we're in high demand this evening."

The elderly woman leaned against the door frame, steadying her weary body. "You did not have to come tonight,

Tsuneoki-*sama*." Korin's voice was gentle. Kind. "If you were involved in any sort of skirmish, it was a risk for you to remain in the city. Your enemies are always searching for you."

Ōkami shook his head. "You were expecting us, Korin-*san*. And I would not have those in your care wanting for anything."

She waved a dismissive hand. "The gold you provided last week will buy the children enough clothing and food for the rest of the month. If we are frugal, there may be some left over for next month as well. Do not trouble your-self, Tsuneoki-*sama*. The Black Clan does so much for us. You protect us. Watch over us as no one else does. Many here in the Iwakura ward owe you debts of thanks for all you do. None among us would ever question your actions. Or your intentions."

The Black Clan protects her? Helps to supply the people in this ward?

Mariko could not prevent a flicker of confusion from passing across her face. Ōkami's body tensed. As he fought to relax, his gaze slid to her, his features remaining tight.

He's irritated that I've been privy to all this information.

"Very well." Ōkami nodded. "I shall return next week with the rest of the funds."

When Korin reached to take his hands in her own, Mariko was gripped by a strange sensation. An odd kind of envy. The wish to be cherished with the same kind of open affection. One without agenda. "May the old gods keep you safe." Korin turned to Mariko. The way the elderly woman studied her made Mariko shrink back into the shadows.

Finally Korin offered her a smile. "And may the new gods keep your young *friend* safe."

"He is not my friend." Though Ōkami's pronouncement was true for them both, his words still stung.

Mariko thought to say something. To respond to either Korin or Ōkami with something equally blithe. Equally biting.

Blessedly the night watchman strolled by at that exact moment, ringing his bell to signify the hour.

"*He* . . . is what?" Korin blinked, clearly confused, the bell behind them tolling into a purpled sky.

He.

The blood drained from Mariko's face.

Korin-san knows I am not a boy. How could she possibly know that?

As the elderly woman's attention shifted from Ōkami to Mariko, her features softened. Her gaze settled on Mariko again. This time with a deeper meaning. "Of—of course he isn't your friend." Korin recovered with a smile. "My apologies." She bowed to Mariko, though her eyes were filled with a knowing light.

Does she think Ōkami and I are—

Mariko almost spluttered aloud.

Before she could react—before she could even think beyond such ridiculousness—her thoughts were swallowed by Okami and Korin-*san*'s continued conversation. A hushed

239

conversation she was no longer meant to partake in. Bracing his arm against the battered gate, Ōkami positioned his back between Mariko and the elderly woman, eliminating the unwanted presence from the rest of his discussion.

Mariko was left to ruminate on all that had occurred.

All she had learned.

The only conclusion she was left to consider was this:

There was far more to the Black Clan than she'd first thought.

Kenshin sat in a corner of the teahouse, wearing a murderous expression. The young servant girl tending to the wounds on his head and hands was careful. Meticulous.

Her efforts were futile.

At the moment, nothing would settle well on his skin.

"You're quite lucky you were not injured further," Minamoto Roku commented as he took a neat swallow of sake from a glazed porcelain cup.

"Luck has nothing to do with it," Raiden interjected. "Kenshin-*sama* was quick to react." He nodded in approval. "In battle, that is among the most important of things."

"Forgive me, but I was not quicker than my attacker, my lord," Kenshin replied curtly. "In battle, that is *all* that matters."

Raiden studied him for a time, his expression perplexed. "The greater question is why did they attack you? I thought they were trying to assassinate my brother. But it was clear at least one of the masked men was aiming for you." He brushed a hand across his jaw. "Or was the boy who jumped from the roof not wearing a mask? I could not be certain."

"I . . . do not know, my lord." Kenshin frowned as he recalled the flurry of movement above him. The crash of a body against his back. The wash of sudden darkness.

Compounded by another, far more pressing concern:

Why had his assailant not finished him off when given the chance? Especially when he'd been afforded the advantage of higher ground?

"These men were far too organized to have been mere drunkards," Raiden continued. "It's clear they were positioned at the teahouse intentionally. But to what end?"

The crown prince smiled as he took another sip of sake. "The true matter of import, brother, is that these masked men were present on the same night we were. They attacked us before we could even get inside the teahouse. Which means someone plotted to lie in wait for us and catch us unawares. I would like to know who it was."

Kenshin said nothing as the attendant—a young girl wearing a kimono that briefly brought to mind the color of Amaya's grey eyes—removed a curved bone needle and a spiral of thread. She began to stitch shut the wound on Kenshin's forehead. Each time the needle passed through his skin, his thoughts wove through his mind.

Consumed with worry for his sister.

Why were these men waiting for them? Did they have anything to do with Mariko's disappearance?

241

His sister's face washed across his vision again.

But it was not possible. It could not be possible.

Was it possible?

A part of Kenshin wanted to ask Raiden and Roku if anyone in the city of Inako knew the identities of those in the Black Clan. If any member of the nobility relied on their services in any capacity. But if Kenshin did ask, then he would be divulging his true intentions in coming to Inako.

And he did not yet trust anyone enough to do that. Not yet. Much less any member of the Minamoto clan. Not when he was still so uncertain as to where their loyalties might lie.

Kenshin watched the steady hands of the servant girl as they moved to stitch the wound on his arm.

Mariko had always been a terrible seamstress.

———————

That night—in his dreams—Kenshin saw a boy in black wearing the mask of his sister's face.

Beneath a pair of saurian eyes.

the hot springs

—✳—

Mariko had not thought this could be possible.

But she was being *rewarded* by the Black Clan. Despite the fact that she'd recently injured their champion at a teahouse in Hanami.

Twice over.

Ranmaru had thanked her personally for everything she'd done to warn them at the teahouse. About the imperial troops. About the arrival of the crown prince. All she'd done to save Ōkami.

And—though the lies blistered her ears—Mariko was not one to return a gift.

She settled into the steaming water, luxuriating in the feel of its silky warmth. It seemed to sap the very weariness from her bones. The sadness from her skin.

It had been so long since Mariko had had a proper bath.

As a reward for all her efforts, Ranmaru had given her leave to travel up the mountain path cut into the outcropping near Haruki's tent. Toward a gathering of hot springs, positioned above the lake that served as another natural boundary of the Black Clan's camp. Of course Ranmaru didn't trust her fully yet—as he'd instructed Ren to remain at the base of the footpath, ready to catch her should she try to flee—but at least it was a beginning. A bare measure of trust.

Trust Mariko desperately needed in order to rise in their ranks.

As she settled against a smooth stone—pausing to let its surface knead the tension from between her shoulders—she stopped to think of all that had transpired last night.

In truth—despite the enormous peril to her brother—it had been a rather successful evening. Mariko had learned a great deal. Experienced things she'd never dreamed of experiencing. Taken part in an actual fight.

Soon Takeda Ranmaru may be asking me *for advice. After that he might even be confiding in me. Telling me every secret I wish to know.*

The possibilities warmed her spirits almost as much as the water warmed her bones.

A cloud of steam eased up her neck as Mariko lowered herself beneath the surface of the hot springs, until the water touched just beneath her chin. She sighed loudly. Such hot springs were a miracle. A miracle heated by the sharp, almost mint-like vapors emanating from the mountain, as well as the earth beneath it. The same combination of elements that produced the bright yellow rocks littering her surroundings. Mariko was familiar with these slightly noxious stones. There had been a time when the ancient mountain in the distance had erupted, spewing molten earth into the sky and acrid ash into the air.

Strange how the same thing that could destroy so many lives could also create such healing waters.

The steam rose before her face, clouding her vision. Mariko untied her hair from its topknot and leaned back, soaking her filthy scalp.

Just as she'd settled into a place of serene calm, the branches nearby rustled. Mariko's head snapped up. She almost yelped at the sight before her.

"What are you doing here?" she demanded of her intruder. Hating that her voice trembled at the last.

Ōkami stood along the edge of the hot springs, studying her coolly. "You're not the only one to have sustained injuries last night."

Mariko leveled him with an equally dispassionate stare. "Wait your turn, *Asano Tsuneoki*."

"Keep speaking to me in such a manner, Sanada Takeo. See if I don't toss you from the water, ass over feet." Ōkami began untying his *kosode*.

Alarm flashed through her, from her nape toward her toes. Briefly Mariko offered thanks to the heat of the water. At least it should mask the rush of color rising in her face.

Her reaction was not because she was about to see Ōkami naked. Mariko had seen naked men before. Nudity did not bother her. But if Ōkami came close to her. If he saw what the water and steam might fail to conceal . . .

All would be undone.

She backed away, then caught herself. Far too hasty. If she fled, Mariko would only draw further attention to herself. Not that she could in fact flee.

As she, too, was naked.

Also there was the matter of Ren, undoubtedly waiting for her to even attempt running, so that he could threaten to cut her into pieces or feed her to Ranmaru's horse or afflict whatever ghastly torment he'd dreamed up for the day.

Mariko kept her eyes steady, all while allowing her sight to blur. Even if she'd seen naked men before, she did not wish to add the image of Ōkami to her memory. Something about it felt . . . unseemly. Untoward.

When a brief image of tawny, lithe muscle cut across her vision as Ōkami entered the hot springs, Mariko swallowed.

"Could you not at the very least grant me this moment of peace?" she grumbled while glancing away. "I did in fact save you."

Ōkami snorted. "Yet another lie. As far as I'm concerned, you nearly killed me. Twice."

"The wound on your back is only a flesh wound." Mariko crossed her arms beneath the water. "And the wound on your head is barely a scratch." A groove formed between her brows. "But I suppose it *is* possible these tiny injuries could be causing you a great deal of pain. If you'd like, I suppose—"

"What?" Ōkami stood suddenly, and Mariko ignored

the way the hot water rolled down the sinew of his arms. The way the steam unfurled above his skin in thick coils. *"Tiny injuries?* Do you have any idea what it feels like to be *stabbed in the back* by a spinning six-bladed dagger?"

Mariko canted her head. "I'm sure Yoshi has a tea that can help ease your pain." She cut her eyes. "And perhaps Yumi can offer her assistance the next time you're in Hanami."

"Tea?" Ōkami pointed at the purple bruise on the side of his jaw. "You honestly think tea will repair the damage of a metal lantern being *swung at my face?"*

"I swung that lantern to save you!" Mariko insisted. "What happened after could not be helped."

"Said the scorpion."

Mariko's mother had once said the very same thing to her. It rankled her to hear the words fall from Ōkami's scarred lips. Her hands balled into fists beneath the water. "I am *not* the scorpion."

"Of course you are. You're absolutely willing to kill something in order to save it."

She gritted her teeth. "I've always hated that story."

A half smile curled up one side of Ōkami's face as he scrubbed the dripping water from his jaw. Massaged the shoulder closest to his wound. Mariko refused to notice the way the water welled in the hollows of his muscles. The way it beaded across his sun-bronzed skin.

No. That was the way of treachery.

Mariko circled her arms through the water. As though she were warding the demons away.

247

"You take to water well," Ōkami commented. "It appears Akira-*san* was right."

It never ceased to needle Mariko immeasurably. How this boy was able to frustrate her with so little effort. "For the last time, I am not water."

"My god, you are stubborn."

"Another reason I cannot possibly be water." Though there was heat to her words, she kept her voice even. "Water is temperamental. It doesn't assume any shape on its own. It takes the shape of whatever is around it. And I have never wished to be controlled by my surroundings."

"And yet you are, all the same."

She splashed water at him.

His smile was thoughtful. "Water is not beholden to anything. It can cut through rock. It can vanish into thin air. With time, it can even destroy iron. You should not see it as a weakness."

"If I am water, then what are you?"

"My father always said I was fire."

This observation surprised her. Ōkami had always struck her as unnervingly cool-tempered. Save for the incident outside the teahouse, Mariko had found him to be almost mild-mannered. At times even cold. Then she remembered Ranmaru's tale by the *jubokko*. Ōkami had burned the tent of his father's accuser.

Mariko found she wished to know more. "You say you are fire as though you don't believe it to be true."

"I believe we are all things, depending on the situation.

Given the right time and the right circumstance, any man or woman can be water or fire or earth or wind."

"You deny the truth of our inclinations."

"No. I deny being a slave to any one thing. In any situation we can choose who we are and choose who we want to be."

"That's . . . true," Mariko admitted.

"Don't sound so surprised. I'm not an absolute fool."

"I never thought you were a fool. I've thought you were lazy. Perhaps even ridiculous at times. But never a fool."

"A lie. You never truly thought I was ridiculous. That's why it bothered you so."

Briefly Mariko recalled the night they'd first met. "No. I actually did think you were ridiculous once. That's what bothered me so."

"More honesty. I like you much more when you're honest, Sanada Takeo."

"But you don't mind me when I lie?"

Ōkami leaned back against a stone, his smile perfectly indolent. "Perhaps. As long as you're not lying to me."

Mariko wanted to splash him again. Wanted to best him in all ways. Wanted to kiss him silent.

The last thought startled her.

Where had it come from? It was so utterly illogical. So fiercely wrong. She'd never wished to kiss anyone before. Never wished to worry any boy's lower lip between her teeth before.

To worry it until his words melted on her tongue.

Ōkami studied her, as though he could sense the tumult

249

of her thoughts. And wished to take advantage of it. "Did you truly know who those men were when they first arrived?"

The question caught her off guard. "Of course I did."

"Liar. You climbed onto the rooftop before they arrived at the teahouse. Why?"

Mariko had suspected he'd known she was there all along. "I thought I saw imperial soldiers when I left to relieve myself. So I climbed onto the rooftop to confirm who they were."

"I don't believe you. I think you were spying on me. And I want to know why."

A wave of shock descended on her. Mariko had not expected him to ask that question quite so bluntly. "If I were spying on you, why would I reveal myself in an effort to spare you?" She pressed her back into the smooth rock along the edge of the hot spring as she considered how best to redirect the tenor of this conversation in her favor. "Did *you* know who all the men were as soon as you saw them?" Mariko filled her voice with accusation. "I didn't recognize one of them."

"I recognized Minamoto Raiden. It took only a moment's work to realize the scrawny little brat at his back was the crown prince. The remaining boy in their company took me a bit more time." He shot her a bladed smile. "Your attempt to redirect this conversation was rather clever, by the way."

Never mind that. Here was a chance for Mariko to learn something of value. Something about her family. "Who was the last boy?"

The angles in Ōkami's face hollowed into slashes. "The

Dragon of Kai. Strange how he did not seem nearly as fear-some in person."

"Who?" Mariko was proud that she did not stammer. Nor did she even blink.

"Another lie. Why are you lying about what you already know?"

"I truly don't know who the Dragon of Kai is."

Ōkami paused. "He's the son of a power-hungry idiot."

Mariko stiffened. "In that sense, you could be speaking about anyone."

"No. Hattori Kano would sell his own soul if it meant currying favor. And he breeds the same kind of idiocy in those around him. Though I will say his son can wield a sword with a passable amount of skill."

Mariko could no longer listen to him speak ill of her family. So she borrowed his own tactic. "What did you say to Yumi that made her cry?"

Two could play at this game of drawing out a reaction.

It frustrated her that Ōkami only narrowed his dark eyes once more.

"I knew you were there. Watching us," he said softly.

"You disappeared. Like you've been disappearing this entire week. When I climbed onto the rooftop to watch the imperial troops, I saw you with her." Mariko chewed on her inner cheek. "And you're a fool to pursue the same girl that Ranmaru loves, too."

A sneer pulled at a corner of Ōkami's mouth. "Too?"

"It's clear you love her."

He paused again. In obvious deliberation. "Of course I love her." Ōkami sank beneath the water, keeping nothing but his head above the surface. The resulting waves rippled against her skin. Reminding her they shared a bath as heated as their words.

The very idea set her heart apace. She was reminded of her earlier thought. Her earlier wish to kiss him silent. How traitorous and wrong it was. How it had become a desire she could no longer deny.

"I see," Mariko said slowly, hating how much everything about him bothered her.

When he did not reply immediately, it became clear Ōkami was still considering something. Perhaps a course of action. Finally he came to a hesitant decision.

"Yumi is my sister."

Mariko's eyes went wide. She caught the relief flooding through her and despised herself even more for it. "You let your sister become a *maiko*?"

"She's safe in Hanami. Safer than she would be here in Jukai forest. And safer than she'd ever be if anyone in Inako found out who she is. Who her family is." He slid closer, and Mariko flattened against the rock, wishing it would move with her. Wrap her like a cloak. "I'm . . . trusting you with this, Sanada Takeo. Against my better judgment. If you tell anyone who Yumi is, I will personally throw you to the *jubokko* and watch it drain you of your life's blood without a moment's thought."

"I told you." Mariko stared back at him. "I'm not afraid of you."

He did not smile. "And you need to tell me you understand what I'm saying."

"Do you want me to promise?"

"Promises mean nothing to me." Ōkami's tone was soft. Severe. "They are words said to assuage any fool who wishes to believe."

"Then what do you want me to say?"

"I want you to tell me you understand that I will kill you—without pause—if you ever betray me." His onyx eyes glittered. "Do you know the story about the rabbit who played with fire?"

He burned to death, along with all his loved ones.

"I understand what you're saying," Mariko replied.

Ōkami's brows lifted in question.

She clarified, though her hands balled into fists beneath the water. "I understand you will set me to flame if I ever betray you."

But not if I destroy you first.

———

Ōkami briefly considered telling Ranmaru about his most recent interaction with Sanada Takeo. Briefly considered telling his friend about his suspicions.

That the slight boy with the doe-like eyes had been sent by their enemies in Inako to spy on the Black Clan.

But whenever Ōkami had voiced his concerns with regard

to their newest recruit, Ranmaru had been unmoved. Almost uninterested. And if Ōkami had to disclose all that happened, he would need to tell his best friend what Sanada Takeo knew about Yumi.

Never mind that it was a lie couched in truth.

A lie meant to test their newest recruit.

Anything Ōkami revealed about Yumi—whether or not it was true—would anger Ranmaru greatly. And after all Ranmaru had sacrificed for him, Ōkami would rather die than cause his friend pain.

As it was, Ōkami had thought long and hard before disclosing this information. But the best way to gain trust was to give it. And Ōkami would murder Sanada Takeo with his bare hands before he let any actual harm come to Yumi.

This would be the first of many tests Ōkami had designed for the young Lord Lackbeard. The wheels of the second test were already set in motion.

Ōkami's suspicion had begun to form the night they'd first met Sanada Takeo by Akira-*san*'s watering hole. It had deepened when he'd caught sight of the boy climbing like an insect across the rooftop. And solidified when Ōkami had pressed a forearm into the boy's throat and heard him all but squeal like a girl.

Ōkami had immediately regretted handling him in such a rough manner. Then felt a wave of irritation at his regret. Everything about this boy was green. Untried. From the soft skin of his hands to the ridiculous way he completed even the simplest task with such unnecessary precision.

The boy had obviously been sent here to ingratiate himself to Ranmaru. To act the part of the bumbling young fool in desperate need of guidance.

Only it had become abundantly clear to Ōkami that Sanada Takeo was far from being a fool. The boy was too clever—in words and in deeds—for that.

Ōkami knocked the hair from his eyes. Refrained from kicking a wayward stone beside his foot. Why had he not just left the boy in Inako, as Ranmaru had suggested?

He'd had the opportunity. Ōkami could have left Takeo in the bowels of the Iwakura district. Takeo could never have found his way back to the Black Clan's camp. Instead Ōkami had felt strangely watchful of him. Almost protective.

Sanada Takeo had been chosen to spy on them for this exact reason.

To prey on their weaknesses. Ranmaru's wish to inspire.

Ōkami's need to protect.

The boy had always made him uncomfortable in a way Ōkami had been unable to adequately articulate. Whenever Sanada Takeo was around, he made Ōkami question everything about himself.

And he did not like it.

His suspicion had only solidified in the grey fog rising above the waters of the hot springs. The best way for Ōkami to confirm it was to watch the boy.

And wait for him to make a mistake.

twisted tales

———✳———

K enshin had spent too many nights in Inako.

He'd attended too many gatherings and been forced to partake in too many insipid conversations. And gleaned virtually nothing of value.

Despite all his attempts to learn whether any member of the nobility bore a grudge against his family, he had turned up empty-handed. Kenshin was not good at manipulating conversations in the same skillful way as his father. The way that enabled him to control the pace of the boat without even touching an oar. Without those around you ever knowing.

No. Neither he nor Mariko had ever been gifted at that. Mariko was far too direct. And he was far too uninterested.

Today Kenshin planned to leave Inako. To return home.

A failure once more. In his eyes. And the eyes of his father.

But he would first revisit the forest and stop to question

the elderly man at the watering hole again. He was lying, and Kenshin no longer had any tolerance for deception. He'd dealt with pretense too often of late.

In an imperial city rife with it.

Kenshin stood beside the curved railing of an arched bridge in the first *maru* of Heian Castle. The glossy finish of the balustrade was red—smooth and cool beneath his touch.

At his back, crisp footsteps drew close. "I hear you are leaving." Roku spoke to him in a measured, lyrical voice. As though he wished to emulate a bird in song.

Kenshin turned to bow. "I have no interest in dallying in Inako any further, Your Highness."

"But you did not find what you were looking for." As usual, Minamoto Roku did not ask questions. He pried in other, far more insidious ways.

In response, Kenshin said nothing. Hoped his face did not disclose anything of value.

"I wish to help you, Hattori Kenshin." Roku's smile formed slowly. Too slowly to be real. "Though my brother has yet to admit it—even to himself—I know he is quite troubled by the death of your sister."

"I do not believe Mariko to be dead, Your Highness."

"Of course." Roku nodded. "I've since learned why those men attacked us at the teahouse."

Kenshin waited, not wanting to ask. Not wanting to be beholden to the crown prince on any score.

"It's information I think you would be interested to

know," Roku continued, smiling once more. He strolled to Kenshin's side, his hands loosely clasped behind his back. "The whispers among several of the *geiko* there said these men were members of the Black Clan."

Roku's words confirmed Kenshin's earlier suspicions. The Dragon of Kai gripped the red balustrade tight. Countless tales surrounded the Black Clan. Tales that had twisted into lore. Ones linking them to exiled *rōnin*. Of murderous men who drank the blood of their victims, leaving their bodies to rot in the shade of skeletal trees. Stories Kenshin had never given a moment's consideration before. He had known the Black Clan frequented certain parts of Jukai forest, but Kenshin had dismissed earlier suggestions that these men had had anything to do with the attack on Mariko's convoy. If the same lore was to be believed, the Black Clan was not disorganized enough to allow a survivor to escape. Mercenaries as celebrated as they did not maintain their livelihoods by allowing their marks to point fingers their way. Besides that, Kenshin had never known them to attack convoys guarded by samurai.

And he'd never heard of the Black Clan murdering young women before. Innocent girls like Mariko's maidservant. It had been a chief reason Kenshin had removed them from consideration at the onset.

In his mind, there were only two reasons for the Black Clan to murder Mariko. One involved a great deal of money. The kind of money linked to those in the nobility.

The other reason involved hatred.

"Permit me to speak frankly, Your Highness," Kenshin began. "I fail to see why this information would be of value to me. Beyond rumor, I have found little evidence to suggest the Black Clan could be responsible for the attack on my sister's convoy."

"Ah"—Roku angled his body, the smooth skin of his face all but unreadable—"but it should be of value to you, Kenshin-*sama*. And there is most definitely evidence."

A part of Kenshin wished to strike Roku across the face. As soon as he realized this truth, Kenshin recoiled from it. These were not the thoughts of a samurai in loyal service to his liege lord. One day Roku would be his emperor. One day Kenshin would be honored to die at this boy's command.

Roku's eyes drifted across the serene waters of the pond. "Have you heard what happened to the last shōgun of the empire?"

"He was accused of treason and committed seppuku."

Roku paused. "It appears a mistake was made in the process."

"A mistake?"

"The traitor Takeda Shingen was executed ten years ago, after being accused by one of his dearest friends, Asano Naganori. The mistake made at the time was that my father allowed Takeda Shingen's son to live. He was only eight when he watched his father die. I believe the emperor did not wish to have the blood of his traitorous friend's son on his hands."

"Forgive the impudence, Your Highness, but I am struggling to understand why this information is of value to my search for Mariko."

Another slow smile, sinister in its bent. "The leader of the Black Clan is Takeda Shingen's son. And I believe they murdered your sister in revenge."

Kenshin blanched in shock. "Revenge? Why would they wish revenge on my family?"

"Your misinterpretation is quite understandable. The son of Takeda Ranmaru wishes revenge on *my* family. Murdering your sister is only the beginning."

"Mariko is not—"

"Of course. She is not dead." Roku waved a dismissive hand, then faced the water once more. "But if she lives, I believe the Black Clan knows where she is. And I would urge you to be wary, Kenshin-*sama*, as it is clear—following the events of that night in Hanami—that a target has been painted on your back as well."

Silence settled between them. Kenshin did not know what to believe anymore.

But he would most certainly find out the truth.

———

From a distance, the Emperor of Wa watched the crown prince speak with the Dragon of Kai. He saw the son of Hattori Kano frown repeatedly. Saw his back straighten with unmistakable purpose.

The web had been spun. Now the spider would wait for its prey to make a fatal mistake.

The emperor smiled to himself.

Roku would make a fine emperor indeed.

Beside him, Kanako toyed with the hundred-year-old carp swimming just beneath the surface of the water, angling for its next meal. She drew it closer, capturing its attention by catching rays of sunlight in the ring she always wore on her left hand. At first glance, the ring was nothing remarkable. Upon further study, a casual observer would note how the stone in its center appeared rather strange. The color within it looked and moved almost like liquid silver. But that was all a casual observer would ever see.

Because when anyone stared at the ring for too long, a cloud of pure white fell across his vision. The observer would need to blink hard. Shake his head.

And forget what he was even looking at in the first place.

Kanako ran her right hand over the ring. The prongs holding the stone in place lengthened. Melted from metal into something much more pliant. Then turned darker. The liquid silver stone formed a spherical body, rising from her finger and scuttling to her nail's edge.

A silver spider—fashioned from the ensorcelled stone—descended from the tip of Kanako's slender finger into the water, its silk a gold glint, refracting the sun's warm rays. The carp remained below the surface, mesmerized, as the spider's legs touched the carp's lips.

Kanako closed her hand into a tight fist.

The spider disappeared.

She walked away.

When the emperor looked down, he saw the body of the motionless carp float beneath the bridge.

And vanish into the waters of the pond.

foxglove

——✳——

The forest smelled of citrus and cedar. In that way of mist and rain.

A late spring shower had livened the air. Sweetening it. Blurring the lines while bringing all else into sharper focus. The rumble of low thunder. The rich green of the leaves. Mariko's feet sloshing through a cool puddle.

It made her want to stick out her tongue and catch raindrops on its tip.

But a boy would never do that.

Would he?

Kenshin had never done that. At least not to her recollection.

Instead Mariko continued trudging along the narrow footpath cut beneath the jagged outcropping of cliffs. Ahead were the hot springs. If she finished her task early enough, perhaps she could sneak in another bath.

At Yoshi's behest, Mariko had spent the last half hour collecting a certain kind of mushroom that sprang to life only when it rained. The cook had told her she would have the most success finding these particular mushrooms around the hot springs, and Mariko had happily left in the late afternoon to oblige. Only recently had she been freed from the constant companionship of her tormenter, Ren, and now was the perfect chance for her to revel in her newfound freedom.

As Mariko hunted through the underbrush—searching for a creamy white stalk and a smooth brown cap—another plant caught her attention from the cliff above. Tiny, vivid purple blossoms, suspended from their stems like bells.

Foxglove.

Mariko remembered her tutor mentioning it once.

The plant was poisonous. When prepared properly, a tea brewed from its petals could slow a person's heart to the point of death.

Her lips pursing in contemplation, Mariko set down her basket of mushrooms and circled the base of the cliff. When she turned the corner and glanced up, she discovered a large gathering of deep purple blossoms, suspended right above the hot springs. The foxglove had apparently burst to life after the rain, many of them still mere buds awaiting their moment to open.

I should collect the flowers. Save them for when I might have an opportunity to use them.

Again Mariko recalled her tutor's teachings. Foxglove had

more than one purpose. She briefly recollected watching her tutor experiment with the stem and seeds of the plant. He'd reduced them to a paste. Then touched the paste with the end of a lighted stick. It had flashed hot and bright—causing Kenshin's face to startle and Mariko's eyes to widen—before burning white and disappearing in a smokeless flame.

That day, their tutor had warned Mariko and Kenshin about the many perils of foxglove.

A plant that could kill in several different ways.

Mariko scanned the cliffs for a time, putting together a plan.

She huffed loudly. There was nothing to be done for it. If Mariko wished to collect the foxglove, she would have to scale the cliffs. She wiped her damp hands on her rain-soaked *kosode*—an exercise in futility—and reached for the nearest handhold to her right.

The surface of the stone was slick. As soon as she braced one foot along a ledge to heave herself up, her foot slid off. With a sigh, Mariko removed her sandals and split-toed socks, knowing her bare feet would offer better traction.

She began working her way up the cliff face to the particular outcropping littered with the most flowers. The bell-like purple blossoms trembled beneath another smattering of soft rain. Below her, steam rose from the hot springs, curling into her face and obscuring her vision. Once Mariko had made her way far enough upward, she began moving sideways, hand over hand, foot over foot.

Soon she found herself stuck a mere body's length from the outcropping of flowers. She reached above and could not find a suitable handhold. Then she reached to one side and her fingers—damp with rainwater—slid from their perch.

Mildly alarmed at her predicament, she toed her way to the opposite side, seeking purchase.

And slipped.

With a screeching cry, Mariko plummeted through the air.

Into the steaming waters of the hot springs.

The instant she landed, all the air was knocked from her chest. Reflexively, Mariko gasped.

And swallowed a mouthful of hot water before passing out.

———————

With a bemused expression, Ōkami had watched Sanada Takeo begin his climb up the mountain face.

Why was the idiot climbing upward when there were plenty of mushrooms to be had on the forest floor? It was only when Ōkami saw Takeo reach for the purple blossoms that he even began to understand.

That little fool hoped to poison someone with foxglove.

Ōkami crossed his arms.

Someone? The fool's intended victim was likely Ōkami himself. Not that Ōkami blamed him. Were he in a similar situation, Ōkami would draw the same conclusion. At the moment, Sanada Takeo would be hard-pressed to find a bigger threat than he, even in a camp full of murderers and thieves. After all, no one else save Ōkami harbored such suspicions against the Black Clan's newest recruit. Nor did they make the effort to spy on him.

Ōkami snorted to himself as he continued watching Sanada Takeo struggle to find a foothold. As though anyone would not recognize foxglove the instant the little shit tried to bring it into camp! Yoshi would smell the green-scented blossoms from a league away.

When Takeo began to slip, Ōkami was not the least bit surprised.

A fool's errand often resulted in a fool's fate.

He'd wait for the boy to fall, then take him to task. Takeo had climbed high, but it was not high enough for it to kill him. Ōkami watched, unmoved, as the boy struggled. Lost all footing. Predictably fell.

It was the sound of Takeo's scream that tore Ōkami from his silent amusement.

It sliced through him.

The sound of Sanada Takeo's scream.

Ōkami was already racing from behind the tree when the boy plunged into the hot springs.

And failed to surface.

———

Mariko coughed loudly. Wretchedly.

Warm water spilled from her mouth as she was turned onto her side. Her vision blurred, then focused.

Ōkami hovered above her, his eyes wide.

Mariko stared up at him. Their chests heaved in unison.

Water dripped from Ōkami's unbound hair into her face. He was gaping down at her, incredulous.

One of his hands rested on the center of Mariko's chest.

Her *kosode* had been ripped open, the muslin bindings across her breasts bared for all the world to see.

An array of emotions passed across Ōkami's face. Shock. Anger. Bewilderment.

Mariko had never thought she'd see so many naked feelings cross his finely chiseled face. The dark centers of his eyes had grown. Now they glistened through the swirling steam like black ice on a mountaintop.

He knows I'm a girl.

"You . . . saved me," Mariko sputtered lamely, trying in vain to keep him from speaking. Keep him from saying anything that might cause her trouble of any kind. Even she knew how ridiculous the words sounded as she said them. How obvious.

"You . . . *liar.*" A mirthless smile began to take shape on Ōkami's mouth. A smile savage in its beauty. A smile that clearly tried to mask the emotions of only a moment before.

His hand still had not left her chest. It stayed there, solid and steady. Unmoving.

Before Mariko could think—before Ōkami's cold smile could fully form—she grasped him by the neck and pulled him toward her.

Her lips crashed into his. Warm water sluiced across her skin.

He tasted like rain and fresh mint.

And—for a breath of time—Mariko's mind was silenced. In that single moment, there was nothing to consider. Nothing to contend with.

Nothing but a stolen kiss beneath a stormy sky.

Ōkami pulled away. "What the hell are you doing?" His words were an outraged rasp. He looked defiant.

But Mariko knew better.

Before his mind had spoken, the Wolf had kissed her back.

"I want you to stop talking," Mariko said. Only honesty would do at a time like this. "Don't you want to stop talking?" She tried to speak over the ragged pounding of her pulse. "Or perhaps not. Tell me—right now—what do *you* want, Asano Tsuneoki?"

He stared down at her. Though the color of his eyes nearly matched their centers, Mariko watched the lines between them blur. Another flurry of emotions passed across Ōkami's face. Confusion. Trepidation. Uncertainty.

But Mariko did not miss that first thought. That first emotion.

Desire.

"Do you feel ridiculous now?" she whispered.

Mariko was met with a trace of humor and a silent challenge.

She responded by stealing another kiss.

Ōkami's hand still rested between them, his long, strong fingers pressed against her skin. And when that hand slid to her neck—when he fitted himself to her and closed his eyes, settling into the kiss—Mariko did not want to let go. Ever.

It was a mistake. All of it. For as long as she'd known him, Mariko had despised the very idea of this boy.

But the truth of him?

The truth was not quite as simple. It was a silent entreaty. A wordless plea.

Don't stop.

Ōkami rolled onto his back, positioning her above him. He braced her chin in one hand, his lips traveling down her neck. To her bared shoulder. Back up to her ear.

Don't stop.

The rain battered down around her. Her heart slammed against her chest. Mariko finally closed her eyes, no longer caring about anything else but the feel of him. His hands at her back. His kisses across her skin. The stars could fall— the moon could crash from the heavens—and Mariko would not care.

When Ōkami broke away, his breath spilled from his lips in jagged slivers.

"Don't stop," she said without thinking.

His response was a wicked smile. Wordlessly, Ōkami rolled again, pinning her beneath his mouth, covering her with his body. He slid lower. Watched her face as he blew a cool stream of air across her bare stomach. A thread of molten amber raced down her spine.

When Mariko trembled—sparks dancing across her skin—Ōkami laughed softly.

Then he kissed her again, and it was a controlled fire on her tongue. The type that threatened to burn into a crashing, thrashing ache. The type of kiss—the type of boy—Mariko had thought to avoid at all cost. The unpredictable type. The dangerous type.

Her hands slid inside his soaked *kosode* to his chest. To feel the rise and fall of smooth muscle beneath her fingertips.

"Who are you?" Ōkami demanded in her ear.

Fitting how the Wolf could speak in such a cold and exacting voice. Yet kiss as he did.

With such abandon.

Mariko knew Ōkami heard each beat of her heart. Felt each of them as she did.

"I'll tell you if you tell me," she said, her words as bated as his.

"You'll lie."

She nodded. "Then we can both be liars." Mariko waited for Ōkami to decide. For him to make the decision to fight back. Or leave the truth alone.

For now.

With a blistering look, Ōkami yanked her topknot free of its bindings. Then he kissed her beneath the chin, so softly, so gently, that it made her gasp. Made him laugh again under his breath. Made her realize that nothing was in her control.

That everything was in her control.

She tangled her fingers in his hair as their lips met. As their kiss deepened. In that moment, Mariko wanted to believe Ōkami would not tell.

At least for now.

They lay beside each other in silence, staring up at the newly uncovered stars.

Close enough to touch but fathoms apart.

Her heart had only just ceased pounding. Her breath had only just settled. All that passed between them were lingering traces of feeling.

Nothing of substance.

Ōkami was stretched out beside Mariko, offering half a smile to no one. As though he was both amused and at war with himself all at once.

"Ōkami—"

"What is your name?" he asked pointedly. "Your real name."

Mariko thought for an instant. Trust was not an option. Not when so much still depended on maintaining secrecy. "Chiyo."

He inhaled, the sound laced with irritation. "You're lying. Again."

"I am not lying, I—"

Ōkami turned toward her, his eyes locking on hers. "Don't draw a line. Unless you wish for me to cross it."

"Well then, don't cross it." Mariko's voice was even, though her pulse skipped.

"You know me well enough to know that is not an option."

An uncomfortable silence stretched between them.

Mariko did know him well enough to know that. Yet she still knew nothing about him. And she wished she could ask him something of note. But—as usual—the Wolf had made it impossible, using only a few simple words. And it only made her want to draw that line and push him past it.

But it was far too risky. Not when he held her secret in his grasp. And not when she'd foolishly entrusted him with a piece of her heart, if only for a moment.

As if in reminder of that fact, Mariko's chest hollowed. She had to redeem herself for such reckless behavior. Behavior so unlike her. These stolen kisses beside these hot springs would have lasting value if she could learn something that served her greater cause. After all—even if Ōkami brought out a wild, uncontrolled part of herself Mariko had not even known existed before—he was still a member of the Black Clan.

Engender trust.

Strike when they least expect it.

"What should we do about . . . this?" she asked in a simple tone. Detached. Much like his typical demeanor. A tone that did not match the sentiments swirling within. One she hoped would prod him to reveal something—anything—of value.

Ōkami looked back toward the night sky. *"Ichi-go, ichi-e."*

Mariko took a deep breath. "For this time only."

He nodded.

"I don't believe that's the intended meaning behind it," she said flatly.

"It's the meaning I give it. Each breath exists for that one moment only. We live for that one moment only."

She paused. "Is that how you wish to live your life? From

moment to moment, without a care for the past or for the future?"

"It's how I live my life now."

"Is that why you choose to follow, instead of to lead?" Here was a chance for her to learn about Ōkami's past. Perhaps even about the source of his powers.

"I have no interest in leading."

"You are a warrior gifted with unique abilities. Does that not give you a certain responsibility?"

"I do not have the gift—or the willingness—to inspire. In battle, my only responsibility is to be the sword. The axe. The fist."

Though Mariko tried to harness the sentiment, disappointment settled across her features.

Ōkami glanced her way. "Don't have expectations of me. Don't look at me and think you should be seeing something else."

"I've never looked at you and expected anything."

"Liar. You see me. Just as I see you."

"You see nothing," Mariko grumbled.

"I see you," he said softly. "Exactly as you are."

The air between them filled with all that remained unsaid. All that should be said.

Yet wasn't.

Worry spiked through Mariko's core, its point all too sharp. "What if—"

"Don't." Ōkami stood without making a sound. "Don't ask me questions to which you don't want the answers."

Mariko watched as he tied his black *kosode* shut.

"I'll keep your secret for now," he said.

"Why would you do that?" She had to ask. Though she cursed herself for uttering the words.

"Because if I don't, there are many who will not hesitate to kill you."

It wasn't a real answer, yet Mariko knew it was foolish to press beyond this.

Ōkami continued. "But I won't call you Chiyo, because that is not your name. And if you ever betray us, I will not stop Ranmaru from exacting his revenge." He paused. "I am not a hero. Don't forget it for a moment. I will not save you again."

Mariko sat up abruptly, her features defiant. "I don't want you to be a hero. And I don't need anyone to save me."

"Good." Ōkami walked away, his steps almost halting. Not nearly as graceful as Mariko had come to expect.

As she watched him fade into the darkness, Mariko found she did not know how to feel. She wasn't sure if she'd kissed Ōkami to keep him silent. Or if she'd kissed him because there was nothing else to be done. Nothing else to do but succumb. All those times she'd hated him. All those times her heart had jolted in his presence.

Did she truly despise him?

Or did she desire him?

Mariko lay beneath the stars for a time. Then came to a decision.

She did not truly care about Ōkami. She was merely using him. Mariko was here on a mission. Here to discover why the Black Clan had tried to kill her. To discover who wanted her dead. And nothing—not even a boy who could kiss her senseless, could kiss her mind into silence—would ever change that.

For this time only.

Ōkami was right.

Tomorrow she would forget this had ever happened.

A Lesson to Be Learned

It had been a long time since Ōkami had outright lied to his best friend.

He'd had no occasion to deceive the leader of the Black Clan. Not in many years.

Ōkami owed him too much to lie to his face. Owed him far too much to ever hide behind the ease of a lie. It wasn't that Ōkami was averse to lying. He lied quite frequently. And with relish.

Often he lied about things that did not matter, merely for the sake of practicing the skill. After all, when one lived a lie, it became important to continue honing the art of deception whenever possible.

But this was a unique situation.

Ōkami knew he should say something soon about—Takeo. Or Chiyo.

Or whatever the hell the girl chose to call herself on any given day.

Chiyo was not her real name. That much Ōkami knew for certain. A gifted liar learned to recognize the skill in others. That night, she'd said "Chiyo" too carefully. With too much thought behind it. A name was something simple. Easy. It should roll off the tongue like unabashed laughter.

Not with such clear calculation behind it.

She'd lied to him. As he'd lied to her.

Never mind that she'd purported to save his life. Twice. Why the girl had done so, Ōkami could not begin to understand. It was clear she'd disliked him at the onset. Found him lazy and trifling.

Just as he wished for others to find him.

But perhaps . . . perhaps her hatred masked an emotion far more troubling than mere dislike. The same emotion Ōkami had struggled to contend with these past few weeks. Struggled to identify, especially as they'd argued with each other. Contended with each other over matters both large and small.

Attraction.

No. *Want*.

Alas, *want* was a weak word for what he now felt.

Perhaps the girl wasn't water, as he'd first thought. Perhaps she was wind. Wind could whip a fire into a frenzy. Make a mighty oak bow. Lash water into mist.

Though he hadn't cared to admit it—even to himself— Ōkami had known something was wrong the first time he'd looked into Sanada Takeo's eyes. The first time he'd touched . . . her.

It wasn't that it was wrong.

It was that it felt strangely right.

And now?

He didn't know for certain what had driven him to promise the girl who lied as freely as she breathed that he would keep her secret. All Ōkami knew was that she fought back— with both words and a strength of conviction—as no girl ever had in his experience. That she saw through his many masks in a way that both unnerved and enchanted him. That her mind worked in a way Ōkami could not take apart and piece back together.

That the moment she'd kissed him by the hot springs, his sight had gone liquid. And that the sound of her sigh was like a sunrise.

The memory thickened his blood. Left him on edge.

Ōkami watched his reflection ripple across the surface of the lake. He looked drawn. Haggard. As a boy, he'd experienced nightmares often. A sleep disturbed by thoughts of anger and retribution. Remembrances of shame and scars of dishonor.

Then, as he'd grown from boyhood into a young man, Ōkami had made a choice.

He would not be burdened by these things any longer. Refused to be burdened by any responsibility he did not elect to take on himself. Since then, he'd thankfully chosen to take on very little.

The fewer obligations he had, the less likely he'd be to fail anyone.

Once Ōkami had made this decision, sleep came to him much more easily.

It had been a long time since he'd had a poor night's sleep. A long time since he'd seen a face marred by exhaustion when he took in his reflection.

Last night had been a bad night.

A night filled with uncertainty.

Ōkami had dreamed of a lagoon filled to its brim with steaming water. Then it had started to drain. Slowly. A churning whirlpool had formed in its center.

The girl's face had drifted past him as she'd glided through the swirling mist.

She'd wandered to the edge of the lagoon. Smiled at him over her shoulder. Beckoned for him to join her. When Ōkami had moved to her side—drawn as a dragonfly to a flame—she'd reached for him. Stepped into the lagoon.

And let the whirlpool swallow her whole.

The entire time she'd watched him—waited for him to join her, even in death—her features had remained serene. A flame in the mist.

Ōkami had stood immobile. Witnessing as the water dragged her under.

Doing nothing.

Even in his dreams, he'd remembered how she smelled.

Clean. Like orange blossoms.

He recalled how she smiled. How her lips would waver at

first, as though she still had not decided whether or not it was wise to show her true feelings to anyone.

Despite everything, Ōkami had admired Sanada Takeo for this. When he'd thought her to be a boy, Ōkami had appreciated how poorly she'd hidden her emotions—how inept she seemed at keeping them in check—despite the fact that the girl clearly knew how to tell a lie.

It reminded him of the small, angry boy he'd been in his past.

A boy who didn't mind lying to others. But despised lying to himself.

Ōkami frowned again at his reflection in the water. Shoved his hands beneath it, splintering the image. He washed his face. Let the water rinse away his memories. Cleanse him of all responsibility.

He was not lying to himself. He did not care about the girl. Ōkami could not afford to care about her. She was trouble, even if she was smart. Even if there was something awkwardly fearless about her.

She was nothing to him. Even though he should have asked her why she'd dressed as a boy. Should have let her know how curious he was about her. How much he wished to know all that passed through her clever mind.

But he would not answer her questions. So he had no right to ask his.

For this one day, Ōkami would not tell anyone about her.

This one day only, he would lie to his best friend.

For this time only.

"I think it's time Sanada Takeo learned how to wield a *katana*. And I think you should be the one to teach him," Ranmaru announced the instant Ōkami entered his tent that morning.

Ōkami's resulting hesitation spoke volumes. "I don't use swords." The Wolf pronounced the words carefully, each one bound in an underlying threat.

Tread no further.

Ranmaru grinned, his expression unaffected, even when met with signs of Ōkami's cool fury. "I think it's time for you to change that." His response was equally underscored with a trace of menace.

Might had to be met with might. Especially on the field of battle.

"With all due respect, I don't really care what you think." Ōkami turned to leave.

Ranmaru stepped into his path, his hands raised in peace. "I understand. It isn't necessary for you to wield swords in battle." His lips thinned into a hard line. "But it *is* important that you not forget from where it is you came."

Ōkami remained stubbornly silent.

The leader of the Black Clan tried a different tack. "Your father was—"

"I know who my father was."

"Good," Ranmaru said quietly. "And you know who my father was."

"I never forget. Not a single day of my life do I forget who your father was."

Hurt flashed across Ranmaru's eyes. It would be different if Ōkami made clear how angry he still was. Showed Ranmaru the pain that shaped his fury instead of rejecting its existence.

But perhaps it was time for them to overcome the mistakes of their pasts. The mistakes of those in their pasts. Ranmaru's anger had long since passed. But Ōkami's?

It was difficult to move past an emotion so long denied.

"Nevertheless . . ." Ranmaru stepped closer. Close enough to make any other man uncomfortable. It was a tactic Ranmaru had learned from Ōkami when they were younger. *Stand in another man's space and watch him squirm.* Ranmaru watched now as the tactic nearly worked on his friend. The Wolf almost stepped back in response. Then Ōkami cut his gaze. And stood firm.

"Nevertheless," Ranmaru said again, "starting today, you will spend two afternoons this week teaching Sanada Takeo how to fight with a sword. It doesn't matter which sword. A *katana*, a *wakizashi*, a *tantō* . . ." He moved his hand in a circle meant to encourage. "All that matters is whether or not the boy can hold his own in a basic fight. If Takeo is to be our newest recruit, he must at least know how to wield a blade."

Ōkami opened his mouth, a slow, cutting retort building, ready to barrel forth.

Ranmaru braced for it. Welcomed it.

There were times when even a howling wolf needed to be silenced.

Then Ōkami closed his mouth without uttering a single

word. He inhaled slowly through his nose. "Fine." His shoulders relaxed. "It won't make any difference anyway. When the boy dies during his first fight, don't blame me."

"At that point, it wouldn't make a difference if I did."

Ōkami snorted. Once more glib and unaffected. "It makes no difference to me anyway." With that, he shouldered past Ranmaru, back into the morning sun.

Ranmaru shook his head.

One day, these lies were going to catch up with his friend.

On that day, Ranmaru hoped he was there to bear witness.

Mariko thought he was joking with her.

Or just wanting to watch her fidget, in that way Ōkami liked to watch anyone fidget when faced with his mocking stare.

"Well," he demanded, "why are you just standing there?"

"I don't know what you want me to do," she shot back. "How you want me—to stand." Her voice trailed off.

Mariko swore she saw the muscles in his jaw leap at that. Then Ōkami cleared his throat. He strode closer, using the tips of two wooden practice swords to tap her legs until she shifted her feet into the right position for sparring. If Mariko hadn't known any better, she'd have thought Ōkami was trying not to touch her. As though she'd been marked by a demon. Or kissed by a plague.

If he is avoiding me, then perhaps I can use it to my advantage.

Ōkami is not the only one who likes to make people uncomfortable.

When the Wolf had glided toward her that morning and ordered her to follow him, Mariko had hated the way her heart had responded, jumping from her chest as though it wished to meet him halfway.

Her stupid heart. It was time she taught it a lesson. Taught it to stay at heel. Here was a chance to get her own back somehow.

If Ōkami was mad at her, then she was mad at him, too.

The next time he thwacked the back of her knee and told her to root herself better, Mariko intentionally crumpled into him. Ōkami jumped back, as though a tendril of fire had leapt his way. She straightened, then smirked at him. He blinked. For an instant, Mariko thought he might smile.

"Do that again," he said in a dangerous whisper. "See what happens."

"Is that a threat or a promise?"

That time, he did smile. But just barely. Then Ōkami stepped an arm's length away. Without warning, he tossed the wooden sword in her direction. Mariko caught it. But just barely.

The practice sword was heavy, its blade fashioned of solid wood. Made to model the weight of an actual *katana*. Its surface was smooth, meant to take on the full blow of an opponent's strike.

Mariko brandished the weapon, hoping she didn't look quite as green as she felt. "Should I not be practicing with a real blade instead of one intended for a child?"

"This is the type of sword we all use when we are not in battle. It is not just for a child."

She held the blade in the air with one hand as her eyes ran the length of him. "You don't want to do this."

"A master of the obvious." He snorted. "Truly I'd rather chew sand." Ōkami walked to her side, his practice sword dangling from his fingertips. "Use both hands. Who do you think you are? Musashi?"

Mariko ignored the jibe about the famed swordsman. "Why are you doing this if you don't want to?"

"Because if I don't, Ranmaru will wonder why. And I don't think it serves you well if his curiosity spurs him to take action," Ōkami finished, his voice low and harsh.

When he leaned forward to adjust the grip of her left hand, his hair fell into his eyes, brushing her brow. A part of her wanted to hold her breath.

Mariko revolted by inhaling deep.

Stupid. So stupid. Wolves were not supposed to smell like Ōkami did. Like warm stone and wood smoke.

"What are you doing?" he asked cuttingly, though his hands wavered above hers. "Stop being so strange."

Mariko settled into her stance. "I *am* strange." She brandished her practice sword. "And you had better learn to appreciate it."

———

Ōkami was in hell.

The first chance he had, he was going to attack his best

friend and leave him for dead. It was only fair after all. Ōkami would rot in hell before he admitted to anyone that he'd been rendered a fool.

Each time Ōkami was forced to touch her, he tallied another way he would make the leader of the Black Clan pay.

"Stop!" he barked. Truly this girl brought out the worst in him. Made him lose the control he prided himself in having at all times. "You're still not holding the blade correctly. Each time you swing it, your hands group closer together. Keep an invisible palm between them, or you'll lose control of the blade entirely."

Fitting that Ōkami was lecturing her on losing control.

She gritted her teeth, her deep brown eyes flashing at him like unfaceted jewels. Her fingers wrapped tighter around the handle. She raised the blade above her head once more.

"Strike," he ordered.

She brought it down, and Ōkami knocked it from her grasp with punishing precision.

"Pick it up," he said, swinging his own blade in a lazy arc.

Her pursed lips reminded him of rosebuds. Not red. Nothing loud and obvious. But blushing pink. Subtle and warm. Just like the way she smelled. As if the color of gold had a scent.

Anger rippled down his throat. If he wasn't more mindful of his thoughts, this girl would inevitably bring about the death of Takeda Ranmaru.

Ōkami inhaled. Exhaled. Tried to speak gently. "Again. This time, keep the blade steady. Move slower. More deliberately."

He demonstrated, the wooden sword cutting through the air in a rush of sound. The movement felt good. Though Ōkami hated using a *katana*—as it brought to mind memories he'd sooner forget—he had to admit he'd missed the feel of the weapon in his hands.

After she repeated the motion ten more times, she eyed him sidelong.

"How many times should I do this?" she asked.

"Until I think you've done it right."

She chewed the inside of her cheek. "Am I not going to learn how to fight?"

"First learn how to hold a sword. If a *katana* is an extension of your arms, your arms are currently broken. Would you encourage a man to fight with broken arms?"

Her eyes shot heavenward. "Why do you not carry any blades?"

"Because I prefer not to carry any."

"You're quite rigid, you know."

Ōkami almost laughed. "And you are not?"

"Have you forgotten already, honored sensei? My arms are broken."

That time, he did laugh.

She wavered for a moment, clearly deliberating her next question. "I've been told a samurai's sword is his soul." Her blade moved into position above her head, ready to practice once more.

A sneer curled the corners of Ōkami's lips. "Only if you

are fool enough to follow the way of the warrior would you ever say something so ridiculous."

"*Bushidō* is about experiencing life in every breath. Seeing life in the simplest of things. There is beauty and honor in that. You yourself said as much."

"If I were you, I wouldn't put too much stock in what I say." Ōkami struck her sword again. This time she managed to keep it in her grasp. "When I fight, I wear a mask. There is no honor in that. And I'm glad of it."

"I think you're lying," she muttered. "And—despite what you may think—I do put stock in what you say. One day I hope to say something that stays with you." She angled her chin.

Ōkami swallowed. This girl unnerved him in a way he could not begin to fathom. He needed to end this exchange. Immediately. "Words are foolish. Promises are useless. Anyone can say anything to get what it is they desire. Believe in actions and actions alone."

"You've said this to me before," she replied softly. "And I still don't believe you are right."

He whipped his practice sword toward her. On instinct, she parried the blow. Ōkami could not hide his surprise at how quickly she learned. Most men he knew did not understand the push and pull of swordplay so readily.

He nodded in approval. "Well done. Don't let it go to your head, though."

She smiled. "My father taught me the touch of true strength

is as light as a feather." With a slight swagger, she brandished her sword, eyeing him with noticeable circumspection. "He also said the deeper you dig, the higher the walls around you become."

"Your father read too many books."

She laughed, and the sound warmed through him. Just like a sunrise.

Without thought, Ōkami moved closer, reaching for her elbows, intent on drawing them toward her center. Giving her better control of the blade. His right foot slid in the space between her feet, his knee grazing her inner thigh.

The instant it happened, Ōkami knew it was a mistake. The sharp intake of her breath. The darting eyes.

His thundering heart.

"You haven't told me not to do this," she said softly, a becoming flush rising in her cheeks. "Nor have you asked me why I'm here."

Against his better judgment, Ōkami replied, "Why would I?"

"Because I'm a girl," she whispered.

Irritation took root in his chest. Not irritation with her words. But irritation with her need to say them and what it meant. Ōkami steadied his gaze on hers. "You are first and foremost a person. A reckless, foolish person, but a person nonetheless. If I ever say you are not permitted to do something, rest assured that the last reason I would ever say so would be because you are a girl."

When her eyes softened, Ōkami knew he'd made another mistake.

But he didn't want to take back his words.

She was without a doubt strange. Maddening. A force to reckon and be reckoned with. And—as she'd demanded of him earlier—he appreciated it.

In that moment, Ōkami knew he was in a great deal of trouble.

All because of a wonderfully strange girl.

A Forest of Blood and Fire

———✳———

Kenshin gasped awake. His chest heaved as he struggled to draw in breath. The ground beneath him was wet, the grass by his fingertips charred. Copper and ash coated his tongue.

He sat up and gripped his throbbing head. When he gazed down at his fingers, he saw they were covered in dried blood. Fear coiled up his spine.

He looked around.

The blood was not his.

No. This was not possible. This could not have happened. He could not have—would *never* have—done such a thing.

Kenshin tried to conjure an image of the last thing he could recall.

Shouts. An angry exchange of words. A refusal to cooperate. Threats blasted both ways. Flashes of blood and smoke and fire, their sources hazy and unclear.

Anger. An uncontrollable rage erupting from his chest, spilling from his lips, whipping into the air around him.

His chest heaved again. Kenshin staggered to his feet, dragging his blade through the charred remains of what was once tall grass along the forest's edge. The kind of tall slender grass that had bent and swayed in the wind. Kane waited in the same place Kenshin had last left him, the warhorse still tethered to a tree trunk at the outskirts of the clearing. Without even bothering to wipe the crimson stains from his *katana*, Kenshin sheathed his sword and heaved himself into the saddle.

His head felt as though it had been split in two and sewn back together. Again Kenshin lifted his hands before his face.

Not his blood. But still his pain.

He did not understand what had happened. Could not understand what might have caused anyone to commit such atrocities. The echo of a scream filled his ears, silencing all else. Except the promise of future torment.

Kenshin squeezed his eyes shut.

It was not him. He had not done that.

He would never do that.

In the shadow of a thorny underbrush nearby, a ghostly grey fox watched Hattori Kenshin reel to his horse. Watched him stare in horror at his bloodied hands.

The fox smiled like a rogue, its eyes warming to yellow, then fading to black. It waited until the Dragon of Kai rode from the clearing.

Then it vanished in a twist of smoke.

In its wake, a black flower blossomed to life, its center pulsing with the beat of a heart.

Drumming out a warning.

Or perhaps a message.

A Murderous Rampage

———✳———

It turned out that Ren—her first and finest tormentor—
was also perhaps one of the finest singers Mariko had ever
encountered in her life.

She'd only discovered this truth in the last few moments.
And it had shocked her. Forced her to appreciate the many
quiddities of life. While riding with the Black Clan toward
the watering hole in which Mariko had first encountered
them, Haruki the metalsmith had begun to sing. In vain
she'd wished to join in—especially since this was the first
time in the three weeks she'd been in their camp that they'd
brought her with them to the watering hole. On several
occasions many of them had left together at night, returning
ribald and robust with drink.

Reminding Mariko of her place, which was always
removed.

Until today.

Haruki's song was a sweet song, with the easy kind of verses that encouraged improvisation. As several of the other members began joining in, the tune became bawdier. Their voices became rowdier.

When Yoshi began to sing of ample bosoms, Mariko quickly urged her steed forward—beyond their earshot—lest the next verse fall to her. She may be pretending to be a young man, but she wasn't quite certain what a young man would most like to sing about when it came to the fairer sex.

Naked women? Certainly.

But what exactly was it about female nakedness that would be attractive? It was just a body. A form. A vessel. Truly it was a puzzle. Breasts were just breasts, were they not? The most fascinating thing about any woman should be her mind, should it not?

Of course not.

Mariko almost groaned when she heard the unmistakable click of Ōkami's tongue at her side. He slowed his warhorse to match the pace of hers. And leaned close.

"Are you not interested in the song, *Takeo*?" he teased. The Wolf looked to be in a fine mood on this late afternoon. Briefly Mariko wondered what his angle might be. What this ploy might cost her.

Then decided it didn't matter.

"I should think you would be far more interested in this sort of song than I, *Tsuneoki*." She grinned.

From the corner of her eye, Mariko caught the curve of his lip. A sly, scarred smile.

"Is that meant to be a testament to my prowess?" Ōkami spoke in low tones, his eyes gleaming. The suggestiveness in his words caused the blood to rise in her neck. Behind them, the sun was starting its slow descent, the darkness reaching for it from beyond the horizon. And Mariko was suddenly reminded. How a night sky darkened words as well. Imbued them with shadowed meaning.

What once was innocent became illicit with nothing but a glance.

The searing warmth of Ōkami's touch that night beside the hot springs. The fire that had burned through her veins.

Mariko shook her head quickly. "It's rather a testament to your ridiculousness."

"Such cruelty." He *tsk*ed. "When all I strive for each day is to convince my shadow I'm someone worth following."

She glanced down at the long, thin silhouette trailing at his back. It looked jagged and uncertain. Appropriate. "Perhaps you should try harder."

"Would it be so hard to say something nice? Just once."

"I shall," she said simply. "After you show me how."

He laughed.

They were far in front of the other men now. Riding side by side.

The *rōnin* and the warrior girl in disguise.

Mariko wanted to hate Ōkami. But the memory of his

hands sifting through her hair. Of the way his eyes turned up when he smiled. The way his entire demeanor softened when he meant it. When he was true.

Ōkami was such an enigma. A boy without honor, who nevertheless did honorable things. Like save Mariko when he could have left her to fend for herself. Or stop to leave money for an elderly woman when he should have been fleeing the imperial city. Like when he kept her secret. Despite the fact that his loyalties remained elsewhere.

Mariko glanced at him furtively. Saw the way his strong fingers lightly grasped the crimson fabric of his reins. Remembered the way his lips shaped his words. Ōkami did everything with the natural grace of a boy absent care. He was not calculating. He was instinctual.

And he really did possess some of the finest hands Mariko had ever seen.

Just as she thought to say something nice—about how well he sat in his saddle—Ōkami cut his warhorse across her path, halting her, his right fist in the air.

The nostrils of his horse flared. Mariko's steed whickered.

Before them was a familiar line of maple trees along the westernmost edge of the forest. The outskirts near the watering hole.

Several wisps of dark smoke curled into the air beyond the tree line. Not the single steady stream they were expecting. Not the smoke from the crumbling chimney of the lean-to. A strange scent suffused the sky.

Burning meat. Mingled with a hint of decay.

"Stay here," Ōkami said harshly, kicking his horse into a gallop.

Without a second thought, Mariko followed after him.

"Stay with the men," he shouted over his shoulder, his brows gathering together.

Anger unfurled in her chest. "You can't possibly be talking to me," she said as she drew alongside him. "Nor can you expect me to follow such an insulting order."

"You idiot," Ōkami said, reining his horse in as they neared the clearing. "I ordered you to stay with Ranmaru because you have a keen eye and a sharp mind."

They stopped at the edge of the clearing, and Mariko's throat caught at the sight.

Akira-*san*'s lean-to was smoldering. As were the rickety tables surrounding it. Across the stretch of cleared land, splatters of blood and patches of scorched earth stained the trampled ground.

A massacre had taken place here.

Several unfortunate patrons were slumped over the tables, long since dead. Some of their bodies had burned in the brushfire.

Ōkami dropped from his saddle. Mariko walked after him, taking stock of their surroundings, even though she could see Ōkami slowly memorizing every detail in sight.

Mariko knew what it looked like to travel alongside a tracker.

If Kenshin were here, he would be doing exactly the same thing.

Beside the smoldering lean-to, they discovered the bodies of the boy and girl who'd served them the last time. The boy had been slashed across his chest. A clean, unbroken line that had nevertheless caused him immense pain. Mariko knew he had not died quickly. The crimson stain circling his body was wide. Dried at the edges. Mercifully the girl had died instantly, a deep wound across her throat.

Mariko and Ōkami paused before the bodies of the girl and the boy, silently grieving their youth. Grieving the loss of life stolen before it could be lived.

A broken voice cut through the silence. A halting cadence crying out into the sky.

"Akira-*san*," Ōkami said as he began moving past the bodies, his steps urgent.

They found the elderly man with the weathered face behind the lean-to. When they saw him lift a trembling hand, they rushed to his side. He'd been stabbed through the stomach. Was slowly bleeding into his body.

A horrifying way to die. A way of pain and suffering.

Blood trickled from one corner of his mouth as he spoke to Ōkami. As he tried in vain to reach for the collar of Ōkami's *kosode* to draw him near.

The Wolf leaned close. "Who was it?" Mariko saw his fists clench.

A low hum rippled from his body.

"S-samurai," Akira-*san* rasped.

In this moment, Mariko realized she had never seen Ōkami truly angry before. Even beside the teahouse that night last week, she'd witnessed a flash of fury, but it was nothing like this. When she'd tried to pry for more information about his powers in those first few days, Yoshi had claimed very little ever warranted the Wolf's wrath.

In order to hate, one must first love, the cook had said.

And Ōkami did not love many things.

Before Akira-*san* could say anything more, Ranmaru came crashing through the burned brush toward them. He skidded to a halt, his face pale. Akira-*san* reached for the leader of the Black Clan, and Ranmaru flew to the old man's side, clasping his bloodied hand tight.

Akira-*san*'s eyes traveled to Mariko. They narrowed. His breaths were becoming shallow and fast.

"Find . . . find the d-dragon," he said haltingly.

Mariko's pulse came to a sudden standstill. An icy vise gripped her chest. Tore through the bindings wound about her breastbone.

"The dragon?" Ranmaru asked.

"Find the Dragon . . . of Kai." He coughed, lines of crimson spurting from his lips. Then he raised a trembling finger, as though he meant to point at something.

Or someone.

Mariko could not hear over the sound of her heart's screams.

It's not possible. This isn't possible.

Akira-*san*'s hand fell as his eyes drifted shut. As the life left his body. Mariko's hand flew to her throat. And her mind was sent into a whirl.

Kenshin. Her brother. Her family.

What have you done?

smokeshields and sorrow

Mariko turned to her work to keep the world around her from falling apart.

She listened while Ranmaru raged about the Dragon of Kai. Listened as he ordered the rest of his men to begin making inquiries as to where Hattori Kenshin might be. As to why Hattori Kenshin would murder an innocent old man and his two young grandchildren in cold blood.

Had Kenshin really done this?

Mariko asked herself this question many times. Too many times to count.

Why would Kenshin do such a thing?

The most disturbing part about its answer was that she could not be sure on either score.

Her brother had always been a man of honor. A man who followed the way of the warrior to the letter. *Bushidō* drove Kenshin as it drove few other men of Mariko's acquaintance.

In order for a man who valued honor and chivalry as Kenshin did to slaughter innocent, unarmed people, he *must* have had a good reason. He had to have one.

But as much as Mariko struggled to come up with it, she could not. Ultimately it was because she knew there could be no good reason.

When she overheard the plans Ranmaru had begun to make—to find the Dragon of Kai and kill him with a thousand cuts—Mariko felt the horror take shape in her soul. And she knew she had to form a plan. At least do something more than sit and worry in silence.

If Ranmaru sent the Black Clan after her brother, Kenshin would have to fight.

He might die.

She did not doubt her brother could hold his own against most of the members of the Black Clan.

But not against Ōkami.

Mariko had to create something to help her brother stave off the Wolf's inevitable onslaught. After all, a predator needed to see its prey in order to catch it.

Ōkami had been decidedly quiet through all of Ranmaru's rages. If possible he'd been even more detached than usual. He did not laugh with Mariko anymore. Instead Ōkami resumed his disappearances from camp, this time leaving every day. Likely journeying to Inako to see his sister Yumi.

Not that Mariko minded.

That fear—that burgeoning worry—drove her to remain apart from all the conversations taking place around her.

Drove her to avoid Ōkami for the few moments they ever crossed paths in camp. Avoid him as he avoided her. At all cost.

Mariko burrowed into her tasks instead. Today she sat outside Haruki's smithy, gingerly filling empty eggshells.

The idea had come to her after an anxious dream. One in which she'd watched Yoshi remove eggs from their casings, leaving the shells intact. Hollow. Then the shells had dissolved into smoke, concealing him from view.

Mariko had woken suddenly. And begun to consider.

A trail of smoke would be an excellent way to conceal a retreat. Or perhaps even conceal an entrance. Especially if the smoke did not precipitate an actual fire.

Smoke was the first sign of a blaze. It usually sent those around it into a panic to find its source. A panic that would help to conceal a marauder's trail.

The next day, Mariko had borrowed a mortar and pestle from Yoshi. She'd begun grinding powders, almost feverishly. First she'd started with a basic mixture. She'd taken the smelly, yellow rocks from the nearby hot springs and ground them into powder. Then she'd mixed them with dried pitch and tried to get them to form a mold in the eggshell.

As could be expected, the stinking disaster had fallen apart in her hands before it could even catch flame.

Then Mariko had recalled something Yoshi had taught her during one of her many lessons about mundane things. An excellent source of tinder was dried animal dung. He'd proven this when he'd taught her how to light a fire.

So she'd mixed equal parts dried horse dung with the

yellow rocks and the pitch, grinding them all into a fine powder. The final addition of soot from Haruki's smithy had stabilized the mixture and made it less noxious to work with.

The last task left to Mariko was to create a mold.

Thus the eggshells.

She needed something that would encase the powders in an almost crystalline structure. Make them easy to transport without falling apart or setting them off at the nearest brush of heat. Yesterday Mariko had remembered the Dragon's Beard candy and how the sweet *amazura* syrup used to make it hardened when left too long away from the fire.

So she'd taken *amazura* syrup from Yoshi and let it melt over a low flame. She'd waited until it hardened before grinding it into a powder. Dusted it across the inside of the eggshell. Then left it near the heat once more to form a shell within the eggshell. A reinforcement that made the eggshells themselves far sturdier.

If this experiment didn't work, she had to start from the beginning.

Mariko carefully measured out the three different powders in the three containers at her feet. She poured each into the eggshell lined with *amazura* glaze.

Then she stood.

As she'd learned early on when mixing these powders, friction caused them to react with one another and form a cloud of smoke.

She rattled the egg twice before throwing it hard on the ground.

It burst with a loud bang. A white smoke rose from the ground, smelling faintly of burnt eggs and horse dung. Tolerable, if one ran away quickly.

At least in one thing Mariko was not a complete failure.

"I'm impressed," Ranmaru said when Mariko showed him the final product. His hand waved through the smoke so that he could see her.

Briefly Mariko considered what it meant that she was providing her enemy—her brother's enemy—with the means to conceal himself from view. Alas, it was too late to hide her success, and—as far as she was concerned—the more smoke, the better. She'd begun working on this project before the events that had transpired in the clearing. When Mariko had wished to earn a place in the Black Clan's inner circle. The only thing that saved her from feeling extreme guilt was the knowledge that she had not shared *all* she'd learned from her experiments.

She had no intentions of giving Ranmaru her greatest invention yet. Despite what her brother had done in Jukai forest, she would help Kenshin best his enemies in whatever way she could.

Mariko steeled herself.

The first chance she had, she would learn the reason Kenshin had murdered so many innocents. After everything she'd experienced while living amongst the Black Clan, she knew appearances could be deceiving. And she wished to give her brother the benefit of her trust, at least for the time being.

"How many smokeshields can you make?" Ranmaru asked.

Mariko hedged. "It's time-consuming."

"I'll send men to help you. Ren and Yoshi will appreciate learning how to do this."

And taking note of my ingredients, as well as seeing what else I am concocting.

"I prefer to work alone," Mariko said. "It's dangerous handling the powders, and an untried hand could set fire to the entire camp."

Ranmaru remained unyielding. "Then train them to handle the powders properly."

"I don't have the time to train them *and* make the smokeshields."

"Why don't you tell me what you need, and I will provide it."

The leader of the Black Clan's unflinching nature was becoming increasingly problematic. Ranmaru rarely saw problems. He saw only solutions, and his eternal optimism grated on her nerves now more than ever.

Mariko thought quickly. Even if she disclosed the ingredients, none of the members of the Black Clan could ever duplicate the amounts. Not without weeks of study. And she would never tell them how she'd managed to harden the inside of the eggshell. "The yellow rocks near the hot springs. Dried horse dung. And ash from Haruki's forge."

"And foxglove." A voice emanated from behind her.

Ōkami.

"Foxglove?" Ranmaru said with a quizzical expression. "As in the poison?"

Mariko refrained from grimacing. "It's true I have foxglove, but—"

Ōkami stepped before her. "Don't try to fool us, Lord Lackbeard," he said in a flat tone. "If you didn't use it for the smokeshields, then why did you need to gather it?"

Again she thought quickly. "I used foxglove sap to line the inside of the eggshells."

Another lie, threaded from truth. Once again, Mariko recalled the experiment her tutor had performed when she was younger. When the paste from the foxglove stems and seeds had flashed a brilliant light. Mariko had realized early on that if she did in fact add the paste to the smokeshield, it would likely explode. Not just emit smoke and fumes.

Alas she'd not yet had an occasion to test her greatest invention yet.

"Interesting," Ranmaru commented.

Ōkami turned toward her, his face tense, as though he could smell the scent of her lies. "Quite."

"Very well," Ranmaru said. "We shall provide you with the ingredients. Can you make fifty smokeshields in the next five days?"

"I can try."

"Excellent." He grinned. "How are your lessons progressing in learning to fight with a sword?"

"They—aren't," she admitted. "I've been spending most of my time working on this."

Partially true. But in actuality it was difficult to pursue any training when one's supposed master was never present in the same place as his student.

"It's important you continue practicing." Ranmaru watched her as he spoke. "Because if you're successful in making these smokeshields, I'd like for you to accompany us on our next raid."

Mariko blanched. "I'd . . . I—"

"I thought you would be pleased," Ranmaru said.

Again Mariko felt Ōkami's eyes bore through her skull.

"I am . . . pleased."

Ranmaru frowned. "You don't sound as though you are."

"May I ask where we are planning our next raid?"

"A land not too far from here," Ranmaru answered. "One that desperately deserves our intervention."

Ōkami glanced down at her. "The province of the Hattori clan."

Mariko's head began to swim, her earliest suspicions confirmed.

Though it did not make the words any easier to hear.

The Wolf continued. "The way to draw out a dragon is by threatening its lair."

Despite the pounding between her temples, Mariko kept her voice calm. Unaffected. "Do we know why he attacked Akira-*san*?" she asked Ōkami, desperate to cling to the first source of her hatred.

The first and most lasting.

Tell me you were there that night. Tell me you were the ones to attack my convoy. Tell me you tried to kill Hattori Mariko and her brother is seeking revenge against the Black Clan for it.

Tell me so I can destroy you and never once look back.

"It doesn't matter why he did it," Ōkami said. "It only matters that he did."

Believe in actions and actions alone.

But Kenshin *had* to have his reasons. Mariko needed to believe he would never do something like this without a reason. Needed to believe it despite all the evidence to the contrary.

"Why would anyone murder someone without a reason?" she said.

"Men like that don't need a reason," Ōkami replied.

Ranmaru sighed. "You will see when we go to the Hattori province. You will see why it is that the emperor has failed his people by putting men like Hattori Kano in power. Our emperor is not strong. He is weak and manipulative. Far more concerned about his own status than he is about the greatness of the empire. If Minamoto Masaru truly cared about his country, he would know its strength lies with its people. And the people of Wa follow those who bring about the glory of our empire.

"It's time to return power to those with the will to rule," Ranmaru continued. "With a strong arm. And a unified heart."

Mariko knew she could not say much. If she spoke out of turn, her words would reveal her sentiments. And her heart

311

could not take any more pain. Not now. "You wish for power to be taken from the emperor?"

The leader of the Black Clan looked to his friend. "Ōkami—"

"Ranmaru wishes for power to return to the shōgun," the Wolf finished.

"Which shōgun?" Mariko asked. "I thought the line of the shōgun had died out years ago."

Ōkami's gaze pierced hers. He spoke softly. "The last in line to be shōgun was Takeda Shingen's son."

Ranmaru.

"So you fight"—Mariko swallowed as she studied Ōkami—"you fight to restore military power to Ranmaru?"

Ōkami said nothing. "The only reason I fight is out of loyalty to my clan. The Black Clan, and all those we serve. If Ranmaru wishes to be shōgun, then I will do whatever is in my power to help him. But I have no designs beyond that."

It was possible Mariko had finally stumbled on the truth. Did the Black Clan have designs on restoring Takeda Ranmaru—a *rōnin*—to the seat of power in Yedo?

And—if so—how did a band of brigands intend to bring that about?

"I told you Sanada Takeo would be useful to us one day, Ōkami," Ranmaru said, his smile tight. Almost menacing.

At that, Ōkami stormed past Mariko, back into the night.

A province of pain

—✳—

Kenshin dismounted from his horse outside the servants' gate.

He was home. Weary. Wretched.

His dreams plagued him. Ever since the day Mariko had disappeared, they'd kept him from having a restful night's sleep. They'd only worsened after he'd lost time beside the watering hole.

Nightmares of an elderly man crying for help. Nightmares of a boy and girl, thrashing through a sea of tall grass, blood spurting from their bodies in crimson founts.

Kenshin banished the thoughts with a shake of his head. He passed through the rear gate of his family's home, his head bowed.

He did not wish to speak to anyone. To see anyone. To allow anyone to see him. It wasn't the shame of his family knowing. His father would not reproach him on this particular score. After all, it wasn't a public failing. At most, Hattori Kano would offer the families of the victims some form of restitution. And Kenshin's mother? Taira Hime would likely frown at her son for losing his temper. Then offer him food before letting the unpleasant incident fade from memory.

The darkness covered him. Torchlight flickered from all corners of the compound. Kenshin's feet carried him automatically to a smaller building, recently reroofed in clean, sweet-smelling straw.

Without pausing to think, Kenshin sat beneath a window on the far right. Leaned his back against the rough white plaster. Hoping the nearness would comfort him.

Even the whisper of a sliding door opening did not disrupt him from seeking solace. Kenshin did not look up when the shadow of a familiar figure fell upon him.

Amaya said nothing. She merely sat beside him.

After a time, Kenshin let his head fall to her shoulder.

"What's wrong?" she asked softly.

He did not reply.

"Kenshin."

"Your shoulder is uncomfortable." He picked up his head. Before he could move away, Amaya caught him by the chin.

"What is it?" she repeated.

"Your shoulder is too bony. You should eat more."

She smiled. "As should you."

He pressed his head to her shoulder again.

"I thought you said it was uncomfortable," Amaya teased.

She reached for his hand, lacing her fingers through his. "It's uncomfortable because you're resting your head. Rest your heart, instead."

Kenshin swallowed. Leaned into her warmth. Let his worries fade, if only for an instant.

"I've made a terrible mistake," he whispered.

———————

The Black Clan rode to a halt on the edges of the Hattori province.

Twilight had fallen. The drone of cicadas cut through the air, the smell of barley and grain suffusing the night sky.

Mariko's heart thundered in her chest. She needed to warn her family. To warn Kenshin what was about to happen.

She glanced sidelong at Ōkami. "Why are we here to raid and ransack these people?" Mariko asked in an even tone. "They have not done anything to you."

"We are not here to raid and ransack them," he said. "We are here to . . ." His head tilted to one side. "Redistribute."

"Excuse me?"

"Hattori Kano has been robbing the people who live and work on his land for years."

"What?" Mariko exclaimed, the fine hairs on the nape of her neck rising. "I've never heard—"

"He lives well beyond his means. And he was recently robbed of his daughter's dowry. A dowry he stole from his people in order to buy his way into influence."

A lie!

Mariko opened her mouth to refute his words. To defend her family's honor. But a creeping uncertainty began to slither across her body. The tiniest seed of doubt.

Hattori Kano was not a bad man.

Even if he had sold his only daughter to further his own prominence. It was not unusual for a man in her father's position to do such a thing. It was true Hattori Kano had always wished for Mariko to be different. Wished for her to forswear her childish wishes and be more than what she was. Those had been his last words to her. But he had not been a bad father. He'd cared for Mariko. Provided her guidance and attention.

A man like this wouldn't rob his own people blind. Not simply for the sake of gaining a foothold in Heian Castle.

Nevertheless, the seed of doubt took root in Mariko's mind.

Her father had traded his only daughter for the barest measure of influence. Not even a seat in the imperial court. And her mother had never once objected. If her father was taking more than his fair share of his people's crops, her mother would not say anything. Her brother would not know to pay attention.

And Mariko?

I've been blind to so much. I've thought I possessed the truth so often.

When in truth I've possessed nothing.

"Do you not believe us?" Ranmaru said. "You look as though you do not."

"It's not that I don't believe you. It's that I can't believe a daimyō would be so careless with his own people."

Ōkami looked her way. "He is only following in the footsteps of his emperor."

"If the thought unsettles you, why don't you journey into the village nearby?" Ranmaru said. "And see the truth for yourself."

"You would trust me?" Mariko asked.

"Of course not." Ranmaru grinned. "Take someone with you."

Without thought, her eyes lifted to Ōkami's. Her heart made the choice for her.

"Return by midnight," the leader of the Black Clan finished. "We will raid the granaries and storehouses then."

———

"So *this* is what you do." Mariko pronounced it as a statement of fact. "This is the true work of the Black Clan. Redistributing the wealth you steal to those less fortunate, like the woman in the Iwakura ward."

Both she and Ōkami wandered through the edges of a village on the southern side of her family's province.

He said nothing in response.

"And you truly think your actions won't hurt the people of this province?" Mariko pressed.

"No," Ōkami said. "Just wound the pockets of Hattori Kano. And if the Dragon of Kai happens to be killed in the process, so be it."

Anguish knifed deep within Mariko's chest. She desperately wanted to protest. To offer some form of counterargument. They did not even know if Kenshin was truly the one responsible for Akira-*san*'s death!

And yet.

Her mind descended in a whirl. The most Mariko could do was stay amongst the raiding party. Perhaps then she could find a way to warn one of her family's servants before it was too late. Before the unthinkable occurred.

And if it should occur anyway . . . Mariko had another weapon at the ready.

She studied the expanse of land before them. Though the sun had already set, many women and children were still working the fields. Cutting away any weeds and fending off the countless insects that always plagued the harvest. The golden stalks of rice were growing tall. Usually Mariko loved the harvesting time. She would wander the fields and get lost among the many reaping baskets, drawing sketches in the mud and crafting new ideas in her mind.

She focused on the best of these memories. On the people working in her periphery.

They were never smiling. And she had never truly noticed.

Ōkami and Mariko stayed to the shadows along the plastered buildings, beneath the thatched roofs, listening to the sounds of the workers as their children squabbled for food and their loved ones returned home from a wearying day's work.

Ōkami paused beside a family gathering for their evening meal near a small fire just outside their tiny home. He handed Mariko a sickle and bade her to follow him into an adjoining field, as though they were workers intent on continuing their reaping. They squatted alongside the tall waves of grain, angling to one side to watch the family eat. In the distance, Mariko thought she saw the yellow eyes of a fox, lingering in the shadows, searching for scraps.

The children were dirty. They smiled even though their meal was meager.

It was clear their mother was injured. She limped as she went to scoop out tiny spoonfuls of millet.

"*Okaa*," the eldest girl said when her mother gave her a bowl of food, "you eat. I'm not hungry." Her eyes drifted to the fields of golden wheat a mere stone's throw from where they sat, stretching as far as the eye could see.

"No, my dearest. I've already had my meal." The woman glanced at her husband, willing him to stay silent.

When the mother sat back down beside him, Mariko watched him quietly give her half his share.

Thankfully, most of the other children did not notice. They smiled and carried on, oblivious to their parents' plight. But the eldest girl knew better. She pushed her bowl beside her parents' and quietly began scooping some of her food into theirs.

The sight startled Mariko. Cut at something beneath her heart. For so many years she had prided herself on being the girl who saw things no one else saw. Who noticed the world not as it was, but as it should be. Her gaze drifted to the smiling faces of the other, younger children present.

At the face of the eldest girl, and the tiniest grooves that now gathered above her brow.

Mariko had countless fond memories of her childhood.

And not a single one of them recalled anything but contentment at mealtime.

Perhaps my mind saw only what it wished to see.

A cold hand of awareness took hold of her throat. In none of those memories could she remember seeing that same contentment in any of her father's workers. When Mariko had wandered past the gates of her family's home, into the fields and paddies beyond, workers had often come to usher her away. The smiles they'd given her had been wan. Aged. As a child she'd often asked why they looked sad. Why they didn't smile more.

Her mother had told her they were merely tired. And then her nursemaid had urged her back inside. This was the way of it. A daimyō owned the land his people worked. In exchange for their lord's protection and care, the people working the lands offered the daimyō tribute.

Was it possible Hattori Kano took more than his fair share?

Mariko recalled her father once saying how ungrateful his workers were. How he provided them with food and shelter and a place to work. And still they were unsatisfied.

The Black Clan intended to redistribute her family's

wealth. Back into the hands of those who worked the fields. Tilled the soil. Reaped the harvest.

All so Mariko could wear fine clothes and attract the attention of the emperor's son. A part of her fought against the rightness of the sentiment. The rightness of seeing these people being granted their fair share. These were her family's people, her family's lands.

But when had Mariko ever once planted a seed or worked in the dirt when it was not out of personal interest? Not until she'd come to the Black Clan's encampment had she even learned the basics of how to live on her own. Indeed this was the first time in her life she had ever held a sickle. And even now it was for the purpose of subterfuge.

As Ōkami had first pronounced that day Mariko had been tasked with carrying firewood, she'd been useless.

It was the truth of it all that had grated her nerves so thoroughly. How wrong it was that Mariko would fight so vehemently against accusations rooted in truth. Had Ōkami accused her of being lazy or slovenly or stupid, she would have laughed.

But when he'd accused her of being useless, it had stung.

Mariko wouldn't be useless now. She saw the truth.

She could make her father see it, too.

Even if they were wrong, they were still her family.

No matter what it cost Mariko, she would warn her brother.

Somehow.

THE RAID

———✳———

They plan to raid the storehouses in the dead of night.

That was all the servant had said to him. Kenshin had chased after the old man. When they'd rounded the corner, he'd grabbed him by his threadbare *kosode*, whirling him around.

The old man's eyes were milky white. He was blind or very nearly so.

Kenshin had cursed to himself. "Do you know who told you this?"

"No, my lord," the old man stammered. "I was told to convey that message, then given a coin for it. That is all I know." He spread his fingers wide as if to prove that was all he had in his possession.

"And there was nothing further? Nothing about who intends to raid the storehouses?"

"No, my lord," the old man said. "It was said quickly, as I was passing by. As though the messenger did not have time to say anything more."

Kenshin removed his grip on the old man's *kosode*.

Someone intended to rob his family. To steal from the stores that fed and clothed the people of his province. That supported the Hattori clan's rise to greatness.

Without a second thought, he turned toward his family's garrison.

Whoever they were, these thieves would not leave this valley alive.

———

Mariko's hands shook as she waited beneath the straw awning. Ōkami leaned into the fall of shadows, watching for the signal.

"You don't have to fight," he said softly.

She turned toward him. "You don't expect me to fight?"

"I have no expectations of you or anyone else. I'm simply saying you don't have to do anything you don't wish to do."

Though Ōkami's words held meaning, the cold precision with which he said them stung. Mariko did not wish to fight against any member of her family or any of the samurai who bore them allegiance. She did not wish to partake in any of this destruction.

But she could not ignore the chance to save lives.

And strangely a small part of her felt responsible for what might happen to Ranmaru. To Yoshi. Even to Ren. And to

Ōkami. The weapon she'd brought with her had the potential to cause damage beyond her wildest imagination. She'd never had an opportunity to test it, and thus had no idea what to expect.

If something happened to Ōkami because of it . . .

She banished the thought.

He was a member of the Black Clan. Likely one of the mercenaries who had been sent to kill her. Even if recent events had brought that truth into question, Mariko would never choose the Wolf over her family. Not if she lived a thousand years.

The call of a nightingale echoed through the darkness.

The call that all was clear.

Using his hands to form a cradle, Ōkami helped propel Haruki and Ren onto the straw rooftop above. He motioned for Mariko to follow. At the last second, he pulled her to him, chest to chest.

"Don't be a hero. You'll make my life harder if you try," he said in a voice barely above a whisper, his eyes two flashing stones of onyx.

Her breath caught. For a mad instant, Mariko thought to kiss him. "Do your job, Tsuneoki-*sama*. And I will do mine." She vaulted onto the roof, trying her best to keep her steps as light as those of Ren. Her heart pounded in her chest as she flattened against the straw, attempting to remain out of sight.

Yoshi and Ranmaru moved like ghosts in the night toward

the storehouse. Toward the same granaries Mariko had played in as a child.

There was no sign of anyone around.

All was eerily silent.

As Ranmaru fiddled with the latch of the storehouse, Ren grasped the edge of the roof, taking tight hold of the wooden frame before catapulting to the ground below.

An arrow sailed from the darkness, striking Ren in the side.

Mariko stifled a cry when she saw him fall. She thought to say something—to point out that they were under attack—but the words remained lodged in her throat.

These were her enemies. Her family's enemies.

Set to rob the Hattori clan.

Even as she warred with herself, it soon became clear that Mariko did not need to say anything. Motion converged in the darkness. As soon as Ranmaru saw Ren fall, he and Yoshi folded into the shadows against the granary.

Torches burst to life across the way.

And the haunted, almost feral face of Hattori Kenshin glowed from the darkness.

Fury roared through his body.

One of Kenshin's men had loosed an arrow too soon. The men endeavoring to rob his family had been warned.

There was nothing to be done for it.

"Show yourselves!" he demanded.

The shadows remained still across the way. Kenshin unsheathed his *katana*, directing his men with a nod. Two foot soldiers whipped across the path, their backs hunched, their arrows nocked as they grabbed the fallen thief by the arms and hauled him before Kenshin.

"Show yourselves, you cowards!" Kenshin shouted.

The young man at his feet was no more than twenty. He'd been shot in the side, the shaft of the arrow protruding from the folds of his black *kosode*. When no further signs of movement or sound emitted from the darkness, Kenshin pressed the tip of his foot to the young thief's ribs, just above his wound.

The boy groaned. Shuddered. Then spat in the dirt beside Kenshin's sandal. "You miserable whoreson." He coughed.

Kenshin leveled the tip of his *katana* at the boy's throat. "Who are you?" he demanded. "Tell me who you are, and you will die quickly. Painlessly. With a measure of honor."

The boy's laughter was harsh. Almost maniacal.

Kenshin pressed his foot down even harder. The boy cried out, then gritted his teeth.

"What kind of loathsome, dishonorable men are you?" Kenshin yelled into the blackness. "That you would allow your man to suffer while you stand by watching, idle?"

Sinister laughter emanated from beneath the awning of the granary.

"I suppose that would make us nearly as loathsome as you,

Hattori Kenshin. A noble samurai who tortures a wounded, helpless boy in an effort to provoke a reaction."

Kenshin flinched. "You drove me to this."

"I expected nothing less from you. The Dragon of Kai . . ." Kenshin could almost picture the faceless sneer accompanying the words. "That you would blame others for your own actions. As though you did not have a choice. Yet you claim to honor *bushidō*."

The fury ignited once more beneath Kenshin's skin. "How dare you speak to me in this fashion? Who are you to dare?"

Another voice tore through the night, this one softer.

And yet infinitely more dangerous.

"We are nothing. We are no one . . ." Footsteps trudged through the darkness. A low hum began to form in the air around him. Strange and full of malice.

"And we are *everywhere*."

From one side, a beast growled. Yellow eyes materialized in the shadows.

The hum grew louder.

Then—as if a giant fist had punched through the center of the earth—an explosion rocketed the entrance of the granary.

And a wall of fire and earth rained down upon them.

———————

She'd done it to save Kenshin. Done it to spare her brother.

Mariko did not care what happened to Ōkami. Did not care at all about Ranmaru.

Did not care that Ren lay wounded at her brother's feet.

When she lit the firegourd. When she rolled to the ground and tossed it before the entrance of the granary. When she provided a distraction enabling the Black Clan to escape.

She had done it for Kenshin.

Mariko shook herself into consciousness. Her head throbbed. She touched her ear and discovered a trail of warm blood trickling from its edge. Then she crawled on her hands and knees toward the safety of a toppled cart filled with chipped porcelain bowls. The explosion from the firegourd had ripped the entrance off the front of the granary. Since the members of the Black Clan had been positioned along the back of the roof and against the sides, they had not been killed by the blast. But several of them had been knocked unconscious, just like Mariko.

Screams echoed into the night as the granary caught flame.

An arrow whistled by her, startling her into full awareness. Sharpening the drone in her ears. Through the fire, she saw Kenshin swing his sword at a black blur.

Her pulse thundered; her throat went dry.

The black blur flashed to a sudden halt. Kenshin brandished his *katana* as Ōkami angled his *bō* to one side, ready to strike.

"Get Ren!" Yoshi cried out from behind Mariko.

Her family's servants barreled into the night, frantically searching for buckets, for bowls, for anything to stanch the rising flames.

Mariko stood rigid, watching her brother make a decision. Watching Ōkami make a choice.

Kenshin moved to attack as Ōkami hurtled into motion. Then—from her place beside the cart—Mariko saw Ren vanish in a smudge of darkness.

Ōkami had rescued Ren instead of attacking Kenshin.

In that moment, Mariko knew she, too, could not just sit here and watch others suffer.

As she stood to help put out the fire, one of her family's foot soldiers caught sight of her. In this young man's eyes, she must look to be just another boy dressed in black. The soldier promptly nocked an arrow to his bow. Before she could think to do anything else, Mariko smashed a smokeshield at her feet, then dashed behind a cart. She unsheathed her *tantō*, her pulse on a tearing rampage.

The arrow missed her, but the soldier barreled through the smoke, intent on cornering her.

He raised his sword, and Mariko knew she had to fight. Had to stop him from firing any more arrows her way. Without hesitation, she tore from behind the cart and flew into his knees. He toppled to the ground, and Mariko raised her *tantō*, brandishing it in a threat. With a look of hatred, the soldier punched her in the face.

Needles of light stabbed at her vision. Mariko grabbed her cheek as one eye welled with tears.

The young soldier tried to stand. Mariko drove the tip of her *tantō* into his hand, pinning it to the earth, the sound of bone grinding against metal causing her to cringe. He screamed hoarsely, then grabbed her ankle when she attempted to run, knocking her back to the ground. They wrestled for his blade, and the soldier reached for the back of her *kosode*, trying to force her into submission. The fabric tore open, just enough for him to see the muslin bindings around her breasts.

His eyes widened in shock. Then cut in unmitigated fury. "You . . . bitch!" He tried to throttle her with his unpinned hand. "What kind of whore fights alongside murderers and thieves? Are you the Black Clan's whore? *What kind of woman are you?*"

Mariko coughed. Scratched at his face. The fingers of her other hand scrabbled across the ground, wrapping around smooth, cool porcelain. In one motion, she slammed a bowl into the soldier's head. He called her another filthy name as she sat astride him.

He'd struck her. Her cheek felt shattered. This boy had tried to shoot her with an arrow. Tried to strangle her. Mariko could kill him, as he wished to kill her. She could kill him, as she had that man in the forest.

This soldier deserved to reap what he'd sown.

Mariko drew back a fist and punched him in the face.

When he spat at her, she punched him again.

For all those times a man had caused her to feel fear. For all those times she'd been made to think something was wrong with her. For all those times she'd been forced to believe a girl was somehow less than a boy.

She struck him again. He called her another filthy name,

and her knuckles met his face once more. Soon she felt nothing in her fist.

"M-Mariko?" a voice stuttered to her right.

Just as she met the eyes of her brother, the roof of the granary collapsed on itself in a flurry of smoke and ash.

And a dark shadow grabbed her and whirled into the night sky.

"Kenshin!" Amaya yelled through a haze of smoke and a shower of sparks.

It couldn't have been his sister.

That scrawny boy with a face covered in a spray of crimson—beating one of his men to a bloody pulp—was *not* Hattori Mariko. Kenshin shook his head, trying to clear his vision.

"Kenshin!" Amaya yelled again.

He whirled around to see her splashing pails of water toward the burning granary.

"There are workers trapped inside," she implored. "They were trying to save some of our stores. If we don't rescue them, they will be burned alive!"

Kenshin's father stumbled to a halt nearby. "Get our men out," he ordered, smoothing the folds of his fine silk kimono while he spoke.

Usually Kenshin was the first to follow any order Hattori Kano doled out, without question. But in this instant, a part of Kenshin could barely register his father's words. He was still lost in the sight of only a moment ago. And he desperately wanted to seek out the crazed young man with a face so similar to that of his sister.

Amaya shoved her hair from her damp forehead and barreled toward the granary.

"What are you doing?" his father demanded.

The fire blazed in Amaya's beautiful grey eyes. "Our men are in there."

"And several servants." His father's face became stern. "Do not risk yourself for the servants. Try to save our soldiers. If you cannot, so be it."

Her lip curled in disgust before she turned toward the burning granary, her head held high. Kenshin raced toward the fire, pushing his way through the smoke.

"Amaya!" he called out.

She was dragging a man from the flames. The sweat was already dripping from her forehead, drenching the collar of her kimono. Kenshin saw from the man's clothing that he was a servant. Amaya was working in express defiance of Hattori Kano's directive.

In the corner, Kenshin caught sight of one of his father's samurai. The man was unconscious, with a wound to his head and a leg stuck beneath a splintered beam. He turned toward the samurai to help.

Amaya called out. "Help me, Kenshin!"

"Leave the servant," Kenshin replied. "Help me with Fumio-*sama*."

"Don't argue with me!" Amaya said.

"My father wants—"

"I don't care what your father wants. Help me save this man. Help me save *this* life."

Kenshin heaved a breath, his eyes wild. Then he grabbed hold of the servant's shoulders and stumbled away from the blaze. His father waited outside, every part of his body tense with fury. Before Hattori Kano could say a word, Kenshin and Amaya fended off the blaze once more and—together— managed to lift the splintered beam and pull Fumio-*sama* to safety.

Another side of the granary bowed inward, consumed by flames. "That's enough, Amaya," Kenshin said, his voice coarse from the smoke.

"There are still two more people inside—a woman and a young boy who works in the granary. We have to help them. They became trapped because they were trying to put out the fire!" She spun to make her way back toward the blaze, undeterred.

"No." Kenshin grabbed her by the wrist.

Amaya's eyes were pleading. "We have to save them."

"Do not risk yourself," his father argued. "The entire structure will collapse at any moment."

Kenshin hesitated. "Amaya—"

With a look of pure revulsion, she returned to the fire.

Kenshin's father took hold of his shoulder, keeping him still. Keeping him beyond the reach of any danger. Again

Kenshin hesitated before firming his resolve. He could not leave Amaya to fight through the blaze herself. The moment he tore himself free from his father's grasp, the walls of the granary buckled.

Without a second thought, Kenshin sprinted toward the roaring fire.

It took three of his father's soldiers to hold him back.

"She's gone," Hattori Kano yelled.

Kenshin stared at the blaze until his eyes burned.

"What a foolish waste of life," his father said before walking away.

MY NAME IS MARIKO

———— ✳ ————

Ōkami let himself be sick. Let himself empty his stomach until there was nothing left. And still the shaking did not stop. Still he felt the cold sweat sliding down his back.

He'd never flown this far before. Never carried a burden like this before.

In the distance behind him, he could see the flames. Hear the shouts. The burning granary and its many victims. Ōkami could only hope the Black Clan had vanished back into the woods, letting the thick veil of night conceal them from prying eyes.

He hoped Ranmaru had been able to take Ren with him. Hoped all his brothers in the Black Clan were spared the effects of that sudden explosion.

When Ōkami had finished emptying his stomach, he wiped his mouth. Though he continued to tremble, he heaved his unconscious burden across his shoulders again.

This girl. This wretched, wretched girl.

This wicked liar.

Mariko. Her name was *Mariko*.

Ōkami had watched the Dragon of Kai see her. Heard Hattori Kenshin call to her with a familiarity that could not be mistaken for anything else.

In truth Ōkami was glad she'd passed out from the force of being hurled through the sky, carried by nothing but wind and smoke. Or perhaps it was a combination of several elements—the explosion this wretched girl had undoubtedly caused, along with being heaved beneath the clouds. Whatever the case, Ōkami could not bear to speak to her. To watch more lies fall from her rosebud lips.

He had to figure out what to do first.

Hattori Kenshin knew who this girl was. There was only one way that could be possible. Ranmaru had told him that Hattori Kenshin had a twin sister.

Her name was Mariko.

Therefore this strange and imaginative girl—this girl who had captured Ōkami's attention with her radiant eyes, who had confused him beyond compare, who had fearlessly sparred with him using words as well as swords, who had befuddled his senses as no one ever had before—was the sister of the Dragon of Kai.

Ōkami almost laughed at himself, even while he choked through the last of his pain. The last of the burden that came with his power. A burden he'd willingly chosen.

In all his life Ōkami had never thought to find love.

Because he'd never sought it. Love was a burden he did not want. When others had described it to be like an arrow or a bolt of lightning, he'd sneered inwardly. Both were things that could kill. Love to him was not a shot to the heart. It was not a sudden, unpredictable thing.

Love was a sunrise. A welter of crimson that rose much like a warning. Slowly and almost in secret.

A secret Ōkami did not welcome.

The girl who'd stolen Ōkami's heart with her lies and her clever, clever mind.

Was the sister of the Dragon of Kai.

Hattori Mariko.

———————

Mariko's head was pounding.

Over and over, she heard her brother's voice. Saw the look on his face.

Mariko?

When she opened her eyes, the first thing she did was cough. Her hand moved toward her lips as she cringed in pain. Her fingers were wrapped tightly in muslin bindings. The room around her was beautiful. Dark wood and silk-screened sliding doors. The scent infusing the air was familiar. Sweet plum and honeysuckle.

Mariko was in the teahouse in Hanami. Her bandaged hands rustled across the elegant covers as she tried to sit upright.

And found Ōkami positioned nearby.

She smiled tentatively. He did not return the gesture.

"Did I pass out?" she asked him.

His features were not cool. Nor were they tinged in amusement. They were filled with . . . nothing. "No."

"Why did I sleep for so long?"

"You were badly injured."

"Well—"

"I drugged you."

Her lips pursed. "Why would you—"

"I told you I owed you an injury. Now we're even."

She blinked sluggishly. "What?"

"I'm leaving you here with Yumi. Your hands need time to heal. Don't try to return to the forest. If by some miracle no one saw you that night, it still won't be possible to keep your secret from them for much longer."

"But . . . I wish to go back," she said. "I—I don't want to leave." As soon as she said the words, Mariko was startled to grasp their truth.

"I don't care what you want."

The coldness of his words cut through Mariko's skin, down to the marrow of her bones.

"Ōkami—"

"Ren might die of his wounds. And we lost two of our men in the fight."

Mariko's eyes widened.

His dark gaze remained heavy-lidded as Ōkami stared at her unfeelingly. "You could have stopped this from happening."

In all the times the Wolf had spoken to her—revealed small glimpses of his truth—she'd never once found him to be grim. And to find him speaking in such a manner about her? It only unnerved Mariko more. "I don't understand what you mean. How could I have stopped this from happening?"

"Don't lie to me anymore, *Mariko*."

Nothing could drown out the roar in her ears. "What?" she stammered.

"I heard the Dragon of Kai call you by name. Hattori Kano had a daughter. We heard she was killed in Jukai forest. Don't tell me you are not she. Don't deny who you are when confronted with the truth. Names have untold power."

"You heard?" Mariko stood, fury imbuing her with sudden strength. "You *heard* she was killed? Don't you mean you were responsible for killing her?"

Ōkami remained so still that Mariko almost reached out to see if time had frozen around her.

"Is that why you're forcing me to stay here?" she continued, her voice beginning to tremble. She should have felt ashamed, but she did not. "Because if Ranmaru learns who I truly am, he will try to finish the job he failed to complete a month ago?"

Ōkami unfolded to his feet. "This is the last thing I can do for you. Stay here until you are healed. Then go on your way."

"Answer me!" Mariko stumbled across the covers. She grabbed him by the front of his *kosode*, trying to hold him still. To force him to answer. "Did you kill my father's men? Did you try to kill me?"

Ōkami pried her hands from his collar, gently pushing her away. "When I return to the forest, I will tell the men everything. If they see you again, they will kill you. Don't look for us. The Black Clan is dead to you."

"Tell me!" she cried.

"Tell me your name first. Say your name. Admit who you are!" His eyes glittered. The first sign of uncontrolled feeling Mariko had seen since she gained consciousness.

She stood tall. "My name is Hattori Mariko."

Ōkami nodded. "If there ever comes a day I try to kill you, Hattori Mariko, you will know it." With that, he left, the doors sliding shut behind him with a final *snick*.

It was always possible—however unlikely—that Mariko had been wrong about the Black Clan. But now that she was confronted with the reality of it, she was not sure what to do.

The beautiful *maiko*—his sister Yumi—entered the room a moment later.

"What did you say to him?" Yumi asked.

"He won't tell me the truth. He won't tell me why he tried to kill me."

She frowned, her lovely features gathering. "I don't believe he tried to kill you."

"Why not?" Mariko cried. "That's what they do. That's who they are! And now I will never know the truth. They won't let me return to the forest. They won't let me return to—" *To the only place I've ever truly belonged.* She began to sob, her words turning ragged.

Yumi set down the tray of food in her hands. She knelt beside Mariko. "If you really think that's who Ōkami is—that that's who Ranmaru is—then you don't deserve to know them anymore, Hattori Mariko."

LOST in the ASHES

———— ✳ ————

Kenshin sat on the ground, his elbows braced against his knees. He stared into the distance, seeing nothing. Tendrils of dark smoke continued to rise from what remained of his family's granary.

But he couldn't think about that.

He couldn't even consider the fact that he might have seen his sister last night. It wasn't possible. A trick of the smoke. A dance of the wind-whipped flames.

Even all thoughts of Mariko were pushed from his mind.

Kenshin could think of nothing else but Amaya.

She was gone.

The fire had killed the only girl he'd ever loved. They'd searched the rubble for her remains, and been unable to find anything of significance. At least two other souls had perished in the fire.

Muramasa Amaya would never even have a proper burial. Kenshin would never see those soft grey eyes—or hear her musical laughter—again.

He should have stopped her. Should have barred her from that final fateful path. But Kenshin was never meant to watch over Amaya. To be the keeper of her heart. He'd told her long ago to find another. To find a man who didn't shoulder his responsibilities. Who wouldn't one day inherit his father's duties. Amaya had laughed at him and said she didn't want Kenshin to be her hero. She'd simply wanted to hold his hand. Let her be a comfort to him, as he was a comfort to her.

Kenshin should have stopped her. Last night. And so many nights before.

"What are you going to do about this?" His father stood alongside him, his face drained. Dour. "The harvest is not for several months. I can increase what I take from those who work our land, but this could possibly ruin us. Now that we've lost your sister's dowry, we may not have enough to last us until the next harvest."

"She's gone," Kenshin said aloud, the words like ash in his mouth as he took to his feet.

They began to walk past the shadow of the charred granary. "What happened to Muramasa-*sama*'s daughter is unfortunate. If this harvest is plentiful, we can give her father a purse of gold. Of course he will always have a place here. But that is not the issue of importance, Kenshin. You are my son. The Dragon of Kai." Hattori Kano's gaze leveled as he eyed his son sidelong. "What do you intend to do about the theft and destruction of your family's property?"

Fury blazed through Kenshin, hot and fast. His father thought to give Muramasa-*sama* a purse of *gold*? How would that even begin to offer recompense for what the revered metalsmith had lost? His father should be at the metalsmith's feet, begging for forgiveness! Asking for atonement. Kenshin turned, intent on confronting his father once and for all. On changing his father's mind. Influencing him to see the good, honorable, righteous path.

Kenshin stopped in his tracks.

This was precisely the way his father had always been. When confronted with an obstacle, Hattori Kano had simply offered money as a means to brush it from his path. Why would his father change his mind for the mere daughter of a famed artisan?

Kenshin knew better than to try to persuade Hattori Kano that the righteous path was the correct one. Indeed he knew better than to convince his father of anything that did not already fall in line with Hattori Kano's established way of thought.

Especially since what Kenshin planned to undertake now had nothing to do with the charred remains of his family's storehouse. Nothing to do with honor or respect.

He would never forget the look of disgust on Amaya's face before she went inside the granary to finish what Kenshin should have started from the beginning.

The last look they'd ever shared.

Before he gutted each of the men in the Black Clan, he would burn them first.

Then, at least for an instant, they would understand his pain.

———————

Yumi floated across the tatami mat, a tray of food balanced in her hands. The way she walked reminded Mariko of a swan gliding across a pond, neck straight and silken feathers impeccable.

"I'm perfectly capable of feeding myself," Mariko said.

"I have no intention of feeding you," the *maiko* replied, her features almost prim in their mockery. "I'm not your servant. I'm merely here to help, as your hands are not yet healed."

"I promise I'll continue taking care of them. May I please leave?"

"You may not. I promised Ōkami I would watch over you. If you're one to make promises, you're one to understand their value."

"I understand nothing." Mariko attempted to cross her arms, but the bulky bindings around her hands prevented her. "And I need the help of no one."

"I see." The beautiful girl's tone was not condescending. Though Mariko knew she deserved to be patronized for being so petulant.

Mariko sighed in defeat. "I thought I possessed all the answers. Or at least most of them. Now I know I understand nothing."

"That knowledge is key to understanding the world, don't you think?" Yumi said as she knelt beside Mariko and handed her a bowl of steaming rice.

Mariko nudged the handle of her spoon with a bound fingertip. "Are you ever angry you were born a woman?"

Yumi sat back on her heels and studied Mariko for a spell. "I've never been angry to have been born a woman. There have been times I've been angry at how the world treats us, but I see being a woman as a challenge I must fight. Like being born under a stormy sky. Some people are lucky enough to be born on a bright summer's day. Maybe we were born under clouds. No wind. No rain. Just a mountain of clouds we must climb each morning so that we may see the sun."

As she let Yumi's words sink beneath her skin, Mariko's eyes drifted across the *maiko*'s perfect face. Across her beautifully sloe-shaped eyes. Her pointed chin and broad lips. Then Mariko's gaze wandered around Yumi's chamber. To the elegantly displayed kimono. To the ivory pot filled with a powder made of crushed pearls. To the pigments prepared from safflower rouge for the lips and cheeks. To the paulownia wood used for the eyebrows. Cosmetics and silks to both mask and enhance a woman's features.

Mariko supposed it was possible all women and men were forced to wear their own kind of masks.

"But how can you say you're not angry?" she asked quietly. "Your brother left you here because there was no other place you would be safe alone. No other place for a young woman to live alone, save a *geiko* teahouse in Hanami."

"My brother brought me here because he was too much of a coward to care for me himself," Yumi said curtly. "It had nothing to do with me being a girl."

Though she was surprised to hear Yumi call Ōkami a coward, Mariko could not help but agree on this score. "We are given less," she continued arguing her point. "We are treated as less. And whenever we make a mistake, it is weighed so much greater."

"The only great mistakes are the mistakes that remain ignored."

Mariko sniffed. "I'm tired of being treated this way."

"Have you felt as though you are incapable of fighting back?"

"For most of my life I have not fought back."

Yumi laughed, and the sound brought to mind a set of wind chimes. "Ōkami warned me you were quite a liar. I see what he meant."

"Why do you believe me to be lying?"

"Because, Hattori Mariko, you are not one to conform to any man's expectations. Is that not—in a way—a manner of fighting back?" She smiled. "Believe me when I tell you I would not want to sleep with my feet pointed in your direction."

"Believe me when I say you would be alone in thinking that." Mariko frowned.

Yumi inclined her head, her expression thoughtful. "There is such strength in being a woman. But it is a strength you must choose for yourself. No one can choose it for you. We can bend the wind to our ear if we would only try." She leaned closer. "Are you not the one who invented a weapon of exploding fire? Did you not bend the will of countless men with nothing but the fruits of your mind?"

"I can bend nothing. I can't even make your brother listen to me. Your entire family is exasperating." Again Mariko tried to cross her arms. Again she was thwarted. "Don't act as though being inscrutable makes you anything more than irritating."

Yumi laughed again, softly and lyrically. A knock resounded at the sliding door to her chamber. The *maiko* stood to answer it, returning with a sealed piece of parchment. While Yumi read it, the edges of her lips became downturned. Her eyes started to narrow.

Without a word, the *maiko* burned the letter.

"What is it?" Mariko asked.

Yumi hedged. Bit her lip.

Mariko set aside her bowl of uneaten rice. "You know something, don't you?"

"I know many things I am never supposed to tell you." It was a leading kind of statement. The sort Mariko knew better than to ignore.

She leaned forward. "Tell me anyway, Asano Yumi. And at least for one day, we can climb the mountain together."

Yumi's smile was pointed. "My loyalty is not to you, Hattori Mariko."

"Then to whom do you owe it?"

"To my brother and his lord, Takeda Ranmaru."

"So why are you even mentioning any of this to me?" Mariko pressed.

"My brother will not return to the city for some time. But I need to get Ōkami a message."

"What is it?"

"Hattori Kenshin is marching on the western edge of Jukai forest." She paused. "In an attempt to rescue his sister."

"Why now of all times?" Mariko cried, throwing back the embroidered coverlet. "The rumors of the Black Clan being responsible for my supposed death have existed for months!"

"I cannot tell you why he is marching on them now. But word must be sent to my brother."

"How did you normally reach him?"

"Ōkami comes here often. Unfortunately I was never told how to find their camp. My brother thought it was far too dangerous for me to know. It was something someone could hurt me in an effort to learn." Yumi sidled closer, tucking her pale green kimono neatly beneath her knees. "Are you certain you could not find their camp if you searched for it?"

"I have no idea how to find it."

Yumi's voice dropped in sudden urgency. "Do you think you could try? You owe them that, at least."

A part of Mariko agreed. She did owe the Black Clan something. As much as they owed her an explanation. If they weren't responsible for attacking her convoy and trying to kill her, then who was? Who had tried to impersonate them that ill-fated night in the forest? "I can try. Do you"—she swallowed—"really think Ōkami revealed my identity to the Black Clan?"

"I have never heard the Honshō Wolf make idle threats."

Mariko inhaled slowly.

"They might not look kindly on you when you return," Yumi warned. "They've slit the throats of other men for less."

With a careful nod, Mariko made a decision. "Will you help me with something?"

"As long as it harms no one, then yes. What is it?"

Mariko wobbled to her feet and began unraveling the bandages on one hand. "If I am marching to my death, then I will march to it as a girl. Without fear."

the shadow warrior

Mariko was not afraid anymore.

As her time with the Black Clan had taught her, avoiding fear made her weak. Embracing it made her strong.

True weakness is weakness of the spirit.

Mariko had lived a life of wealth and privilege. A life spent blissfully unaware of the suffering around her. A life she herself had never fully appreciated. Her mother did not give without expecting something in return. Her father only ever took.

And Kenshin?

Kenshin gave to others from a sense of honor and responsibility. But his honor and responsibility had failed him that night. Mariko had watched him torture Ren. Had seen the aftermath of his attempts to find her in Jukai forest. The bloodied bodies of innocent young men and women. Of an old man much beloved by many.

Only a few days ago, Mariko had been the reason such chaos had unraveled before her very eyes. Her invention had wrought havoc on her people. Undoubtedly hurt some of them. And she did not yet know what had happened to all the members of the Black Clan.

Her . . . friends?

Yes. If they were no longer her enemies, perhaps Mariko could one day consider them her friends. Certainly Yoshi. He'd only ever been kind to her. Offered her guidance and delicious food. Laughter in moments when she desperately needed it. And Ranmaru had been a strange source of reassurance for Mariko. This boy with an almost mysterious air to him, who nevertheless came across as approachable and direct in all of his dealings. Even Ren—her erstwhile tormentor—well, on second thought, Mariko supposed he could never be a friend. Not unless she could catch him unawares with a few strategic strikes of her own.

And Ōkami? No. They could never really be friends.

Mariko wasn't sure she wanted to be the Wolf's friend anyway. Could she ever be friends with a boy after dreaming of the way his calloused hands felt on her bare skin? Of the way his scarred lips felt pressed against her own?

She supposed not.

Mariko had never had friends before. Real friends. Ones who were not threatened by her family or by her strangeness. Her strange desire to learn about anything and everything.

Not until Mariko had first gone to the forest dressed as a

boy did she ever realize how small her world had been. What it meant to be truly challenged. What it meant to be truly happy, in a world where no one questioned her place.

The Black Clan might reject her.

They might kill her.

Ōkami had said he would tell them. He'd said he no longer felt any obligation to keep her secret. Not when she'd betrayed them as she had, by helping her brother.

Their enemy.

Mariko stopped in the clearing where Akira-*san* had perished. Where Kenshin had lost his way. The burned lean-to was still standing. She looked to the trees. Studied the jagged silhouette of the mountain in the distance.

A silhouette she'd often studied while at camp.

Everyone had told Mariko she would never be able to leave their encampment. That she could not run.

But could she make her way back if she tried?

Northeast. If Mariko trekked in that direction, it would be possible to find some kind of path. Some evidence of where the encampment was.

Unlikely. But possible. These were odds Mariko could work with.

She began walking northeast, keeping the mountain in her sights.

If there was any chance of finding the Black Clan's encampment without stumbling into a trap, Mariko hoped a girl would be the first one to do it.

The sun had descended behind the trees. A white-gold glow limned the horizon.

Nightfall was imminent.

Soon Mariko would be lost in Jukai forest. Lost amongst the *yōkai*. Lost amongst the *jubokko*. Lost amongst those she'd recently betrayed.

She trod carefully, searching for signs of black flowers. Sniffing the air for the scent of blood. Seeking vines covered in thorns. Watching for anything that seemed out of the ordinary.

Fear kept her alert. She would always let it feed her. Never let it consume her.

Mariko stopped in her tracks when a pair of yellow eyes formed in the darkness.

A pair of yellow eyes she recognized well.

When the beast took shape around them, Mariko held her breath. It eyed her as it had before, its head tilting to one side. Then it leaned back on its haunches and howled. The sound was low, but it began to widen, to layer with the weight of many voices, large and small. It echoed through the trees, ricocheting into the night.

She was not afraid.

Then the beast turned. Waited for her to follow it.

That time before—with the filthy man who had trailed after Mariko the night her convoy was attacked—the beast had warned her.

She would trust it tonight. A part of her understood she'd

almost expected the beast to find her again, as it had that first time.

It padded through the dirt and dead leaves. Mariko realized it moved without making any noise. When she tried to draw close, it whipped its head back at her.

The beast was edged in dark smoke. Perhaps even fashioned of it. She followed it up an incline. Until they came across a pool of freshwater. Though it was full dark, the beast stepped with an otherworldly sure-footedness. Then it dissolved on a wisp of wind, its eyes fading into black. Mariko stood within a tight grove of trees. The chirruping of insects halted, and the gentle sound of rustling leaves ceased.

She heard nothing.

Then, from the darkness, a single torch began weaving her way.

It flickered through the branches as it approached her.

Mariko's heart raced, but she was not afraid.

She was strong. Free.

Other torchlights took shape around her. They all drew toward her like water gathering near a dam. Shapes materialized behind each ring of fire. Darker, thicker shadows, enveloped in night. But corporeal.

They were all masked. All dressed in black. Thick lines of black ink had been drawn across their eyes. Mariko knew they saw her. Saw a girl, dressed in a simple pale pink kimono, its hem stained from her trudge through the forest.

A figure moved to the head of the converging shadows. He

stood before her. Mariko knew based on his stature, based on his bearing, that it was Ranmaru.

"To be a shadow warrior, the forest must accept you first," he began. "It must see you as its equal. As its ally." His eyes glowed yellow for an instant. He winked at her once.

Mariko remained still, her heart immobilized in her chest.

The beast. The beast formed of smoke and shadow.

It was Ranmaru.

Which meant the leader of the Black Clan had known all along that Mariko was a girl. She longed to ask him why he'd kept her secret. Why he'd helped her in the forest after her convoy had been attacked. Only to disappear as she was set upon by a drunken fool.

There would be time later for her questions. Now was not that time.

"The forest led you here tonight," Ranmaru continued with a meaningful smile. "Only those it deems worthy are granted this gift."

Mariko lifted her chin, accepting the forest's embrace. Accepting that she had truly found her place here, in a grove of enchanted trees, with a band of mercenaries dressed in the color of night.

"Hattori Mariko . . . do you agree to fight and die for your fellow shadow warriors?"

"Yes."

"Do you agree to fight for justice, irrespective of honor?"

Mariko cleared her throat with conviction. "Yes."

"Do you agree to see all those before you as your equal, regardless of birth or rank?"

"Yes."

"Do you agree to use all manner of subterfuge—even lying, cheating, stealing—to achieve our shared goals?"

"Yes."

"And will you die to protect this secret?"

She did not hesitate. "Yes."

"Today you become *kagemusha*. Today you swear to serve and protect all those in need." Ranmaru walked back when he finished.

No leaves rustled nearby. No sound emitted from his footsteps. No wind carried with it the scent of warm stone and wood smoke. But Mariko knew Ōkami moved toward her. Her body leaned forward of its own volition, drawn like drying leaves to a river's edge.

Ōkami stepped before her.

"Close your eyes," he said softly. In one hand he held a small earthenware pot filled with a black liquid.

She let her eyes fall shut, reveling in the darkness. Embracing her fears.

"Be as swift as the wind. As silent as the forest. As fierce as the fire. As unshakable as the mountain." His words swept over Mariko as Ōkami's fingers brushed slowly across her eyelids, covering them with the same black paint they all wore. His touch was a flare of heat across her skin. When he finished, the wind took flight once more. The trees rustled with a sudden swish of air, and the branches creaked in celebration.

As though the forest itself were welcoming her.

Mariko tossed in her tent, sleep eluding her.

She did not understand why she could not rest.

The Black Clan had welcomed her. Not a single one of them had turned his back on her, though they all knew who she was. Though they all knew what she had done.

She'd deceived them. Infiltrated them. Cheated her way through their ranks. Outsmarted and betrayed them, several times over.

And they'd welcomed her for it, as though she'd always been one of their own.

No one in her life had ever welcomed Mariko for being herself. Not her parents. Never those in the nobility. Even Kenshin had wished her to be different. Wished her to conform, at least in the smallest of ways.

She had done none of those things.

Now there was nothing to fear. And still Mariko could not sleep.

Only when she paused to stare at the sloped ceiling of her tent did she understand why dreams continued to elude her. Ōkami had not spoken to her. Save to tell her to close her eyes. Save to recite the refrain he'd once said to her in passing.

For the rest of the night, the Wolf had leaned against a

twisted tree trunk as Yoshi had come to take her in a rather energetic embrace. As Ranmaru had clapped her on the back, his grin simultaneously knowing and secretive. As each member of the Black Clan had—in his own way—demonstrated his solidarity. Their sense of kinship with her.

Perhaps Ōkami did not want Mariko to be here.

Perhaps he had objected and been overruled by a higher authority. Overruled by the forest itself. The trees must have known better than they that Hattori Mariko belonged—above all—beneath the forest's sighing branches. Perhaps because she was far more inventive than all the men put together. Or perhaps the forest simply knew this was where someone like Mariko—a lost girl in search of a place to call home—could plant roots and flourish.

She tossed again, kicking up her thin woolen blanket. Wishing she'd had a chance to tell Ōkami that Ranmaru had always known she was a girl.

Wondering if this revelation was worth seeding enmity between the two friends.

When the flap of her tent rose—washing cool night air across her skin—Mariko yanked a throwing star from beneath her pallet and sat up in the same motion.

Ōkami crouched outside the entrance.

"Throw it or put it down." He did not sound angry.

But Mariko did not discard the throwing star immediately.

He waited. "Are you going to invite me in?"

"Those are the words of a villain."

"I *am* a villain. A deceiver. The son of a traitor. And so much more."

"I know."

"So then are you going to invite me in?"

"If I don't?"

"Then I will never ask for an invitation again."

Mariko moved aside, tossing off her thin blanket. She wore nothing but her white underrobe, but it did not matter. From him, she had nothing to hide. "Stay or go. I leave it to you. But you are welcome always. In all ways."

Ōkami dipped inside the tent, letting the flap fall behind him. Mariko did not ask why he'd come to her tent in the dead of night. She dared not hope to ask, the blood pounding through her veins.

He cast her a searching glance. "I was unfair to you earlier."

"I lied to you," she said simply. "And I hated you."

"I wanted to hate you," he said. "It would have been easier to hate you. But I couldn't." Ōkami lay beside her, long and lean. "One day, I will tell you everything. About who I was. About where I came from."

Mariko stretched out next to him, her fingers laced across her stomach. "I don't care who you were. I only care who you are now. And that you are with me tonight."

He turned toward her. "Always. In all ways." Ōkami stroked a thumb along her jaw. Mariko leaned into his touch as he framed her face between his hands. As he kissed her eyes closed.

"Look at me." It sounded innocent.

But nothing Ōkami ever said was innocent.

When Mariko opened her eyes to meet his, she saw a night full of stars.

"To me, you are magic." His voice was soft. It slid over her skin like silk. The words he spoke were firm and unyielding. Steadfast. It gave Mariko comfort. For she, too, was equally unyielding. Equally steadfast.

She kissed his wrist, then reached for the loose collar of his *kosode*. Her hands brushed away the fabric, baring him to the darkness. When his fingers grazed the muslin of her thin underrobe, it sent a shiver down her back. The slide of the ties through his fingers was like a spark igniting in the dark.

"I want to lie here next to you tonight," Ōkami said.

"How unfortunate for you," she murmured. "Because I want much more than that."

He smiled. His lips pressed beneath her chin, and Mariko wrapped both arms around his neck, drawing him over her.

Ōkami took hold of her wrists, pinning them above her head with one hand. Then he dragged a fingertip along the edge of fabric at her chest, loosening it, pulling it away.

All too slowly.

She sighed in frustration.

"So impatient. You've always been so impatient." With his teeth, he spread apart her underrobe. Every bit of unveiled skin, he kissed, his breath a whisper and a promise.

Mariko brought him back to her lips. "You're trembling," she teased.

"I'm cold."

"Liar. Tell me something true."

"You first."

She swallowed carefully. "I am not a maid."

"Neither am I." He laughed as she shoved a hand in his face.

"Ōkami?" She looked into his eyes. "To me, you are magic, too." Mariko rested a palm against his chest. "My heart knows your heart. A heart doesn't care about good or bad, right or wrong. A heart is always true."

All trace of amusement vanished from his expression. "I may lie every day of my life, Hattori Mariko. But my heart will always be true."

She could ask for nothing else. Mariko crushed her lips to his. He caught her against him, swallowing her sigh with a kiss. Causing her to catch flame as his tongue swept into her mouth. She let the fire burn through her until every thought in her mind was nothing but a wisp of smoke.

And Mariko felt it. The magic of a night sky filled with stars. Of a haunted forest with demons hidden in its folds.

Of a liar, cloaked in truth.

She felt it with every brush of his lips, every touch of his skin to hers.

The searing warmth of this new emotion. This hope she dared not name. A part of Mariko knew better than to touch this kind of flame. Knew better than to let anything deliberately burn her. But she returned Ōkami's embrace. Returned each of his kisses. Every touch. Until nothing at all existed between them.

But shared breaths.

And unspoken promises.

Lies.

And unshakable truth.

The Black Orchid

———— ✳ ————

Kanako watched her son, Raiden, sit across from the son of her enemy. She watched him laugh. Watched him listen intently. Interject occasionally.

Her face was cool and calm. Though her blood boiled from within.

The emperor dreamed of a world in which both his sons held power. Roku as emperor. Raiden as shōgun.

For years, Kanako had smiled at this. Smiled and gifted the emperor tastes of her power. Tastes that had intoxicated him. Kept him in her thrall. It had not mattered to her that the emperor's evil hag of a wife mistreated her daily. Spoke down to her. Belittled her at every turn. It was not unusual for an emperor to have several consorts. For an empress to abase them out of jealousy or spite.

But Kanako had watched for nineteen years as the hag had mistreated her son.

Openly mocked him. Openly called him a whoreson.

Kanako could stomach anything when it came to herself. But she would not stomach any more of the tiny she-devil's contempt for Raiden.

The emperor was her lover. Her son was her beloved.

There was no contest when it came to Kanako's loyalties.

She wandered away from the first enchanted *maru*. Wove through the next set of gates. Then another. And another. Kanako paused before a flowering orchid tree. When she raised her hand, the surface of its leaves shimmered. Distorted.

The tree had been bewitched years before, by an enchantress of great skill. Kanako waved her hand across the blossoms. Removed a purple flower at its base. She gently drifted past the vines along its bottom. Vines that snaked toward her feet, then curled back, as though they'd wandered too near a fire.

A mirrored surface shimmered to life before her. Kanako touched a finger in its center and watched eight concentric circles ripple from the point of contact.

She stepped through the mirrored surface, into a garden absent color. Everything around her was rendered in shades of grey and white. Of black and silver. Her skin was milky, her kimono a stark contrast. A layered arrangement of painted silk.

A man waited beneath a yuzu tree. Its citrus scent wafted toward her, sharp and fresh all at once.

The man stood, dressed in a formal *hakama*, his features solemn.

A dark grey fox with golden eyes ambled across a corner of the enclosed garden. Stopped. And waited.

"I've come with another task for you," Kanako said to the solemn man.

"Then I am to reemerge from this place?"

"It is time." She conjured a silk purse from nothingness. The silver pieces within clinked together as she passed it along to him. "You must tell my son to go into Jukai forest. The fox will show you the way."

"How does the fox know?"

"The fox is a creature of the forest. It always watches. Always knows." Kanako smiled warmly. "Tell Raiden to seek out the Dragon of Kai."

The man's gaze hardened. "Hattori Kenshin."

"You were unsuccessful in the forest the first time. But here is another chance to remedy your mistake. Find the Dragon's sister, and you will find the one we seek. The one who will set this course on its rightful path."

"What am I to do with the Dragon once I am done?"

"It is immaterial to me what happens to Hattori Kenshin. Bring me a way to control the leader of the Black Clan. A way to exert influence over the son of Takeda Shingen. If he will not come to me of his own volition, then I will pull his strings from afar and wait."

"This is what the emperor wishes of me?"

Kanako bowed. "I serve our emperor, in all ways. And you serve him in the greatest of ways."

The man nodded and returned her bow.

Kanako passed him the flower in her hand. The orchid had turned black. She breathed deep of its perfume. Blood and heavy musk. "Take care not to damage our prize, Nobutada-*sama*."

"Of course." For an instant, his eyes glazed over. Distress washed across his face.

The distress of a man in conflict with his soul.

"The emperor will not look kindly on you should you fail," Kanako reminded him, imbuing her words with steel.

Nobutada nodded, setting his spine straight. "If need be, I will die to bring an end to this conflict."

"Of that I have no doubt." She smiled. "You are the finest of samurai. A true tribute to your way." Her eyes drifted across the sea of grey and silver before her. To the immense white oak tree in the distance. And the distortion in its center. "If Hattori Kenshin should cause you any trouble, do not hesitate to inform me." Kanako wandered closer to the white oak. "I am caring for something he desperately wishes restored to him. Your lord will be grateful to us for our consideration."

Nobutada bowed once more.

Kanako waved her hands across the thick trunk of the white oak. The mottled surface of the bark shifted to reveal a young woman, fast asleep in an enchanted slumber.

Half of her face was badly burned.

A Mountain of Fire

———✳———

The next day all the men of the Black Clan were put to work fortifying the camp's position against the Dragon of Kai's oncoming onslaught.

All the *men*.

Mariko protested loudly when she was sent once more to work alongside Yoshi. Blank faces and solemn stares were the only replies with which she was met.

Finally—after three days spent preparing food—Mariko stood her ground before evening mealtime, tightening the dark silk cord wrapped around her middle. As before, she'd donned the clothing of a warrior, but she now chose to augment her garments with elements more suited to her status as the camp's only female.

"I would hate to think," she began in a stern voice, "that my place is manning the cast-iron pot simply because I'm a woman."

"Why would you think that?" Lines puckered across Yoshi's brow. "You did not protest before."

"Give me something meaningful to do."

"Do you not find providing sustenance meaningful?" He huffed.

"I did not mean to insult you."

"Nevertheless you did."

Though Mariko had never been gifted in the art of placating, she attempted to do so now. She took a step back and channeled her best attempt to emulate Yumi. "You're being entirely too sensitive, Yoshi-*san*. I am merely stating that I'd be of far more use developing a way to reinforce the existing defense structures than I would be stirring a simple pot of bean curd."

Yoshi turned to yell into the darkening woods. "Ōkami!"

"What are you doing?" Mariko said under her breath in exasperation.

Ren limped from the bushes, the wound in his side still causing him obvious pain. "What did you do now, woman?" he seethed, his face wan, the color in contrast to his eyes.

"Nothing you need concern yourself with, *boy*," Mariko retorted.

Ōkami shoved through the underbrush, his arms coated in a thin layer of sweat. He waited, and Mariko ignored the way the setting sun struck the angles of his face. Brought his muscles into sharp relief. "Why did you shout for me, Yoshi-*san*?"

Yoshi pointed at Mariko. "She was condescending."

"What did you want me to do about it?" Ōkami raised his eyebrows.

Yoshi shrugged. "I thought you might . . . talk to her. After all, she might . . . listen to you," he grumbled.

Ōkami started to laugh. Then promptly turned and walked away.

Mariko smothered a smile. And refrained from watching the Wolf's tall figure vanish from sight. It would do no one in the camp any good to know how often she looked for him, even at the most inopportune moments.

With a heavy sigh, she turned back to the steaming iron pot.

Arrows screamed into the dirt nearby, their feathers notched to create sound.

"Warning arrows." Yoshi dropped the bowl of ground ginger, and it broke into pieces as soon as it struck the forest floor.

Mariko scrambled up the hill as several members of the Black Clan rushed to look at the color of the arrows' feathered fletchings. Ranmaru stopped short beside Mariko, his sword already in hand.

Red.

Which meant that armed intruders had been sighted in close proximity to camp.

"How did they find us so quickly?" Mariko's whisper was hoarse.

"A dark magic haunts these trees," Ranmaru said. "Like calls to like. If the soldiers have a way to commune with the *yōkai*, then it's possible one of the spirits has led them past our traps."

The ground beneath them grumbled.

Ranmaru looked behind them. "The mountain is talking again."

"What is it telling us?" Mariko felt the warmth of Ōkami's presence at her back.

The Wolf pointed over her shoulder to the tree line. "That we are out of time."

When Mariko saw the crests flying above the row of mounted samurai in the distance, she nearly collapsed.

The crest of the Minamoto clan. Alongside the crest of her own family.

At the head of the troop sat her brother.

The Dragon of Kai.

He'd begun in the clearing. The fateful clearing where his sight had left him. And all that remained was feeling.

The feeling of being threatened. Of being lied to.

Of being hunted.

Kenshin had lashed out that day. Cut down any and all who strode near. When he'd awoken, he'd found his sword covered in blood. The bodies of the old man and the boy and girl who'd worked alongside him had seared into his vision.

In his dreams, it was the fox that had saved him.

It was the fox that saved him now.

When Kenshin had begun searching through Jukai forest for any signs of the Black Clan, the creature had led him to another watering hole. Where an enormous man—nearly three heads taller than anyone else present—with a broken wrist sat drinking himself into a stupor.

This disgruntled giant had told him to ride toward the mountain. To gather Takeda Ranmaru's topknot. And bring it back to him so he could collect a bounty from a nearby daimyō. A bounty that would allow him to regain the respect of his men.

Kenshin had been pleased when Raiden had first offered to accompany him. To help rescue his sister. The feral creature Kenshin had seen that night through the flames around the granary was not Mariko. She'd been crazed. Savage. So unlike the gentle scholar Kenshin had always known.

It must have been these men—these bloodthirsty mercenaries of the Black Clan—who had turned her into such an unimaginable version of herself. Who had made her descend to her baser instincts in order to survive.

Kenshin would destroy each of these men—tear them limb from limb—for what they had done to his sister. For what they had done to Amaya.

But all was not lost.

Mariko had warned him. Indeed that message could have come from none other than his sister. She'd told the blind man to seek Kenshin out. To save the granary.

Just as he intended to save Mariko today.

He would root out this evil from Jukai forest, once and

for all. With the emperor's son and his sister's betrothed at his side. With the might of the empire at his side.

Hattori Kenshin would right the wrongs of this forest.

And learn exactly what its trees had to hide.

———————

The mountain grumbled once more, this time even louder. As though it were warning everyone present that the sun was on the cusp of disappearing. That all light was about to be lost. Mariko grabbed her *katana* and searched for Ōkami. The Wolf had moved to direct other members of the Black Clan into the trees, as they'd decided early on.

What they lacked in numbers they planned to make up for in higher ground. Mariko was supposed to have climbed into her post immediately. But she'd stopped to help Ren. Her erstwhile tormenter still had not gathered enough provisions or adequate weapons for the pending siege.

And now they were out of time. Not all of them would make it to their assigned posts. Not all of them would be able to fend off the attack.

When the arrows started to rain down through the trees, Mariko knew they'd also lost the option to flee. Her eyes flitted across the rapidly darkening underbrush, searching for something, unable to find—

"Follow me." Ōkami moved alongside her, sure-footed, even through the rising gloom. He hoisted Mariko into a tree before climbing into position at her side.

"*Anate!*"

The call for another volley of arrows echoed from the woods beyond.

Ōkami grabbed the wooden shield and yanked Mariko against his chest. The solid beat of his heart thudded in her ear as arrows pounded into the shield and struck the branches around them.

The thunder of hooves followed soon after the last arrow volley. When the mounted samurai came into range, the Black Clan began firing back.

Mariko reached into her pouch of throwing stars. And took a deep breath.

Ōkami ripped an arrow from the tree trunk before firing it into the first wave of charging cavalry. "Fight back, Hattori Mariko. I know he's your brother. But his men are not making the distinction. And neither should you."

"I know." She gritted her teeth.

"The only power any man has over you is the power you give him." Ōkami fired another shot, and a soldier tumbled from his horse below.

At that, Mariko rolled her shoulders, took aim with her throwing star, and hurled it into the darkness.

She'd managed to injure three samurai and take down another warrior from his steed before she noticed something. Mariko could not see her brother anywhere. If she knew Hattori Kenshin at all, she knew her brother would be at the vanguard of any fight.

Something was wrong.

Mariko looked past the trees. And saw torches in the distance.

But they were not normal torches.

They were immense. Rounds of fire bigger than Yoshi's iron cauldron.

"We have to get down." She gasped. "Tell all the men to climb down from the trees at once."

The Wolf loosed another arrow. "What?"

"Do it now, Ōkami!"

Across the way they heard a shout. Mariko saw Yoshi tumble from a tree to the ground, breaking several branches along the way. Ōkami whistled loudly before vaulting to the forest floor to help him.

At that moment, the first ball of fire was catapulted in their direction.

And the sound of men screaming in terror began.

The Phoenix

---✳---

"I t is over," Kenshin shouted to the trees.

Smoke curled in the night air before Mariko's brother. Blood scented the leaves at her sides. Fire smoldered against the forest floor. She strained once more to see any signs of Ōkami and Yoshi, but could not make out anything beyond the wall of smoke to her left.

"Reveal yourselves," Kenshin said grimly. "Return my sister. And the rest of your men might live through this night."

"And if I refuse?" Ranmaru replied. His back was to a tree trunk beyond her brother's view. The leader of the Black Clan smiled at Mariko as he spoke, but it did not touch his eyes.

"I will set fire to every tree in this forest."

Ranmaru's laughter was bitter. "Then you—and your sister—will burn with us."

"This forest is not yours to control anymore," Mariko's betrothed said, his voice clear and firm.

"I was wondering why you chose to show yourself today, Raiden-*chan*."

"Who is that?" Raiden said, urging his horse forward.

Ranmaru stood, his back still to the tree. "We played together as children. Would you know me if you saw me now?"

"Show yourself." Mariko watched Raiden dismount from his black warhorse. "You have taken my bride prisoner. I propose a trade. Return Hattori Mariko to me, and I will return something of great value to you."

"And if I refuse? Will you then burn your bride as well?"

A breath of tense silence passed. "Reveal yourself." Raiden turned to the samurai behind him, taking hold of a sheathed sword from the warrior's hand. "And I will give you that which your father lost so many years ago."

To Raiden's right, a grey fox shifted into view, staring at Mariko through the smoldering trees. Before darting back into the shadows.

"I have no interest in anything you might have to offer." Ranmaru did not even look to see what it was. Instead he reached for Mariko's hand and squeezed it once.

The torch at Raiden's side rendered his smile sinister. A smile that would—on any other occasion—be pleasing to most young women's eyes. But never to Mariko's. Not after this night. "I think you do not know what it is I possess."

Ranmaru sighed quietly. "I think you do not know what it is you seek." Nevertheless the leader of the Black Clan let go of Mariko's hand.

And moved into view.

Ōkami wiped the blood from Yoshi's mouth as he listened to his dearest friend barter with the son of his greatest enemy.

Yoshi coughed again, and more blood trickled from his lips.

"You can't die yet, old man," Ōkami said with a sad smile.

"And you can't tell me what to do, you ungrateful boy. You gave up that right long ago." He returned the smile, then winced.

Ōkami glanced at the wound in his side. At the blood leaking from the arrow puncturing Yoshi's stomach.

Slowly killing him.

"Are you going to let him do this?" Yoshi whispered.

Ōkami wiped the blood from his mouth once more.

"Don't let him do this," Yoshi continued in an urgent whisper. "The young lord has done everything he can to make up for what happened those many years ago. For what his father did. Please forgive him."

"There is nothing to forgive, Yoshi-*san*."

"Then don't let the young lord die to keep your secret."

"I would die before letting anything happen to him." Ōkami inhaled slowly. "And it didn't begin as my secret."

"It was always your secret. The young lord made it to protect you." Yoshi cringed in pain. "Now it is your turn to protect him. Do this for me. Do this for your father." He reached for Ōkami's hand. "Be as swift as the wind. As silent as the forest."

Ōkami wrapped both hands around Yoshi's bloodied fist. "As fierce as the fire. As unshakable as the mountain."

"Rise from the ashes," Yoshi said. "And take your rightful place."

The leader of the Black Clan moved forward warily. The sound of bowstrings being tensed murmured through the branches.

Mariko watched Ranmaru shift toward her betrothed. For an instant, she was unnerved by how much bigger Minamoto Raiden appeared. Ranmaru was not small. But Raiden was far broader in the shoulders. His armor and the twisted horns curling from his helmet made him seem more powerful than Ranmaru in all the ways that mattered. Especially on the field of battle.

Like the remainder of her shadow warrior brethren, Mariko crouched forward, brushing her thumb across the surface of her last throwing star.

Ready to strike.

She tried to ignore the hurt that filled her eyes when she glanced her brother's way. Mariko could never take aim at Kenshin. Her brother had asked after her. But he'd not attempted to make a trade before raining arrows down upon the Black Clan. Before catapulting spheres of fire into the trees. Any of which could have killed her. Any of which nearly did.

Her brother had been more concerned with causing harm than he'd been with finding a solution.

Just like her father.

Ranmaru paused before Raiden. He stood tall. Fearless.

With a wicked gleam in his eye, Raiden unsheathed the sword in his hands. Mariko flinched from the sight.

The metal of the sword was not fashioned of normal steel. It gleamed white, like a flash of lightning. Like something enchanted with an otherworldly light. A vague memory began to take shape in the deepest recesses of Mariko's mind. An old story, whose words were just beyond her grasp.

Ranmaru did not reach for the sword.

"Do you not recognize this weapon?" Raiden asked.

Ranmaru's back was to Mariko, but she saw his hands turn to fists. "You have no right to that sword."

"I have every right."

"Your father murdered mine in cold blood. Return that sword to its rightful owner."

"Return my bride."

"A girl is not a sword. And no price is worth that trade."

Raiden took a step forward. "You truly believe that? This sword has been in your family for a thousand years. Your ancestors would turn over in their graves to see you disregard its significance."

"My ancestors"—Ranmaru took a breath—"would never agree that a weapon is worth a life."

Raiden brandished the sword, swinging it from one side to another in a slow arc. "It's a magnificent blade. I've never seen its equal. When I was told to return it—to offer the sword in exchange for my bride—I thought the same as you do now. That no weapon could be worth a life." He brandished it once more. The final arc brought it within reach of Ranmaru's face. Raiden held it there for a breath. The sword remained an eerie, almost pearlescent white. As though diamonds had been ground upon its surface.

Ranmaru remained staunchly unmoved. Though Mariko watched his fists open and close twice.

"You do not recognize this sword. And it does not recognize you," Raiden said slowly. *"Who are you?"*

When Ranmaru failed to answer, Mariko's heart missed a beat. The lost story took its place on her tongue with a sudden, seizing clarity.

The Takeda sword. The Fūrinkazan. It had been taken from the Takeda clan when its family had fallen from grace. An enchanted weapon. A sword of light.

A sword meant to be carried only by a member of the Takeda clan itself.

A flurry of words collided in her mind, searching for order amidst chaos. Seeking truth amidst lies. Then the sword began to glow. Faintly. But surely. Its blade began to warm and flicker. The light emanating from its core was pure white.

From the shadows, a sinewy figure moved into view, through a haze of smoke.

His hands and face were covered in blood. He walked as though he were weary. Old.

Broken.

Mariko watched, frozen in place, as Ōkami stepped closer. Still soundless. Stalking through the night.

Raiden kept the sword steady. His features drew together in confusion, then smoothed as Ōkami—the Wolf—stepped beside the leader of the Black Clan.

His best friend.

With a satisfied smile, Raiden nodded at Ōkami. "I've heard a great deal about you, Takeda Ranmaru."

———————

The only son of the last shōgun stopped before the elder son of his mortal enemy. The man who had brought about the death of his father.

Ōkami did not flinch from the sight of his father's sword. The Takeda sword. A weapon he had considered lost. And good riddance to it.

The Fūrinkazan was a weapon meant for a man of truth. A man of principle.

Not a pretender. Not a thief. Not a liar.

Not a coward.

And yet the sight of it in Minamoto Raiden's grasp had ignited a long-dormant emotion. A feeling rich with strife. Rich with history. Replete with vengeance.

Ōkami had denied it for so long.

And his dear friend? His best friend. The son of Asano Naganori. The boy who had—for nearly seven years—assumed his mantle. Ōkami had never asked him to do so.

Tsuneoki had done it to keep him safe. Had done it to make amends for the betrayal of his father. The actions that had led to the death of Takeda Shingen.

But—at his core—Ōkami had known there was more to it. More that his best friend had not yet said. He'd hoped Tsuneoki would tell him in time.

He owed his dearest friend this. He would not allow Asano Naganori's son to perish in his stead. Or answer for his own reticence.

"What is it you want, Minamoto Raiden?" Ōkami asked.

Ōkami. It was a name gifted to him when he'd first entered the fighting ring not long after he'd bartered the last of his family's wealth to gain his abilities. A story for another time. From another life.

The Honshō Wolf.

He had never corrected anyone. He had sought only to learn. To destroy. To know what it felt like to feel truly powerful. To truly understand what had been stolen from his family.

Raiden studied him, taking in his bloodied appearance. No doubt pleased to see how broken and weary Ōkami appeared. "My bride was captured on her way to Inako."

The way he referred to Mariko as *his* irritated Ōkami immensely. Almost as much as the pompous cut of the fool's armor. "Not by me or by any of my men."

"It does not matter. She is here now."

Ōkami breathed through his nose. "Are you quite certain of that?"

"We are," the Dragon of Kai said curtly.

"She does not answer to you," Ōkami replied in equally arrogant fashion.

Hattori Kenshin moved forward, attempting to intimidate his quarry. "She answers to her family. To her duty."

"Mariko answers only to herself," Ōkami said without flinching.

"Mariko?" A smirk began to form across Raiden's face.

"She is one of us," the leader of the Black Clan answered simply. "And you will not lay a hand on any of our warriors."

Raiden laughed as though the entire idea were ludicrous. "If she chooses to side with you, then I cannot help her."

At that, Hattori Kenshin stepped forward. Though he tried hard to conceal it, Ōkami saw the horror wash onto his features. Bloom across his face like a brushfire.

"Mariko!" he yelled. "Where are you?"

Not a sound emitted from the shadows and smoke.

"Mariko!" the Dragon of Kai called out once more, his voice increasingly desperate.

Again not a single answer.

"Put Takeda Ranmaru in chains," Raiden said as he reached for his reins and began retying the chin guard on his helmet. "And kill anyone left standing."

Mariko heard the hum begin to gather even before Raiden made his final pronouncement. She grabbed Ren and handed him her sword.

She would prevent any more blood from being spilled this night, no matter the cost. Mariko could not bear to lose anyone she loved.

"Kick me and strike me if you have to," she said to Ren in an insistent tone. "Make them believe you hate me. Trade me for your safety."

Ren's eyes widened as Mariko swiped mud across her face and clothes.

"Don't just stand there!" she said. "Here's your chance to hate me as you've always hated me."

Ren swallowed. "I'm—I'm truly sorry," he said simply. "It wasn't what I wanted to feel, Lord Lackbeard." With that, he shoved her from the shadows.

"Try not to limp," she said through gritted teeth. "Be strong. Unafraid."

The sword at her back faltered.

"Stand tall, Ren," she whispered. "The only true weakness is weakness of the spirit."

The men before her shouted when Mariko and Ren came into view. The hum around Ōkami only increased in intensity. Ranmaru—or rather Tsuneoki—put a hand on the Wolf's shoulder. Only then did the hum slowly begin to dissipate.

Mariko halted her march ten paces away. Ren cleared his throat. In a flash, he positioned the blade of the *tantō* at her throat. "You wanted your bride, Minamoto Raiden? She is here. I'll return her to you in one piece. Under one condition."

Raiden dropped his reins. "Why would I want a bride who has betrayed me?"

"This ridiculous girl?" Ren laughed maniacally. "She couldn't even betray herself. Cried herself to sleep most nights. Look at her. She's filthy. When we took her prisoner, we had no idea who she was."

Kenshin moved forward. "Mariko? Is this true?"

It wasn't the sight of her brother that moved her to tears. It was the thought that those she cared for—her friends, the boy of her heart—the thought that they might die that made Mariko's sight begin to water. The tears gathered and spilled over, trailing down her muddy, bloody face.

"Kenshin," she said, her voice quavering, "please take me away from here. My lord Raiden, these men kidnapped me. They are liars and thieves. They have treated me abominably."

The son of the emperor remained unmoved. He continued to address Ren and not Mariko. "Even if she is my bride, what makes you think we would trade Hattori Mariko for the lives of all the men left standing?" Raiden said, his hand still resting on the hilt of his *katana*.

In that moment Mariko had her first taste of hatred for her betrothed. And she knew it would not be her last.

"Because it is not just one life to be traded. Leave the rest of my men alone. And I will go with you as well," Ōkami said quietly.

No!

Mariko fought back the urge to cry out. To scream in protest.

But Minamoto Raiden smiled his menacing smile. And the deal was done.

Ren pressed Mariko into the fold. Kenshin swept closer, and Mariko ran the rest of the way. As she passed Asano Tsuneoki—the real son of Asano Naganori—her eyes met his for a moment. They glowed yellow and feral as he nodded once.

And the look was a promise. The beast would be at her back. Keeping watch. Always.

Kenshin took her in his arms. Held her tight. The tears continued to spill down Mariko's face unchecked.

Over her brother's shoulder she saw Raiden shove Ōkami until he was kneeling in the mud. Watched as imperial soldiers bound his wrists in chains. Mariko closed her eyes tight, willing away the image.

"I'll take you home," Kenshin said softly.

"No," Mariko said. "There's nothing left for me at home. Take me to Inako." Her tear filled gaze bore into the face of her betrothed, daring him to lay hands on Ōkami again. "If my lord Raiden will still have me, I'm ready to begin my life in the imperial court."

"Are you certain?"

The tears burned in her eyes as she watched smiling, taunting imperial soldiers drag Ōkami to his feet. "I have never been more certain of anything in my life."

An Ending

————✴————

This was to be an unusual tea ceremony.

In an unusual location. At an unusual time of night.

But then her emperor had always been an unusual man.

Her Imperial Majesty Yamoto Genmei, Empress of Wa, slowly made her way to the moon-viewing pavilion, each step itself a journey. A reminder.

Her nerves were wound tight within her. But she did not show it. Years spent living in Heian Castle had taught her better than to wear her every emotion for all the world to see.

The emperor had asked her to join him for tea this night.

It had been years since he'd asked her to partake in anything together. Years since he'd asked her to share in anything under the stars. And the moon-viewing pavilion was one of his favorite places to be on a warm summer's eve. In fact, this particular pavilion had been built for *her*. For his whore, Kanako.

Genmei paused in her steps. She reached into her sleeve and drew out a tiny glass vial. Slipped a drop beneath her tongue and took a deep breath, letting the tincture spread down her throat. Cool her burning nerves.

She lifted her head high. And continued down her path. The emperor had asked her to join him this night. It had not been a mistake.

Genmei reached the moon-viewing pavilion. The emperor was already there, his hands behind his back, his head turned to the stars. He looked her way after she removed her lacquered *zori* and bowed at the top of the steps.

"I'm pleased you are here," he said with a smile.

"My sovereign asked me to come."

"You could have refused."

"I have never refused you anything."

"All the same, you could have done so tonight."

Genmei dipped her head. "My life has been devoted to serving my emperor."

The emperor smiled again. He directed her toward the tatami mat positioned before the iron tea brazier. "Will you join me for tea?"

Again Genmei bowed. "Only if I may be allowed to serve it."

The emperor nodded warmly.

The silks of Genmei's elegant kimono and *tabi* socks brushed across the mats as she knelt before the brazier. With utmost care and precision, she began by folding a piece of clean orange cloth in three, then rolling it into a neat bundle. Using one side of the cloth, she lifted the lid off the iron brazier.

The emperor knelt across from her. Settled into position, his features almost kind.

Genmei used the long-handled bamboo ladle to spoon out steaming water into a small glazed porcelain bowl. She rinsed the bowl out, then—with another side of the orange cloth—wiped it clean before carefully portioning three tiny scoopfuls of pale green *matcha* powder into the porcelain bowl.

With a bamboo whisk and another ladleful of steaming water, Genmei mixed the tea until it was frothy and light. Each of her movements was precise. Calm. Artful.

Such was the tea ceremony. One of harmony. Respect. Purity. And tranquility.

She wiped the edges once more before turning the bowl toward the emperor. Serving him with an almost hesitant smile.

There was so much between them. So many unspoken sentiments.

The emperor drank deep from the bowl. Set it down.

Genmei rinsed it and repeated the process so that she, too, could drink from the same bowl. Share in the same ceremony of harmony and respect.

"I have been unkind to you," the emperor said quietly, when Genmei had finished drinking her tea.

She said nothing. Refused to allow hope to enter her mind.

Hope was a poison to her world.

"It was not my wish for things to happen in such a way. But I do wish for things to change in the future," he continued.

"Forgive me, my sovereign, but how can things ever change when—when *she* is still here?" Genmei said, her words laced with venom.

"Kanako is my royal consort. She is not leaving Heian Castle." The emperor's tone was firm. "But I do want to mend things between us. I do want to create a bridge between our worlds."

"Why?"

"Because I look at our son, and I want our son to be better than we are, Genmei." The emperor sighed. "I want him to see a better example."

"Roku *is* better than we are."

"I know I can be better. That we can be better." The emperor stood and made his way to the steps of the moon-viewing pavilion. He waited for Genmei.

Something he'd never done before.

Each of her movements guarded, Genmei joined him. They donned their *zori* and walked together toward the pond's edge. Waxy lily pads glistened beneath a ghostly full moon. Frogs and cicadas sang together in discordant chorus.

The emperor cleared his throat. "There is hatred between us."

"There is," Genmei agreed.

"Will you not agree to become better than our hatred? For the sake of our son?"

Genmei turned toward him. Looked her emperor in the eye.

He coughed as he met her gaze. His face became flushed.

There was a time she would have given anything to hear him say these words. To hear him say he cared about her—cared about their future—even in the barest of measures.

The emperor coughed again, a fist raised to his lips. Awareness began to take shape in his eyes. They bulged as his fingers grasped at his collar.

He tried to shout. But his voice remained lodged in his throat.

Genmei stood silent. She watched.

Tranquil. In harmony with herself.

As the Emperor of Wa keeled over into the pond beside his favorite moon-viewing pavilion.

Genmei looked at her husband for a moment.

"No, my sovereign," she spoke softly. "We cannot become better than our hatred. But to protect our son from your mistakes, I *will* do whatever is necessary." With the toe of her lacquered sandal, she shoved his head beneath the water.

Then Genmei breathed deep. Waded into the pond. And began screaming.

"Help! Someone please help. The emperor has fallen!"

Above them, a swallow with iridescent wings took flight on a gust of wind.

Vanishing into the night.

Glossary

———✳———

Akuma—an evil spirit from folklore

amazura—a sweet syrup

anate—the command for "fire," as in "to fire an arrow"

ashigaru—foot soldiers

Bansenshukai—the ancient manual on the *shinobi no mono*, or the art of the ninja

bō—staff

boro—patchwork fabric worn by maidservants and peasants

bushidō—the way of the warrior

-chan—a diminutive and expression of endearment, as in Chiyo-*chan*

chūgi—loyalty; one of the tenets of *bushidō*

daifuku—a confection of glutinous rice stuffed with bean paste

daimyō—a feudal lord who is typically a vassal of the shōgun; the equivalent of an English earl

dō—chest armour

Fūrinkazan—a sword of light, associated with the Takeda clan; it is inscribed with the phrases *As swift as the wind. As silent as the forest. As fierce as the fire. As unshakable as the mountain.*

geiko—geisha

gi—integrity; one of the tenets of *bushidō*

Go—a complex strategy board game for two players; using black and white pieces called "stones," the goal is to surround a larger territory than your opponent

hachimaki—headband

hakama—traditional clothing of pleated trousers over a kimono top

haori—type of coat

honshō—true

ichi-go, ichi-e—one lifetime, one meeting; i.e., "live in the moment," "for this time only"

jin—benevolence; one of the tenets of *bushidō*

jinmaku—camp enclosure

jubokko—vampiric tree

kaburaya—a whistling arrow

kagemusha—a shadow warrior; man behind the scenes

kanabō—a spiked club or truncheon

kata—set combinations of movements for martial arts practice

katana—type of sword

koku—a unit of measurement, typically associated in feudal times with land

kosode—simple robe worn by both sexes

kunai—type of dagger

maiko—apprentice *geiko*

makoto—honesty; one of the tenets of *bushidō*

maru—castle bailey

meiyo—honor; one of the tenets of *bushidō*

naginata—bladed weapon on a long shaft

norimono—litter, vehicle; palanquin

obi—wide sash

okaa—mother

ponzu—sauce containing citrus, vinegar, and soy

rei—respect; one of the tenets of *bushidō*

rōnin—masterless samurai

ryō—gold currency

-sama—a term of respect, a little more formal than *-san*, as in Mariko-*sama*

samurai—a member of the military caste, typically in service to a liege lord or daimyō

-san—a term of respect, as in Akira-*san*

saya—scabbard

sensei—teacher

seppuku—ritual suicide

shamisen—stringed instrument

shinobi no mono—the art of the ninja

shodo—calligraphy

shōgun—military leader

sumimasen—thank you

tabi—split-toed socks

tantō—blade shorter than the *wakizashi*

tatami—a woven mat traditionally made of rice straw

tatsumura—a rare type of silk gauze, used to fashion priceless kimono

tsuba—hand guard of a sword

uba—nursemaid

umeshu—plum wine

wakasama—young lord

wakizashi—blade similar to but shorter than the *katana*; samurai traditionally wear both blades at once

washi—a type of paper commonly made using fibers from the bark of the *gampi tree*

yabusame—mounted archers

yōkai—forest demon

yoroihitatare—armored robe

yūki—courage; one of the tenets of *bushidō*

yuzu—a small citrus fruit with a tart flavor similar to a pomelo

zori—type of sandals

acknowledgments

*"You must understand that there is more
than one path to the top of the mountain."*
—*Miyamoto Musashi*

I've written seven novels, several of which will—thankfully—never see the light of day. Whenever I finish writing a book, I always take a moment to reflect on what the experience has taught me. In many ways, writing *Flame in the Mist* was a bigger challenge than anything I have ever attempted professionally.

It was also one of the most rewarding.

Of course, it often takes a village to point me in the right direction. To my compass—my agent, Barbara Poelle—I am thankful every day for you. Your wisdom, your guidance, your humor, your candor—this dream of mine would never be possible without you.

To my editor, Stacey Barney: will there ever be enough words to express my gratitude? I think not. So instead let's clear out a few more restaurants and make sure every place we visit is haunted by the echoes of our laughter.

To the team of amazing people at Penguin: I am always struck by your limitless passion. The work you do—and the work you enable me to do—is beyond important, now more than ever. To Kate Meltzer and my tireless publicist Marisa Russell: you never fail to keep this ship of ours on course. Thank you, a thousand times over. A wealth of gratitude for Carmela Iaria, Alexis Watts, Doni Kay, Chandra Wohleber, Theresa Evangelista, Eileen Savage, Jen Besser, Elyse Marshall, Lisa Kelly, Lindsay Boggs, Sheila Hennessey, Shanta Newlin, Erin Berger, Christina Colangelo, Colleen Conway, Judy Parks Samuels, Tara Shanahan, and Bri Lockhart. And a special note of thanks to Kara Brammer for all of your ingenious ideas.

These last few years, I've been privileged to meet and interact with so many amazing bloggers, librarians, readers, and book lovers across the globe. Thank you so much for the laughs, the fan art, the letters, and the shared excitement. You are the reason I do what I do. A shout-out to Natasha Polis and Christine Riccio: that bird in San Diego will never be the same after seeing us.

To my writing sisters—Joy Callaway, Sarah Henning, Ricki Schultz, JJ, Roshani Chokshi, and Traci Chee—I can't wait to see what the future has in store for us as we continue this journey together.

To the early readers of *Flame in the Mist*—Sabaa Tahir, Marie Rutkoski, Dr. Jan Bardsley, Misa Sugiura, and Sarah Nicole Lemon—your notes and your guidance and your love were invaluable. This book would not be what it is without you. Any errors or oversights within the work are mine alone.

Among the greatest gifts of this career have been the friendships I've made with so many astoundingly talented writers. To Beth Revis, Lauren DeStefano, Sona Charaipotra, my tour wifey Dhonielle Clayton, Victoria Aveyard, Adam Silvera, David Arnold, Nicki and David Yoon, Victoria Schwab, Jason Reynolds, Daniel Jose-Older, Brendan Reichs, Soman Chainani, Margie Stohl, Kami Garcia, Megan Miranda, Gwenda Bond, Sarah Maas, Cassie Beasley, Lauren Billings, Christina Hobbs, and Nic Stone: thank you for all the laughter and the wonderful late-night chats. Lo, I don't think I can go to Vegas again without you. Brendan and Kami: thanks for braving the super spider in our quest for the One Ring.

To Marie Lu and Carrie Ryan for being constant sources of love and support. I always leave our times together wishing we could hang out more.

To my assistant, Sarah Weiss: thank you for making sure I dot every *i* and cross every *t* with your signature style and grace.

To Brita Lundberg, Heather Baror-Shapiro, and the wonderful team at IGLA: thank you for all your endless work and unceasing professionalism.

To Sabaa: every seven I see, I thank the stars for you.

To Elaine: there are no words to express how much your friendship has meant to me. Through the good and the not-so-good, you have always been my light on the distant shore.

To my family: my siblings—Erica, Ian, Chris, and Izzy—

thank you for your love and support. Here's to many more years of celebrating nothing and everything as only we can do. To my parents—Umma, Mama Joon, Baba Joon, and Dad—thank you for a lifetime of love and guidance.

To Omid, Julie, Navid, Jinda, Evelyn, Isabelle, Andrew, Ella, and Lily: thank you for being there through every joyful event and for weathering any storm in the best way possible: together.

And to Vic: It doesn't matter what path we take up the mountain. It only matters that you are there with me.